VIRTUALLY
MARIA

VIRTUALLY MARIA

JOHN JOYCE

POOLBEG

Published 1998 by
Poolbeg Press Ltd,
123 Baldoyle Industrial Estate,
Dublin 13, Ireland

The Arts Council
An Chomhairle Ealaíon

A catalogue record for this book is available from the British Library.

ISBN 1 85371 824 6

Cover design by Poolbeg Group Services Ltd
Set by Poolbeg Group Services Ltd in Garamond 10/13.5
Printed and bound in Great Britain by
Cox & Wyman Ltd, Reading, Berkshire.

ABOUT THE AUTHOR

John Joyce was born by the sea, in Weymouth, Dorset, and moved to Ireland in 1977. He was awarded a European Union Fellowship for Science Writers by the Glaxo Corporation the following year, and in 1980 set up the trade magazine *Aquaculture Ireland* for the emerging fish-farming industry in Ireland. He is also author of the "Captain Cockle" series of children's books, published in Ireland by Poolbeg Press, a keen amateur cartoonist, and a founder member of the *Resonance* writers' group in Dublin.

He lives in Dublin with his wife Jane and their children Jenny, William and Jessie. He is currently working on a number of fiction projects, including the next book in the Gilkrensky series.

ACKNOWLEDGEMENTS

I would like to thank Kate Cruise O'Brien, Gaye Shortland and everyone at Poolbeg Press, my personal "Editor-in-Chief" Lola Keyes-McDonnell, and my friends Antoinette Dawson, Sue Conaty, Elizabeth Hyland and Gillian Markey for reading this manuscript, as well as Peggy Cruickshank and company, John Kelly and the members of the writers' group *Resonance* for their help and support over the years.

Technical assistance was provided by: Richard Keyes-McDonnell of Logitech, California, and Brian McNamara of the Irish Marine Data Centre, on the virtual reality, computer viruses, e-mail systems and computers – real and imagined – that feature in this book; Dr Madeline Gordon on matters medical; and Nekane Bilbao-Altuna on behavioural psychology. Additional insights came from Maelíosa de Burca at the Japanese Department, Dublin City University: *Arigatō gozaimasu*! Mystic guidance came from Michael Poynder, author of the book *Pi in the Sky*, and help generally from friends and contacts in Cairo, Cork, London and Tokyo too numerous to mention individually.

A special word of thanks is also due to my agent Celia Catchpole for her encouragement and support, and to John Sherlock, screenwriter and scriptdoctor extraordinaire, for his words of wisdom on plot structure. Also to Bernard and Mary at the Tyrone Guthrie Centre at Annaghmackerrig, and the Arts Council for the peace to finish the second draft.

Finally, I would like to thank my family for sharing their home with Theo, Jessica, Maria and the gang for so long, and in particular my wife Jane for her patience and understanding.

This book is lovingly dedicated to you.

Thank you.

FOR JANE

"To cross at a ford means to attack the enemy's weakest point, and to put yourself in an advantageous position. This is how to win in large-scale strategy . . . You must research this well."
Miyamoto Musashi – from *A Book of Five Rings*

"Those who are saved from their own greed shall be the successful."
(Surah 14:91) From the Koran

"What may it profit a man if he gains the whole world – – and loses his own soul?"
(Luke 9:25) From the Bible

VIRTUALLY
MARIA

PROLOGUE:
THE DEATH OF MARIA

BETRAYAL IS AN UGLY WORD. IT LURKED IN THE DARK CORNERS of Maria Gilkrensky's mind like a spider, tugging at its web of suspicion so that she could not sleep. Theo had changed, ever since that bitch Jessica Wright had got him tangled up with the Japanese. Where his mind had once been open to her, where they had once been friends and lovers, he was now closed – obsessed. Everything was about "control" and "keeping ahead". Conversation was dominated by "strategy meetings", "risk minimisation" and of course, by that bloody Wright woman.

Maria's arm stretched out across the empty space in the big double bed, where Theo should have been, but wasn't. How long had it been since they'd last made love? A week? A fortnight? A month? It seemed the only time they talked was when they argued. And they did that every day.

Now there was nothing left, nothing except a cold, hard anger, like ice against her heart.

Maria lay alone in the darkness, listening to the ebb and flow of her own breathing. Then, when she could stand the silence no longer, she sat upright, pulled the duvet around her like a cape and walked to the window.

Dawn was coming – a new day. She could see the dull red glow of the sun to the east, blotting out the stars. There was her valley, spread out before her – the meadow, the heather, the forest near the pheasant farm, the brook and the old rickety bridge where Theo had taken her photograph on the day she'd agreed to marry him.

A new day? Or would it be just like all the others they'd lived together recently? The Theo she had loved had died the night before, when he'd stormed out of the dining-room after her ultimatum. Maria looked across the courtyard and up to his workroom. The light was still on.

That bloody computer! Didn't he believe she'd meant what she'd said?

Maria Gilkrensky felt the anger rise in her throat and let the duvet fall from her shoulders, so that it puddled around her feet. Then she stripped off her nightdress and pulled on her clothes. She had made a decision.

She was leaving.

By the wardrobe was the rucksack she used on her solitary walks around the Wicklow hills. She would stay with friends in Dublin for the time being, until she could find a flat near the practice, or until Theo came to his senses – if he ever would!

She looked around the bedroom for something to write him a note on, but there was nothing. Nothing except the black slab of his old laptop computer on the low table next to the bed. She pressed the catch on the lid and opened it, manoeuvring the trackerball to take the cursor through *Exchange*, *Compose* and *Video*, until the red *Recording* light shone above the machine's internal camera. Then she tried to compose herself, pushed a strand of coppery hair out of her eyes and started to speak.

"Theo. You *knew* what I'd do if you went back to that bloody machine of yours last night. So I'm recording you a message on the only thing you ever listen to. I'm going, Theo. I'm leaving you! I can't take this any more . . . this being alone."

Her face turned away from the screen and her hand reached for the keyboard to end the recording. Then it stopped. She could feel the stinging tightness in her throat and the tears welling up in her eyes

"Theo! I hate this! Why can't we just talk like we used to? I know we're so different, you and I. But I love you, Theo . . . I really do!"

The door of her old yellow Mini creaked as she opened it, threw her rucksack into the back and pulled herself into the familiar seat. In the near-darkness, she had no trouble in pulling out the choke or fitting the key to the ignition. There was a laboured heave of the tired engine and . . . nothing! She tried again, and again. After all these years and all the miles it had done, for it to let her down now!

All at once, Maria Gilkrensky felt totally alone, as if the little car had somehow conspired to fail her, just as Theo had done.

This time the tears burst through, taking her by surprise. For a moment she fought them back, gripping the steering wheel tightly – as if it were the only solid thing left in her universe. Then a great wave washed over her, and she collapsed, locked in the misery of her loss.

What could she do? Where could she go? Theo must not find her like this!

In the rucksack was one of the electronic keys to his sleek BMW. Maria hauled the bag from the back seat, slammed the little car's door with all the strength she could muster and ran across the courtyard.

In the stillness, the only sounds in the room were the regular rasp of breathing and the low purr of the computer working tirelessly on the desk where Theodore Gilkrensky was slumped asleep. His head rested in the crook of his right elbow, his long body sprawled awkwardly on the swivel-chair, and all around him was the debris of his night's work – abandoned coffee cups, plates of congealed food and piles of computer manuals, flow charts and spreadsheets that spilled onto the floor.

Then, another sound – a strident electronic *beep*. The

computer screen cleared, displaying a narrow white band with the words *Incoming Message*.

Gilkrensky snorted and jerked upright, rubbing his fingers over the rough stubble on his chin.

Christ! Was that the time? Maria would kill him! She'd threatened to leave if he ever did this again . . .

Then the memory of what he had finally accomplished during the night burst upon him like the rising sun.

Minerva worked! After all the false starts and dead-ends. After all the problems with the biochip, the neural net and the months of stumbling around in the dark with the software – Minerva *worked*!

"What is it?" he asked.

A crude caricature of a female face, barely more than a cartoon, flashed onto the screen. A disembodied electronic voice said, "A video message."

"Who's it from?"

"Your wife. Maria."

"Play it for me, please."

Gilkrensky watched in disbelief as Maria's message told him she was actually leaving. But that was impossible! Hadn't she always been the first to insist they should each have lives of their own? Didn't she realise how important this project was?

The sound of her car engine turning over and the slam of its door echoed up from the courtyard, bringing with it the sudden realisation of what life would be like if she was gone. Without waiting for the end of the message Gilkrensky rushed to the window, just in time to see her getting into the BMW.

The last thing he saw, before the explosion tore the car into a million flaming fragments, was her tearful face . . . looking up at him.

I

THE CRASH

"This is Cairo Tower calling all helicopters on the field. We have an emergency. What is your flight status? Over!"

The call took a few seconds to register with Leroy Manning. In his mind he was a thousand miles and a quarter of a century away, at the beginning of his quest for the perfect woman. For him, it was the long, hot summer of sixty-nine, and he was in his father's Buick on the way to Cape Canaveral with Patsy Miller. In the marshes on either side of the road alligators basked in the sun and, shimmering on the horizon way ahead of them, was the tall white rocket that would land a man on the moon.

It had been a week like no other, before or since.

All of Florida had sat with their eyes glued to their TVs for news from Mission Control. Offices had opened late, schools had closed early. And on the day Neil Armstrong made that "one small step for a man", Leroy

Manning had made his own giant leap towards manhood in the darkness of a drive-in movie.

"I'm going to be an astronaut," he told Patsy afterwards, as they lay in each other's arms looking up at the stars. And she hugged him even tighter. A year later, he had joined the United States Army in the hope of learning to fly.

"Calling all helicopters! I repeat! This is Cairo Tower. Is there anyone out there who can take off? Over!"

Leroy jerked upright, swung his feet down from the top of the helicopter's console, and squeezed the radio trigger.

"Cairo Control! This is Golf Romeo Charlie! I'm almost done with refuelling. What's your problem? Over!"

"We have a plane down! We must get medical teams out there. How soon will you be ready?"

Manning's fingers flicked a circuit breaker, bringing the fuel gauge on line. Through the canopy he could see flood lamps snapping on at the military airbase, lighting up the grey hulls of transport planes and the dark, insect shapes of other helicopters. Around the medical centre blue lights sparkled, rushing out across the runways, and above the normal whine of the busy airport, he could hear the rising wail of sirens.

"Cairo Control! I'm all set to go right now! Over!"

"Thank you, Golf Romeo Charlie. We're sending a medical team to you. Out!"

Manning slid back the pilot's door and shouted to the figure in overalls who was tending the fuel line.

"Hey, Ahmed! Cut the gas! I'm gonna crank her up!"

Ahmed raised his hands to Allah.

"Mister Leroy! You cannot leave without signing for this fuel!"

"To hell with it! Pull back the line or I'll break it off!" And he slammed the door shut.

One of the blue lights swerved away from the military base and raced towards the fuel depot. Manning reached down to the centre console and ran his hands over the switches and circuit-breakers, checking their positions. He glanced over his shoulder to make sure Ahmed had dragged the fuel line clear and was standing by with the big red fire extinguisher, just in case. Then he reached up and pushed the igniter circuit-breaker above his head, rolled the throttle to the starting position and squeezed the starter trigger.

There was a shrill whine, as the high-speed starter began to move the fifty-foot rotor blades – painfully slow at first, and then blindingly fast as they blurred into a disc over his head. The main turbine fired, and Manning watched the exhaust-gas temperature gauge rush past the red line, steady, and fall back into the green. Only then did he give a thumbs-up sign to Ahmed, who put down his fire extinguisher and turned to face the oncoming lights.

An old Mercedes ambulance skidded to a halt just beyond the reach of the spinning rotors, and disgorged a medical team onto the tarmac. Ahmed slid back the rear passenger door of the helicopter and helped two orderlies load folding stretchers between the seats.

Nurses slung black medical bags onto the floor and climbed aboard. The front passenger door popped open and a doctor, wearing an unbuttoned tweed jacket and an expression like a frightened owl, hauled himself into the co-pilot's seat. Manning passed him a radio headset. Without it, they would never be able to hear each other over the din of the machine.

"Please! We must go quickly!"

"Where!"

"To the west. About five miles beyond Giza. There were two hundred people on that plane!"

"Jesus!"

Manning checked that Ahmed was standing clear. Then he twisted open the throttle on the collective as he pulled it back. The rotor noise changed to a heavy *whop-whop-whop* as the wide blades bit the air and the nose came up. The big Bell 214 lifted off the tarmac, hovered for a moment, and began to slide across the airfield, gaining speed as it climbed into the darkness.

In a moment, the lights of Cairo were spread out below. There was the bright necklace of the motorway, stretching into the city. There were the gleaming columns of the tourist hotels, the bracelets of stars on the bridges over the Nile and the dim lattice of the Cairo tower. Ahead of them was the dying glow of the sunset, the alien shapes of the pyramids on the Giza plateau, and a strange, dark cloud . . .

At first Manning thought it must be a thundercloud, because of its size. Then he saw it dip and thicken into a single black column rising straight up out of the desert . . .

"Christ!" he thought. "They're on fire!"

Leroy Manning was no stranger to death. He had seen bodies before – in Vietnam – men who looked as if they were just sleeping, had it not been for the neat red holes in the head or the chest. Bodies of men who died in explosions – strange twisted corpses with limbs and faces missing – and the oddly crumpled bodies of fallen air-crews. But of all the ways of dying Leroy Manning had seen in his thirty years in the air, fire scared him the most. In Vietnam, Leroy and his buddies had been issued with pistols when they flew out over the jungle – big Colt .45 automatics with wooden hand-grips – just in case they had to crashland. Leroy's friends made a big show of these guns. They even practised shooting beer-bottles off the wooden fence out past the canteen. But Leroy didn't need to. He knew what *his* pistol was for. When you're crushed inside your cockpit and the fire is coming to get you, you don't need marksmanship to put the barrel in your mouth and pull the trigger.

So Leroy shuddered when he saw the oily flames at the base of the great column. He could see the hard shape of the crashed aircraft, with its high T-shaped tail, the entrails of escape chutes bursting from the emergency exits, and the reflection of fire on its wings.

He imagined what was burning inside that fire, and his flesh crawled. God help them!

Leroy swung the helicopter round the nose of the smashed aircraft, away from the fire, and flicked on the spotlight. Then he played its brilliant disc over the sand, looking for . . .

"Jesus! There's hundreds of them! How the hell did they walk away from that!"

Around the wreckage, standing singly or huddled in groups, were the dazed survivors, squinting up into the spotlight or shielding their eyes against the flying dust – couples huddled together, parents trying to comfort children . . .

The doctor pointed to a man in a white shirt who was waving at them frantically.

"Put us down over there, please. There is someone badly injured!"

"Some-*one*!" shouted Manning. "They should *all* be dead!" And he turned the helicopter to hover over a patch of clear ground. The Bell settled onto the desert, throwing up dust and sand, whipping at the clothes of survivors and forcing them to cover their faces. Yet the man in the white shirt ran straight to the helicopter as soon as it touched down and tore open Leroy's door, flooding the cockpit with the sickly sweet stink of burning rubber.

"For God's sake, we must have a doctor out here now!" he shouted above the whine of the turbine. Leroy could see the epaulettes of a flight captain on his shoulders.

"Hey! I'm the *pilot*! *He's* the doctor!"

Behind them, the rear doors of the Bell were slamming back as the medical team tumbled out onto the sand. The captain ran around the nose of the Bell, grabbed the doctor by the arm and dragged him to the closest huddle of survivors. Manning stayed in his seat, watching as the flames licked up the tail of the burning aircraft from the smashed engines.

His eyes fell on a black leather bag resting between the rudder pedals on the co-pilot's side of the cockpit – the doctor's medical kit!

"Hey, Doc! You left your bag!"

"Over here!"

Manning climbed out over the skid, taking the bag with him. Above his head, other helicopters were arriving, playing their own searchlights over the crowd and whipping at the column of smoke.

"Over here! Quickly please!"

Manning pushed his way through the survivors and passed the leather bag to the doctor, who was kneeling over the body of a stewardess. With his thumb, the doctor peeled back her left eyelid, and shone a torch into it. The black pupil in the centre did not shrink from the light. Neither did the pupil of the right. He gave the torch to Manning and motioned for him to hold it steady. Then he gently lifted the blood-soaked hair covering the woman's right temple. Beneath the matted gold, glistening white bone showed through the slash of a deep wound.

"Hold the light still, *please!*"

He gently pressed a field-dressing over the gash, wrapped the woman in a blanket tucking it carefully under her chin, then supervised as she was strapped into one of the aluminium stretchers.

"Are there any other casualties?"

A small, dark woman in a pilot's jacket stepped forward. Her hands were bound in blood-stained bandages.

"Just me. I cut them on the wreckage. There's nobody else. I've checked."

The doctor stared over her shoulder at the shattered aircraft, the rising column of smoke and the crowds of dazed survivors.

"Are you sure?"

"No. Thank God!" said the Captain. "It was a bloody miracle!"

He was watching the stewardess as she was carried towards the Bell. "Only Julie was hurt. One of the kids in first class was out of his seat when the machine stalled the plane. She got up to grab him and was thrown against the bulkhead before she could get strapped in. I'm going to crucify the people who made us carry that bloody machine!"

"What machine?" asked Manning as he turned back towards the helicopter.

The captain saw the logo on Leroy's flight jacket and stabbed at it with his finger.

"The machine that crashed the plane of course! You'd

know! You work for them! It was the Daedalus unit that brought us down. It gave us no warning before it went berserk. There was nothing I could do! I'll kill the man who made us use that bloody robot if anything happens to Julie!"

And he stood there on the sand watching Leroy, as the body with the golden hair was loaded gently onto the Bell, ready to be lifted back into the night sky above Cairo.

II

JESSICA

IN LONDON, PREPARATIONS FOR CHRISTMAS WERE WELL UNDER way. Pearl strings of lights criss-crossed the streets, giant figures from the latest Disney cartoon hung outside Hamley's toyshop and at Trafalgar the sparkling cone of a Christmas tree towered into the sky. From the top-floor restaurant of the Olympiad Hotel in Grosvenor Square, the city was an ocean of stars, as far as the eye could see.

"Do you mind if I use a tape recorder?"

The question hung in the air for a moment, threatening to shatter the fragile rapport that had built up between the man and the woman over dinner.

Then the chief executive of the Gilcrest Radio Corporation motioned to the waiter to pour the last of the Chateau Coutet into the journalist's glass and said, "Not at all. Whatever suits you best."

They were discreetly hidden in a secluded alcove, well away from the few remaining diners. The woman was handsome rather than pretty, tall, and in her early forties. She had rich, chestnut-brown hair, a strong slim body, and quick searching eyes that watched the world from behind a pair of dark-framed glasses. The man was large and avuncular, with a soft beguiling voice and a face that told of many such meals in fine restaurants. Both wore business suits, and both continued to circle each other in carefully guarded conversation, like two world-class chessmasters.

The journalist produced a small cassette recorder and set it down on the starched white tablecloth, where it sat like a malevolent insect amongst the glittering crystal. The Record button was pressed, and the formal interview began.

"Ah . . . this is the third time in a row that GRC has won the medal of honour at the Hamburg electronics fair," said the journalist. "How do you account for this string of successes?"

It was an easy enough question – to start with.

"I like to think it's because of our dynamic management team, our committed workforce and, of course, because of the new technology we continue to produce at the right price."

So far so good. The chief executive was tired after a long day in Hamburg, where the award for GRC's new "SmartMate" had been presented, and would have liked nothing better than to slide into a long, luxurious bath with a decent glass of whiskey. But the corporation press office had insisted on this last important interview. The journalist was one of the most widely read business commentators in London, with influence enough to make or break the SmartMate. It was even suggested that the CEO might take one along – as a gift.

"And, of course, quite an achievement for a . . . " The journalist paused.

"For a woman?" suggested the chief executive. "Really Robert, I'm surprised you can survive in this day and age with an attitude like that."

There was an awkward silence.

"For someone so *young*, my dear Jessica," smiled the journalist, raising his glass. "Here's to youth!"

Jessica Victoria Wright, chief executive officer of the Gilcrest Radio Corporation, raised her glass in return.

"Wine him and dine him, and give him the full press kit," her people had told her. "But never forget, he has a mind like a steel trap."

"I really am *awfully* sorry I couldn't make Hamburg," sighed the journalist. "But when you get to my age, flying is such a bore. Tell me, what is this new toy of yours everyone's raving about?"

Jessica Wright took a flat, black case the size of a paperback book from her handbag, and put it down next to the journalist's tape recorder. Then she opened the lid to reveal a screen, and fold-out keypad.

"This is SmartMate," she explained. "It represents a new generation of personal business machines."

"Oh, Jessica! Not *another* organiser?"

"Not at all. Watch!" And she switched on the little machine, raising the words *Welcome to SmartMate* in white on a blue background, rapidly followed by a menu sheet.

"SmartMate contains all the elements of a modern office in a case small enough to carry in your pocket. It's a one-gigabytes-capacity personal computer, with two SmartCard ports, video phone, fax modem, and Internet. It can operate anywhere in the world via the GSM satellites and," she added with a smile, tapping the journalist's cassette recorder, "it can also be used as a Dictaphone."

"Touché," chuckled the journalist, turning the SmartMate to examine the screen more closely. "And I imagine that, since this must be the work of your brilliant chairman, the notorious Dr Theodore Gilkrensky, it's way ahead of anything the Japanese have to offer."

"Absolutely."

"You say the video phone operates *anywhere* in the world?"

"Anywhere the satellites can reach."

The journalist picked up the machine and turned it in his hands.

"I suppose it's *terribly* expensive?"

"We intend to retail it at just under a thousand pounds initially, including VAT. But, of course, you must accept this one with our compliments. To review for your paper, you understand."

The journalist shut down the SmartMate and slipped it into his jacket pocket.

"My dear Jessica, what can I say? GRC has done it again." Then he leant over and picked up a blue and white folder from the floor. "I suppose all the tedious technical specifications are in this press kit?"

"Indeed. Liqueur?"

"Jessica, you spoil me! A large Hennessy, if you please."

The waiter cleared the table, brought the brandy, and retreated.

The journalist opened the folder and spread its contents on the white tablecloth. Amongst the press releases, technical specifications and glossy brochures was a portrait photograph of a darkly handsome man in his late thirties. There was a confident smile on his face and a twinkle in the hypnotic brown eyes. The journalist held the photograph up between his thumb and forefinger.

"And how is the good doctor these days, Jessica? Still in the pink?"

"Dr Gilkrensky is very well, thank you."

The journalist slowly turned the photograph for a moment, before laying it, face down, on the table.

"So all the stories one hears are untrue?"

Jessica Wright stiffened. Images flashed in her mind – Theo in a hospital bed . . . in the rest home . . . on the island – in pieces.

"Stories, Robert?"

The journalist leant forward and pressed the Stop button on his cassette recorder.

"Jessica, off the record. There was a time when Theodore Gilkrensky personally launched *every* new product from GRC, and took great pleasure in doing it. This time last year we'd have had him hanging outside that window from one of those helicopters of his, with a glass of champagne in one hand and this SmartMate in the other. He wouldn't be in hiding on some God-forsaken Irish island while GRC sends you out to have a cosy fireside chat with me. What's wrong?"

"Nothing's wrong, Robert. It's all there in your press kit. Theo is tied up with an important new project right now. But when it's ready, I'm sure he'll come back and announce it personally . . . like always."

"Is this the priceless new super-computer? The one that's supposed to save you from the Japs?"

"That's right."

"The one he's been working on for the past five years?"

"Ah . . . yes."

The journalist swirled his brandy, watching the alcohol condense against the glass.

"Jessica. I've been watching you ever since Theo put you in charge of his father's company. And to be honest, I never thought you'd survive. You were a one-product electronics manufacturer with nothing but Theo's gadgets and his father's money to keep you going. But, I have to hand it to you, you played it smart. You made your money on the electronics, and you spread your risks – hotels, an airline, state-of-the-art research and development companies – and every year or two Theo would come up with some amazing breakthrough that would take the world by storm. The SmartCard, that robot pilot, the interactive video parks. How much is it all worth now?"

"About twenty billion."

"But two years ago, you slipped up, didn't you? Mawashi-Saito, one of the largest conglomerates in Japan, somehow managed to get its hands on a twenty-five per cent shareholding. And what does the famous Doctor Gilkrensky do? Nothing, that's what. Until this . . . this SmartMate of his. And even then, he doesn't promote it himself. In spite of the fact that it represents the only good news from GRC in years."

The journalist put his glass down on the table.

"I think the good doctor has lost it, Jessica. I know this business inside out and, frankly, this SmartMate is nothing more than a handful of old developments, miniaturised and cobbled together. Oh, you can frown at me over the top of your glasses with those beautiful brown eyes of yours but I think that since his wife was killed, Theo Gilkrensky has fallen apart. This mythical super-computer he's supposed to be working on is nothing more than a smokescreen to keep the other shareholders from selling out."

Jessica Wright pushed her glasses back up on the bridge of her nose, took a deep breath, and said, "Robert, there's nothing wrong with Theo, or with GRC. Off the record, yes, Maria's death did shake him up pretty badly. They were very close and, because of the circumstances under which she was killed, we had to be careful about Theo's public appearances. But look at our financial performance since Mawashi-Saito came on board. It's better than ever. So I don't think any of our directors . . . "

An electronic chirrup warbled from the journalist's jacket pocket.

"That's not *my* bleeper!"

"It's the SmartMate, Robert. Could you take it out please?"

The journalist slid the case out of his pocket and laid it on the table. Jessica Wright opened the lid and pressed a key. The screen was filled with the image of a young man with slicked-back hair. He peered anxiously at Jessica and the edges of the screen, as if to see if she was alone.

"Good evening, Tony."

"I'm sorry to call you at this number, Jessica. But your own SmartMate wasn't answering."

"I left it in the suite. Is there a problem?"

"Can you call me back straight away? Something's come up."

"Can it wait, Tony? I'm in the middle of an interview."

"I'm afraid not. I've already rung the hotel to have your car brought round. Call me when you can, all right?"

Jessica Wright smiled at the journalist, who shrugged his shoulders, then she shut the SmartMate's lid and handed it back to him.

"Saved by the bell, my dear Jessica," he said, turning the case in his hand. "And just when our interview was getting interesting. But don't worry. Just to be patriotic, I'll give you a good review on this little machine of yours, and hope you'll pass on my regards to the good doctor. If there is ever any chance of a personal interview with him . . . ?"

Ten minutes later, Jessica Wright was behind the wheel

of her black Jaguar, rushing eastwards beneath the lights of Oxford Street. The return call to Tony Delgado, made from the privacy of her personal suite at the hotel, had shaken her – an air crash near Cairo, involving a plane flown by one of Theo's machines. Tony didn't have many of the details yet but the story was all over CNN, and the word was that the autopilot was to blame.

Damn!

The heel of her hand ground down on the horn as a taxi tried to pull out in front of her.

Damn! Damn! Damn!

She had spent years building up GRC with Theo. Then months and months of holding things together after he fell apart. Just when she thought she had won the other shareholders away from Mawashi-Saito, *this* had to happen. It would destroy Theo's credibility and deliver GRC to the Japanese on a bloody plate!

She shot through Holborn and Cheapside, narrowly dodging a red light at the Bank of England, and swerved the XJ6 into King William Street. There in front of her, towering above the shop fronts and the grim stone buildings, was a tall glass monolith showing lights in the office windows at its summit. On the very apex of the building, standing proud against the night sky, were the glowing red letters GRC.

The man who had spoken to her on the SmartMate was waiting as she stepped out of the lift onto the ninth floor. Tony Delgado, assistant chief executive, smiled nervously and ran the fingers of his left hand through his hair.

"Sorry about this, Jessica."

"Any more news?"

"Only bits and pieces. I called Neil Martin and got him out of bed – he's waiting for you in the boardroom. The press office is going crazy. We've taped the latest CNN broadcast and all the networks are looking for a spokesman. I put out a covering statement, but I was waiting for you before I went any further."

They hurried down the wood-panelled corridor towards the main executive suite. Jessica flung open a door to her right, marched across a reception area and past a desk where an older woman rose to meet her.

"Mr Martin is waiting for you. And the video's set up."

"Thank you, Sheila. You'd better hold all calls for half an hour."

They swept through another door and into the boardroom. Beyond the windows, the lights of Tower Bridge and HMS Belfast glittered on the Thames. Standing in front of the large video screen, which dominated the remaining wall, was a thin, worried man.

"All right, Neil. Let's see it!"

Neil Martin, GRC's press officer, fingered the remote control.

"You won't like it."

On the screen, a grim-faced news reporter sat behind a desk. In the top left-hand corner of the picture was a still photograph of a plane in flight. The words *Air Crash* formed a banner across the bottom.

"And news just in from Egypt: there has been a plane crash involving an airliner belonging to the GRC subsidiary, Exair. The aircraft is reported to have smashed into the desert just minutes after take-off from Cairo, at around nine this evening, local time."

The still photograph of the plane expanded until it filled the screen and then dissolved into video footage of the crash site. Flames were leaping from the tail section and pouring into the dark sky. The camera zoomed in to focus on the GRC logo.

"Shit!" hissed Jessica.

"As yet, casualties are reported to be light . . ." continued the reporter as the picture changed to show helicopters arriving at a hospital. " . . . with estimates of only a handful of fatalities amongst the two hundred passengers."

"Thank God!"

"It gets worse," said Martin.

"So far, there are no firm facts as to the cause of the accident, but early reports are of a failure in the Daedalus robot-pilot system."

The camera zoomed in on one group of arrivals and steadied on a stretcher carrying a blonde woman. For an instant it focused on her still face, and then she was swallowed up by the bustle of reporters and hospital staff around the emergency room.

The picture was cut and replaced by a close-up of the reporter in the studio.

"The Daedalus autopilot was developed by the well-known electronics tycoon Dr Theodore Gilkrensky, for his GRC corporation, and fitted to all the jets in its Exair fleet two years ago. A spokesman for the corporation said this was the first incident of its kind in over a million flying hours, but that all aircraft using the system had been advised to switch to manual control pending an investigation. Dr Gilkrensky himself was not available for comment. Meanwhile, in the Chilean earthquake . . . "

Tony Delgado was scanning a fax page.

"The news broadcast was wrong, as far as we know from our Cairo office. There have been *no* reported fatalities, and only one serious injury."

"The woman on the stretcher?"

"She's a stewardess. Nobody else was hurt, apart from a lacerated hand, a couple of cases of shock and a few sprained ankles from the escape chutes."

"Well, that's *something*," said Jessica, clutching at straws. "All those safety features we built into that plane paid off in the end."

"It's still a public relations disaster, whichever way you try and dress it up," said Martin.

"And nothing about the SmartMate award?"

"The crash will wipe it right off the map. Would you buy a computer from a corporation whose robots crash planes?"

"Shit!" hissed Jessica again through her teeth. "It couldn't have come at a worse time. The board decision on the Japanese share offer is only a week away. What time do you make it, Tony? I left my watch in the suite."

"One forty-five."

"Right, I want VIP treatment for all the survivors – the best health care, hotel beds, the works – whatever it costs! And I want uniformed flight crews to make themselves conspicuous on all Exair flights until we have this problem with Daedalus sorted out. Neil, put a call through to that professor Theo has working over in Florida – the one who designed the plane – and tell him to get an investigation team together. Then have our people in Cairo dig me up as many hard facts as they can. I'll meet you in the press office in ten minutes and we'll see what we can salvage from this mess!"

Four and a half hours later, Jessica Wright was back at her desk in the boardroom. Detailed statements had gone out to the national newspapers, with short interviews to all the main dailies and sound-bites for the radio stations. At least four television crews were expected before breakfast, to cover the morning news.

She could feel the tiredness creeping up on her behind the adrenaline. She could have done with a few hours' sleep in the "overnight room", but there wasn't time. Thoughts of Tony Delgado surfaced. She had left him downstairs on the phone to one of the radio stations. At least *he* was someone she could rely on in a crisis.

There was a knock at the door and Jessica's personal assistant set a large china mug of strong tea carefully down on the glass-topped desk.

"Thank you, Sheila," said Jessica, as she cupped the mug in her hands she tried to find comfort in its warmth as she stared out at the darkened city, frightened and alone.

3

THEO

JESSICA WRIGHT WAS NOT A SENTIMENTAL PERSON. NOBODY could survive as chief executive of one of the largest corporations in the world by being sentimental. But she had spent a great deal of time in searching out that china mug.

Her father had drunk his tea from one exactly like it, as regular as clockwork, at half past ten in the morning and at three in the afternoon in the family sweet shop in Lowestoft when she was a little girl. Before her brothers had grown up, she had helped him behind the counter, knowing the price of all the sweets filling the big glass jars, and feeling the weight of the thick copper pennies in her hand. She learnt the basics of economics early, did Jessica Wright. She learnt the difference between "wholesale" – the price you bought something for – and "retail" – the price you sold it at. But most important of all, she learnt that "profit" – the difference you kept for yourself – was the only measure of success that really

29

mattered. She never stole sweets from the shop, the way her brothers did, because that would upset the profit. And she was always careful to take her time when giving change – putting large notes in a special clip on top of the till until the amount was agreed – so there could be no mistake.

Then, when Jessica was in her teens, her brothers started taking an interest in the business. Jessica fought her ground. She said they didn't care if the shop made a profit or not – as long as they could dip into the till now and then. There were scenes. Jessica was banished back to the flat upstairs to help her mother. Then more scenes, until her family packed her off to college in Norwich to study economics to her heart's content. It was no surprise to anyone when she passed her exams with distinction and won a business scholarship to Harvard for her MBA.

And what had they taught her about crisis management at the Harvard Business School? Approach the problem logically. Gather all the information you can. Analyse it – with as much expert help as you can muster, then make your moves accordingly.

And there was only one expert in the world who could really help her now – Theodore Gilkrensky himself.

She had met him in Boston, towards the end of her first year at Harvard. Jessica had been determined to be at the cutting edge of business technology, and had exchanged a year's worth of canteen lunches for a primitive word processor, one of the first on campus. But there were problems.

"The screen keeps jumping," she complained to a classmate who was consuming a large salad in the cafeteria while Jessica watched. "It wobbles like an earthquake right in front of my eyes. If it loses my thesis, I swear I'll throw the bloody thing out of the window!"

"Have you checked to see if the hard disc is full?" said an English voice behind her. An English voice! After almost a year submerged at Harvard, Jessica was sure she must be slipping into a mid-Atlantic twang herself. She turned in her seat to see who the fellow-expatriate might be.

Sprawled easily on a seat at the table behind her was a young man in a brown leather jacket, with a crumpled white shirt, jeans and a pair of running shoes that had seen better days. His face was thin and pleasant, with a hint of mischief in his smile, and thick, dark hair brushed back over his ears. But what startled Jessica was the unsettling energy in his eyes – their directness – as if they could see right through her.

"I beg your pardon?" she said.

"Computers only have a limited amount of space in their memory," said the man, leaning forward. "Once that memory gets full, the machine starts to overload and play tricks. If you're not careful you could overheat the chip and the whole system will crash. That's why I asked if you'd checked the hard disc."

"I wouldn't know how."

The man gestured at the empty space on the table in front of her and smiled.

"If you're not eating, and the machine's not too far away, I'll do it for you," he offered. "Computers are my thing. My name's Theo, by the way. Theodore Gilkrensky. I'm working down the river at MIT."

Jessica felt her classmate nudge her beneath the table. She, at least, had heard that name before.

Five minutes later, Jessica Wright was watching Gilkrensky's long hands as they fluttered over the keyboard of her word processor. It was like watching a concert pianist perform.

At a loss for anything more intelligent to say, she said, "What part of England are you from?"

"I was born in Farnborough, where the airbase is. My father has a big factory there."

"Your name doesn't sound very English."

"It's not. My father was a Pole. He was working in Germany when the Nazis came to power and had to get out. He'd just married a gypsy girl, and could see what was about to happen. There look! Your hard disc's full. Don't you ever download anything onto floppies?"

"I just keep pressing 'ALT SAVE' all the time," said Jessica. "I didn't know there was a limit."

For an hour they sat and talked while he moved files to and fro. She learnt he was working on something very advanced called a "neural net" computer, that his father was rich and that, like her, he was lonely.

That Saturday they met at the New England Aquarium on Central Wharf and strolled down the long spiral walkway as it wound around the four-storey glass tank.

"All the fish remind me of Lowestoft," said Jessica. "When I used to go down and watch the fish market sometimes with my father."

"Do you miss home?" asked Gilkrensky.

"Sometimes. I remember my father bought a lobster one evening for a treat. It was the most luxurious thing I'd ever tasted."

The following Saturday he picked her up from her apartment on an old Triumph motor-bike and took her to the Museum of Science, where they sat in a steep row of seats in the OmniMax cinema. A helicopter flight unfolded before them with such vivid realism that Jessica said, "It must be fantastic to fly."

The following Friday he called her and asked if she could meet him near the swimming-pool in Charlesbank Park not far from the Science Museum.

"Be there at noon. And don't be late," he insisted. "It would be very awkward if you weren't on time."

Which left her in a state of curiosity that carried her onto the south bank of the Charles river well ahead of schedule. It was unlike Theo to *insist* on anything. He was normally one of the most relaxed people she had ever met.

She heard the little helicopter before she saw it. She had been watching the long racing rowboats practising up and down by Harvard Bridge, and the panting joggers pounding the Charles River Esplanade. Behind her, in a playground, children whooped, cried, whined and laughed on the swings, roundabouts and slides. Then suddenly, the thumping chop of the helicopter was very

33

near – nearer than she had ever been to one before. The joggers on the footpath and the children in the playground looked up, and then she was staring at the white underside of a bright blue helicopter that circled once, before settling in the centre of the park, scattering leaves and paper cartons in all directions. Jessica held her coat against the down-draught peering at the blurred image of the pilot behind the glassy nose. Behind her, on Starrow Drive, a fat policeman was getting out of his patrol car and waddling across the grass to see what the matter was. It must have landed to bring someone to the hospital, thought Jessica. If Theo was here he'd know all about it.

The policeman was getting nearer.

A small crowd was gathering.

Then the pilot's window slid back.

"Hurry up and climb in, Jess!" shouted Theodore Gilkrensky. "I'm not supposed to land here!" And he leaned over to open the passenger door. She ran to the helicopter and climbed in. Theo strapped her in and gave her a set of headphones. Through the perspex she could see the joggers watching in envy, the children on the climbing-frame open-mouthed, and the policeman calling frantically into his radio.

They flew up over the Charles Dam and out across the Navy Yard, passing the tall masts of the *USS Constitution* on their right. Jessica was grinning from ear to ear. It's like when I was a child, she thought, and my father took me on my first merry-go-round. She looked across at Theo and he was grinning too.

They flew out along the estuary, heading north-east over Mystic Bridge, Chelsea and Revere until they reached the ocean. Then Theo turned the helicopter to fly parallel to the coast, across the Nahant peninsula, out around the lighthouse at Lee Mansion, and over the fishing village of Marblehead. Below them, dozens of yachts and motor-cruisers scratched white arrowheads on the sea.

"Just like Lowestoft?" shouted Gilkrensky over the noise of the engine.

"Yes," laughed Jessica. "Just like Lowestoft."

They landed at a small airfield outside Salem and spent the afternoon touring the town. Theo took a great interest in its New Age shops, explaining the origins and uses of all the crystals, pendulums and potions, before buying her a gold chain with a slice of brown agate on it. He said it matched her hair. Later they wandered down onto Pickering Wharf and Theo directed her gently to the small rustic inn, where he had booked a room. The smell of cooking wafted out into the air like the music of the Pied Piper.

"Hungry?" he said. "I've ordered lobster!"

"You can read my mind."

"It's the gypsy in me," said Gilkrensky.

Their affair lasted for his remaining nine months at Boston. Theo was exciting company and no two days were the same. There were walks around the bookshops in the Faneuil Marketplace, whale cruises on the bay, weekend trips to Cape Cod on his old motor-bike and, best of all, long lazy Saturdays in bed. On those timeless afternoons, Jessica would lie amongst the crumpled sheets, looking up at the sunlit ceiling and wonder where their relationship was going. She told herself it wasn't love. She said as much, and he agreed. She was lonely. He was lonely. They were together. QED! But, even though they were "just friends", it annoyed Jessica that he would not let her see inside his heart. Behind the energy and the drive, there was always part of his soul he kept hidden away in reserve . . . but for whom? One Saturday, Jessica was determined to find out.

"What was your defining moment?" she asked, as she lay naked and warm in the afterglow of their love-making, with her head pillowed on his chest.

"My what?"

"The moment in your life that made you what you are."

"How do you mean?"

So Jessica told him the story of her father's sweet shop. About how she had been forced to watch her brothers run it into the ground, and how she had determined to achieve enough control in her own life never to let that happen to her.

"Now you," she said, rolling over in the bed so that she could watch his face.

Gilkrensky stared at the ceiling for a long time. Then he said, "I suppose it was at the Farnborough Air Show when I was about nine or ten. My father's company had a stand at the exhibition, promoting some new gadget he'd invented. There were lots of business clients around and my father's partner, Lord Rothsay, had his Japanese contacts at the show, all busily taking notes. My father wanted me on the stand, so that he could show me off to his customers, but there was also a fun fair just outside the exhibition hall, and more than anything I wanted to ride on the chair-a-planes, the ones that make you feel as if you're really flying . . . I've always loved flying . . . "

"Go on," said Jessica.

"My mother was at the show as well, and knew what I *really* wanted to do. She took one look at me, one look at the fun fair and said, 'Come on. Let's go!'"

"So you went to the fair?" said Jessica.

"We never got there. We were hardly off the stand when my father came rushing over and asked us where we thought we were going. My mother said he was being ridiculous and there was an almighty row, right there in the exhibition hall, with me watching. They were going at each other, in front of all those people, as if nothing else in the world mattered. Finally, I couldn't take it any more. I turned and ran outside into the crowd. The main air display was about to start and there were thousands of people, pushing forward to get a good view. When you're small, all you can see are trousers, jackets and dresses, nothing else. And you can't see where you are because the bodies block your view. I was lost for two hours before they found me, just running backwards and forwards in the crowd, trying to see where I was . . . "

His voice tailed off and he stared into space, as if he were living it all over again.

"Funny," he said at last. "The things you remember."

Jessica kissed his bare shoulder.

"And why do you think that was your 'defining moment'?" she said softly.

Gilkrensky was still looking up at the ceiling. Finally he reached down and stroked her hair.

"I don't know. My mother and father were so different. He wanted me to work, and she wanted me to stop once in a while and enjoy myself. Then she died when I was twelve, and my father got his way. Perhaps that's why I get so obsessive about work, and why I've been looking for someone to 'take me to the fair' ever since."

"And do I?"

There was another long silence. And Jessica knew, if ever there was to be a "defining moment" for their relationship, this was it.

"We'll always be friends. Won't we, Jess?" said Theodore Gilkrensky at last.

The affair ended when he finished his research and left to take the results back to his father. There were no scenes, no tearful goodbyes. He even offered her a job with his father's company back in England, which she politely turned down, saying that she was her own woman and would look him up when she'd made her first million by herself.

"I bet you'll do it too," he told her when they parted at Logan airport. "I'll be watching out for you."

And then he left.

Look at it this way, the logical part of her brain reminded her as his plane taxied onto the runway, it wasn't love. We had an easy friendship born out of mutual convenience for as long as we were together. Nothing more, nothing less. It was only when the aircraft finally disappeared into the clouds that the illogical part of her soul wondered what it might have been like to spend the rest of her life with him.

And from then on, wherever she was in the world, a single red rose would arrive on the anniversary of that night in Salem when they had first made love.

The roses used to annoy Roderick Thorpe, when she went to work for him as chief executive of his family's Olympiad hotel chain back in England. Jessica had had a number of jobs since Boston, gradually working her way upwards, but it was obvious to her that if she was to make that first million she had promised Theo, she had to be a shareholder, with a piece of the action.

And that was how she got involved with Roderick Thorpe.

His group had hotels all over the country and needed a manager who knew what they were about. Jessica already had a job with a similar group but, over coffee, Roderick Thorpe offered what Jessica wanted most – a five percent shareholding, subject to performance.

It had been a long hard slog. The Olympiad chain looked impressive on paper, until you examined the books. Every hotel seemed to be a law unto itself and nobody seemed to be managing costs. To bring the group into profit represented a definite challenge.

But Jessica did it.

She called in the accounts of each hotel and went through them in meticulous detail, ruthlessly pruning those that didn't pay. Then she put together a strategic plan to change the image of the group – concentrating on the more profitable conference venues in London, Birmingham and Manchester.

She only made one mistake.

She fell in love with Roderick Thorpe.

She knew it wasn't smart. Thorpe was married. He had a bad reputation. But Jessica didn't care. She was on top of the world, and life was as full and exciting as it had been in Boston with Theo. Only this time it was better. Jessica was in control.

Until Thorpe dumped her.

He said he was sorry, but the chain had not performed as well as the board of directors had hoped. They had decided not to renew her contract.

At first she thought it was a joke. She showed him the books, the bank balances, the brochures for the fine new hotels and conference centres. But he wasn't listening.

He had been using her to save the business. Now his wife wanted him back, and had rattled her father's share holdings to get her way. Jessica had to go.

That night in her flat in London, after a long evening's journey through rage and despair, Jessica lay on her bed, trying to drink herself to sleep. There had been no "golden handshake", no severance pay, no shares in the business and, of course, no first million.

She was pouring herself another stiff gin and tonic, and cursing because all the ice was gone, when the doorbell rang. Through the haze of alcohol, she noticed it was a quarter to one in the morning, and for a moment thought it might be Roderick – but then again, he had a key. She stumbled from the bed, threw cold water on her face, tidied herself up and staggered to the door, making sure the security chain was on.

"Miss Jessica Wright?" said a uniformed courier.

"Yes."

"Package for you. Sign here please." And he handed her a single red rose, together with a small parcel containing a mobile phone. There was a note attached.

"I'm thinking of branching out into the hotel business and need someone with experience. Please call me. Your friend – Theo."

"Would you like some more tea?" said Sheila as she laid a fax sheet on Jessica's desk.

"No, thank you. What's that?"

"The latest report from Cairo. You should get some sleep before the television people get here."

"What time is it now?"

"Almost a quarter past seven. Abigail has just come in, so I'll go and get a few hours' rest myself."

"Thank you, Sheila. Before you go, could you copy this to the island and tell the Chairman I'll call him in ten minutes to discuss it."

"Do you think he'll be awake? It's still very early."

"Don't worry. He'll be up."

Jessica Wright put the china mug down gently on the glass of her desk. For a moment she allowed herself the memory of Roderick Thorpe's face on the day, some weeks later, when she had forced the sale of his hotels to Theo's new corporation, and the pleasure of replacing the name-plate on his private suite at the London Olympiad with her own.

Would Theo be able to handle what she was about to tell him? If she could be there when he got the news it would help, but there was no time. Bringing her eyes to focus on the paper in front of her, she leant forward to read her notes in preparation for her report to her Chairman, friend, and former lover, Dr Theodore Gilkrensky.

4

THE EIGHTH RICHEST
MAN IN THE WORLD

IN THE GREY TWILIGHT OF THE EARLY MORNING, MAJOR
Jonathan Crowe could hardly tell where the sky ended
and the sea began. Fat raindrops shouldered their way
towards the sill on the other side of the bullet-proof
glass, and the last wind of the dying storm shook the
rhododendron bushes near the helipad.

We'll need to cut those back, he thought, and made a
note on his checklist. All through the storm, the weather
had played tricks with the new security system. Waves
had given false echoes on the radar and the wind,
rattling doors and windows had kept Crowe up half the
night as it broke the contacts on the alarms. The only
things that hadn't given trouble were the microwave
motion sensors, but it was early days for them too.

Crowe slipped the clipboard under his arm, picked up
one of the radio headsets from the desk and made sure
his security badge was in place. Then he opened the

guard-room door and walked down the corridor to the main office in the east wing. One of the secretaries was already up and typing a technical report from a Dictaphone.

"How long does he usually run for?" asked Crowe.

"Sorry, Major?"

The girl lifted the earphones and stopped typing.

"How long does the chairman run for?"

"About an hour in the mornings. But it's very wet today. So I expect he'll cut it short."

Just so long as he doesn't go beyond the perimeter, thought Crowe, or he'll trigger the motion sensors and we'll have to reset those as well.

Crowe had been head of security for GRC for less than a year, and was acutely aware of his responsibilities regarding the chairman. Mistakes had been made in the past, and the chairman's wife had died. Crowe was determined that no such mistakes would happen while he was in charge.

Sliding the battery-pack of the radio-link into his pocket, Crowe eased the headset over his left ear and spoke into the microphone.

"Gerald? Where are you? Over."

"Just completing our second lap, Major . . . we'll be back in about five minutes . . . Over."

"Carry on. Out!"

The high-resolution fax machine dedicated to head office business started to whirr, spewing paper into a red wire tray. Catching sight of the word *Urgent* on the cover sheet, Crowe picked it up and started to read.

"Oh, my God!" he said softly, and searched the windswept landscape beyond the office windows.

"Gerald? Tom? You'd better get the chairman back in here fast. There's an urgent fax from London and they'll be calling him about it in a few minutes. Over."

"We're coming up near the helipad now, Major . . . you should see us in a moment. Over?"

"Roger that. Out!"

Above the hiss of the rain, Major Crowe heard a regular slapping sound, like a slow handclap. Three running figures in line abreast came round a curve in the path, each one dressed in an identical jogging suit with a waterproof hood and cape. From a distance, it was impossible to tell the figures apart – just one of the many security precautions on Crowe's list.

Crowe gathered up the remaining pages from the wire basket and checked them against the cover sheet to make sure they had all been received. Then he tapped the secretary on her shoulder and asked her to take the message to the chairman, while he considered the security implications of what he had just read.

The girl stapled the pages together and walked into the corridor. As she went, a closed-circuit television camera observed her from above, and a scanner in the ceiling recognised the identification badge she wore above her left breast. At the end of the corridor she entered the guardroom, with its TV monitors, security controls and grey-painted desks. One of the bodyguards was peering down into a monitor as he wiped the rain from his face. He looked up at her and grinned. It was

Thomas, the blond one who tried to chat up all the girls. The quiet one from the North, the dark man who never smiled, would be in the shower. They always worked like that when they changed shifts. One of them was always on watch.

"Good morning, Helen. Will you come and scrub my back for me when Gerald's finished in the shower?"

"Maybe I will, and maybe I won't. But right now there's an urgent fax to go straight to the chairman, if you'd be so kind?"

He was very good-looking. But Helen had seen him sparring with Gerald in the gym one evening, and it had scared her.

"You can go right in, Helen. Or would you like me to body-search you first?"

"Ah! Would you ever grow up, Thomas? That attitude of yours'll be the death of you one of these days!"

The door to the inner sanctum opened.

After the stark brightness of the guard-room, the study beyond was soft and dark, like a well-furnished cave. The only light came from a lamp on the desk at the far end of the room and a bank of video monitors facing it from beneath the window. In the centre of the room was a small conference table piled high with papers, and along each wall an odd assortment of books, manuals and video cassettes jostled each other on crowded shelves, spilling into roughly stacked heaps on the floor.

But the desk itself was perfectly clear, except for three items – the lamp, a slim black briefcase, and a simply framed photograph of a young woman sitting on the rail of an old wooden bridge against a green wall of sunlit trees. She was wearing a forget-me-not-blue dress that set off the coppery red of her hair, and she was smiling at the photographer. It was easy to see the love in her eyes.

"What is it, Helen? Gerald said it was urgent."

"It's from Miss Wright in London. You're to read it straight away, so she can call you in a few minutes to discuss it."

The man who had been staring out at the rain stopped drying his hair with a towel, and turned to face her across the desk.

"Thank you," said Theodore Gilkrensky and reached out for the message. In the light of the lamp, Helen could see the scars running like melted wax across the back of his left hand. There was a thin scar on his face too, from beneath the dark tousled hair, over his left temple, and down into the closely cropped beard. For a moment, Helen watched the tired brown eyes scan the fax pages, wondering what he was thinking as he read, then she turned and left. It was a sad face, she thought as the door hissed shut behind her, but nothing remarkable. Hardly what you'd expect from the eighth richest man in the world.

Gilkrensky scanned the pages once, said "Oh shit!" and sank into the leather swivel-chair. Then he read the fax sheets again, searching for any hope in the blunt businesslike wording. Finding none, he slapped the pages down on the desk and lay back, staring up at the ceiling.

"Shit! Shit! Shit!"

The chirrup of an incoming call sounded from the bank of video monitors. Gilkrensky ignored it. He could feel the sweat rising on his skin and a buzzing in his ears.

The video warbled, louder this time.

Gilkrensky glared at the papers on the desk, willing them to go away. The video console bleated at him again. This time the sound was continuous. Gilkrensky sank back further into the chair and raised his hands to cover his ears.

In London, Jessica Wright waited for Theo to take her call. The first television crew was arriving at eight and time was running out. Tiredness was starting to get the better of her. If only Theo would bloody well answer!

"Is he *there*?"

"I'm sorry Miss Wright. He was in the study a moment ago. I'll try him on the intercom."

"Please do. It's very urgent."

There was a few minutes' delay. Then Theo's face filled the big screen in Jessica's office – a face she still found unfamiliar. The short beard, the tousled hair, and the sad haunted eyes were a far cry from the confident, handsome man she had built a business empire with.

"We have an emergency, Theo!"

"I can see that, Jess. I'd say it was pilot error."

"That's not what the pilot says. He's all over CNN insisting it was your Daedalus that crashed the plane."

"But that's impossible. You know the number of

safety features Bill McCarthy and I built into that thing. Even the back-up systems have back-up systems, and the main neural net is supported by three logic-based peripherals. Those systems have . . . "

"Theo. This isn't about the machine. It's about public confidence. If we can't find a way to recover from this story in the next few hours our reputation is going to go down the toilet. The SmartCard, the computers, the SmartMate . . . everything!"

"Then get the press office onto it! Get Bill to fly over from Florida with a team! He'll soon show them that . . . "

"Theo! I wouldn't ask you if this wasn't so crucial, but I need you to come to a press conference in London right away."

"Get somebody else, Jess. Get Pat O'Connor from the lab here, or Gerry Ross from the Microelectronics Centre in Cork. They'd . . . "

"You're the only one with all the facts on Daedalus, Theo. It's *your* machine!"

"Jessica. I'm in the middle of very important work on the Minerva system. We have the interface perfected now."

"But this is vital!"

"No way!"

"Theo! I need you!"

"No!"

Jessica Wright glared at the image on the screen. It was five to eight. The television crews would be arriving at any minute. She took a deep breath to steady herself.

"Theo. I have to call an emergency board meeting to

49

discuss this crisis anyway. That's my job, and there's still that vote of confidence hanging over our heads regarding the Japanese."

Gilkrensky stared at her blankly from the monitor.

"I can't leave the island, Jess."

Jessica Wright's fingers curved around the handle of her china mug. Her thumb pressed against the rim.

"Jesus, Theo! You've got to do something! Offers have been made to the other shareholders by Mawashi-Saito, and if you're not here I am *not* going to take responsibility for what might happen at the meeting. The whole fucking corporation might as well pack up and move to Tokyo!"

Gilkrensky shifted uneasily in his seat.

"All right, Jess. I hear you. Send the jet to Cork and I'll get my notes together."

"I'll keep you updated. There's material coming in all the time."

"Whatever. Have the Dublin office requisition another chopper and contact Helen to tell her what time it'll arrive. I'll have to use the one we have on the island to send Major Crowe ahead to arrange security."

"OK. I'll see you later. Oh! And Theo . . . !"

But Jessica Wright was already looking at a blank screen.

The intercom on her desk buzzed.

"The BBC people are here, Miss Wright."

With a tiny snap, the handle of Jessica Wright's china mug came away in her fingers.

5

MARIA

THEODORE GILKRENSKY SLUMPED BACK BEHIND HIS DESK, staring into space. After all the months he'd spent trying to lose himself in his work after Maria's death, he was being dragged back. Back from the security of the island, his study and his personal routines for coping. He ran his hand over the smooth black surface of the briefcase. After nine months of unremitting sweat since the explosion, the Minerva 3,000 was fully operational. He'd perfected a new biochip that could survive without a complicated support system, new software that would make the most of its unique capabilities, and the most sophisticated user-interface the world had ever seen . . .

His eyes wandered to the photograph of Maria, and from there to the rows of books lining the room. Most of them were hers – everything from standard medical texts to works on astrology, Richard Wilhelm's translation of the *I Ching*, Colin Wilson's book on *The Occult*, El Fiky's review on *The Pyramids of Egypt*, books on earth energies, ley lines, and the book on Celtic magic she'd been reading on the day they'd met . . .

It had been in the old library at University College, Cork. Gilkrensky was working at the new Microelectronics Centre, down by the river Lee, and had walked over to the main campus to look up references on company law for ammunition in his forthcoming battle with Lord Rothsay.

Because the June examinations were due, every space in the college library was filled, and every microfiche reader was in use. Then, off in a quiet backwater of the sea of earnestly bent heads, a machine became free and Theo claimed it, laying out his books while he went off to the main files to hunt for the references he needed.

He returned, only a few minutes later, to find his claim challenged. All his research material had been piled into a neat stack on the floor, and in their place were scientific papers on geomagnetism, reports on visits to early prehistoric settlements, a map of Stonehenge and a large photograph of a Celtic brooch overlaid with tracing paper. Gilkrensky glared around at the bent heads nearby, but none of them would meet his eye.

He was just gathering up the tracing paper, the photographs and the books, when he noticed the faint smell of patchouli oil and a voice behind him hissed, "And what do you think you're at?"

Turning sharply, he found himself transfixed by a pair of angry green eyes in a sea of coppery hair.

"I was using this machine. Those are *my* books!"

"And how could you be using that machine when you were away mooning about in the stacks?"

She was simply dressed, in a white cotton blouse, a denim skirt and sandals. Gilkrensky looked into her eyes and felt his resolve slipping.

"I . . . I was looking for a reference," he replied, recovering enough to wave the glossy black microfiches at her.

"So was I!" she snapped. "And now I come back to find you throwing me out of my place."

Heads were starting to rise all around them.

"Ssshhh!" hissed one of the other students.

"Isn't that exactly what you've done to me?" said Theo.

"And why not? Everyone knows this is where I work in the evenings!"

Gilkrensky was floundering. Clutching at straws, he pointed to her picture of the Celtic brooch and the swirling ink-lines.

"This is the technical section," he said. "'Arts is up on the first floor."

"There's no space up there! And besides, who are you to tell me what research I'm to be carrying out. You mechanists are all the same. Your thinking never leaves the rails of your blinkered imaginations!"

"And your does, I suppose?"

"Indeed it does. Do you know that the complete geometry of the solar system was laid out in the design of that brooch, over two thousand years ago!"

"Really!" snorted a student. "I'm going to call the librarian." Several other heads nodded.

"You can call the gardaí and the Local Defence Forces for all I care!" retaliated the redhead. "But I'm not budging!"

The other student fought her ground. "We'll see about that, Mary Anne Foley! Everyone knows you have no business here anyway!" And she marched off in search of reinforcements.

Mary Anne crossed her arms defiantly on her chest as she watched her go. Then suddenly, when the student was out of sight she muttered, "Judas!" and bent quickly to snatch up her material. "Now look what you've done. My library card expired ages ago, and if that old bat of a librarian catches me again, I'll be barred from campus."

"I'll help you," offered Gilkrensky, and by the time the irate student had returned with the librarian, the microfiche reader was empty.

"The least you can do is buy me a cup of coffee," said Mary Anne, once they had reached the safety of the college quad.

"And why should I do that?" asked Gilkrensky with a smile, knowing full well he would have bought her almost anything in return for a few more moments of her time.

"Because I have no money, and because I know who you are," she replied, softening slightly. "You're that rich mechanist that's working on some sort of super-computer down at the Maltings. Besides, I want to talk to a mechanist about a theory of mine."

"And you are?"

"Doctor Mary Anne Foley. But my friends call me Maria."

"I'm Theodore Gilkrensky. But my friends call me Theo. Where would you like to go?"

"I'll drive," she told him.

She drove a battered Mini, with paintwork pimpled by rust, bald tyres and the boot-lid tied down with string. The place she drove to was a pub on the west side of city, where grassy banks sloped down to the river Lee where it was still small enough to wade across. As she drove past the greyhound track and down the Western Road, towards the setting sun, he learnt she had qualified in medicine at Cork and joined one of the Irish Third World relief agencies, because she wanted to "make a difference". In Africa, she had seen poverty and hardship beyond comprehension, but she had also seen the remote tribes deep in the bush, where the materialism of modern man had not yet reached.

"These were the people who never came to the relief camps," she explained, once they had corralled the little Mini in the pub car park and found a table by the river. "They were in tune with the seasons, the natural energies of the earth, and the phases of the moon. They were happy. It was only when we forced our own values on them, and then failed to keep our promise that the real poverty set in. We have a lot to answer for in Europe. We think we have a better way of life and ram it down everyone's throats."

Gilkrensky looked across the pub garden, at the sleek cars lined up in the car park, and across at the sad curve of a willow as it dipped into the river. In the setting sun, the light had caught the colour of Maria's hair and forged a coppery halo.

"And you're going to change that?"

"No. People aren't going to give up their televisions and their cars and their semi-detached houses on my say-so. I can only look after my own destiny, and show others the way."

"And what way is that?"

She looked up from her coffee and fixed him with her green eyes. Suddenly he felt completely transparent, as if she could see every part of him. It was a feeling he had never experienced before, not even with Jessica.

"I want your opinion on that," she said. "What with you being a mechanist and all. But first I must be sure you seriously want to know."

"Yes. I do."

"Because I've been hurt before, you see. If I tell you my theories and you laugh at me, I'll never speak to you again."

"I promise I won't laugh."

Again the green eyes appraised him.

"No. I believe you won't. Very well then. You are a mechanist."

"A what?"

"A mechanist. A scientist. Somebody who believes in a mechanical universe, in the laws of physics. You believe that electrons make atoms, atoms make molecules,

molecules make proteins, proteins make flesh, flesh makes people. According to your way of thinking, the earth and everything on it are all part of a gigantic living machine. Am I right? And when we die, our flesh rots back into proteins, and molecules and atoms, and the whole process starts all over again."

"And you mean there's more?"

"Of course there is," she insisted earnestly. "And you, as a scientist know it too, only you can't see the truth right in front of your eyes. What *is* an atom? Just a ball of tiny sub-atomic particles that quantum physics tell us are nothing more than energy."

"Yes," said Gilkrensky, wondering where this was leading. "I understand."

"But do you *really*? Do you actually understand that this means *everything* in the whole universe – you, me, the table we're sitting at, the river and everything in this world we see around us, is nothing more than energy."

"Of course."

"Then what happens when you die?" She said triumphantly, springing her trap.

"My body rots."

"Your *body* rots. But what about the real you – the real Theo Gilkrensky living inside that mechanical body of yours. What about *that*?"

"I suppose, if I'm lucky, I go to heaven."

"Yes. And where is 'heaven', geographically speaking?"

"Aren't we straying into religion now?"

Maria's eyes sparkled.

"Exactly! That's the very point of it. All the religions in the world speak of an 'afterlife' – a reality after death. In China it's called 'Tao', in Hinduism it's called 'Brahman', in Islam they call it 'al Haaq – the reality', and in Christianity we call it 'heaven'."

"I . . . I suppose so."

"I've had religion shoved down my throat ever since I was a child, but it's only in the last few years I've really thought about it scientifically. Have you ever seen a baby born? Have you ever seen its face the very moment it opens its eyes?"

"No."

"I saw it once, when I was in Africa. I delivered a little black baby, and for an instant, when she opened her eyes, I was looking into the face of the wisest, kindest person I'd ever met. It was a person coming back to live again on earth. She was coming back from energy into matter, to live on the material world all over again."

"So when we die, our real selves leave the body behind and go back to being energy?"

"Yes. That's what 'heaven' really is. Inside we're immortal. We live forever, dipping down from the field of energy you call 'heaven' into material bodies to spend time on earth. You are not a body with a soul, you are a soul made of energy who is temporarily inhabiting a body." And she sat back on her bench, minutely examining his face for the first trace of ridicule.

"So? What do you think?" she asked finally.

"About us being nothing but energy?"

"Yes. Doesn't it explain everything? About heaven, and God and how Christ could rise from the dead? Doesn't it explain why people sometimes feel they've lived before, how you can heal someone with nothing more than your hands, and why I saw the wise old person in that baby's eyes?"

He knew his answer was vitally important to her, and something deep within him even understood, although the leaps in logic she'd made were way beyond anything he'd ever been taught.

"It . . . It sounds like something my mother would have believed," he said at last.

Maria smiled.

"Why? Was she a philosopher?"

"No. She was a gypsy."

Even before she spoke, he knew he'd committed a serious crime.

"You *were* making fun of me all along!" she said coldly. "I told you if you laughed I'd never speak to you again."

"But it's *true*! My mother *was* a gypsy. She believed in fate and the future, and ancient remedies, and all the things you've been talking about. I can't rationalise what you've just said in terms of science, but I believe you! It does explain a lot."

"And my mother was the Queen of Siam!" snapped Maria. "Come on. I'm getting cold. Where do you live?"

"I'm not living anywhere. I'm staying in a hotel."

"Which one?"

"The big one next to the college."

"Jury's?"

"That's it," he said, almost ashamed.

"I'm glad you paid for the coffee then."

Maria refused to believe his protests of innocence all the way back to Cork. She refused his offer of a drink, to clear the air. She simply handed him his books and dismissed him with a crisp "goodnight".

He watched her Mini bump over the speed ramps as it left the hotel, knowing he had to see her again. She had struck some chord deep inside him and suddenly, he felt incomplete without her there to talk to. For a long time he lay fully clothed on his bed, staring at the ceiling, puzzled at what he was feeling, unsure of what to do.

Then he looked up her name in the phone book. But she wasn't there. She must live in a flat, he thought, and was suddenly aware of an acute and illogical pang of jealousy that she might not be living alone. He'd never felt like that about anyone else before.

All through his work next day in the Microelectronics Centre, his thoughts kept slipping back to Mary Anne Foley. He even made carefully couched enquiries, but nobody seemed to know her. At lunch-time he visited one of the more serious bookshops in the city, made a purchase, and contrived to be at the microfiche readers again that evening.

She was nowhere to be seen. So he took his books outside and searched the campus, carefully examining the groups of students taking the evening air, until he saw the familiar shock of coppery hair.

She was bent over a file of papers, beneath a cherry tree on the far side of the quad, deep in heated conversation . . . with a young man.

Gilkrensky felt an unfamiliar cocktail of emotions just then. There was betrayal, that what he thought they had shared was not for him alone. There was fear, that this might be the partner he imagined she lived with . . . who understood her . . . and loved her.

And there was relief, that he had found her again.

For a moment he watched her face as she argued her points, seeing the green eyes flash and the sun pick out the highlights in her hair. Then he summoned up his courage and walked across the few yards that separated them.

"Hi!" he said. "Did they throw you out of the library again?"

Maria's face lifted from the paper she was debating.

"They did *not*," she said coldly. "I chose to stay out in the sun. Besides, I wanted to discuss something with Liam here and, as you know from experience, they don't let you talk in the library."

"How's it going?" said the young man and shook Gilkrensky's hand.

"This is my friend Theo," said Maria. "He says he's a gypsy and yet he lives in a hotel. I was telling him my theory of the universe last night."

"Good to meet you," said Liam. "Do you think she's mad, too?"

"Theo did not laugh at me *once* throughout my lecture," said Maria sternly. "And he's a rich gypsy. So he should know."

"She has her family driven demented with this stuff," said Liam, implying a familiarity with Maria that made Gilkrensky's heart sink. "Ever since she came back from Africa, she's been spouting on about magic and tribal dances and ancient mumbo-jumbo. Her mother will hardly take her to Mass for fear she might scare the priest."

"That is *not* so. I always respect other people's beliefs."

"Do *you* understand her?" said Liam. "I don't think anyone else in the world does."

"Not yet," said Gilkrensky. "But I think this person would. It seems to me you both think the same way, and I know *he's* not mad." Then he took the book he'd bought that day and handed it to her. It was *The Tao of Physics* by Frithoff Capra.

Maria smiled up at him, and the light of heaven shone again.

"Ah, Theo! You weren't making fun after all! I've been looking all over for this book."

"You must be someone special," said Liam getting to his feet. "There aren't many people who come looking for Mary Anne once they've been through her theories once. Let alone share them with her."

"You did," said Gilkrensky, needing to know.

The young man smiled.

"I'm forced to," he said. "I'm her brother. I'll see you around, I'm sure."

And he winked.

Gilkrensky saw Maria every day after that. They spent

hours walking on the West Cork beaches, browsing in bookshops, or meandering through the woods talking about anything at all. Later they spent evenings alone in her top-floor eyrie of a flat, overlooking the lights of the city from a Victorian tenement off Waterloo Road, eating pizza and drinking red wine. On the first night they made love, in the candle-scented darkness of her bedroom, she held him to her with an urgency that surprised him. And then, when the last wave of passion had broken inside her, she cried softly in his arms.

Gilkrensky lay awake afterwards, watching as she slept under the soft glow of the candlelight, trying to solve the mystery of this wonderful, magical woman. The next morning, after they had made love again, he asked her about the tears. But whether they had been from the joy at having found him, or over some secret sorrow in her past, she would never say.

They were married the following spring, in the happy chaos of an Irish country wedding. Her father could hardly conceal his sense of relief as he gave the bride away, her sisters only *just* kept their jealousy under control, and her brothers gathered up the more drunk and daring of the guests for a midnight swim in the sea.

When GRC diversified into Ireland, Theo made his base in a converted country house her family had once owned in one of the prettier valleys south of Dublin. Maria set up a practice in alternative medicine in the city, and seemed to adopt every charity under the sun.

And through all the ups and downs of their time

together, through all the fights that came later, he had loved her. He had finally found someone to "take him to the fair."

Theodore Gilkrensky sat and stared at her beloved face in the photograph for a long, long time, lost in those green eyes. Then, when this private meditation was over, he leant forward, opened the lid of the slim black briefcase on the desk and started to work.

6

YUKIKO

"There is no place in the Sekigushi *ryu* for someone who does not honour tradition."

Yukiko listened to the words with a sense of impending doom. Everything about the Sekigushi *ryu*, which had taught swordsmanship and other ancient skills for the past five hundred years, was based on tradition. Everything – from the monastic simplicity of the room in which she now sat, to the gruelling sessions with arcane weaponry – was rooted in tradition and *bujutsu*, the way of the warrior. Sekigushi *ryu* was the most exclusive school for swordsmanship in Japan, with an endless waiting-list. There could be only one fate for a student who did not adhere religiously to its strict code of ethics – disgrace, dishonour, and dismissal.

Suddenly, the sweat that had soaked Yukiko's simple black cotton uniform since the beginning of the evening's training session felt cold on her skin.

"*Hai, sensei!*" she said.

The dying light of the winter evening, reddened to the colour of blood, played over the room. It lit the polished wooden floor, the simple brush paintings of birds and butterflies that the late Master Okuda had hung on the walls, and the single flower in a porcelain vase his son had placed on the desk to honour his memory. Outside the window, the roar of a jet landing at Narita airport sounded like the thunder of another age.

"Do you have anything to say?"

"No, *sensei*."

Taisen Okuda did not look like an adept in a dozen ways of dealing death. He was a small man, with the thin, pinched face of a country priest, and misty eyes that always seemed to be fixed on higher things – even when they were probing an opponent's guard for the slightest hint of weakness.

"Tell me about your encounter with Hasagawa."

Yukiko chose her reply carefully. Hasagawa was Okuda's protégé, a strict traditionalist from one of the oldest families in Japan. He was a master of archery, *karate*, *aikido* and most of all *ken-jutsu* – the way of the sword. By many he was considered to be the best. But, like many of the older conservatives in Japan, he was a confirmed bigot.

Yukiko wondered how much Okuda knew, or suspected.

"It was merely a practice *karate* session, *sensei*," she suggested. "I asked Hasagawa if he could help me improve my sparring."

"Hasagawa tells me you challenged him."

So he knew.

"*Hai, sensei.*"

Okuda considered this response for a while, as his grey eyes tested hers.

"Why?"

"Hasagawa called me a '*gaijin*' and worse. He said there was no place for anyone of mixed race at the *ryu*. I have been a student here for many years, and was awarded the third scroll by your father before he died. It was my duty of honour to challenge him."

"And then what happened?"

Yukiko described the match carefully. It had taken place in the sparring square of the main *dojo,* as if it had been a demonstration exercise. Referees had been appointed, and the contestants briefed. Yet the barely hidden anticipation of the students gathered to watch told a different story. Hasagawa was an adept, a master. Yukiko, the only woman ever to be admitted, was feared for her aggression.

There was blood in the air.

The first round had been over in less than five seconds. Both contestants had bowed and assumed the fighting stance. Each stared into the other's eyes – probing. Then Hasagawa exploded forwards with a loud "*kaia*" scream as he flailed the air in a volley of knife-hand strikes. Yukiko had hardly seemed to move. And then, there was Hasagawa, lying sprawled on the wooden floor.

The contestants moved to their corners and bowed again. This time, Hasagawa avoided Yukiko's gaze, testing her defences with carefully planned strikes before committing himself. But he was too slow. There was a flurry of movement, the slap of a body on wood, and once again Hasagawa was glaring up at Yukiko from the *dojo* floor. The referee in Yukiko's corner raised his hand. The match was over.

For a few moments Okuda contemplated this account. Then he said, "By what means did you defeat him?"

Yukiko saw the hidden danger behind the question, and knew Okuda already had the answer. It had really only been a matter of time.

"I do not understand, *sensei.*"

"I think you do, Yukiko. I think you know very well. Tell me about your visits to Kyoto."

"I go there to further my studies, *sensei.*"

"And you never thought to tell me, or my father before me, until now? What things do you learn there?"

Yukiko did not answer. She knew that masters of the pure form of *bujutsu*, as taught at Sekigushi *ryu*, frowned on the "black arts" she had been immersed in over the last two years. Perhaps Okuda had known for some time, and been waiting for a chance to lure her into the open, so that he might dismiss her. Today, his protégé Hasagawa had provided it.

"If you will not give me an answer, then I will supply one for you," said Okuda slowly. "The school you attend in Kyoto teaches skills of which nobody can be proud. That you feel the need to learn them, I can only put down to your sex and your ancestry. You have deceived me in this, and it has only been my father's debt to your uncle which has kept you here. In spite of my regard for him, I have no choice. You must leave now and never return."

"*Hai, sensei.*"

There was nothing more to be said.

Yukiko bowed and rose from the floor, looking around the room for the last time. Sekiguchi *ryu* had been the one rock in the swirling waters of her troubled life. Her training sessions the metronome against which she had measured time.

She closed the thin screen behind her and walked around the sacred *dojo* floor to the locker room beyond, seeing the years of her training, from adolescence to womanhood, there in the polished wood.

Sitting on a bench close to her locker was a young man with a pleasant moon-shaped face. It was Sasaki, the student who had been her referee.

"I fear the worst," he said. "Is it so?"

"*Hai.* I have been asked to leave."

Sasaki considered this, while his head moved sadly from side to side. "I thought as much. Did I not warn you, many times?"

Yukiko opened her locker, and was moving her few possessions into a black holdall.

"You did, Sasaki-*san*. But I had to go my own way."

"Why, Yukiko? Were you not happy here?"

She gently took a slim bundle from her locker. It was about half a metre long and wrapped in oiled cloth. Carefully, reverently, she placed it inside the holdall and closed the zip.

"There is a great sadness in you," said Sasaki at last. "But also a great anger. We can all sense it, and I know Okuda *sensei* can, too. That above all, must be why he asked you to go."

Yukiko turned and faced him.

"I am a woman and I am a *gaijin* – a half-caste. Okuda has been waiting for an excuse to throw me out ever since he inherited the *ryu* from his father. And today I lost control and betrayed myself by beating his favourite student – a person like him, who is obsessed with tradition and blinded by prejudice. *That* is why he told me to go!"

Sasaki shook his head.

"Once again you are angry," he said. "But you are right in one thing. Hasagawa is a traditionalist, and he will demand a traditional settlement. Would you like me to come with you to your car?"

"No, Sasaki-*san*. You have been a good friend. But I must face him on my own."

It was fully dark by the time Yukiko left the *ryu*. The cold white light of the moon had replaced the blood-red glow of the sun, and it shone on the sea of carefully raked pebbles in the formal Zen garden, casting deep shadows around the rocky islands, the hedges beyond, and the narrow lane leading to the car park.

Yukiko could sense Hasagawa's presence in the darkness, as well as his intentions – they had taught her this in Kyoto. So she stood still and waited, until a short stocky figure stepped from the alleyway, blocking her path.

"We have unfinished business, *woman!*" snapped Hasagawa. "You used witchcraft against me, and I demand a rematch – *shiniai.*"

He was still dressed in the black cotton *gi* of the *ryu*. Tucked into his belt on the left side was the gracefully curving sheath of his *katana* – a beautiful handmade sword of unbelievable sharpness – a priceless heirloom that would have been handed to him by his father on the day he reached manhood.

"I have no wish to kill you," said Yukiko, bowing her head. "I have been dismissed from the *ryu*, and all that is behind me now."

"I spoke the truth when I called you a half-breed without honour," hissed Hasagawa. "You defile the memory of our late Master Okuda and the *ryu* itself by thinking you are above its teachings. Then you defeat me with trickery. I demand *shiniai* – a duel to the death."

Yukiko considered this latest in a lifetime of insults, feeling the familiar madness rise, burst, and fall back . . . under her control.

"We will move to the lawn then," she said flatly, taking her black holdall with her. "This is not the place."

The lawn was below Okuda's darkened window. Yukiko knew he was watching. She could sense his presence behind the half-drawn blinds, and in that instant knew Okuda had arranged everything – from Hasagawa's insult to her own presence here on the lawn – to be this way. Now, Okuda *sensei*, she thought, we will see where tradition takes you. Then she reached down for the black holdall, and slid out the oilcloth package. Carefully, lovingly, she undid the string and unfurled the cloth.

Lying in its centre was a *wakizashi* – a smaller version of Hasagawa's *katana* – a short sword in a delicately inlaid scabbard bearing the cherry blossom of the Funakoshi family. She pulled the belt of her cotton *gi* from her bag, wrapped it around her waist and tucked the short sword into it. Then she turned and faced Hasagawa, who sneered at her in disbelief across the moonlit lawn.

"What is this, woman? You mock me again! Where is your *katana*? Nobody fights with a *wakizashi* – that is a suicide sword!"

"It belonged to my parents," said Yukiko simply. "You challenged me to *shiniai* and I have chosen my weapon. If you do not want to fight me, you can always withdraw."

Yukiko could sense the swirling emotions of mistrust and contempt inside Hasagawa as he faced her. But stronger than any of these, she could feel Hasagawa's supreme confidence in his own ability as a master swordsman. Hasagawa was a known *sensei* of *iai-jutsu*, the art of drawing a sword and striking an opponent in one blindingly fast movement. He would be certain of victory against any other student at the *ryu*, including her, in a traditional match.

That would be his undoing.

"As you wish then," said Hasagawa. "We will begin?"

"*Hai.*"

They both bowed solemnly in the moonlight, and

knelt facing each other on the tightly mown lawn with their right knees forward. Yukiko saw Hasagawa's left thumb move his sword free of the scabbard, ready for the draw. Her body relaxed totally as her mind focused below her own navel, on the seat of her inner power. Her eyes were fixed on Hasagawa's, and in that instant, the two swordsmen became one.

Hasagawa was not afraid of death. As a true disciple of *bu-jutsu*, he accepted it as an inevitability. Far better to die in one glorious stroke, than to waste away without dignity inside a maze of tubes in a hospital bed, as Master Okuda had done. Therefore, having challenged the *gaijin* woman to *shinai* as Okuda *sensei* had suggested, Hasagawa welcomed her as an honoured guest in the duel, and focused himself on the task in hand. He sought to calm himself with his breathing, so that he might reach that solid rock within from which to spring.

But it was gone!

As his gaze was drawn into Yukiko's, all his composure and strength drained away. All the years of training were suddenly sucked out of him by those remorseless black eyes.

It was witchcraft!

At a stroke he had gone from warrior to child, alone and frightened in the darkness. And as a child, he lashed out artlessly with his father's beautiful *katana* – at empty air.

The last thing he felt was the piercing chill of her short sword deep inside him, as it slid through his solar plexus, his diaphragm and up into his heart. Then the great *katana* dropped from his hand as he fell forwards onto the wet grass, dead.

Yukiko stood above his body like a statue in the moonlight, as the madness ebbed away. Then she carefully wiped the *wakizashi* in the oilcloth before sliding it gently into its scabbard. Finally, she turned to Okuda *sensei*'s darkened window, bowed, and walked off into the night.

7

HOSTILE TAKEOVER

JESSICA WRIGHT SNAPPED AWAKE IN HER CHAIR AT THE DISCREET knock on the boardroom door. The morning had been hell – a minefield of media inquiries, order cancellations and reassuring calls to major customers. She had just closed her eyes for a second . . .

Standing in the doorway was a short, broad-shouldered man with a thickset neck, dark brown hair in a military cut, and a neat moustache.

"You wanted to see me, Miss Wright?" said Crowe. His voice was clipped and precise, with the slightest west country burr on the "r" of her name – born in Dorset, or so it said on his file. He had served with 21 Commando until seriously injured in a helicopter crash in the Falklands and invalided home. From there he had set up his own security company, specialising in high-tech computer surveillance, and had done contract jobs for GRC, until Theo had made him chief of security following Maria's death. Crowe had been at the farmhouse in Wicklow, about to undertake a review of security systems, on the day she had died. It had been Crowe who had pulled Gilkrensky back from the bomb-shattered wreck, saving his life.

Jessica tried to shrug off the tiredness.

"Yes, Major. I'm sorry to drag you back here to London, but we have a crisis on our hands. Come and sit down."

Major Crowe took a seat at the board table facing the window, while Jessica turned his file face down on her desk.

"How are things going in Ireland?"

"Very well, thank you, Miss Wright. I've insisted we upgrade the security on the island, and I was just checking everything out when the balloon went up."

"Has there been any progress in the investigation into Maria Gilkrensky's death?"

"I'm afraid not. None of the terrorist groups have claimed responsibility and because both cars were destroyed in the blast, there's precious little forensic evidence to go on. We can't tell whether the bomb in the BMW was triggered by the ignition, if it was set off by remote control from somewhere else, or even if Mrs Gilkrensky's Mini itself was tampered with, forcing her to use her husband's car."

"What are you saying?"

"Well, if the bomb was triggered by someone watching the house, someone who knew who they were killing when they pressed the button, then we have to consider the outside possibility that the whole thing was stage-managed to look like an attempt on the chairman, while the real target was Maria Gilkrensky herself."

Jessica shook her head.

"And how is the chairman, now? Psychologically speaking?"

Crowe hesitated before he answered.

"The lads tell me he keeps pretty much to himself. Work on the new computer is going well, and the boffins from Cork are quite excited."

"Any other visitors?"

"Nobody except the scientists, and a few other specialists from time to time. Dr Gilkrensky doesn't leave the island, apart from the odd helicopter flight to Cork airport to fly the jet. And there haven't been any séances for months . . . "

"Séances?" Jessica had heard rumours, but had never known if they were true.

"Just after Mrs Gilkrensky died and we set up the house on the island, there was a gaggle of spiritualists who had to be security-cleared. Then the whole thing stopped at about the time he had the last breakthrough with the computer. It was as if he didn't need them any more. Good thing too, in my view. It used to spook the staff like mad. Only last week . . . "

"But I thought you said the séances stopped months ago?"

"So they did. But you know how people are, once word gets round. Only last week one of the girls claimed she heard the chairman having a long conversation with his dead wife after everyone else was asleep."

Jessica's mind was wandering. She found herself staring out through the rain-streaked windows into space as she thought about Major Crowe's ghost stories. Well, if anyone had the right qualifications to be a witch it was Maria Gilkrensky, she thought, and felt the old stirrings of jealousy rising up again. Jessica had only met her once, but once was enough – more than enough – to establish the rules of engagement between them.

It had been at the opening of the new GRC electronics plant in Cork. The event had been arranged with the usual Gilkrensky flair. Theo had arrived by helicopter, grinning and waving to the cameras. There had been a lot of speeches by local politicians. The Lord Mayor had cut the ribbon across the threshold, and pressed the button to start the machines. Theo was being asked all the right questions about job creation and investment. Everything was going beautifully.

Maria had arrived quietly by car on her own, parked well away from the VIP area and only shadowed Theo from a distance, as if she did not want to be part of what was going on.

Jessica had already made it her business to know a great deal about the new Mrs Gilkrensky. Part of her excused this curiosity as simple interest in her friend Theo's welfare. But she also had to admit to good old-fashioned jealousy. If Maria had been any other woman in the world, Jessica would have had the comfort of knowing that Maria had only chosen Theo for his money. But Maria was not interested in money, or anything to do with it. The car she drove was a battered Mini. The clothes she wore would not have looked out of place in a charity shop and, when Theo finally spotted her and dragged her into the limelight, her discomfort at the trappings of success was thinly disguised.

As Theo moved on with the main group of VIPs to tour the plant, leaving Maria on her own, Jessica took the plunge and introduced herself.

"Mrs Gilkrensky? I'm Jessica Wright."

"I know," said Maria, fixing Jessica with her green eyes. "My husband knew you in Boston."

That was it.

There were no pleasantries. No refined sparring with words. No attempts to build bridges or forget the past. The message was clear. You knew my husband once, but now he is mine. Stay away!

Maria turned, put down her glass of mineral water on the groaning buffet table, and walked back to her car, leaving Jessica to stew in the most intense cocktail of jealousy and loss she had ever experienced.

It wasn't simply that Maria was beautiful. Jessica herself was a striking woman, and other lovers since Theo had told her so. It wasn't that Maria was intelligent and accomplished in her own right. Jessica was the chief executive of a major multinational corporation and handled transactions involving millions every day.

What galled Jessica – what ate at her deeply, at a level she hardly acknowledged existed – was that Maria had reached that inner sanctum of Theo's soul which she herself had longed to touch, and been denied.

That hurt.

She had let the only man she ever really loved slip through her fingers that day at Boston airport. Fool! She told herself. I should have swallowed my pride, left everything behind, and jumped on that plane with you, Theo. Fool! Fool! Fool!

On the morning when news of Maria's death had come to her, as she ate her solitary breakfast in her Grosvenor hotel suite, that secret, lonely part of Jessica Wright rejoiced. "The bitch is dead," it said. "Now Theo is mine."

"In your capacity as head of security, I would like you to sit in on the board meeting this afternoon, Major," said Jessica, snapping back to the present. "And to do that I will need to brief you on the Japanese involvement in GRC. You know they have a twenty-five per cent shareholding. Do you know how they came by it?"

Crowe hesitated before he spoke.

"I heard there was bad blood about that," he said carefully. "A disgruntled shareholder called Rothsay sold out. But I don't know all the details."

"Then I should fill you in. GRC was originally formed as the Gilcrest Radio Company back in 1937. The original shareholders were Leo Gilkrensky the chairman's father, and this shareholder you speak of, the flier Lord Stephen Rothsay. Each of them held twenty-five per cent, and a gentleman's agreement never to upset that balance of power. Then there was one of the major aircraft companies in Farnborough, with twenty per cent, a pension scheme consortium with another twenty per cent, and an investment bank with ten. At the start, the company was very successful, particularly with the war coming when it did, but Lord Rothsay was a very high liver, with an eye for the ladies. After the war, he found he could make more money by selling Leo Gilkrensky's ideas to competitive interests in Japan.

"When old Leo died, his son Dr Theodore Gilkrensky asked me to take over as chief executive. Lord Rothsay was still up to his old tricks, but it was impossible to prove and I got nowhere convincing any of the other board members. Then there was a scandal . . . Rothsay was caught cheating on his wife and left the country. But that didn't stop him selling GRC down the drain. The chairman had to get Lord Rothsay out. And to do that, he had to have a majority shareholding. So I worked out a . . . er . . . scheme, to get it for him.

"Between us, we let it be known that work on the new neural-net biochip was going nowhere. Without the biochip to keep us ahead of the pack, people assumed the Gilcrest Radio Corporation was doomed. And you can guess what happened to the price of the shares."

"They fell," said Crowe.

"Exactly. They fell so low that both the Farnborough aircraft company and Lord Rothsay got cold feet and dumped their shares. The aircraft company sold at a rock-bottom price to a certain merchant bank in London, a bank which had been specifically instructed to buy those shares for a third party."

"And that third party was Dr Gilkrensky."

"Yes, Major. With the twenty-five per cent holding his father had left him, that brought Dr Gilkrensky's shares up to forty-five per cent of the company, one step nearer to the majority shareholding he needed. Or so he thought."

"And Lord Rothsay?"

Jessica stared at the rain-swept window again, watching the fat drops race each other down the glass. The tiredness was really catching up on her now.

"That's the irony of it all," she said in a distant voice. "He sold to the Japanese."

They had sent no limousine or helicopter to meet Jessica Wright at Narita airport that day on her first, and only, visit to Tokyo. And it had been a two-hour journey by taxi to the Mawashi-Saito building in the Shinjuku business district, where she had been shown to a vast boardroom on the forty-second floor. The walls were bare, except for a simple ink-drawing of a bird on a bamboo branch.

Across the city, through the haze, she could see Mount Fuji and Tokyo Bay to the east. But her eyes kept coming back to that picture. To her, it seemed crude, like something a child might have done. And she wondered why such a rich and powerful company as Mawashi-Saito should choose to give it pride of place in this, their holy of holies.

"Do you have any idea what you are looking at, Miss Wright?"

Standing in the doorway to her left was a short, compact Japanese with iron-grey hair. He was dressed in a dove-grey business suit, a brilliant white shirt and a black tie of knotted silk. Beside him was a young woman, an "office lady" in a smart company uniform, with raven-black hair tied in a tight bun and delicate, gold-framed glasses. To Jessica, she seemed tall for a Japanese – head and shoulders above the man – and her eyes seemed red, as if she had been crying.

"You mean the picture?" asked Jessica.

The man could have been any age between fifty and seventy. His stern face was a mask that gave nothing away.

"That is precisely what I mean, the picture. Do you know what it is?"

"No. I don't."

The man and his assistant sat at the polished lake of the boardroom table. They did not ask Jessica to do the same.

"That picture is an original ink-drawing by one of our greatest artists, Miyamoto Musashi. You have heard of him?"

"No. I'm afraid not."

"Musashi was the greatest swordsman who ever lived. His masterpiece was his *Book of Five Rings*, the *Go Rin No Sho* as we call it. I'm sure you must know of this book?"

"I cannot say I do."

"It appears there is much you do not know about

Japan, Miss Wright. I am therefore surprised our chairman should send you on such an important mission, rather than coming to see me himself. Perhaps he is trying to send me a message?"

Jessica noticed that the woman in the office uniform had stopped taking notes, and was watching her for a reaction.

"There is no insult intended, Funakoshi-*san*," said Jessica, pulling out a chair from the table so that she could sit down. "I am the chief executive of the Gilcrest Radio Corporation, and as such the most important person in the organisation after the chairman."

"You know my name at least," said Funakoshi. "What else do you know?"

"I know you have succeeded in doing what no other businessman has ever been able to do, in merging two major Japanese companies together, in this case Saito Electronics and the Mawashi trading house. I know the Mawashi-Saito *kobun* is among the top five in Japan, which makes you one of the most powerful men in the country."

"Look out of the window, Miss Wright, and tell me what you see."

"I see the city, the mountain, and Tokyo Bay."

"Indeed. In 1945 I stood on this spot and watched the great American battleship *Missouri* on which our surrender was signed. I was only ten years old at the time, starving and covered in lice; both my parents were dead, and my baby sister was lying sick at my side. Japan suffered three and a half million casualties, Miss Wright.

A quarter of all the buildings were destroyed here in Tokyo. Now, look again. What do you see?"

"Your country has done well."

"It has. You are standing on the most expensive real estate in the world, where land sells for fifty thousand US dollars per square *metre*. Japan is the most powerful business nation on earth. Do you know how that was done?"

"Mr Funakoshi. What are you driving at?"

Funakoshi turned and pointed to the picture on the wall.

"*Giri*, Miss Wright – the code of selfless duty and obligation we Japanese live by – and the position you find yourself in today."

"I don't understand," said Jessica.

"I did not expect you to," replied Funakoshi. "Mawashi-Saito, and indeed everything in Japan, is built upon a code of ethics, the triumph of *giri* over *ninjo*, our personal feelings and desires. Dr Gilkrensky acquired his majority shareholding in the Gilcrest Radio Corporation by devious means, by 'sharp practice', as you would say. Such a thing is unheard-of, here in Japan. There is no such thing as a hostile takeover. We call that a "hijack", the word for it is the same. In artificially collapsing the price of your shares and acquiring a majority shareholding over Lord Rothsay, you not only broke the agreement he had with Dr Gilkrensky's father, but also swindled him out of a great deal of money."

"I understand that, Mr Funakoshi," said Jessica, thinking of Rothsay's own deception in selling Theo's secrets. "But do you not have a saying in Japan that 'business is war'?"

"Indeed we do, Miss Wright, and now Mawashi-Saito has a twenty-five per cent interest in your company."

"It is only a minority shareholding."

"As you speak of war, I would draw your attention back to the works of Musashi. If you were familiar with them, you would recognise our tactics as what he called 'crossing at a ford.' Put simply, Musashi says that one should always attack an enemy at his weakest point. You say our seat on your board is a minority one. That is true. But it gives us access. And who knows, if the other shareholders decide to sell, it could become a controlling interest in time."

"What is it you want, Mr Funakoshi?"

"Two things. Firstly, I am interested in Dr Gilkrensky's neural-network biochip. I hope we can come to some mutually agreeable arrangement whereby Mawashi-Saito can manufacture it here in Japan under license."

"That will not be possible."

"Why not?"

"Look at the experience of IBM. They granted licenses to manufacture their computers to Japanese companies and suddenly found themselves pushed out of the Japanese market. GRC will manufacture the biochip and sell it to you on our terms."

"But I am part of GRC now, Miss Wright. I have a seat on your board of directors. Think on my offer. Discuss it with Dr Gilkrensky. I can work in partnership, or in opposition. In opposition, I will win. Please consider partnership."

"And the second thing?"

Funakoshi leant forward. For the first time a trace of emotion sounded in his voice.

"I wish you to know that Lord Rothsay did not recover from the blow you dealt him over this matter. Early yesterday morning he was found at his apartment here in Tokyo. He had taken his own life."

Jessica could no longer meet Funakoshi's gaze, and glanced instead at the young woman by his side. For an instant, it was as if a mask had slipped. Through the gold-rimmed glasses the most intense look of animal hatred Jessica had ever seen burned at her across the boardroom table, bringing with it a terrible, chilling realisation. Then the look was gone, and the woman was an "office lady" again, busy with her notepad.

"I'm sorry," said Jessica.

"So am I, Miss Wright. He was my friend. I will see you at our next board meeting."

8

CRISIS MANAGEMENT

THE STORM, WHICH HAD CAUSED SO MUCH HAVOC TO MAJOR Crowe's security systems on the island, had reached London. Rain lashed at the windows of the GRC boardroom, and on the skyline, there were flashes of thunder to the west.

"I realise both of you have been made substantial offers by Mawashi-Saito for your shares in GRC," said Jessica. "And that, in the normal run of events, you were to give me your decision in a week's time, on Christmas Eve. But we have to set that aside and concentrate on the crisis in hand. It's in all our interests to exonerate the Daedalus unit and restore confidence as fast as we possibly can. I've outlined one possible strategy for doing so, based on advice from our technical people and the press office. I've outlined it to you in advance of the meeting to get your reactions, and to make sure I have your support before we're joined by the Japanese."

"And the chairman," said Sir Robert Fynes, whose pension fund represented ten per cent of GRC. "Have you discussed it with him?"

Sir Robert was an impressive man, with a broad honest face. His grey eyes appraised Jessica minutely, reminding her that he had not approved of her appointment as chief executive by Theo, or the way she had masterminded the Lord Rothsay affair behind his back.

"I spoke to the chairman early this morning," she said. "But he may've been too upset about the crash to take in all the details. That's why it's important we know what we want to get out of this meeting. Tony, have there been any more developments?"

Tony Delgado combed his fingers through his hair. Jessica knew he had been without sleep for at least as long as she had, and it was beginning to tell. There were grey rings under his eyes.

"We've had a whole flood of problems in the wake of the crash," he said. "Many of the advance orders for the SmartMate have fallen through, and that deal we were doing with the Taiwanese to install Daedalus in their commercial air fleet has been put on ice pending an enquiry."

"The cost of all this is mind-boggling," said Giles Fulton of the investment consortium who owned the remaining shares in GRC. He was a small, neat man with a large balding head, thick glasses and the sharpest business mind Jessica had ever come across.

"And it will go on rising, if it isn't settled," she said. "If

GRC can't regain the ground it's lost over this Daedalus incident, you'll both lose out whether you sell to the Japanese or not. The value of your shares will plummet and the Japanese may well reconsider their offer. I'd say that any amount of money we spend, or any action we take, that succeeds in exonerating us, is well worth it."

"Anything?" said Sir Robert, reminding Jessica of her proposal.

"We're losing money hand over fist as it is," offered Tony Delgado, coming to her aid. "The adverse publicity alone has already completely eclipsed the launch of the SmartMate."

"I see your point," said Fulton. "But why should the Japanese support the proposal? Surely they could just sit back and let GRC fall apart. Then they could pick up our shares for a song?"

"They might," said Jessica. "But don't forget that Mawashi-Saito own a valuable parcel of GRC shares themselves. If they let this crisis go too far, and confidence tumbles, their own shares will become worthless too. It all depends on the corporate strategy their board of directors adopts. We're taking a gamble, gentlemen. It could go either way."

"Excuse me, Miss Wright," said Sir Robert, pointing through the rain-dashed window, to where a blue and white helicopter was climbing upwards over the Thames to the helipad above their heads. "But I think the chairman is about to arrive."

Theodore Gilkrensky unclipped his seat belt, took the

black briefcase from the man behind him, and peered out through the windscreen. Through the driving rain, he could see four men in yellow oilskins, each guarding a corner of the helipad, and Major Crowe directing operations from the shelter of the stairwell. Beside Crowe was Tony Delgado, holding his coat tight against the wind.

Gilkrensky pulled on his own leather jacket, tucked the briefcase under it to keep off the rain and stepped out over the skid, ducking under the spinning rotors as he ran to the stairwell.

"Good to see you in the flesh, Tony. It's been a long time."

"Too long, sir. It's great to have you with us again."

"I suppose you haven't met my new baby-sitters yet. This one is Gerald Maguire. Gerald, meet Tony Delgado."

Delgado offered his hand.

"Pleased to meet you, I'm sure, sir," said Maguire. His voice was soft and controlled, but his hand remained deep in the pocket of his bulky anorak, as if he was holding something.

Gilkrensky leant forward and grinned.

"Whatever you do, don't make any sudden moves, Tony," he said and laughed, moving down the stairs and into the warmth of the building.

Since his retreat after Maria's death, Jessica Wright had not met Theo face to face. In spite of the many video calls, she still found it hard to accept how much he'd changed. The thin, bearded figure in the worn leather jacket who greeted her in the boardroom bore little resemblance to the man she had once loved in Boston. His eyes, which had held such fire, now had a haunted look about them, and the wonderful hands she had once admired were rippled with scars.

"Hello, Jess," he said.

And deep inside, Jessica Wright wept. Had she not been in the corporation boardroom, in front of half a dozen directors and staff, she would have hugged him.

"Mr Chairman," she said at last, holding out her hand. "I'm glad you could come."

"Let me take your coat, sir," said Sheila Browne, and turned to hang the leather jacket on the coatrack near to door. It was protocol at board meetings for her to take the minutes and manage any teleconferencing that needed to be done from the big master-terminal to the left of the chairman's seat. But when she turned back from hanging up Gilkrensky's jacket, she found he was already sitting in her place. She frowned at Delgado and he leant over Gilkrensky's shoulder.

"Would you mind sitting in your normal seat, sir?"

"I'd rather sit here, if that's all right with Sheila?" said Gilkrensky. He placed his briefcase on the floor next to the master-console and connected it to one of the communications ports with a thick grey cable he had taken from his pocket. Tony Delgado watched him for a moment, and then shrugged.

"I'll sit in the 'hot seat' for today then, shall I, Tony?" offered Jessica. "I'm sure Sheila won't mind."

She took her place at the top of the table, facing the teleconferencing screens. To her right sat Major Crowe, scanning the nearby rooftops over Tony Delgado's shoulder.

"Very well then," said Jessica. "Could we have the teleconference links please, starting with Japan?"

Sheila Browne had already started to lean across Gilkrensky's left arm to press the appropriate key on the master-console. But before she could touch it, the key lit up of its own accord. She drew her hand back in surprise.

On the wall at the far end of the boardroom table, the largest video monitor blinked into life. The scene was almost a mirror-image of their own boardroom, with a long table totally clear of paper, surrounded by a dozen earnest Japanese. On the wall behind them, Jessica would make out the ink-drawing by Musashi.

"I thought we were just speaking to Funakoshi alone," she hissed to Delgado.

The familiar figure, in the seat of honour furthest from the door at the table in Tokyo, could be heard as clearly as if he had been in the boardroom with them.

"I hope there has been no misunderstanding, Miss Wright. In view of the seriousness of the situation, I thought it would be wise to have my colleagues on the board of Mawashi-Saito here to participate in the meeting. Ah! I see we are honoured by the presence of our distinguished chairman! How are you, sir?"

Gilkrensky bowed his head to the Mawashi-Saito board. They bowed back in unison.

"I am well, Funakoshi-*san*. Time heals all wounds. Would you introduce us to the members of your board, please?"

Funakoshi obliged. Each Japanese bowed individually as his name was called.

"Now," said Gilkrensky. "Could we have Bill McCarthy in the plane, please?"

Once again, the keys on the master-console moved of their own accord and one of the smaller screens, flanking the main monitor, came to life – catching a big-boned man with dark, curly hair and a heavy moustache in the act of lighting a pipe. He swatted the resulting cloud of smoke away from the screen and peered into the room through a pair of half-rimmed steel glasses.

"Well, well! Look who made it to the party. How are you, Theo? I like the beard . . . suits you."

"I'm fine, Bill. But you of all people should know it's unsafe to be smoking a pipe on an airplane."

Professor William McCarthy, formerly of MIT and the US National Aeronautics and Space Administration, and currently head of avionics research at the Gilcrest aerospace facility near Orlando, Florida, scowled at the teleconference lens.

"Yeah, you're right. But hell! We don't arrive in Cairo for another hour and a half and if I can't have a smoke I'm gonna go crazy. I'll have one of the flight crew stand behind me with a fire extinguisher if it will make you feel any better."

"I trust you, Bill. Have you read the reports?"

"Sure have. Read them over breakfast. It seems to me, ladies and gentlemen, that the outcome of this incident simply emphasises the safety of the Whisperer aircraft design. After all, how many low-altitude crashes do you remember where ninety-nine per cent of the passengers actually walked away from the wreck?"

"Professor, that might be the case with the aircraft itself," said Jessica. "But our problem is with the Daedalus autopilot, which is accused of crashing the plane in the first place."

"I agree with Miss Wright," added Sir Robert Fynes. "As a damage-limitation exercise, we could well emphasise the low casualty rate and the safety of the plane. But GRC is in the business of making computers – safe, reliable computers – and customer confidence will continue to fall until we prove we still can."

Tony Delgado looked up from a sheaf of fax messages.

"Sir Robert's right," he said. "As Professor McCarthy knows, there's a massive contract hanging in the balance to supply Whisperer jets to Virgin Atlantic. We know Branson's people are actively looking elsewhere now, and word is out that we could lose the deal to Boeing. So it's imperative we find out if, and why the Daedalus failed, as fast as we possibly can."

"The central core of the Daedalus unit, the part that contains the main memory and the neural-net chip, is protected by a titanium casing and is virtually indestructible," said Gilkrensky. "If we can get access to that core with a computer powerful enough to interpret the data, then we can find out what caused the crash."

"And we assume that finding such a powerful computer which is portable enough to take to Egypt will be no problem for GRC," said Funakoshi from Japan.

"How is work progressing on the new Minerva prototype, Mr Chairman? Is there any chance of having it ready in time to meet this emergency?"

Jessica Wright glanced suspiciously at the briefcase on the floor, and then at Gilkrensky, who showed no reaction other than to place his hands palms down on the table in front of him.

"I've had difficulties in writing appropriate software to allow the operator to interface with such a powerful system, Funakoshi-san," he replied. "In the meantime, I will make arrangements to have a 2,000 model available."

"With respect, Mr Chairman, that is exactly the response your people in Ireland gave us six months ago, when we inquired as to the progress of the Minerva project. And we have still not been allowed to view even the schematics of the 3,000 biochip design."

"New developments take time. As to the security arrangements, I'm sure your board of directors can appreciate that a project with the revolutionary potential of Minerva must be carefully protected. If it were ever to fall into the hands of a competitor, GRC would lose all control of its development, as well as the huge profits that would certainly accrue. We're merely protecting your twenty-five per cent investment in our corporation, Funakoshi-san. That's all."

"A system with the promised capabilities of the 3,000 model would have been invaluable in recreating the events of the crash using the new virtual-reality system your scientists have developed for the theme parks," persisted Funakoshi.

"That's true. But I'm sure the 2,000 model can cope with the interface well enough. Now, Sir Robert and Giles, do you have any points you'd like to make?"

The board meeting had moved to its most sensitive issue – the unveiling of Jessica's plan. Neil Martin joined the meeting from the press office, and laid the groundwork. The point he stressed, over and over again, was that any public relations campaign to restore confidence in the corporation, however skilful, would be a total waste of time unless the GRC autopilot could be proved blameless.

"So I think it's clear to everyone that exonerating Daedalus is our top priority," said Jessica.

"And we can start on that as soon as we get access to either the unit itself, the flight recorder or both," cut in McCarthy. "One should corroborate the other. And we'll need to talk to the flight crew . . ."

"I was thinking the chairman should join you in Cairo," said Jessica, taking the plunge.

Gilkrensky's head snapped up from his console. Major Crowe looked at her in surprise. But Jessica avoided their eyes, addressing her remarks to the group.

"We've agreed that exoneration of the Daedalus is our prime concern. A full investigation of the crash might take weeks, during which the corporation could find itself bankrupt, even if the unit *was* proved to be blameless. But if the chairman takes a personal interest, and flies out to Cairo in an aircraft fitted with a Daedalus unit then . . . "

"I'm not going!" snapped Gilkrensky.

"Theo! Let me finish!"

"Jessica. It's no use you springing this on me in front of the whole board. I'm not going and that's final!"

"Excuse me, Miss Wright," said Crowe. "But it will be impossible to guarantee the chairman's security in Egypt."

"Why don't we put it to a vote?" said Sir Robert, ignoring him.

"But Miss Wright!" insisted Crowe. "The security implications are . . . "

"You are here only to observe, Major!" snapped Jessica, cutting him dead. "We will discuss security later. Sir Robert, you were saying?"

Sir Robert Fynes glanced at Crowe. Then he said, "I think it's a good plan. You've heard the public relations man. Our shares will be worthless if confidence in the Corporation continues to slide."

"Here, here!" said Giles Fulton. "Let's put it to a vote."

Gilkrensky turned on him.

"You'll lose! I own forty-five per cent of the shares!"

"Mister Chairman," said Funakoshi softly. "*We* have not voted yet."

The board members of Mawashi-Saito were conversing rapidly in Japanese. Gilkrensky turned to Jessica Wright, but she just kept looking straight ahead at the video screen.

"Listen, all of you!" he said. "I can't afford to go. Firstly, Bill McCarthy's already on his way to Cairo in a jumbo jet packed with experts and equipment. He can do a far better job than I can. Then . . . there's the Minerva project. How can I complete it if I'm out there grubbing around in the desert?"

Funakoshi returned to the screen.

"With all due respect, Mr Chairman, it is our opinion that GRC can ill afford for you *not* to visit Egypt. By going, you are demonstrating your deep personal interest in solving this problem, which is essential for the image of the corporation. To the world, Dr Gilkrensky, you *are* GRC. So it occurs to us, as it obviously has to Miss Wright, that if you travel to Egypt in a plane flown by the Daedalus system, you are showing the world you have no hesitation in trusting your life to it. We support Miss Wright's proposition, and we would vote for it. I believe that would give fifty-five per cent in favour."

Gilkrensky sat slowly back into his seat. His hands were trembling.

"It looks as if I'm going to Egypt," he said.

Following the adoption of Jessica's plan, the board meeting descended into a simple discussion of logistics. Professor McCarthy listed the equipment he would need to interrogate the Daedalus. Neil Martin and Tony Delgado were full of ideas to extract the maximum publicity from the chairman's flight. Only Gilkrensky was silent, as the conversations ebbed and flowed around him. Once or twice, Jessica caught Major Crowe's eye, and knew he would be seeking an interview with her once the meeting was over.

By six-fifteen the discussion was drawing to a close. McCarthy was knocking out his pipe, ready for landing in Cairo, and Tony Delgado had finished giving Sheila Browne detailed instructions regarding the GRC executive jet.

"Would anyone like a drink now that's settled?" he said, opening one of the concealed cupboards in the oak-panelled wall.

"I'd like a word in private with the chief executive," said Gilkrensky, in a tone that silenced all other conversation in the room.

Sheila Browne looked at Delgado. Sir Robert Fynes and Giles Fulton exchanged glances and Jessica Wright stopped gathering up her papers.

"Would you like us to wait outside, sir?" said Crowe.

"If you'd be so kind, Major."

"I can't believe you did that!" snapped Gilkrensky, when he was sure they were alone. "You engineered the whole bloody thing and then got the Japanese to back you up. Funakoshi hasn't made you an offer as well, has he?"

Jessica Wright sat motionless in the chairman's seat with her hands clasped tightly in front of her, staring at the empty video monitors. When she thought Gilkrensky's anger had subsided enough for her to reply, she said quietly, "I'm sorry it turned out this way, Theo. But it had to be done. I'd been meaning to speak to you about it before the crash happened."

"What had to be done? Talk about what?"

Only then did she turn to face him. Her eyes were very bright, as if she were on the verge of tears.

"Theo, you're rotting away on that island. And we've had nothing worth a damn out of those laboratories of yours for the last two years. Funakoshi is right. To most of the world you *are* the Gilcrest Radio Corporation. And look at you! You're falling apart!"

Gilkrensky pulled back the seat Major Crowe had occupied and sat facing her.

"What about the SmartMate, Jess? And the Minerva?"

"I was talking to that journalist Robert Stark last night, Theo. He said SmartMate was just a collection of old ideas . . . miniaturised and cobbled together . . . and . . . he's right! The Japanese will have something better within months!"

"But the Minerva, Jess! It's ready to go!"

"Is it, Theo? You've been working on it for five years now. And every time I ask for a production schedule, so we can organise a sales campaign, you tell me it isn't ready . . . It's either the biochip, or the software, or the user interface . . . or some damned thing!"

Gilkrensky lifted the briefcase up from the floor and laid it gently on the boardroom table.

"This is it," he said. "It's ready now."

Jessica eyed the case with suspicion.

"Then show me!"

"I . . . I'd rather not. Not here."

"Why not?"

"It's just that . . ."

"*Why* can't you show me? You say it's ready! It's on the bloody table right in front of us!"

"Jess. Don't ask me to . . ."

Suddenly all the pressure, all the frustration and all the anger of the past twenty-four hours burst through Jessica's worn-down barriers. She lashed out with her arm, sweeping the Minerva along the length of the table, sending empty water jugs and half-filled glasses spinning and spilling on the polished wood.

"I'll tell you why you can't show it to me!" she screamed. "Because it doesn't bloody well work, that's why! I've been breaking my heart trying to keep this corporation afloat, buttering up the shareholders, fending off the Japanese and taking God knows what risks to protect our investments. And all you've been doing is moping around on that bloody island of yours lighting candles to Maria! She's *dead*, Theo! She's been dead for almost a year! And I need you *now!*"

Gilkrensky ran to the other end of the boardroom table, where he wiped the spilled water from the Minerva casing.

"Do you hear me, Theo? You can't turn me off! I'm not on some bloody video link, like I was this morning. I'm right here in the room with you . . . and I need you, Theo. I need you to go to Cairo and fight for what we've built together. I need you . . . I need you!"

Gilkrensky looked back, to see her slumped forward on the table with her head in her hands, sobbing. Gently, he laid the briefcase on one of the boardroom chairs, and walked back to sit beside her.

"Jess? Jess, I'm sorry. But Minerva *does* work. It works better that you could ever imagine. The reason I can't show it to you is personal to me, but I'll fix that as soon as I get back from Cairo. Perhaps you're right. I do need to get off the island for a while. It's just that I wasn't ready before now. Jess?"

Jessica Wright lifted her head. Her dark chestnut hair had fallen across her face. She swept it away. There were tears in her eyes.

"I was very jealous of Maria," she said softly. "She made you so happy. I never did, did I? Not in any way that really mattered."

Gilkrensky could feel her pain. He reached forward and took her hand.

"We're very much alike, you and I," he said. "Both Scorpios. Far too intense for each other."

"But still friends?"

"We'll always be friends."

She lifted his hands in hers, remembering the way they had touched her in Boston. She ran her fingers over the scars for a moment, and then kissed them gently.

"Thank you," she said.

"For what?"

"For picking me up when Thorpe threw me out. For having confidence in me, and for standing up to all those people who said I couldn't handle this job."

"They didn't know you like I did. And besides, it's easy to call the shots when you own the company."

"Well, forty-five per cent of it anyway," said Jessica, forcing a smile.

"Perhaps."

In the distance, they could both hear the purr and chop of the helicopter returning from refuelling.

"Are you sure you want to go through with this, Theo? It's not too late to call it off."

"I'm sure."

Gilkrensky bent over and kissed Jessica Wright gently on the forehead. Then he picked up the Minerva and went out, leaving her in the chairman's seat at the top of the board table.

Jessica remembered Logan airport.

"What *have* I done?" she said softly.

9

INTELLIGENCE GATHERING

YUKIKO WATCHED THE MONITOR ON HER DESK AS THE BOARD OF
Mawashi-Saito signed off from the teleconference with
GRC. Then she shut the small black case in front of her
and slipped it into the jacket-pocket of her grey office
uniform, stood up and walked to the window. From
there she would be able to watch the sun rise over
Tokyo bay while she waited for the call to come.

She did not have long to wait. The call from Miss
Deshimaru came just as the first glow was reddening the
sky. And in less than a minute Yukiko felt the familiar
churn of conflicting emotions, as she stood before the
man who had been her guardian and taskmaster for most
of her life.

"Good morning, uncle! You wished to see me?"

Gichin Funakoshi returned her bow.

"*Hai*, Yukiko-*chan*. You saw the teleconference?"

"I did. From my office."

"And what is your opinion?"

Yukiko thought carefully before she answered. She was aware of her unique position within the *kobun* and of the value her uncle placed on her opinion regarding western competitors.

She owed him a huge debt of obligation – of *giri* – and could not disappoint him now.

"With the greatest respect, uncle, I wonder if you were wise in supporting Dr Gilkrensky's trip to Cairo. Surely, it is in the interest of Mawashi-Saito to see GRC's crisis deepen and their share prices fall?"

Funakoshi smiled.

"It is not the shares I want. They are merely a means to an end. Was I right about the Minerva project? Does Dr Gilkrensky have it ready?"

"Yes, uncle, he does."

"You are sure?"

Yukiko reached into the pocket of her jacket and laid a brand-new GRC SmartMate on the desk between them, opening the lid to reveal the screen.

"I received this unit a few day's ago by courier from my contact in London. You will see from this latest message that Dr Gilkrensky lied to you when he spoke of problems with the Minerva software. He actually had a working prototype at the teleconference just now, small enough to fit inside a briefcase. He was using it to control the teleconferencing and analyse the proceedings as you were speaking."

Funakoshi nodded slowly as he recalled the board meeting, searching his own memory for clues.

"Is your contact reliable?"

"Both reliable . . . and *very* highly placed."

"Are you sure? I do not want a repeat of that regrettable incident in Ireland last March."

"There will be no mistake this time, uncle."

Funakoshi nodded slowly.

"Then I was right to support Dr Gilkrensky's expedition to Egypt. If Minerva *is* working, and portable enough to carry, then he has no choice but to take it to Cairo. It is his best chance of interpreting the data from the Daedalus in time to save his corporation. You realise how important this Minerva unit is to us, Yukiko?"

"I do, uncle. Its neural net contains biological material that should allow it to actually 'think' as a human being would, making associations and value judgements beyond the reach of conventional systems."

"Quite so. It represents the next generation of computers, and as such is quite priceless. Up until now, GRC has not allowed us to view the device or be involved in any part of its development, in spite of much pressure exerted from this office. To make matters worse, that botched attempt at industrial espionage last spring forced Dr Gilkrensky to replace his security staff and move his whole laboratory to an offshore island facility, making any further – ah, intelligence gathering, impossible."

"I understand, uncle."

"You still have no explanation as to what happened that day?"

"No, uncle, I do not. I chose my agents unwisely. It

appears they had a personal agenda of their own. I will not let it happen again."

"I hope not, Yukiko. For the memory of your mother I have watched over your advancement here at Mawashi-Saito and, as you know, your father was my friend for many years before he died."

"Yes, uncle."

"But since his death I sense a change in you. Is your mind on your work, Yukiko? Can I trust you as I always have?"

"You can."

Gichin Funakoshi regarded his niece for a moment, undecided. Then he said, "In that case, let us examine the situation together and decide what we must do. Miss Jessica Wright has presented us with a unique opportunity. Dr Gilkrensky is about to step outside the walls of his fortress, bringing the Minerva 3,000 with him. He will be travelling to Cairo, a city where there has been an increasing level of terrorism in recent years."

"We have contacts there, uncle."

"Indeed we do. For the past few years an Egyptian electronics company, which is little more than a front for one of the lesser-known Islamic fundamentalist groups, has been begging me to sell them satellite communications technology, so they can broadcast their message to the world. We might be able to operate anonymously through them."

Yukiko hesitated.

"Are you sure that is wise, uncle? It has been my

experience that such groups can be very unreliable. Would it not be more effective for me to simply steal the biochip from Dr Gilkrensky myself?"

Funakoshi pondered this for a moment.

"No, Yukiko, I would prefer not to involve you directly. Should you fail, you might be traced back to the *kobun*. That must not be allowed to happen. Therefore, I expect you to contact this group and arrange for them to steal the machine for you. Can you do this?"

"I think so. But to be sure I will need to go to Cairo and speak to their leaders myself."

"Then do so. I understand it would suit you very well to be out of the country just now. That little upstart Okuda, from the Sekigushi *ryu*, contacted me last night. An 'unfortunate accident', he calls it. He can hardly admit to himself that his prize disciple was beaten by a woman, and blames the defeat on secret training you have been undertaking at a . . . less conventional *ryu* in Kyoto. Is this something you should have been informed me about before?"

"I am sorry I did not tell you, uncle. I took on the extra training merely to broaden my range of expertise. So as to serve the *kobun* better."

Funakoshi nodded slowly but his eyes never left hers. "I see. In any event, it would be useful if you were not available for questioning. Miss Deshimaru will make the necessary flight arrangements."

"At once, uncle."

Funakoshi leant forward.

"Nothing is to happen to Dr Gilkrensky," he said

slowly. "Is that clear? I am aware of your deep personal interest in him, as you must be of mine and frankly, I am still far from satisfied with your explanation concerning events in Ireland. Success comes from putting *giri* before *ninjo*, in everything, Yukiko! Without Dr Gilkrensky, GRC – and our future in this new technology of his – is dead. You *will* obey me in this! Even if it means losing the Minerva, Dr Gilkrensky is not to be harmed. Do you understand me?"

"*Hai,* uncle."

Yukiko thought of Hasagawa, the last man who had stood before her. She remembered how her father and mother had died, and a debt of *giri* she herself had vowed to pay. Then she bowed to her uncle and made her way to the door.

10

LEROY

Leroy Manning was angry and hot. Angry, because he and his helicopter had been pulled in from the crash site outside Cairo to ferry a gaggle of Corporation fat cats to their plush hotel. And hot, because they were keeping him waiting.

He had spent most of the first night after the crash flying survivors either to the University Hospital or, if they were luckier, to complimentary suites at the Corporation hotel. Boy! Was GRC ever going to take a bath over this!

Then the next day, the big jumbo jet from Florida had arrived, spewing out men, equipment and portable cabins that had to be flown out to the wreck. Leroy had felt a pang of homesickness just talking to the technicians and one old guy, with a lumberjack shirt and a thick moustache, had even worked on the space programme in Florida . . .

Leroy remembered Patsy Miller, and the long, hot

summer of sixty-nine. He had been very innocent then, and so had she. Making love had been a wonderful adventure, a magical conspiracy. He remembered the first time – the breathtaking sight of her as she lifted her sweater over her head, the feel of her nipples as they hardened in his hand, the slide of her panties down over her knees, the soft warmth between her legs as he fondled her awkwardly in the back seat of his father's car. She had been his first love, and he thought she might be his last, until her letter reached him in Vietnam.

With Su Lin, it had been nothing more than sex. She had been one of the bar girls down at the officer's club in Saigon and had dazzled him with the energy and imagination she brought to the bedroom. After the sweet fumblings of Patsy Miller, and all her pleadings to be gentle, not to "come too soon" and to make sure he was "protected", Su Lin was a revelation. He remembered the feel of her oiled fingers on his chest, as she massaged him – the heat of her breath on his belly as she slid down the bed – the touch of her breasts against his thighs, and the sweet, sure, stroke of her tongue . . .

The closest he had come to marriage was with Sarah Jane – the tall, blonde Texan who worked as secretary in the helicopter company he'd joined when he came home from Vietnam. Sarah Jane loved horses, helicopters and sitting naked with a glass of mulled wine in front of the fire. If ever there was a woman he felt a friend to, it was her. And Leroy needed a friend just then. He was waking up in the middle of the night covered in sweat, and losing his temper at the smallest things for no reason at all. She told him to get help on the day he broke her nose.

Rosalie had been a nurse at the centre where Leroy had gone for treatment. She had seen a lot of "Vets" by then, but something about Leroy's sense of loss troubled her greatly. For a while it had been easy to simply let go and be smothered by her cottonwool kind of love. It was only when she started telling her friends about "her man Leroy" and hinting about engagement rings, that alarm bells began to sound.

To escape her, and the velvet trap he was falling into, he had moved out and signed up with an old army buddy who flew tourists over the game reserves in Africa.

That was fine for a while. But the tourists wanted to go lower and lower, and it wasn't always a camera they were shooting with. One hot afternoon, when the air was thin and the updrafts were at their most treacherous, a rich German had decided he wanted to chase a lion with a helicopter.

That had been Leroy's first serious crash. Afterwards he had lost his taste for dangerous flying.

To make ends meet, while he got his nerve back, he had started doing "milk runs" for a guy he'd met on an aircraft carrier off Vietnam. The man was now a big wheel in a multinational corporation with interests all over the place, and there were lots of nice, safe jobs to do around Cairo, or flying people and equipment up and down the Nile Valley. When Leroy had started with the Gilcrest Radio Corporation he'd only meant to stay for six months. That had been eight years ago.

Leroy twisted in his seat to pull a crumpled packet of Marlboros and a lighter from his pocket. Across from the helipad, the dead brown concrete stretched past the feeder lane to the main runway. Beyond that, a sombre row of transport planes squatted shimmering in the late afternoon heat, sullen beasts of the field compared to the brightly painted airliners that glistened on the commercial runway.

"I do not think you should be smoking."

Standing on the tarmac was an army officer with dark glasses resting on his hooked nose, just above a neat black moustache. Leroy took in the "State Security" emblems on his uniform and his rank badges.

"Come off it, Colonel. I've been flying these things since I was eighteen!" Then he lit the cigarette and took a long drag, blowing the smoke out into the tired air.

"How long will it take you to start up?"

"About two minutes. Why all the security?"

"You do not know?"

"I was just told to ferry a bunch of executives to the Nile Olympiad. They didn't say who."

The portable radio in the colonel's hand buzzed. He raised it to his ear, listened, and then spoke in Arabic, far too quickly for Manning to understand.

"You will start now, please," he said at last in English. "The jet is about to land."

"OK. You're the boss. Hey! Ahmed! Get the fire extinguisher while I crank her up!"

Manning went through the start-up procedure, pressed the starter button and heard the turbine fire. In a moment the great blades were slicing the air in great whooshing sweeps, forcing Manning to shout above the noise.

But the colonel was speaking into his radio again.

Outside, on the airfield, two things happened at once.

From the military airbase on the far side of the field, three black Land-Rovers crossed the main runway and took up position around the end of the feeder lane in front of Manning's helicopter. The canvas hoods at the rear were not fully fastened, and Manning could make out the dull reflection of light on gunmetal.

At the same time, a beautiful blue and white executive jet flashed into sight and hurtled down the runway past the transport planes. The sun glinted on the wing-tip fuel tanks and the tinted windscreen.

"Why all the firepower?" shouted Manning. "I thought Howard Hughes was dead!"

"So did I, but I do not think he worked for GRC."

"No. I mean, who is it?"

"Since you will meet him shortly, I do not see any harm in telling you. It is your chairman, a man called Gilkrensky."

"No shit?"

"Definitely 'no shit', I assure you."

Leroy stubbed out his half-smoked Marlboro and threw it out onto the tarmac while he watched the approaching aircraft, as it manoeuvred onto the feeder strip ahead of him.

Wow! Only Mister Theodore, Jesus H Christ,

Gilkrensky! The "G" in GRC! Coming for a ride in this little old helicopter of mine.

The plane was fifty yards away and moving closer.

Now that was definitely *the* way to travel. Air-conditioning and champagne all the way.

The nose of the executive jet was close now. It slid delicately into the circle formed by the helicopter and the waiting Land Rovers. As the whine of its jets died, the colonel barked an order into his radio and jumped down onto the tarmac. The rear flaps of the waiting vehicles were thrown open, and a score of black-uniformed state security police moved into a tight cordon.

Each one was carrying a Kalashnikov assault rifle.

Airport security gone mad, thought Leroy, and peered into the cockpit facing him to see who his opposite number in the jet might be.

It was almost like looking into a mirror.

Behind the tinted perspex a tall, bearded man in a loose, white shirt was pulling off his headphones as he shut down his engines. As Manning watched, the man slipped on a worn leather jacket and disappeared back into the cabin. Manning immediately felt a kinship. The man was an obvious rebel like himself. It'd be a pleasure to make his acquaintance.

"Please be ready to take off straight away," shouted the colonel.

Manning watched as a short, stocky man in a neat suit peered out of the passenger door of the jet, examined the security cordon around the waiting helicopter, and ushered out two heavily-set guys who Leroy immediately recognised as ex-military, followed by the bearded pilot. The group moved quickly beneath the churning rotors and were ushered into the Bell.

There was a rush of introductions, which Manning didn't hear. Then the short, stocky guy, who was obviously the "big man" himself, started to get all steamed up that the jet pilot had slipped into the co-pilot's seat next to Manning.

There was a clicking of seat belts and the thud of the passenger door slamming, cutting out some of the din from the rotors.

"OK, Colonel?" shouted Manning.

"The Nile Olympiad Hotel. As fast as you can!"

Manning smiled at the man with the beard and leaned closer to him, so that he could be heard. "Do you ever feel like a goddamned taxi driver?" he said out of the corner of his mouth.

The man smiled in sympathy as Manning twisted the throttle, pulled up the collective pitch lever, and heaved the big helicopter into the air above the watchful eyes of the security police.

Fifty feet below, and a hundred yards to the right, Yukiko watched the helicopter from the observation deck of the Arrivals hall – just another Japanese tourist in a light blouse and skirt. The binoculars she was using were unremarkable, but anyone watching the index finger of her right hand would have seen the slightest movement, as she pressed a concealed button next to the focusing ring. And had the noise of aircraft not been so overpowering, anyone listening closely might have been able to make out the faintest click and whirr as the hidden camera inside took picture after picture in quick succession.

Leroy Manning watched the man in the co-pilot's seat run his eyes over the control panel.

"You're running a bit thin!" he shouted to Leroy above the noise of the engines. And yes! Goddammit! He was right. Leroy had set the choke to "manual" while he had been idling at the airport and had forgotten to reset it when he took off.

He passed the stranger the only other radio headset in the helicopter and motioned for him to plug it in. There had been no time to refit the others following the stripping out and hurried replacement of the passenger seats after the airlift from the crash. Without them, nobody in the back would hear a word above the clatter and whine of the engines.

"Thanks. Have you flown one of these yourself?"

"Not for some time. We use JetRangers at home, but we're thinking of changing to Aerospatiales because the spares are easier to get from France."

"I've been flying Hueys like this for the past thirty years. They're a peach! A bit heavy on the controls compared to the smaller choppers, but you can live with that. Want to try?"

"Sure. Whenever you're ready."

The man settled his feet on the dual-control rudder pedals, reached forward for his joystick and took the collective from Manning. The old Bell shimmied slightly as the stranger got used to the feel of the controls. But Manning didn't notice. He was staring at the burn scars on the back of the man's hands, feeling his own skin crawl. God! That must have hurt.

They flew on in silence for a few minutes, while Manning tried to think of something to say. Finally, he jerked his thumb at Major Crowe, who was sitting behind him in one of the fold-down seats, glaring at Leroy's new co-pilot.

"What's it like flying with him?"

"It has its moments. I think he'd rather have me sitting back there in the cabin than riding up here with you."

"Yeah?" said Manning, puzzled. "Just follow the road there at about a thousand feet."

"You got it!"

The grey and brown "Z" of the airport runways slid beneath them as the man followed the tall security towers along the new Suez Road motorway towards the city. The helicopter skimmed over scatterings of shanty town dwellings that gradually congealed into the outskirts of Cairo. Soon the view below them was dominated by domes, minarets and television aerials. Cars jostled each other like coloured corpuscles in clogged grey arteries. Ragged tatters of clothes hung from makeshift lines on the rooftops.

Manning took back the controls, opened the throttle, and the helicopter gained height above the city. Among the confusion of packed buildings along the east bank of the Nile, Leroy could make out the grey oasis of Tahir

Square, the forbidding statue of Rameses by its own lake, and the endless flow of traffic – red and white buses, black and orange taxis, trams, cars, motor-scooters laden with goods, the generous sprinkling of cyclists and pedestrians – all managing to avoid each other in the whirlpool, as if by magic.

Beyond the square, rising like a block of shimmering ice above the confusion of other buildings on the Corniche, was the tower of GRC's Nile Olympiad Hotel. The painted letter 'H' was clearly visible on each of the rooftop helipads.

"Nice piece of real estate!" shouted Manning into his radio microphone.

"It's not my favourite. The one in Vancouver's far better. I had them build it from scratch down by the aquarium."

Manning looked the bearded pilot up and down, taking in the faded jeans, the worn leather jacket and the scuffed jogging shoes. Since when did GRC ask its pilots where to build their hotels? Nobody'd ever asked him!

"They must think a lot of you to let you dress like that," he said.

The man grinned broadly.

"It's one of the advantages of being chairman," he said.

And Leroy Manning had the sickening feeling of having made a terrible mistake.

Nobody spoke for the remainder of the flight. Leroy's flying had suddenly become stiff and precise – a departure from his normal fluid style. And when the helicopter touched down on the southern helipad of the Nile Olympiad Hotel, it was in the exact geometric centre of the marked circle.

"Can you be back here in an hour?" shouted Gilkrensky, taking the Minerva from Major Crowe and stepping out onto the roof. "I'll have to visit the crash site."

"No problem," said Manning.

"Great! And don't forget that auto-choke!"

The two bodyguards, Thomas and Gerald, ran smartly to check the stairwell, followed by Gilkrensky, Crowe and the Egyptian army colonel. At the bottom of the first flight of stairs, away from the noise of the departing helicopter, the Egyptian officer turned and offered Gilkrensky his hand.

"I'm sorry we did not get the opportunity for proper introductions," he said. "My name is Selim, of state security. Your safety here in Egypt is my responsibility."

"Outside this building, perhaps!" said Crowe.

"Everywhere, Major. And in the meantime you will find this southern section of the penthouse floor has been sealed off, with access only by these two lift-shafts and the stairs to the helipad. You, Dr Gilkrensky, have the presidential suite at the end of the corridor, with Major Crowe and the other two gentlemen to the left. The boardroom, should you wish to use it for conferences and such, is to the right. Now, if it is convenient, I would like to talk to you about security arrangements outside the hotel."

"Could you give us five minutes?" said Crowe. "We need to unpack some things."

Colonel Selim frowned. "If that is what you wish."

"Thank you," said Gilkrensky.

Crowe led the way to the end of the corridor, opened the door of the presidential suite and went in, followed by Gerald Maguire carrying a heavy suitcase. Beyond the door, there was a small reception lobby leading to a short corridor, with the main lounge to the right and the bedroom to the left. At the end of the corridor was a fire escape.

"That'll have to be sealed off and alarmed for a start," said Crowe. "Gerald, you and Tom get the machine set up around the front door while I check out the rest of the suite. Dr Gilkrensky, you wait here in the corridor for a moment, please."

Gilkrensky watched through the lounge door as Crowe pulled a flat, black box, the size of a cigarette packet, out of the suitcase and began running it over the pictures and fittings. Thomas and Gerald were busy arranging a cable around the door-frame leading to the corridor.

"Can I come in now, Major?"

"I think it's clear, sir. I noticed before we landed that the window glass is mirrored on the outside, so nobody will be able to see in."

"Hmmm," nodded Gilkrensky, and walked to the window. Below him was the broad stretch of the Nile, with Tahir Bridge, the Cairo Tower, and the exclusive Gazirah sporting club. On the horizon, he could make out the clean, hard lines of the pyramids beyond the jumble of domes and minarets.

"Ah . . . Please try not to stand in one place too long, sir," said Crowe. "I don't think the glass is bullet-proof."

"How could anyone shoot me if they can't see in?"

"Thermal imaging. But they might not be able to tell who they were shooting at."

"That's a comfort," said Gilkrensky and sat down on the plush sofa.

A knock on the outer lobby door was followed almost immediately by a loud buzz.

"Metal-detector works anyway," said Crowe.

Colonel Selim was standing in the doorway, sliding his dark glasses into his breast pocket. His heavy automatic pistol was being held for him by Gerald Maguire. Selim did not seem too pleased about it.

"You will excuse me, Colonel," said Crowe. "But I insist there are no firearms in this suite. It's nothing personal, you understand? Purely a precaution."

Selim's eyes narrowed slightly. Then he smiled.

"I understand perfectly. But in return, I suggest you move your metal detector and your guards back closer to the lift. If an enemy has managed to get this far, there is very little to stop him. Purely a precaution, you understand."

It was Gilkrensky's turn to smile.

"Thank you, Colonel. Would you like to come in? You wanted to talk to us about local security."

"That is correct. No doubt you are aware of the activities of extremist groups here in Egypt? Such activities date back to the time of the English occupation, but they came to a head when President Sadat angered the fundamentalists by aligning Egypt with the West to get American aid. These people protested against him. He in turn threw over fifteen hundred of them in jail, and then paid for it with his life when he was shot."

"Why hasn't there been an Islamic revolution here, like there was in Iran?"

"Because the level of violence employed sickens the majority of Egyptians, so that the terrorists have no popular support. Not long ago a fourteen-year-old girl was killed in an assassination attempt against the prime minister. And a motor-cycle bomb intended for the minister of the interior, killed four innocent people and injured nineteen bystanders. Then there was that incident outside the museum, not far from here, when a busload of tourists was machine gunned and, of course, the terrible massacre at Luxor. Normal people do not condone such activities in a civilised society."

"Do you see these extremists as a national threat?" asked Crowe.

"No. I do not. They are merely a handful of gangsters in the pay of Iran. The main threat is to our tourist industry, since their activities inevitably attract press coverage."

"And in my case?" said Gilkrensky.

"Your case is different, sir. You are an internationally known figure, the head of a multinational corporation, a very rich man. Anywhere in the world, you would represent a target for kidnap or assassination."

"I'm flattered."

"The honour is a double-edged sword, I'm afraid. Therefore we must take reasonable precautions. I will station a team of men in the lobby of the hotel, and another on the roof, guarding the helipad."

Crowe frowned.

"I can't allow any man I cannot personally vouch for onto the roof of this building, onto this floor, or anywhere near the chairman."

Colonel Selim sat back in his chair.

"You are in my country. It would be wise to take my advice."

"I'm fully aware of that, Colonel. And I'm grateful for any help but, as I understand things, we are not dealing with an enemy who might only attempt an assassination from long distance with a high-powered rifle or a remote-controlled bomb. We are potentially faced with fanatics who believe in a holy war. They might walk right into this suite with their pockets packed with explosives and blow us all to hell, in the belief that they would be assured of a place in heaven."

"That is correct, Major."

"And such an assassin could be anyone. Remember, President Sadat was killed by men from his own army, officers from good families, who believed they were doing the right thing. With the greatest respect, Colonel, for all I know you could even be such a person yourself!"

Selim grinned.

"I suppose I should be shocked, Major. But for once it is refreshing to deal with a man who has done his homework. I will therefore confine my activities to the lower floors of the hotel, as long as I can be sure you have sufficient staff to secure the presidential suite itself. Can I ask what your travel plans are outside this building?"

"In general terms, you may. We plan to limit such travel to the wreck of the aircraft itself, the airport, and whatever government offices it might be necessary to deal with in order to investigate the crash. Wherever possible, the chairman will travel by helicopter. It will be returning in a few minutes to take us to the crash site."

"Good. If you need an escort for your flight, I can provide one. We have two armed helicopters, which are part of the regular city patrol."

"Thank you, Colonel. But that won't be necessary."

"Very well. Now that we understand each other's position, there are formalities, such as visas and registration with the authorities. I can be dealing with those while you wait for your helicopter to arrive."

II

THE FUNDAMENTALIST

Yukiko was dropped by taxi next to the bus station in Tahrir Square. When she was sure that the taxi had pulled away, she walked inside, found an empty toilet cubicle in the washrooms and, ignoring the smell of stale urine, opened the red travel-bag she was carrying and pulled out a heavy *galabia* robe that covered her from head to toe. Then she turned the bag inside out to reveal the blue lining, stuffed the binoculars inside, and went to hail another taxi.

This taxi took her further to the west, across the Nile on Tahrir Bridge and onto the exclusive Gazirah island, which is home to many museums, embassies, and some of the most expensive residences in Cairo. The taxi turned north along the bank of the river, passing the Cairo Tower and the Sixth October Bridge, the bowling greens and croquet lawns of the sporting club and on towards the Marriott hotel. There were more fine hotels on the other side of the Nile, including the Olympiad, which Yukiko glanced at briefly.

Just south of the Twenty-sixth July Bridge the taxi dropped Yukiko, who once again waited until it was out of sight. Then she walked past several fine apartment blocks with names dating back to the British Empire – "Park Lane", "Nile View" and "Dorchester House" – until she came to the address given to her by her contact, stepped up and rang the bell.

The man who answered the door could have been a successful athletics instructor at any of the smart sports clubs on the island. He was tall and muscular, with jet-black hair, olive skin and a neat moustache. He had been described to Yukiko as a top fashion photographer and his luxurious apartment, overlooking the river to the east, contained a complete darkroom and photographic studio. It was no surprise then, to find an expensive Nikon camera with a powerful telephoto lens, sitting on a tripod just far enough back from the window to be invisible from the outside. Yukiko's gaze followed the direction of the lens. It was pointed at the top floor of the Nile Olympiad.

She opened the travel-bag and handed him the binoculars.

"These pictures were taken at the airport less than an hour ago. They show the target and the men in his security team. You know how to extract the film?"

The man turned the binoculars in his hands.

"I'm surprised they sent a woman on such an important mission as this. But yes, I know how to extract the film."

Yukiko said nothing, but watched as the man pressed

a button near the focusing ring, rewinding the film inside back onto the spool. Then, when he was sure the exposed film was safe from the light, he twisted the barrels of the binoculars apart. There was a click, and nestling inside the black metal was the unmistakable yellow canister of a Kodak 35 millimetre film cassette. He handed the binoculars back to her.

"I will develop these and assemble the group," he said. "Then I will call you to confirm."

He smiled, but his eyes remained cold.

They were the eyes of a fanatic.

Once the Japanese woman had left, Zaki El Sharoud made sure his apartment door was securely locked. Then he took the Kodak cassette to his darkroom, lifted a black plastic developing-drum from the shelf, opened it to remove the spindle and laid it on the work surface in front of him where he could find it easily in the dark. He switched off the light, prised open the film cassette with a kitchen bottle-opener and threaded the film inside onto the plastic spindle, before replacing it in the developing-drum. When he was satisfied that the lid was tightly screwed down, he reached for the light-switch and turned it back on.

In a water-bath set for twenty degrees centigrade were bottles of developing-fluid, stop bath and fixer. He unscrewed the top of the first bottle and carefully poured it into the developing-drum. It was strange, after the many thousands of photographs he had processed in his career, that he could never develop a film without thinking of that unique set of pictures he had taken on that fateful October day.

He had been twenty-three then, and just appointed to the Cairo newspaper *Al-Ahram* as a junior photographer – ideal cover for what he *really* wanted to do. None of the old hacks on the paper minded when the new hot-shot, fresh from university and his compulsory army service, asked to be assigned to the predictable and tedious ritual of the Sixth October parade. They even joked that Zaki might as well take the rest of the day off and send in last year's photographs instead. The parade was always the same they said, nothing will change.

They were wrong.

Zaki arrived early and set up his equipment directly opposite the presidential viewing-stand, with a clear view of the parade route up and down the Sari El-Quasr El-Aini. Around his neck were two cameras, a Nikon with a 500 millimetre catadioptic lens, and a Pentax with a normal telephoto. In his pockets were roll after roll of fast Tri-X film and, taped to his chest beneath his clothing, with its throat-microphone and ear-piece hidden by the hood of his light anorak, was a miniature radio.

The day was fine and bright, ideal for photography. The crowd gathered, as it always did, and the VIPs arrived. Zaki raised the Nikon and started to take portrait shots from long range. There were the ministers, important officials, representatives from other countries, Vice President Hosni Mubarak and, in the centre of the viewing-stand, magnificent in his Cardin uniform with the two gold lotus blossoms on the collar, was President Anwar Sadat himself.

Zaki trained the powerful lens of his camera down the line of the parade, past the oncoming artillery, towards a single approaching truck. Then he turned back to the presidential stand for any signs of alarm or increased security.

There were none.

"It is clear," he said softly into the throat-microphone. "God be with you!" Then he raised the Pentax, and began to shoot again.

Click!

Sadat sits smiling and clapping, almost half-heartedly, as a flight of air-force jets roar overhead.

Click!

The single truck stops, directly in front of the presidential stand. Four soldiers jump out. They are firing Kalashnikov assault rifles.

Click!

Sadat thinks this is part of the parade. He actually rises to applaud.

Click!

The soldiers continue to advance on the President. Their guns are levelled. Sadat realises his mistake.

This is an assassination!

Click!

Sadat is shouting, "Boy! Stand where you are!"

Click!

Sadat is hit. He falls to the ground. Mubarak is

sprayed with blood and hit in the hand by a ricochet. He throws himself down as the assassins advance.

Click!

A grenade is thrown. It fails to explode. In the shooting, the Omani ambassador and a Coptic bishop are killed.

Click!

The shooting stops. Sadat is dead! With a bullet-hole between the embroidered lotus blossoms on the collar of his beautiful uniform.

Click!

In the terrible silence that follows, the leader of the assassins shouts, "I am Khalid al-Istambuli! I have killed Pharoah, and I do not fear death!"

Zaki El Sharoud placed the processed negatives under a clean sheet of glass, and made a contact print with his big Durst enlarger. Then he ran a powerful magnifying glass over the individual frames, comparing the faces in the pictures with the face he had seen earlier that day on a CNN news broadcast. Finally, he selected a frame containing the portrait of a tall thin man in a leather jacket. The man had a sparse beard, and was carrying a black briefcase.

"I have you," said Zaki El Sharoud, and set up the enlarger to make a full-sized print.

12

CRASH SITE

GILKRENSKY HAD NEVER EXPERIENCED ANYTHING QUITE LIKE THE desert before. Its horizon with the sky split the world into just two colours: blue, and a swirling yellowy brown that rolled in frozen waves beneath the scurrying helicopter.

The crash site began with a strange gash in one of the larger dunes. Further on there was another, surrounded by twisted shards of metal. Then a long, wide tear in the smooth sand, littered with scattered luggage which had burst on impact or been torn open by looters, spewing clothes out over the desert.

Finally, rising hard and crooked above the rolling sand, was the giant metal "T" of the aircraft's tail-fin. Below it was the wreck. Gilkrensky could see the black stains of fire damage, spreading from the engines under the tail and collapsing the fuselage roof to just behind the cockpit. Only the forward section of the hull was intact, and that was being picked clean by the milling ants of the investigation teams.

"Well done, Leroy!" he shouted into his radio microphone. "How did you find the wreck so quickly?"

Manning had been on his guard for most of the flight out, trying furiously to think what he might have said to Gilkrensky earlier. But, what the hell! If he'd said something wrong, he'd be out of a job by now.

"No problem! I just followed the investigation team's satellite beacon. The boys from Florida fixed themselves an up-link last night, when I flew them in."

On the sand below, just off the port wing of the crashed airliner, were two portable cabins linked by thick cables to a mobile generator. As the helicopter touched down, a big man in a lumberjack shirt and denim slacks shuffled out, shielded his eyes against the flying sand and ambled over to meet them.

"Theo!" he roared above the engine noise. "Good to see you, son. Pity it isn't under better circumstances, but there you are. Hey! Is that what I think it is?" And he pointed to the black case containing the Minerva.

Gilkrensky nodded.

"Yes, Bill. But don't say it too loudly, or everyone will want one!"

"Point taken. I can't wait to see it in action. Have you brought the virtual-reality gear?"

"I have. Who's on-site?"

"Well, the official investigation team is all here. Then there's a whole bunch of Egyptians, representing the country where the crash happened. Then there's me, wearing two hats – one as a representative of the state of manufacture and, of course, one as the company who made the plane. There's an English guy from the Ministry of Transport in London, and a guy called Malone from the Civil Aeronautics Administration. Now, who've you got with *you?*"

"This is one of my bodyguards, Gerald Maguire. And this is our new head of security, Major Crowe."

"Security eh? There's no shortage of that around here. I had some colonel out here giving us the once-over the minute we arrived. He put a cordon of troops around the aircraft last night. Claimed it was to protect it from looters."

"That would be Colonel Selim," said Crowe. "We had a long talk with him earlier."

"Cold sort of a fish, eh? Still, he seemed to know what he was doing. Do you want to get a look in the cockpit?"

"Yes please, Bill. Have they found the 'black box' yet?"

"No, they haven't. I'd say the radio beacon crapped out when it was ejected onto the sand during the crash. And I'll tell you something else that's worrying. The Daedalus unit is smashed. I don't think you'll get any information out of that either."

"Smashed?" asked Gilkrensky. "But that's impossible!"

"Yeah. I know. It's impossible during a *normal* crash. But it looks as if some looters got into the cockpit before Selim arrived and went crazy with a fire-axe."

"The titanium casing should have protected the main memory chip."

"You'll see for yourself in a minute. The Egyptians are very wary about me going anywhere near it and, by the same token, I've insisted they stay out of the cockpit in case they might screw anything up. I thought I'd wait until you got here before I tried to access the Daedalus's memory, just in case. Come on, let's take a look."

McCarthy led them to a light aluminium ladder propped under the cockpit door. Using one hand on the rungs, and one hand to carry the Minerva, Gilkrensky followed him into the fuselage, the darkness, and the smell.

"Pretty damned awful, isn't it," sighed McCarthy. "Fire started in the rear after the passengers got clear and ate its way towards the nose. You see, we only use special gelled kerosene instead of standard aviation fuel, because it doesn't burn as easily. Then that burned itself out and the internal extinguishers killed it, just aft of the cockpit. See the way the seat covers are still intact? All fireproof material, but it doesn't stop them smouldering."

Crowe stepped forward and touched a shapeless object on the cabin floor with his foot. It was a child's doll. McCarthy bent down and picked it up, running his thick fingers through its blackened hair. For a moment he was a million miles away. Then he said, "Don't worry, Major. She walked away from this one. Aircraft safety is a kind of obsession with me, and I designed this plane to be the safest in the world. You see the seats? They all face towards the rear of the plane. In a crash all the impact is absorbed by the seat itself, instead of firing the passenger forward like a bullet out of a gun. You'll notice from the crash report that the only serious injury was to the stewardess who was out of her seat when the incident happened."

"You saved a lot of lives with this plane," said Crowe.

McCarthy gently sat the doll in the first passenger seat, facing aft.

"Pity I didn't do it years ago," he said sadly. "Then my eldest daughter Angie, and her kids might still be alive. OK, Theo. Do you want to . . . Theo?"

Gilkrensky had vanished into the cockpit and was sitting crossways in the pilot's seat, hunched over the smashed casing of the Daedalus.

"Somebody really went crazy in here," he said, shaking his head. "Why the hell would they do that?"

All around him were the empty eye-sockets of smashed VDUs and ripped-out panels. The plastic throttle controls were broken off, exposing the metal bars underneath, and the simple joysticks were shattered. One had been torn right out of its panel, leaving a trail of coloured wires on the cockpit floor. As Crowe stepped onto the flight deck, his shoe crunched on broken glass.

"Here's your culprit," he said, pointing to a heavy fire-axe that had been thrown down between the pilot's rudder pedals. "I wonder why they didn't take it with them, if they were looters. It must be worth something."

"Looks like there was a fight!" said McCarthy.

The fabric of the co-pilot's seat was smeared with the unmistakable black stain of dried blood. There were drips of it on the control panel around the Daedalus unit. Gilkrensky lifted what was left of the shattered cover.

Someone had hit it very hard, splitting the plastic so that it came away in two sections. Beneath the cover, the unit was wrecked. The screen was smashed in, the keypad hammered into a confetti of shattered plastic, and the inspection cover had been peeled back like a half-open can. The jagged metal was smeared with blood.

"Looks like someone was trying to pull the core out of the plane when the inspection cover jammed on them," said Gilkrensky.

"Industrial espionage?" suggested Crowe. "Perhaps they were after the neural-net chip?"

"No point. The 1,000 model we use in Daedalus is available commercially. The Japanese and the Americans have been copying it for years."

"Perhaps the looters thought it was a radio?"

McCarthy laughed.

"Aw, come off it, Major! This is a multi-million dollar airplane we're talking about here, not a stolen car."

Gilkrensky pulled a penknife from his pocket and prised open a thin plastic panel, low down on the pilot's side of the Daedalus.

"We could sit here and speculate all day," he said. "But I think it'd be more use to see if we can extract the information we need from the main memory chip and get out. Would you two mind making sure I'm not disturbed for a minute or two?" And he pulled a grey plastic cable from his pocket, attaching one end to the port he had just uncovered, and the other to a similar socket in the Minerva.

Crowe and McCarthy stepped out of the cockpit into

the cabin. At the far end, they could see a pair of Egyptian officials picking their way towards them. From the cockpit they heard Gilkrensky say,

"Copy input and commands from master unit and all peripherals for the last forty-eight hours."

"What's that, Theo?"

"Nothing, Bill. Just talking to myself."

McCarthy stepped forward behind Crowe to meet the two Egyptians. From the cockpit, McCarthy heard Gilkrensky's voice dictating another command to the Minerva, and for an instant, McCarthy could have sworn he heard a woman's voice answer.

13

THE CREW

"The Egyptians seemed pretty upset that I was in the cockpit," said Gilkrensky, after they had returned to McCarthy's main caravan. He laid the Minerva gently on the fold-out table next to the metallurgical X-ray machine and looked back out of the doorway at the wreck.

"I don't think it was that," said McCarthy. "Under the Convention, we have the right to examine the wreckage, to have full access to all the evidence, and to question witnesses. What I think really pissed them off was that you wouldn't let them see what you had in the briefcase."

"I can't let them see the Minerva. It's one of the only two prototypes there are."

"Did you manage to extract the information?"

"I won't know until Minerva processes it. The main Daedalus chip may have been too damaged to recover anything usable. Why don't you take one of the other portable computers up there and see if you have any luck. Better still, do it in front of the Egyptians, so they can see it's all above board. We can use it in the official enquiry."

"So why take your own copy with the Minerva?"

"Because, if the information from the Daedalus autopilot is usable, I want to analyse it well ahead of anyone else. I don't like surprises, Bill. Did you say we had the right to question witnesses?"

"I did, and we do. But if you're thinking of questioning the flight crew, I suggest you ask that CAA guy Malone, or another independent witness to sit in with you. Otherwise it's going to look like you're trying to intimidate them."

"OK. Let's go and find this Mr Malone. Have someone call the hotel and ask them to have Captain Danvers and his crew meet me in the boardroom in an hour. There's a lot of things about this incident which just don't add up."

The helicopter landed on the roof of the Nile Olympiad at just after five that evening. Anyone watching it closely would have seen its tail wag slightly on the final approach. Gilkrensky had persauded Leroy Manning to let him take the controls again, and he was still finding them difficult to master.

"Don't worry about it," said Manning. "That's called the 'Huey Shuffle' and everyone flying one of these babies for the first time does it. Did it myself. It's because the pedals are so sensitive and make it easy to over-control."

"Thanks," said Gilkrensky. "I'll try it again later." And with McCarthy, Crowe and Martin Malone, he ran to the stairwell of the hotel and down into the corridor of the presidential suite.

Thomas Hargreaves was there to greet him. "The flight crew are waiting for you in the board room."

"Thank you," said Gilkrensky, and opened the door.

Facing him across the table, with their backs to the Nile and the western city, were five people in clean Exair uniforms. They all rose as he entered, and looked at him nervously.

"Ah . . . Good evening, ladies and gentlemen. My name is Theodore Gilkrensky. This is Professor William McCarthy who designed the plane, and Martin Malone from the Civil Aeronautics Administration."

The man in the centre of the group put out his hand.

"I'm Captain Robert Danvers," he said. "And this is Margaret Spalding – my first officer, Brian Griffiths – our engineer, and Sarah and Melanie – our cabin staff. Juliette Maxwell, our chief stewardess, cannot be with us. She's still in hospital, as you probably know."

"I'm sorry. How is she?"

Danvers glared at him. He was about to speak when Margaret Spalding cut across him. She was a small, neat woman with black hair and a thick Liverpool accent.

"She's going to be all right," she said flatly.

For a moment there was an awkward silence.

Then Gilkrensky said, "I'm glad. Please sit down everyone."

There was a scraping of chairs around the table.

"I'd like to thank you all for coming here today at such short notice, and to say I wish we could have met under different circumstances. This is not an official enquiry, you understand, simply an initial investigation into the circumstances of the crash, particularly in light of what's been said in the media about the . . . "

"I take it you're referring to me, Mr Gilkrensky?" said Danvers. He was a large man with a ginger moustache, freckles and bright blue eyes that glared across the table.

"That's right. I . . . "

"What I told the reporters is true. Your machine crashed the plane and that's all there is to it." His hand went to his jacket pocket and pulled out a small cassette recorder, which he placed in the no-man's-land of the table between them. "Now I know this is not an *official* enquiry, but I have to protect myself and my crew by insisting there's a record of this conversation."

"Aw, come off it fella . . . !" began McCarthy.

But Gilkrensky said, "That's OK. Can you run through the events leading up to crash for me, please?"

"There's very little point," said Danvers. "It was all routine. We'd punched the flight co-ordinates into that machine of yours, and it took us up as sweetly as you please at first, heading for London. Then, out of a clear blue sky, the collision and low-altitude warning-alarms went off and the machine put the plane into a steep climb, so steep that it stalled. If you know anything about aerodynamics, you'll know that stall situations are particularly dangerous on planes like your Whisperer with high T-shaped tails. If the plane climbs too steeply, the turbulent airflow from the wings causes the engines to surge and interferes with the tail's ability to lift the rear end of the aircraft. So she literally falls backwards out of the sky."

"It's called 'deep stall'," offered McCarthy.

"I know what it's called," snapped Danvers. "I also know that when you're sitting up there with the lives of two hundred passengers in your hands, you don't have time to debate it academically – you just act! And that's what I did."

"What *did* you do?" asked Gilkrensky.

"I switched off the bloody robot for a start! The stall-warning gong was going crazy and I could feel the tail dropping away. So I did the only thing that would bring lift back to the wings."

"Which was?"

"I hit the emergency parachute we use for braking. That snapped open, pulled the tail up, and suddenly I had control again. But we'd fallen too close to the ground to regain lift, and there was nothing I could do but crashland."

Gilkrensky nodded. "You did very well."

"And how would you know?"

"I'm a qualified pilot – fixed wing and helicopters. When exactly was Miss Maxwell injured?"

One of the stewardesses said, "It must have been when the parachute opened. All the passengers were still strapped into their seats. But this little boy got up to go to the lavatory as soon as the seat-belt sign went off. The alarms sounded, and Julie went to get him. She had him in her arms when the nose went down and she was thrown against the bulkhead."

"What about the child? Was anyone else injured?"

"No," said Danvers sharply. "The kid was OK."

"But there was another crew member hurt. It's in the accident report."

"Just a few bumps and scrapes. Nothing to write home about."

Gilkrensky looked at Danvers, and then at the tape recorder between them.

"So you're telling me Daedalus suddenly put the plane into a steep climb, stalled it, and then failed to recover control?"

"That's right," said Danvers.

"Miss Spalding?"

"That's what happened."

"And there was no interference with the unit that any of you are aware of?"

"I only switched it off after I was sure it wasn't going to recover the plane," said Danvers slowly. "I gave it every reasonable chance, considering I had two hundred lives on board."

"So you've said. Do you still insist the machine was at fault?"

Danvers leant forward across the table.

"I object strongly to the word *'insist'*, Mr Gilkrensky. I am not *'insisting'* anything. I am, along with the other members of my crew, simply stating the facts as they happened. Your machine failed, and the plane crashed. That's all there is to it."

Gilkrensky stared back at him.

"Technically, I still find that hard to believe. Daedalus would have compensated for the deep stall through its back-up systems in less than five seconds. It . . . "

Danvers exploded.

"For God's sake, man! We're not talking about a theoretical exercise here! I was *not* going to gamble with the lives of two hundred men, women and children while I waited to see if your bloody machine would get its act together! You and your precious corporation have tried to take the human element out of flying, and you've failed. Your bloody robot doesn't work and your aircraft is unsafe! As far as I'm concerned this interview is over until the official enquiry!"

Danvers jerked to his feet so fast that his chair toppled backwards onto the floor. Then he stormed out of the suite. His crew exchanged glances. One by one, they followed him out of the room.

The last to go was Margaret Spalding, who reached forward to retrieve Captain Danvers's cassette recorder. Her hands were heavily bandaged so that she couldn't turn it off. Gilkrensky reached forward and pressed the button for her.

"You've hurt yourself, Miss Spalding."

"I burnt myself on the wreckage," she said calmly. "Now sir, I think we'd be grateful if you left us in peace until the enquiry."

"That is understood," said Martin Malone.

"Thank you," she said, and went to join the rest of her crew.

"If you don't need me anymore, Dr Gilkrensky, I'd like to get back to the crash site," said Malone.

"Yes. Of course," said Gilkrensky in a distant voice. "Leroy will fly you back."

McCarthy opened the door for him and then turned back into the room. Gilkrensky was still slumped in his seat, staring out at the setting sun.

"That Captain Danvers really hates me, doesn't he, Bill?"

"They've all been through a lot, Theo. An investigation brings out the worst in people anyway. You've got to expect that."

"Is there any way this thing can be proven, one way or the other?" said Crowe.

McCarthy drew a deep breath and sighed.

"The 'black box' flight recorder is the only officially admissible evidence. But it might be damaged, or have only basic information that wouldn't give enough detail to figure out if Danvers's story is true. Conversation in the cockpit is recorded, but the tape is usually recycled so that only the last thirty minutes before the crash are retained."

"So you can see it all boils down to what's on the Daedalus memory chip, and whether or not the official enquiry will admit it as evidence," said Gilkrensky.

"That's right, Theo. And we've never had to use it this way before."

Gilkrensky seemed lost in the view to the west, towards the desert, and the wreck.

"Of course not. I developed that system so we'd never have another plane crash. And now look at us! Danvers was right. I tried to remove human error. Isn't that what Dr Frankenstein said when he made his monster? His wife was killed too, wasn't she?"

"Aw, come off it, Theo! You're being too hard on yourself."

"Did either of you notice how Danvers hogged the whole interview?" asked Crowe. "It was almost as if the crew had rehearsed it in advance and agreed that he'd do all the talking."

"He's their captain after all," said Gilkrensky.

"But you saw Miss Spalding's hands, didn't you, sir?"

"I did. She said she'd burnt them on the wreckage."

"Perhaps," said Crowe. "But just to be sure, I'd like to do a bit of research on my own over at the hospital. If that's all right with you?"

At that moment, on the other side of the Nile, visitors were arriving at a fashionable address – four men and a woman – who would have been coveted guests at any cocktail party in the city.

The owner of the fine apartment took a heavy brown envelope from the top drawer of an antique bureau, and spread the contents on the low coffee table. It was a collection of professional eight-by-ten-inch black and white photographs, each slightly grainy from the enlargement of the fast Tri-X film, but still showing excellent detail.

"As you all know," said Zaki El Sharoud, "there was a plane crash outside the city two nights ago, which caused considerable embarrassment, and immense financial loss, to the company which owned it. Yesterday, they flew in a whole army of technicians in a specially fitted-out jumbo jet. This afternoon they interviewed the flight crew at the corporation hotel. But of greatest interest to us is this . . . "

Zaki pointed to the first photograph, which showed a group of men disembarking from a private jet.

"This morning, there was a great deal of security activity at the airport. Nothing ostentatious, as there might be for a visiting dignitary or head of state, but serious activity for all that. The whole operation took less than five minutes, but it was not fast enough to stop us obtaining these pictures. Look at this one carefully. The tall man with the beard is none other than Theodore Gilkrensky himself, the chairman and majority shareholder in the Gilcrest Radio Corporation. He is one of the five richest men in the world."

El Sharoud looked around the group for a reaction. The men nodded. Only the woman had a question.

"Why is this man so important to us?" she asked. "There are many rich men in Cairo who would be easier targets."

El Sharoud went to a carved bookcase and pulled out an international business directory, opened it at a marked page, and handed it to her.

"This man is important to us, not so much for what he is worth, but for what he controls. The Gilcrest Radio Corporation is essentially a holding company with interests in computers, airlines and aerospace, a chain of hotels, recreational facilities, food companies and, most importantly, a communications group. Gilcrest Communications has been involved in smartcard development, virtual-reality theme parks, alternative phone and video systems, and the launch of communications satellites. It is this last area which holds the key to a great victory for Islam."

"How?" asked the woman.

El Sharoud smiled.

"Because mass communication is today's most powerful weapon. During the war in the Gulf against Iraq, when a single Muslim power opposed the combined forces of the West, who controlled the satellite news?"

"The West, of course."

"And because of this, only one side of the story ever reached the world. Yet, during the successful Islamic revolution in Iran, the voice of Ayatollah Khomeini reached the ears of thousands of his followers, who could not even read, on smuggled audio cassettes."

The woman nodded.

"Satellite television is the fastest-growing news medium in the world," continued Zaki. "It can reach anywhere that a person can set up a 'devil dish'. All over Islam, western consumerism, profane images, political propaganda and even pornography are being beamed directly into people's homes, and it is destroying their faith. Yet if we had access to a satellite channel, think of what we could accomplish! We could spread the word of Allah across the globe. Our masters have decided this man is the key to a new dawn for Islam, and we have been chosen to bring that about."

The woman looked up from the book. Then she pointed to one of the photographs on the table, showing the armed cordon of state security guards around Gilkrensky's plane.

"He will be a difficult target."

El Sharoud settled himself into a white leather chair.

"That is true. According to my research, there has already been one unsuccessful attempt on his life, and so now he has his own private army of bodyguards, led by an ex-major of the British commandos. The presidential suite of his hotel is a sealed fortress and the lower floors are swarming with state security troops. Today, he ventured outside the hotel. But this was in a private helicopter, which is kept under guard at the airport and flown by a corporation pilot. Yes, he is a difficult target. But for the power he can bring us, he is worth the risk."

Gamal, a short powerfully built man who had served with Zaki during his time in the army said,

"Have our masters given you a plan?"

"This is where you, and Abdul and Sarwat, must advise me. This man's obsession with security is also his greatest weakness. You see how all his defences are designed to prevent an attack from below? Now please tell me if this is feasible . . . "

Zaki's plan to kidnap Theodore Gilkrensky was both daring and well-researched. Like all good plans, it made full use of the special talents of each member of the team. By the time El Sharoud had finished, none of the men had any doubt that it would work.

When they had gone, the woman said,

"You have convinced them. They will follow you."

"And you?"

"You know I will."

"Even though yours is the most difficult task of all?"

She was Abdul and Sarwat's sister Farida, the most beautiful of the fashion models who came to Zaki's studio – tall and slim, with shining black hair that flowed to her waist, and eyes so dark he thought he might drown in them. Of all the women he had known, and there had been many, she was the one for whom he had the most respect. There had been times when he had looked into her eyes, that he thought what it might be like to forget the past and begin again with her. But the Holy War – the *Jihad* – was everything to them both.

"I will do what must be done," she said. Then she left.

Zaki El Sharoud gathered up the photographs from the table, put them back in the envelope with the negatives, and carefully placed the package on the fire, where it flamed and spat into ashes.

Behind him, the door to the bedroom opened slowly.

"You briefed them well," said Yukiko. "But you forgot to mention the briefcase."

El Sharoud looked up from the fire.

"I do not like to lie to my people," he said. "If they are to believe this is a simple kidnap, then I must be free to explain the mission as I see fit. Surely your masters in Tokyo have told you that. When we are successful, and the communications satellite is ours, who is to know whether or not it came from Japan or from this man's company . . . as long as it comes?"

"You will have your access when my company has the briefcase," said Yukiko. "But you must deliver Gilkrensky to me. That is my *personal* condition."

"You will have him," said Zaki El Sharoud.

14

CABARET

THE HELICOPTER TOUCHED DOWN ON THE ROOF OF THE NILE Olympiad at 10.35 p.m., after its last trip of the day. Its landing-lights flashed on the painted concrete, cutting off the helipad from the rest of the night as if the machine was resting in a large room. Leroy Manning gingerly removed his headset as the engine idled, massaged his scalp with his fingers, and waited for his passengers to disembark.

Next to him, Gilkrensky was popping the buckle on his seat belt. "Tired?" he shouted above the engines.

"You know how it is. The last few days have been hell!"

"Then why don't you switch off the chopper and leave her here for the night. There's bound to be a bed for you in the hotel somewhere. That would be OK, wouldn't it, Major?"

"I don't see why not," yelled Crowe. "Just get Hargreaves to fix you up a security badge."

Manning flicked off the engine and waited for the blissful silence as it died.

"And if you're not tired, there's always the nightclub!" said Hargreaves as the rotors ground to halt. "I saw a belly-dancer in Turkey once. Gave me a hard-on for a week."

"Whatever turns you on," said Manning and started pulling the dew-covers for the engine out of their lockers. Still, as long as he was in the hotel anyway . . .

The nightclub, on the wing-tip of the hotel farthest from Gilkrensky's penthouse, was tacky and touristy . . . and empty. Glass walls on three sides looked out over the city, while the wooden dance-floor was an island in a sea of tables.

It must seat three hundred, thought Manning. And there's less than a dozen people here!

"Are we too early?" asked Hargreaves.

"You're always too early for Cairo cabarets," said Manning. "They're nightbirds. Here, let's get a table over by the stage!"

A uniformed *maitre d'* intercepted them, saw the security badge and corporation logo on Manning's flight jacket, and stopped in his tracks. Then he removed the "reserved" sign on the table they had selected, wished them a pleasant evening, and slid off to get the menus.

"I'll order," said Manning when they came. He ran his eyes down the ornately scripted lists, picked what he thought might be acceptable, and ended with, "Two bottles of Stella Export beer, with the blue label."

"It's dearer, but it's stronger than the local brew," he added.

The beer arrived, along with a selection of small bowls of shrimps, strips of meat, chicken wings, hummus and stuffed vine-leaves.

"It's called *mezze*. Here, you can dip your bread in it. What do you think of that meat?"

"S'OK!" said Hargreaves with his mouth full.

"It's deep-fried brain. That's OK! Spit it out into this," and he held out an ash-tray.

The main course was beef and veal, served with a sauce and vegetables, which was more to Hargreaves's taste. At least he could see what it was. All around them, people were starting to arrive. Manning ordered another pair of Stella Exports – what the hell! The company was paying! – he lit a Marlboro while he waited for the dessert. A group of German tourists eyed them suspiciously, then took the other reserved tables on the far side of the dance-floor and ordered a round of drinks.

Things started to move at around one a.m. An Egyptian singer, who reminded Manning of a bit player in a gangster movie started to grind his way through a medley of Dean Martin songs, each worse than the one before.

"It gets better," said Manning. "Trust me!"

At half past one, a wedding group arrived from a reception downstairs. The guests clapped as the bride and groom danced nervously in front of the stage. The singer was getting into the swing of his act. More and more people were coming in. A large group of Japanese took the remaining tables around the dance-floor. And by two o'clock the place was full.

"I told you," said Manning. "Nightbirds!"

Then the singer bowed and left. A large band moved in, taking up the whole stage.

"That'll be for your belly-dancers. They're a really big deal around here."

"So who's on tonight?" said Hargreaves, draining the last of his beer.

"No idea. Just enjoy, eh?"

The new orchestra tuned up noisily. The lights dimmed, and the spotlight fell on the singer, who had returned to act as Master of Ceremonies. For a moment he spoke in rapid Arabic. There was a round of applause and the bride and groom stood up, happily embarrassed, and sat down again. Then more Arabic, far to fast for Manning to catch, and a wave of laughter. Finally the singer said, "Ladies and gentlemen from overseas, I would like to welcome you to the Rooftop Club of the Nile Olympiad Hotel. Without further ado, may I introduce you to our star of the evening, the one and only . . . Mirium!"

"Oh shit!" said Manning, who'd seen her before.

Mirium was a large and energetic woman, overflowing with personality and body fat. She teased the bridegroom mercilessly, gyrating in front of his table and running a silk scarf around his neck. The German tourists loved it. The wedding party applauded. The Japanese shot roll after roll of film.

"You'll notice she's wearing a body stocking, so that nothing shows," said Manning, when there was a lull in the music. "Something we have the fundamentalists to thank for."

"Yeah, I did. Service to mankind if you ask me, given the size of her."

"It's an art form. Not a strip show."

Mirium finished her act to rapturous applause, waving and laughing at the crowd as she mopped her face with a handful of paper tissues from a box at the side of the stage.

Then the singer was back. He took the microphone from its stand.

"Ladies and gentlemen, it is not often that an old hand like me has the chance to introduce you to a great new talent. But tonight, I have such an honour. Making her debut here at the Rooftop Club, I present . . . Camille!"

The lights dimmed. The singer withdrew, and there was a single drumbeat, cutting short the applause and any ripple of conversation.

To the left of the stage, a bright disc of the light picked out a veiled face that peeked innocently around the curtain. Above the veil were the largest, darkest eyes Manning had ever seen. Their eyelids fluttered.

Another drumbeat.

The girl stepped lightly out onto the stage, with the spotlight still only on her face. The dark eyes blinked.

Drumbeat! And the spotlight drew back.

Standing proudly in its glare was a long, lithe figure wrapped in strips of coloured silk over an electric-blue body stocking. Her shining black hair, held by a jewelled clasp, flowed in a river to her waist.

There was silence in the room.

Drumbeat.

The girl began to dance, in graceful fluid movements, as her hands rose above her neck. Between the finger and thumb of each hand she held a tiny pair of brass cymbals, that tinkled as the music flowed with her.

Dom, dom, dom – dom dom dom!

She was a beautiful butterfly, dipping across the dance-floor in her own pool of light, raising her arms, elbows bent, lifting her breasts against the taut material of her costume. Her hands slid through her hair to the back of her neck. A strip of silk fluttered to the floor. Manning watched it go, mesmerised.

The music swelled and flowed. Camille was less than six feet away from him on the dance-floor. The cymbals tinkled. Her hands fluttered around her slim waist, just above her groin. Another strip of silk fell away. Manning looked up at her eyes, and imagined himself with her, in a private room . . . dancing . . . holding . . . touching . . .

The body stocking hid everything, and nothing. It clung to her like paint. There were the high, perfect breasts, the flat belly, the tantalising valley below. Leroy Manning, who had watched every belly-dancer from Pyramid Row to the Nile Hilton, and been bored by them all, had never seen anything like it.

The girl was spinning in front of him. Bright eyes flashing, long hands teasing at knots.

Another flash of falling silk.

And another, and another . . . She was in a frenzy now, sweeping across the stage from table to table in a whirl of dazzling blue and flowing hair.

Another strip of silk fell to the floor.

My God! She was good!

Suddenly, Leroy realised he was sweating. It was as if he was a kid again. In the back seat of his father's Buick with Patsy Miller, touching the warm globe of her right breast for the first time. He could feel himself getting hard and moved his chair closer to the table so nobody would see. But nobody cared. Hargreaves was hypnotised. The German tourists stared, open-mouthed. The Japanese hadn't taken a single picture.

Camille was kneeling in the centre of the dance-floor in front of him, with her legs spread. Her fingers combed through her hair, caressing it as a lover might – as he might. Her belly started to writhe in waves, slowly at first and then building, until she was in the grip of a passion that seemed to reach out and suck him in. Faster and faster, until . . .

The last strip of silk fell away.

Leroy Manning was looking into the most beautiful face he had ever seen. There was the innocence of Patsy Miller in the liquid brown eyes, the sexuality of Su Lin in the full moist lips, and the magic of Sarah Jane in her smile. The very essence of every woman he had loved and lost, right there in front of him – his perfect woman!

"I've found her!" he said out loud. But his words were swept away by the frenzy of frustrated energy that exploded in a thunderous round of applause. The Germans were on their feet. A ripple of lightning burst from the Japanese camera-flashes. The wedding guests were ecstatic. The bride eyed the groom suspiciously.

Camille bowed low before him. Her shining hair kissed the ground. And she was gone.

"My God!" breathed Manning.

"Yeah! You're telling me," panted Hargreaves. Beads of sweat were running over his large face. He rubbed the cold bottle of Stella on his forehead and crossed his legs. "What wouldn't I do for a few minutes alone with her right now!"

"She's Muslim," snapped Manning a little too quickly. "You haven't a hope."

"Yeah? I suppose a classy bit of stuff like that's not for the likes of you and me . . . still, I wouldn't mind seeing what's under that body stocking."

Manning stared at the stage curtain while his pulse returned to normal. She probably has some rich sugar-daddy somewhere, who keeps her in the life . . . Then he thought of the face he had seen when the last veil fell, and the look of innocence in her eyes.

No! She was his perfect woman. Beautiful and unreachable. She probably lived with her Muslim family somewhere in the city and honoured her mother and father by putting herself through college. When she was ready, she would find a perfect Muslim man and settle down to a happy Muslim life.

He wished that for her.

"Shit! Look at the time!" said Hargreaves. "It's nearly three. I'd better be getting back. If I'm not there when my watch starts, the Major'll have my balls for breakfast!"

"Whatever turns you on," said Manning, still staring at the centre of the dance-floor.

Hargreaves got up, signed the bill, and hurried to the exit. All around Manning, the club had dissolved into happy chaos as members of the band, wedding guests, and tourists mingled at the tables, swapping jokes with the bride and groom. The voluptuous Mirium had adopted the group of Germans, who were laughing at the tops of their voices.

Manning reached down and pulled out his packet of Marlboros, but it was empty.

"Shit!"

All at once, he felt painfully alone. There were the bride and groom, about to start a new life together. There were the other wedding guests in twos and threes – couples, families, uncles and aunts. There was Mirium, laughing and joking with a table of people she didn't even know.

And there was his perfect woman, come and gone!

Leroy Manning crushed the empty cigarette packet in his fist and dropped it into his beer glass. Then he stood up, walked to the door, and closed it on the laughter behind him.

Nothing left really, but to hit the sack – on his own.

Then, in the quietness of the corridor, he heard a woman's voice raised in protest. There was a man's voice too, insistent, slightly slurred, coming from behind the side door leading to the backstage area. Manning reached out and pushed it open.

The voices stopped.

Glaring at him, above the turned head of a woman, was the singer from the cabaret. His slick black hair was ruffled and his bow tie was undone. His hands gripped the woman's shoulders tightly, pulling the material of her loose *galabia* robe down over her shoulders, revealing the electric-blue body stocking.

She turned, and Manning stared into the eyes of his perfect woman. There was the proud face, the sculptured neck, the dark innocent eyes and a hint of that perfect body beneath the robe. For a moment, Leroy Manning was paralysed.

Then he said, "Are you having a problem?"

The singer swore rapidly in Arabic. Then he saw the security tag on Manning's jacket.

"There is no problem, sir! It is a personal matter!"

The woman pulled the singer's hands free, and flipped the hood of the *galabia* back up over her head.

"What do *you* say?" said Manning.

"I think I need someone to see me to a taxi. This man is drunk."

Once again the singer's eyes darted to the logo on Manning's jacket. Then he snorted, threw up his hands, and staggered back into the din of the club.

The woman watched him go. She turned to Manning and offered her hand.

"Thank you. He is a pig. Did you like my dance? It was my first time."

Manning shook her hand and took the duffle bag she handed him. Together they walked towards the lift.

"Er . . . I thought it was fantastic. My name's Leroy. And you're Camille?"

"Oh no," she said, smiling at him. "That is my stage name. During the day I work as a model. My real name is Farida."

15

VIRTUAL REALITY

"I'm sorry to call you so early, Jess," said Gilkrensky. "But we have an important meeting here in the hotel in ten minutes. We might even be able to push the Egyptian authorities for a preliminary hearing to examine new evidence from the crash."

Jessica Wright hugged her dressing-gown tighter around her naked shoulders. Her SmartMate was on the table in the lounge and Theo's face was on the screen. He seemed to be sitting in the sun. Jessica looked out at the thin sleet falling against the darkened window overlooking Grosvenor Square and peered at her watch. For him it was just before nine. For her it was six forty-five – a.m.!

"What new evidence, Theo?"

"They found the 'black box' flight-data recorder from the wreck last night. It had been buried deep in the sand by looters, so its radio tracer was impossible to detect until our people were right on top of it. Bill's been through its recordings with the investigation team, but it's not going to tell us very much."

"Why not?"

"Because it was only set to record time, speed, altitude and acceleration. We can't use it to tell whether Daedalus made an error during the flight, whether it was switched off during the flight, or even if it was switched on at all!"

Jessica was groggy with sleep. She had difficulty taking everything in.

"Why wouldn't it be switched on?"

"CAA regulations require flight crews to do an obligatory number of flights on full manual control, even if they have Daedalus aboard, just to keep their commercial licenses. But such flights are always notified well in advance. This one wasn't."

"I thought you said Daedalus recorded all its own flight information."

"It does, and I managed to recover it, even though the unit was badly smashed up."

"That's good news, Theo. So what's the problem."

"I had to use Mar . . . I mean Minerva to do it. Even the upgraded 2,000 computer Bill McCarthy brought wasn't powerful enough to handle the data linkages."

"And?"

"Well, that's it, Jess. If I use the Minerva 3,000 to display the data, then everyone will see it. Can you postpone the board meeting for a couple of days until after Christmas?"

"Surely you can demonstrate the data without people seeing the computer that's driving the presentation?"

"It's not that, Jess. It's just that I need a couple of days to reprogram the interface, all right? I didn't have time to remodel it before we left, and . . . and it's highly personalised to me. It could be embarrassing."

"Theo! We're losing millions every day on this. The other shareholders are breathing down my neck. If I try and stall the Board meeting, they'll lose confidence and sell out to Funakoshi like a shot. Show it to the enquiry now. It's only going to be half a dozen people at most."

"I just need a couple of days, Jess!"

"We don't have it, Theo. If the information exonerates Daedalus, use it. Then we can tell the world and stop ourselves sliding into oblivion!"

Gilkrensky looked beaten.

"All right, Jess. You win."

"And call me when the enquiry is over. All right?"

But he had already signed off.

The door to Jessica's bedroom opened and a man peered into the lounge. He was dark and good-looking, with deep brown eyes and ruffled hair.

"Who was it?" he said, walking over to her.

"It was Theo, from Egypt. He's obsessed about some modification he made to that precious computer of his. He probably has it talking like Donald Duck or something."

"You worry about him too much, Jess," said Tony Delgado, as he slipped the dressing-gown from her shoulders. "Come back to bed."

There was a knock at the door of the presidential suite.

Gilkrensky quickly shut the black case of the Minerva and said, "Come in!"

"I have the results of my little investigation," said Crowe, handing him a thin folder. "I'd recommend you read it carefully before you go next door to the meeting."

"We're supposed to start in five minutes," said Gilkrensky.

"I know, but the stewardess who was injured regained consciousness last night, and I managed to talk to her. She gave me a possible motive for what might have happened."

"Thank you," said Gilkrensky, and started to read.

"Before we consider the evidence presented by the Corporation, I think it would be valuable to recap on what we have heard so far," said Colonel El Wassef, the chairman of the enquiry. He was a large, fleshy air force officer with prominent lips and a regulation services crew cut. "We have heard from the crew of the aircraft that they made a normal take-off from the airport here in Cairo on the evening of Wednesday the eighteenth of December, assisted by the Daedalus auto-pilot. We have heard that, shortly after take-off, the autopilot malfunctioned, and threw the plane into a stall."

The crew of the plane nodded.

"The evidence from the aircraft's official flight recorder confirms the testimony of the crew, in so far as it is able," continued the colonel. "And voice recordings from the cockpit also confirm an emergency took place.

But I understand the manufacturers of the aircraft have new information they wish to submit."

"We do, Mr Chairman," said Gilkrensky after a moment's silence. "We would contend that Daedalus did not fail."

He was sitting at the far end of the conference table from El Wassef. To his left was Bill McCarthy, and to his right was Major Crowe and the flight crew of the aircraft – Danvers, Peters and Spalding. Martin Malone of the CAA was at the head of the table next to the chairman.

On the table in front of Gilkrensky was the black case of the Minerva 3,000. A thick cable reached back to a squat box on the floor, and from this box, smaller cables stretched to blue and white plastic headsets on a small table near the door.

"And how do you intend to prove this?" asked El Wassef.

"With data from Daedalus itself."

Gilkrensky saw Margaret Spalding turn to face him, but he continued.

"The unit was badly damaged, but the basic memory chip was not so fragmented that we couldn't recover enough material for a simulation of the events leading up to the crash."

"I protest," snapped Danvers. "We already have the official technical information we need from the flight recorder, and *that* corroborates the facts!"

"But Daedalus has much more," said Gilkrensky. "Even though it was not switched to autopilot mode, it . . ."

"Daedalus *was* switched on!" insisted Danvers.

"You've already had three people *and* the official flight-recorder data tell you that!"

"As I was saying," said Gilkrensky evenly. "Even though Daedalus was not controlling the flight, it still recorded every action of the flight crew, and more importantly, every word spoken in the cockpit since they entered it!"

Danvers looked hunted.

"I wasn't aware we were being spied on! This evidence is inadmissible!"

"I'm afraid not," said Martin Malone. "There was a whole new set of regulations drawn up regarding cockpit voice recordings when Daedalus first came in. You'd have got a notice about it."

"Bloody cheek," snapped Danvers, and glanced at Spalding.

"Please, ladies and gentlemen," insisted El Wassef, looking at his watch. "I would like to get on. You mentioned a simulation, Dr Gilkrensky?"

"I did, Mr Chairman. I've combined the data I extracted from the Daedalus memory chip with one of the computerised flight-simulation programmes we use to train pilots on the Whisperer jet. The result has been loaded onto this computer, and can be displayed to you using advanced virtual reality through those headsets over there. Major, Bill, if you'd be so kind."

Crowe and McCarthy handed a headset to each of the flight crew, El Wassef, and Martin Malone. Danvers turned the thing in his hand before he put it on. It was like a baseball cap, with headphones over the ears and eyepieces fitting snugly from below the peak. In the darkness, he could hear Gilkrensky's voice over the headphones.

He was afraid of what he might see next. How much had that damned man found out? Margaret had said . . .

All at once, Danvers was looking at a soft blue background. A white sign flashed up onto the blue, saying,

"Gilcrest Communication Systems: Simulation Programme 33 – Whisperer 106. Standard Daedalus Flight. Prepared in conjunction with GRC Aerospace, Florida. Copyright GRC. All rights reserved."

Then the sign vanished, to be replaced with the words,

"Modified for Minerva 3,000 interface: TIG/Maria."

Danvers heard Gilkrensky say,

"If you pull the blinds, Bill, you and Major Crowe can follow the simulation on the wall monitor. Now, ladies and gentlemen. Could I ask you each to state your name please, so that Minerva can recognise you?"

Danvers spoke first, followed by Spalding and Peters. El Wassef and Martin Malone followed suit.

"Right then," said Gilkrensky, with a resigned sigh. "Can we start the programme, please?"

All at once, Danvers was back in the pilot's seat of the Whisperer.

The realism of it took him by surprise. It was so lifelike! There was none of the cartoon quality he was familiar with from other VR demonstrations. There were the shadows beneath the controls, the displays on the cockpit VDUs, the lights of Cairo airport beyond the cockpit window. Even the heads of individual screws on the control panel and the textured material of the seat were real.

"Wow! That's some detail," said McCarthy.

"It's a new system we've developed for the theme parks," said Gilkrensky. "We did a lot of work on it with NASA and Chapel Hill."

"The resolution must be phenomenal!"

"It is. The best conventional television eyepieces on the market only give 480 by 640 scan pixels. These headsets use twin lasers to project an image directly onto the back of the eye. That gives us 6,000 by 4,000! It's as if . . . "

"Do you mean there are laser beams being fired into my eyeballs!" gasped El Wassef.

Danvers could hear him pulling off his headset. He was about to do the same, when a woman's voice beside him said,

"Don't worry about that now, Captain. It's perfectly safe."

Danvers turned his head sharply. The image moved with him instantly. There was none of the motion sickness he had experienced from time-lag in other demonstrations.

Sitting in the co-pilot's seat to his right was a beautiful woman in a forget-me-not-blue dress. Her coppery hair fell in a cascade over her shoulders, and her brilliant green eyes fixed him with a concerned smile.

"Oh my God!" said Crowe.

Danvers heard a sharp intake of breath.

"Aw, Theo!" gasped McCarthy. "You didn't."

"I told you I didn't want to use Minerva, Bill," said Gilkrensky.

"Is there a problem, Theo?" asked the woman, turning in her seat.

"No," said Gilkrensky. "Ladies and gentlemen. Before we continue I should explain that the computer I'm using to drive this simulation is a very advanced biochip prototype. It has the option to programme the 'help' menu into the image of any person, or thing, that the user might be comfortable to dialogue with. If I'd had time, I would have deprogrammed this particular image out of the machine. But I hadn't. So I'm sorry. I hope you'll excuse me."

"She's lovely," said Malone. "Who is she?"

"She was my wife," said Gilkrensky.

16

THE GHOST IN THE MACHINE

"MARIA, COULD YOU TAKE US THROUGH THE SIMULATION, PLEASE?
Starting with the entry of the crew into the cabin."

Danvers saw the figures on the cockpit clock change,
and heard his own voice say,

"That's the outside checks done, boys and girls! Let's
get this show on the road. Margaret, could you finish
your scan check? I'll go through the defects list from the
last flight."

"Roger, Skipper."

There were rustling paper noises in the headphones.

"There's the check list for you to sign," said Spalding.
"Do you want me to programme the Daedalus, or will
you do it?"

Danvers knew what was coming next.

"Fuck the bloody machine," he heard himself say.
"We'll do this one on 'manual'."

"But Skipper, you have to notify the company twenty-
four hours in advance if you're going to do that!"

"Listen, Margaret! I've just about had it with this fucking company! I want to do a bit of old-fashioned flying for a change, all right? If anyone asks we'll say we had an instrument failure."

"Skipper!"

"On my authority as captain! Now . . . "

El Wassef cut across the simulation.

"Why did we not hear all this on the voice tape from the official flight recorder?"

Maria smiled. A pair of gold-rimmed glasses had appeared on her nose as if by magic, indicating she was in "information" mode.

"Because the voice recording on the 'black box' recycles every thirty minutes, Colonel. By the time the aircraft crashed, it had already started re-recording over this section of the tape."

"But the plane crashed five minutes after take-off!"

"Just watch for a moment, and you'll see."

On the simulation, Peters the flight engineer said,

"News from the tower, Skipper. They say there's going to be a thirty-minute delay."

"Hell's bells!" snorted Danvers. "What's the problem this time?"

"Unscheduled arrival on the main overseas runway. We have to hold."

"Bloody typical! Those gypoes couldn't organise a piss-up in a brewery!"

"I beg your pardon," snapped El Wassef.

The gold-rimmed glasses were back on Maria's nose.

"Captain Danvers is perfectly correct, Colonel," she

informed him. "76.2 per cent of all commercial flights out of Cairo are delayed for an average of 21.6 minutes. Although it must be said that figures for other international airports can be just as high."

"Maria. Can we stick to the simulation please?" said Gilkrensky.

The virtual woman in the seat next to Danvers actually frowned.

"Theo, I was only trying to be helpful."

The gold-rimmed glasses disappeared.

"Thank you. Please continue."

"I object!" shouted Danvers, ripping off his headset. "This is nothing more than a computer-generated speculation designed to frame me for this accident and let that bloody machine of yours off the hook!"

"The data is authentic, Captain," said Maria calmly from the wall screen above El Wassef's head. "In another three minutes and fifteen seconds, you will find it matches the official voice recording exactly."

Margaret Spalding laid her headset down on the conference table.

"The computer's right, Skipper," she said sadly. "We can't go on lying any more."

Danvers was shaking.

"Damn! Damn! Damn!" he said softly.

"I think it would be useful if we broke there for a few minutes," said Colonel El Wassef.

Spalding looked across the table at Gilkrensky.

"Could I speak with you in private please, sir?" she said. There were tears in her eyes.

"You have to understand the pressure the skipper's been under," said Spalding.

She was perched on the edge of the leather sofa in the lounge of the presidential suite. Gilkrensky was sitting in a chair opposite her, with Major Crowe at the far end of the room, just out of earshot.

"I know," said Gilkrensky, and laid Crowe's manila folder on the low table between them.

"How much do you know?"

"I know Captain Danvers was having . . . domestic problems. I know they were coming to a head."

"He was . . . having an affair with Julie Maxwell. It'd been going on for years. But his wife clung to him like glue. He was going back to make a final break with her after this trip."

"I see."

"Do you *really*? Bob Danvers was at the end of his tether when he took control of that plane last Wednesday. He'd called his wife and told her about Julie. He'd even let it slip that they were planning to go into business together."

"I know. A flying school?"

"Well, his wife went mad. She threatened to take his kids, the house, everything! She told him she'd use her father's influence to make sure he'd never be able to raise the money he needed. That was the final straw. The skipper was already in debt up to his ears."

"Did Captain Danvers tell you all this?"

"No, sir. Julie did. She was in tears at the hotel before

we left. The skipper was being put out to grass by Exair anyway. He wasn't getting past the six-monthly medical checks the way he used to. He's fifty three-now, and they retire you at fifty-five."

Gilkrensky looked down at her heavily bandaged hands.

"Did *you* smash the Daedalus after the crash?" he said, as gently as he could.

Tears had started to well up in Spalding's eyes again. She looked very small on the big sofa.

"I did. I knew if Captain Danvers took the blame for the crash it would be the end of everything for him. So I smashed and smashed at that damned machine with the axe, but all I did was chew up the casing. Then I went crazy and tried to pull out the memory chip, but it wouldn't come. I cut my hands on the metal."

"Captain Danvers is lucky to have you as a friend."

Spalding wiped the tears away with her bandaged hand.

"He was good to me, Mr Gilkrensky. It's not easy for a woman to make in this business, even now. And I've wanted to fly since I was a kid. When I joined Exair, Bob Danvers made sure I got the opportunities due to me. I didn't want to see him crucified for wrecking that plane, particularly when it wasn't his fault."

"But the plane crashed while it was under his control. The Daedalus wasn't switched on."

"There was an alarm. It went off for no reason at all. The skipper's mind was full of his own problems when it happened and he over-reacted. If your computer

simulation is as accurate as you say it is, then you'll see
I'm telling the truth when we go back in there."

"Thank you, Miss Spalding."

"I want you to know I'm well aware of what I've
done in covering up for Bob Danvers, and how that must
look to you and the rest of the enquiry. But I did it
because I owe him a great deal, and . . . well, there's a
lot of us pilots who feel the same way he does about that
machine of yours."

Margaret Spalding looked directly into Gilkrensky's
eyes for the first time.

"I might as well tell it to you straight, now that I've
gone this far. We feel you're taking our life away from
us. Flying is what we do, and you're turning us into
nothing more than baby-sitters for that machine of yours.
Bob Danvers feels that way I know, and so do I!"

"I take it we can resume," said Colonel El Wassef.

Danvers watched Gilkrensky from the far end of the
table. The hostility in his eyes had been replaced with a
dull resignation.

"Yes, Mr Chairman. We can."

"If you'd all put your headsets back on?" said
Gilkrensky.

Once more the soft blue screen was in front of them.
Then the cockpit returned, and Maria said,

"Welcome back, ladies and gentlemen. I hope there
wasn't a problem?"

"None at all, Maria. We were just discussing some
discrepancies in the data."

"I hope that's cleared up now. Personally, I'm satisfied the simulation programme is as accurate as possible."

"I'm sure it is. Could you run it again from the take-off, please?"

The lights outside the cockpit began to rush forward.

"One hundred and twenty knots . . . " said Peters's voice on the simulation. "Vee-One! . . . Vee-R!"

"Rotating!" said Danvers, and the runway lights fell beneath the nose of the aircraft, to be replaced by stars.

"We are now airborne," said Maria. "The control tower has just told us we are over the middle marker. Captain Danvers makes a turn to the north-east. Standard westerly departure."

"Eighty-five seconds into the flight," said Spalding's voice in the cockpit.

"We are climbing out over the city," continued Maria. "The undercarriage has gone up, and we are at nearly two thousand feet on a heading of 295 degrees."

"There!" said Danvers's voice. "Nothing wrong with that, was there? You can switch off the seat-belt sign now, Margaret."

"This is when it happened," said Danvers to the room.

Suddenly, the cockpit was flooded with the blood-red glare of a warning light. An ear-splitting whine whipped everyone's hands to their headsets.

On the simulation, Danvers shouted,

"Christ! We're too low! Pull her up, Margaret!"

They all saw the short control sticks jerk back and the instruments swing wildly.

"It took me by surprise," said Danvers. "So I just reacted . . . and pulled back on the controls."

"Would you like me to pause the simulation, Theo?"

"Yes please, Maria."

All action in the virtual cockpit froze. The piercing whine was silenced.

"That was Daedalus," said Gilkrensky. "Even when it's not actually flying the plane, it keeps a watching brief on the height, speed and angle of the flight. That was the low altitude alarm. It triggers if the plane drops below five hundred feet, or if there's an obstacle in its path."

"But we were at two thousand feet!" said Danvers.

"Yes, you were. I don't know why the alarm went off. Do you, Maria?"

"No, Theo. It's very puzzling. The aircraft was climbing into a clear sky. There are no mountains around Cairo and there were no other aircraft in the flight path."

"That's what spooked me," said Danvers. "I thought we were about to hit something, and that's why I pulled the stick back so hard."

"Please continue, Maria," said Gilkrensky.

The cockpit came back to life. Amber lights were now flashing on the panels in front of both the pilot and co-pilot. The control sticks were shaking visibly.

A loud *ding-dong-ding-dong* klaxon was ringing.

"We were stalling at that stage," said Danvers. "I've been in flight simulations of deep stalls before, and I know it's ninety-nine per cent impossible to recover from them. So I did the only thing I could. I released the emergency parachute in the tail."

The simulation jerked violently before their eyes. El Wassef jumped in his seat. The screams of frightened passengers burst in on them. There were loud crashes from behind.

"That was when Julie was hurt," said Danvers.

Lights leapt and spun outside the cockpit window. The instruments raced. The *ding-dong* klaxon and the screams filled the room.

"My God!" said El Wassef out loud.

"It was all I could do to save them," said Danvers.

The virtual cockpit spun and settled. There was a roaring, rushing sound . . . a thundering scream of tearing metal . . . and then silence.

"But you *did* save them," said Gilkrensky. "Well done."

"What would have happened if Daedalus had been flying the plane?" asked El Wassef.

"Up until the incident, everything would have been the same," said Maria. "Captain Danvers made a near-perfect take-off."

"And then?"

"It is impossible to say with certainty. The low altitude warning system incorporates the radar, altimeters, and high-precision landing-sensors. Any one of them could have triggered the alarm."

"These high-precision landing-sensors, what are they?"

"Daedalus uses a dual system of laser beams and high-frequency sound waves to measure distance from the ground at low altitudes. I cannot tell from the data presented to me, if it was these sensors which originally triggered the alarm or one of the other systems."

"But do you have any theories, Maria?" asked Gilkrensky.

Maria smiled.

"There are three possibilities, Theo. Either the Daedalus *was* at fault, something outside Cairo *did* actually get in the way of the plane, or some phenomenon was interfering with the aircraft's sensors so as to mimic an obstacle in its path. As a start, I would recommend examining a similar aircraft fitted with Daedalus. I could then link myself to its computer systems and see if I could diagnose the fault."

"And if there is no fault in the Daedalus system?"

"Then the only option is to repeat the flight exactly with an identical aircraft, and see if it happens again!"

Gilkrensky found Bill McCarthy, and the smell of sweet tobacco smoke, waiting for him in the lounge when he returned from a long discussion with Danvers and Colonel El Wassef. He set the Minerva gently down on the low coffee table, lay back onto the sofa and lifted his feet onto the arm-rest.

McCarthy glared at the black briefcase. Then he took his pipe from his mouth and said,

"I'm worried about you, Theo!"

"What's to worry about, Bill? We know Daedalus didn't crash the plane. El Wassef has agreed to bring forward the official hearing and the CAA will almost certainly exonerate GRC as soon as we can find out what triggered the alarm. Then Jessica can have her press conference. Funakoshi will back off, and the corporation will be saved! You should be congratulating me!"

"That's not what I'm worried about, and you know it!"

Gilkrensky rubbed his eyes.

"I don't. Tell me!"

"Aw! Come of it, Theo! This is Bill McCarthy you're talking to! I know how cut up you were about Maria's death. I know how losing someone you love can change your life, believe me! I've been there. But this, this . . . freak show with Maria as the Minerva interface. Jeez, Theo! You're only torturing yourself."

Gilkrensky stopped rubbing his eyes and stared up at the ceiling.

"Listen Bill, Minerva is not Maria. I know that. It's just a 'help' menu image I made up from photos and SmartCard messages so I could . . . relate to the system better during the start-up."

"Then why does it call you 'Theo'? Why do you call it 'Maria'? Why does it wear her clothes and speak with her voice? Shit Theo! I was devastated when Angie and the kids died in that plane wreck. Planes were my business. But I accepted it. I was angry about it. I mourned her, and I moved on! You'll keep denying Maria is dead for as long as her image is in that machine."

Gilkrensky twisted on the sofa and sat up.

"Do you have a photo of Angie and your grandchildren, Bill? Something to remember them by?"

"Yes, of course!"

"Would you tear it up if I asked you to?"

McCarthy said nothing.

"Then don't ask me to destroy that image of Maria, because that's all it is – a picture! Something to remember her by! I didn't invite you into the Minerva system. You, and Jessica, and that bloody enquiry forced me to let you in. Only the 3,000 model would do, remember?"

McCarthy sat down on the chair opposite Gilkrensky and took a long draw on his pipe.

"But Minerva's more than just a picture, isn't it, Theo? That machine can pass the 'Turing test'!"

"What do you mean?"

"You know very well what I mean . . . Alan Turing! The genius who cracked all those Nazi codes during the war with a primitive computer . . . the man who gave us the first definition of artificial intelligence. He said that once a person who is talking to a machine can no longer tell if they are talking to a computer or another human, then that machine has intelligence! Minerva's like that, Theo. Your new 'Maria' is no longer a picture, is she? She's alive!"

"So? Congratulate me! Another breakthrough for GRC!"

"Yeah. But you need to go forward, my friend. You don't need to spend the rest of your life carrying Maria's soul around in a box!"

Gilkrensky stood up suddenly, knocking the low table and spilling cold coffee onto the carpet.

"Look Bill. I hear what you're saying. But I'm tired. I was up all night working on that simulation in there. So, before I say something I might regret, let me get some sleep and I'll see you at the airport this evening for the tests."

"The ones 'Maria' suggested?"

"The ones Minerva recommended. Now please, just leave me alone!"

17

PILOT ERROR

"JUST WHAT THE HELL DO YOU THINK YOU'RE DOING?" SNAPPED Jessica Wright. She was standing at her desk, surrounded by faxes from Exair Airlines, e-mail print-outs from GRC Cairo, memos from the accounts office, and even a terse note from Funakoshi in Tokyo, which had all been waiting for her when she returned from her morning's press briefing.

"I'm conducting an experiment," said Theodore Gilkrensky from the screen of her open SmartMate. "I thought you'd be pleased!"

"I *was* pleased you were able to clear the Daedalus, Theo. Of course I was. But to pull a fully booked commercial aircraft off a scheduled flight, just to run experiments on it, is going way over the top. I've had the CEO of Exair onto me, complaining. The Japanese are worried, and Giles Fulton has been leaving messages for me all over the place, saying you're about to run up a bill for hundreds of thousands of pounds."

"Only about a hundred and forty thousand, actually. I've checked. Between putting the passengers on other flights, the cost of fuel, airport charges and crew time, it comes to . . . "

"You mean you're actually going to take the plane *up*!"

"We have to, Jess. We've run every conceivable computer diagnostic on the Daedalus system of this plane and they all check out. There's nothing physically wrong with Daedalus on the ground. The next step is to find out if there's something peculiar to this airport, or the area around it, that made the system malfunction."

"Couldn't the local airport authority, or the CAA do that?"

"It's *my* system, Jess. I have to find out why."

"You're not taking this personally, are you Theo? I thought you wanted to get this over as quickly as possible and come home!"

Gilkrensky thought of Margaret Spalding and her fear that he was taking the pilots' livelihood away from them.

"Perhaps. But *you* manoeuvred me into coming out here in the first place, don't forget."

"All right, Theo. Don't blow a fuse! Just remember all this costs money, OK?"

On the screen of the Minerva 3,000 in Cairo, Jessica's image was replaced by that of Maria.

They were on the flight deck of the Whisperer aircraft under close security in the GRC hanger at Cairo airport, with Gilkrensky, McCarthy and other members of the GRC Aerospace team aboard running battery after battery of tests, assisted by the Minerva, which was installed at the flight engineer's work station aft of the pilot's seat.

"Miss Wright is upset," said Maria. "But I can't really see why, when you compare the relatively small cost of this experiment against the revenues GRC will gain when Daedalus goes into full service on all the airlines. I estimate that . . ."

"Are you sure there is no other way to do this?"

"I'm certain, Theo. Now that we've checked out an identical Daedalus unit, the only other variables are conditions in the local area. I'm sure Professor McCarthy will confirm that."

Bill McCarthy regarded the computer suspiciously from the flight-deck doorway.

"She's right, Theo. It's the only option left."

"She?"

"Hell! You know what I mean. Your computer! It's going to take me a long time to get used to her . . . it . . . whatever."

"I'm sorry about that, Professor," said Maria. "Theo has programmed my information files with all your original work on the Whisperer design. I was hoping we might discuss them, as well as the designs for the new 'Hi-Lift' prototype you're working on."

"I'd rather not. Not until you're someone different. You see, I knew the real Maria Gilkrensky, and talking to you like this gives me the creeps."

"If that is what you wish," said Maria, and vanished from the screen.

In her place was a message reading,

"Welcome to Minerva 3,000. Personalised Interface Facility has been temporarily suspended. Please interact by stating identification and user number."

"She's sulking," said Gilkrensky.

"Jesus, Theo! You've gone *way* too far with that thing!"

"It's only a quirk of the interface programming. Minerva will continue to monitor the experiment through its link with Daedalus, and if we need to consult it, I'll speak to Maria myself."

"Then God help us all!" said McCarthy, shaking his head, and went to make final arrangements for the flight.

At 7.55 p.m. local time, the Whisperer jet was lined up on the approach to the southern runway, pointing west. Captain Danvers was in the pilot's position, with Gilkrensky in the co-pilot's seat to his right. McCarthy was at the flight engineer's work station facing the Minerva, with Martin Malone and Margaret Spalding on fold-down seats at the back of the flight-deck. In the passenger cabin behind them, were Colonel El Wassef and the other members of the crew, accompanied by the remaining GRC Aerospace scientists.

"Can everyone see what we're doing?" said Gilkrensky into his radio headset.

"Perfectly," replied El Wassef. "We can all see the flight-deck on the in-flight television screens."

"OK. Are there any other pre-flight checks we need before we get clearance?"

Danvers said, "No. Daedalus is programmed with the same flight plan we would have filed on Wednesday. It'll follow an identical course to the one I flew manually."

"Exair 601. Your clearance?" said a voice from Cairo tower.

"Go ahead," replied Danvers.

"Your ident will be six six one five. Exair 601 cleared for take-off. Standard westerly departure."

"Thank you, tower," said Danvers. "Exair 601 cleared for take-off." He glanced at Gilkrensky, accepted his nod, and pressed the 'engage' button.

There was a slight jerk as the brakes came off and the aircraft trundled forward to the runway. As it rolled forward, Gilkrensky watched the robot testing the flight controls, the rudder and the ailerons. Then the aircraft bumped gently off the taxiway, onto the very end of the runway, turned until it was pointing down the long avenue of lights, and stopped.

The big brake-pedal between the rudder controls depressed. The four black throttles in the centre of the instrument panel moved forward and, behind then, the noise of the engines mounted to a shrill whine. Gilkrensky saw Danvers watching the gauges closely, even though his hands, like his own, were in his lap.

"Ninety-four per cent take-off power," said McCarthy. "Ninety-six per cent . . . ninety-eight per cent . . . And away we go!"

The brake-pedal lifted, and the aircraft began to roll. On either side of the plane the runway lights flashed past. Gilkrensky could feel the acceleration pushing him back in his seat.

"One hundred and twenty knots," shouted McCarthy. Then, "Rotate!"

The control columns to Gilkrensky's left and Danvers's right pulled back. The nose of the aircraft came up. Below them, the runway lights fell away and vanished.

"So far, so good," called McCarthy above the whine of the labouring jets. They all felt the thud as the undercarriage retracted.

"Heading?" asked Gilkrensky.

"We're just coming up to the middle marker," replied Danvers. "Then we'll turn to 295 degrees."

"Eighty-five seconds into the flight," said McCarthy.

The gyrocompass indicators started to turn. The digital readout below it settled on 295.

"Height?"

"Just over two thousand feet. If it's going to happen, it should happen now!"

Gilkrensky watched the controls and indicators. He could see the black safety-bar over the big red 'disengage' button on the Daedalus, down to his left. He could feel his body tensing, and the pressure of the seat belt around his shoulder. Beneath his shirt, the sweat was coming.

There was silence in the cockpit.

Then McCarthy said,

"Three minutes into the flight."

Gilkrensky turned in his seat.

"But the incident happened just after eighty-five seconds!"

Colonel El Wassef's voice sounded over the intercom.

"What is happening?"

"Nothing! That's the problem! Nothing at all!"

McCarthy said, "It must have been a once-off. Some sort of phenomenon that just happened to one plane on one flight. We're on the same course, at the same height, in an identical aircraft . . ."

"But not at the same time!" said a voice from the Minerva.

"What is it, Maria?"

Her image appeared on the screen in front of McCarthy. She was frowning through her gold-rimmed glasses.

"I would like to point out, Theo, that in the actual flight last Wednesday, take-off was delayed by thirty minutes and forty-five seconds. We may be in the right space, ladies and gentlemen, but we are thirty minutes and forty-five seconds early!"

"You should have reminded us before we took off!" snapped McCarthy.

Maria's image flounced its head.

"You did not ask me for this information, Professor. In any event, you gave me a direct instruction that I was not to speak to you again. You said I gave you 'the creeps'!"

"That's all we need," sighed McCarthy. "A computer with attitude!"

Gilkrensky twisted round to face the Minerva screen.

"Sorry, Bill! Everyone! The software for the Minerva is still experimental. The biochip is actually rewriting it as it goes along. So you can see why we get these 'glitches' from time to time. Maria! You *know* that when information you learn or derive is relevant to a decision a user might make, it *must* be passed on immediately!"

"Professor McCarthy's direct personal instruction to cease communication acted as an override. Unless you would like me to re-prioritise my instruction web?"

"That won't be necessary. But it's vital we return to the spot where the incident occurred, at the same time it occurred. Could you interact with the Daedalus to manoeuvre this aircraft back in a circle?"

"I can," said Maria. "If that is what you wish?"

"Of course we do!" hissed McCarthy.

"I do not recognise that voice command. It has been deleted from my user file by personal request."

Gilkrensky smiled.

"I think she wants you to say 'sorry', Bill."

McCarthy muttered under his breath.

"She certainly passes the Turing test OK, Theo! All right, Maria, I would like to speak to you again . . . please."

"Good evening, Professor. Welcome back to my user file. Is there something I can do for you?"

"Yes. Can you bring us back to where we want to be, at the correct time?"

"I can. But it will mean causing some disruption at Cairo airport. There will have to be seven diversions and delays to give us a safe flight corridor over the next thirty minutes."

Gilkrensky glanced at Danvers, Malone and Spalding. McCarthy nodded.

"All right, Maria. We've come this far. Let's go for it!"

"We are just passing over the southern runway of Cairo airport," said Maria, twenty-five minutes later. They had turned to the north in a huge sweep over Ashun, Benhah and the Eastern Desert, before returning to Heliopolis and the airport. Gilkrensky and Colonel El Wassef had spent an anxious time on the radio, talking to Cairo control, but the flight had eventually been cleared.

"I hope this experiment proves fruitful," said the colonel. "You now owe a great many favours to the Cairo control tower."

"I hope so too," said Gilkrensky. "How are we doing, Maria?"

"We are back on the original Daedalus course for last Wednesday's flight, and within five seconds of the original time line," said Maria. "The incident point is now only thirty-three seconds away. I would advise everyone to make sure they are strapped in."

"We'll see," said Gilkrensky. "Give us count, please!"

"Twenty-five seconds to incident point."

"What if the flight becomes uncontrollable?" asked Danvers.

"It shouldn't," said Gilkrensky. "We're ready for it."

"Fifteen seconds!"

Danvers' right hand flicked back the safety-bar over the "disengage" button on the Daedalus.

"I'd rather not take any chances with all these people on board."

Gilkrensky said, "Please don't touch that! It'll ruin the experiment!"

"Ten seconds . . . nine . . . eight . . . seven . . . "

"I won't compromise the safety of this plane!"

"Six . . . five . . . four . . . "

"You won't have to. Just give the machine a chance!"

"Three . . . two . . . "

"Here we go again," said Spalding nervously.

"One . . . - We are now at the incident point!" announced Maria.

The plane flew on, straight and level.

Gilkrensky turned in his seat.

"It looks as if you were right, Bill. It was a once . . . "

A high-pitched scream pierced his ears. The cabin was flooded with the glare of a red warning-light. The Whisperer surged forward as the Daedalus opened the throttles and pulled back on the controls.

Spalding screamed, "It's happening!"

Danvers was trying to push the control stick forward with both hands, but Daedalus was in control. His right hand darted for the safety-bar on the "disengage" button. Gilkrensky grabbed his wrist.

"You mad bastard!" yelled Danvers. "You'll kill us all . . . "

Suddenly, the red light was gone! The warning tone

was silent, and the plane righted itself in the sky. For a moment, the pitch of the jet engines rose and fell as the robot re-orientated itself. Then the steady whine returned as the plane settled into level flight.

Gilkrensky let go of Danvers's wrist.

"Did you do that, Maria?"

"No, Theo. For me to interfere would have compromised the experimental result. In spite of the initial discomfort, we were in no real danger. So I simply observed."

"Then the robot corrected itself," said McCarthy.

"Yes, Professor. Had Daedalus been flying the plane last Wednesday night, it would've corrected for the momentary lapse in the system before the plane went into the fatal stall, just as it did tonight!"

El Wassef's voice boomed over the intercom.

"Can someone please tell us what is happening?"

"Tell them the machine could not have crashed the plane last Wednesday night," said Captain Danvers slowly. "Tell them it was pilot error."

Under Maria's control, the Whisperer turned to port and followed the same great circle into the Eastern Desert.

"Can you trace what caused the lapse in the Daedalus, Maria?" said Gilkrensky. He stood up from the co-pilot's seat and moved to stand behind McCarthy at the engineer's station.

"The signal that caused the malfunction came in on both the laser receptors and sound-wave receivers as a massive return surge, that misled the system into thinking the plane was very close to the ground. This sent an emergency signal straight to the central binary processor. Therefore the neural net did not have time to cross-reference this input with readings from the radar and altimeter before the emergency procedure was started and the plane was put into a steep climb. But three point seven seconds later, when the neural net had found that the emergency was not justified, Daedalus took corrective action, and levelled off the plane."

"What the hell is there, out here in the desert, that could interfere with the system like that?" asked McCarthy.

Danvers said, "It could be a powerful military radar of some sort. They're quite common in the Middle East."

"Or a microwave satellite transmitter?" offered Spalding.

"We could ask the colonel to contact his air-force friends and find out," said Malone. "Does your computer have any idea what the source of the signal might have been?"

"I do, Mr Malone," said Maria. "Based on the fact that no conventional type of installation I am aware of could have generated the unique signal we have experienced."

"Unique?" said Gilkrensky staring at the Minerva. "You mean you know what's doing this?"

"Yes, Theo. Both the laser and sound-wave receptors on the high-precision altitude system were triggered at the same time. Yet we saw no light beam, and heard no noise before the klaxons went off. Whatever it is, gives the same signal as light and sound, and yet behaves like neither. In my experience, this is unique!"

"So what's doing this?" said Malone. "What was below us when the incident occurred?"

"During both incidents with the Daedalus system, the aircraft in question was directly above the Giza Plateau," said Maria, "and the Great Pyramid of Cheops . . . "

18

CHANCES

THE WHEELS OF THE WHISPERER JET KISSED THE RUNWAY OF Cairo airport at 9.16 p.m., and the aircraft rolled down the taxiway back to the GRC hanger. Gilkrensky remained behind on the flight-deck as the investigation team filed down the gangway onto the hanger floor and left. Finally, there was just himself, Captain Danvers, and Spalding on the plane.

"Thank you for what you said about pilot error," said Gilkrensky. "It makes things a lot easier."

"For you perhaps, Mr Gilkrensky," cut in Spalding. "But not for Captain Danvers."

Danvers sighed. "Let it go, Margaret. I had too much on my mind and I panicked, that's all. I'm only glad I didn't perjure myself in front of an official investigation. I'd have been thrown out of this business for sure. And you with me!"

"And this way?" said Gilkrensky. "What are your chances of keeping your licence?"

"With your machine taking at least some of the blame for the incident by sounding the alarm, my chances at an official enquiry shouldn't be too bad. But I'm getting close to retirement age, and I'd say my flying days are numbered. Pity! It was my life!"

Gilkrensky leant back on the pilot's seat.

"I understand you plan to open a flying school?"

Danvers glanced at Spalding.

"That was the plan. But there are other . . . er . . . domestic factors which now make that impossible."

"Like money?"

"Yes," nodded Danvers sadly. "Like money."

"Flying's a big part of my life too," said Gilkrensky. "And I need refresher courses from time to time to keep me up to speed. If it's all right with you, I'd like to invest."

Leroy Manning's Bell helicopter lifted off from the apron outside the GRC hanger and chopped its way westwards towards the city and the Nile Olympiad Hotel. For the first time, Gilkrensky had given the co-pilot's seat to Major Crowe, who said very little, leaving Leroy free to daydream about his previous evening's brief encounter with his "perfect woman".

Behind him, Gilkrensky was installed in the passenger compartment with the Minerva on his knee, deep in conversation with Bill McCarthy. On either side of them, Thomas Hargreaves and Gerald Maguire kept watch.

"So, what do you think of Maria's theory about an energy beam interfering with the Daedalus?"

"I don't know, Theo," said McCarthy. "It's pretty way-out stuff. An energy beam that is neither sound or light, but acts like both! The idea that it might be coming from the Pyramids! It isn't natural!"

"I agree! It has to be man-made."

"No! Not that. The Minerva . . . Maria . . . whatever you want to call it. You've put too much of your wife's personality into that thing, and *that's* not natural. That's what I mean. All that crap it was spouting about earth energies and ley lines on the flight back!"

"Maria studied natural energies. She wrote a book on ancient belief systems."

"I know, Theo. And that was fine in the *real* Maria. I even admired her for it. But to have that New Age nonsense coming out of a state-of-the-art computer! Hell! If you bring the Minerva to the official enquiry, and it starts going on about cosmic forces, you're going to lose a lot of credibility. And no serious customer's going to spend money on an artificial intelligence that believes in 'Pyramid Power'. Do yourself a favour, Theo. Reprogram it!"

Gilkrensky looked down at the black briefcase on his knee.

"The pyramid theory would be worth investigating, though. If there were no other explanations."

"Take it from me, Theo. El Wassef will find a perfectly sound reason for whatever energy source spooked the Daedalus. Then we can put in a safety feature to overcome it, and all rest easier in our beds."

"Perhaps you're right," Gilkrensky said. But he did not sound convinced.

Leroy was like a kid again.

He'd spent the whole day flying people and gear between the crash site, the hotel and the airport, and as he flew there had been just one word going through his head – Farida!

They had spent an hour together the previous night – just talking – in the coffee shop on the ground floor of the hotel. She had let the hood of her *galabia* fall around her shoulders, and to him she'd looked more innocent, and sexy, and beautiful, and wise, than any woman he'd ever known.

"You look so sad," she'd said. "Have you had much pain in your life?"

He told her about the States, and about his tour in Vietnam. About the flying jobs, the crash he'd had, and the work he was doing for Theodore Gilkrensky. Farida seemed particularly interested in that. She said Leroy must have had an exciting life, and wished she could learn to fly a helicopter too.

"Perhaps when this job is over and there aren't security goons breathing down my neck all the time, I'll show you."

"That will be good. I'll be here every evening this week. We can meet again."

And for Leroy Manning, those last four words had offered more magical promise than any phrase since Patsy Miller had said, "You can kiss me now, if you want to," all those years ago.

So Leroy did not mind being asked to sleep over for another night in the hotel. Far from it! He even sat through another dinner and cabaret at the Rooftop Club, just to watch Farida dance again. This time it was with Gilkrensky's other bodyguard, Maguire – a thin, catlike man with a hard Belfast accent. Maguire rarely smiled, and all the time during the show, his eyes were on the doors, the windows, and his watch.

"What do you think of her?" asked Leroy, as he enthusiastically applauded Farida's finale. Her performance had been as riveting as the first time he'd seen it, and word must have spread, because the nightclub was packed to capacity, with condensation running down the windows and cigarette smoke obscuring the ceiling.

"I think a man would want to be careful," said Maguire. "You remember where you are now."

Then he got up from the table, and walked back to his duty inside Major Crowe's secure area.

Manning sat staring at the empty stage, wondering what he'd meant. Did Maguire know how he felt about Farida? Did he see her as some kind of threat?

Then she was there in front of him, in a simple sweater and skirt.

"You look sad again! Did my dancing not make you happy?"

"Oh, it did. Come and sit next to me."

"Who was that man with you tonight? I could see him through the curtains while Gamal and Mirium were on. He did not smile, even though some of Gamal's jokes were quite funny."

"He doesn't smile very much. He's one of my boss's goons – security!"

Farida thought for a moment.

"It must be difficult working with him. Are there many others like that?"

"Only two. The man who was here last night, and the one they call Major Crowe. He's in charge."

"Your boss must be a very important man to have three soldiers working for him, and you to fly his helicopter. There are many soldiers downstairs also, but they are Egyptian. They search me when I come to work and tell me it is security! Do they make such big security on your helicopter?"

They talked late into the night. Manning loved the way she smiled, and the interest she seemed to take in what he had to say. They touched hands, and suddenly Leroy Manning didn't feel so old and tired any more. All at once there was more to life than living as a flying tramp in a country far from home. Now there might be a future, with Farida.

But later, when he leant forward to kiss her goodnight in the foyer of the hotel, she turned her head away.

"Not here," she said, and squeezed his hand. There was a message there in that touch. But whether it was a promise or a put-down, he could not say.

He was still thinking about it the next morning, as he undid the guy-ropes holding down the big, wide rotors of the Bell on the roof of the Nile Olympiad. Across the city, the amplified wail of the *muadhdin* called the faithful to prayer from the minarets.

If she is Muslim, then she should not want to be with me. So why does she come?

Gerald Maguire's warning echoed in his head, but he pushed it away. She was his perfect woman, and such a perfect woman would never betray him. Would she?

He made sure the rotors were swinging free, and the condensation-covers were off the turbine vents. Then he opened the cockpit door and started to go through the pre-flight checks. Thomas Hargreaves appeared on the roof to ask if he was clear to go.

Manning said he was, but asked Hargreaves to stand by with the fire extinguisher while he fired up the turbine. As he finished the final checks, he said, "That guy Maguire you work with. Is he always such a drag?"

"Ah, don't you mind Gerald. He had it rough in Northern Ireland, that's all. We all had a bad time up there when we were in the Marines, but Gerald got hardest hit. It's made him a bit paranoid ever since."

"How come?"

"He got involved with a girl – in deep, way over his head. Then one night we got ambushed at a road block near a place called Auchnacloy. We lost three men, and they lost two. It turned out she'd been working for the IRA all along."

"And what happened to her?"

Hargreaves looked up from the fire extinguisher he was holding.

"She was one of the two they lost," he said. "And it was Gerald who shot her."

The big helicopter lifted off the roof of the Nile Olympiad, turned gracefully above the river, and disappeared towards the west.

It was followed closely by the single eye of an 800 millimetre catadioptic camera lens, mounted on a tripod in the front lounge of an exclusive apartment across the Nile.

"They do not seem to operate to a timetable," said Zaki El Sharoud. "Nothing predictable."

Farida shifted uneasily on the leather couch. "The helicopter comes and goes as the rich man orders it."

"And how many people fly with Gilkrensky when he leaves the hotel?"

"The pilot Manning, the head of security Major Crowe, and one or both of the other bodyguards. They normally work in shifts, but sometimes these coincide and they work together."

"Are they armed?"

"I think so. I have not had a chance to see them up close, and I did not want to press Manning with too many questions, in case he suspected."

"So far, you think he does not?"

"I don't think so."

"Then you'll need to get closer to him. The southern helipad on the hotel has enough room for what I have in mind, but it would be too risky to try it in darkness tonight. We must know the time of his first flight tomorrow morning as soon as we can. Do you think Manning trusts you enough for you to spend a night with him in the hotel?"

Farida said nothing. Her legs were tucked up in front of her. She was hugging them to her tightly and rocking, small and helpless, on the large settee.

"Do you think that will be a problem?"

"I . . . I do not like to touch him, Zaki. Is there no other way we can get control of the helicopter?"

Zaki turned from the window and knelt in front of her on the floor. His heart sank as he said,

"Farida, there *is* no other way. You will be in the hotel and you are close to this man Manning. We have the other arrangements made and we are ready to strike. If we delay, we risk losing the opportunity of a great victory for Islam. I know I'm asking more than you can bear, and it hurts me to ask you. But it must be done."

Their eyes met.

"Hold me," said Farida softly. And she cried in his arms.

19

THE EXPERT

THE UPPERMOST FLOOR OF THE MUSEUM OF EGYPTIAN Antiquities is closed to the public, allowing an academic calm to pervade the upstairs corridor that follows the spine of the building. In one of the offices furthest from the dome overlooking the front entrance of the Museum, one of its more senior staff was taking advantage of this peace to undertake some serious study.

The office was hopelessly old-fashioned. Three walls were lined with bookshelves groaning under the weight of dusty journals and brown-stained papers. The remaining wall was panelled with dark wood like a Victorian study, and dominated by a huge, fake chimney-breast.

There was a reverential knock at the door, and a serious young woman with thick glasses peered in.

"Do you have that *National Geographic* article by Roberts, Professor? The one from January of last year?"

Professor Ahmed El Fiky peered at her over the rims of his steel-framed glasses. Then he lay down his pen on the drawing board, scratched his beard with a podgy, childlike hand, and said,

"The one with those diagrams you were so interested in?"

"The one's I used in my slide presentation for my thesis, yes!"

"I cannot think why you used them. The one's in LeMesurier's book were far more accurate."

"But they do not show up as well on a projection slide, Professor. There is no colour, and the texts are difficult to read. The ones in National Geographic are easier to understand."

Professor El Fiky eased himself down from his high stool, eased the yellow-covered magazine from beneath a pile of papers, and handed it to his student.

"It is a sorry day for Egypt," he said, scowling at her kindly, "when the greatest museum of antiquities in all the world has to turn to the National Geographic for its reference material!"

"Thank you, Professor."

"It is my pleasure. Now run along please. I have much work to do."

Professor El Fiky watched her go. He loved his students, as they loved him, although many of them often remarked that, for all his enthusiasm and wit during lectures, he seemed a sad and lonely man.

And they were right, for he had seen much sadness.

In 1968, a bomb dropped on Cairo by an Israeli jet had killed his wife and son, and smashed his comfortable apartment in Heliopolis into rubble. From there, he and his only surviving child, a daughter, had moved to the overcrowded chaos of the Shubra district, where circumstances had forced them to take a tiny flat in an alley off Geziret Street. In those days, he had provided everything for her. Now, it seemed she provided everything for him.

There was the sound of running footsteps from the corridor outside and Omar, one of the old museum guards, burst into the room.

"Professor! Professor! There is an important message!"

El Fiky peered at the old man, who was standing to attention in his threadbare uniform and black beret.

"Omar, my friend. Be calm! What can be of such importance to make you run around the museum like a madman?"

"A message, Professor! Please come at once!"

"Can I not simply take it on the telephone here in my office?"

"It is not a telephone message, Professor. The switchboard is closed for lunch, and I do not know how to make it work. It is a messenger from one of the big new hotels on the Corniche. He says a very important man, a rich Russian I think, would like you to visit him."

"I thought the Russians lost interest in Egypt when Nasser died, years ago!"

"I am not sure what the Russian wants, Professor. But the man from the hotel said it was something to do with the Pyramids."

Professor El Fiky had only been inside the Nile Olympiad once before, at the wedding of a friend's son, and its decadence disturbed him. He knew that only a mile away, two hundred thousand homeless people were squatting in public cemeteries – while others lived in shanty towns where rubbish and human faeces were simply thrown up onto their corrugated-iron roofs. Yet here he was, being led across the air-conditioned splendour of the vast hotel lobby, with cool white pillars rising to the high ornate ceiling, plush red couches and chairs arranged in discreet groups, and a white marble staircase zigzagging to untold opulence above.

"Could you come this way, please Professor?" asked the messenger. He had a special plastic key card for the lift and, having swiped it in the slot, pressed the button for the twelfth floor.

"We are very privileged to have this great man as our guest," he bubbled excitedly. "He owns this hotel, and many like it in other countries. I have not seen him, but I am told he is one of the richest men in the world."

"I see," said El Fiky coldly, eyeing the security camera above their heads. "It appears that great wealth does not always bring peace of mind."

"Perhaps."

The lift stopped, and they were shown into a long corridor without windows. A short, stocky man, who looked like one of the instructors El Fiky had had during his compulsory military service years before, greeted them.

"My name's Crowe. Are you Professor El Fiky?"

"That is correct."

"Then follow me, please."

Crowe led him to a small ante-room where another man sat at a desk. From the ceiling above there was a loud buzz.

"Do you have any metal objects on your person," said the second man pleasantly, taking the book El Fiky had brought with him and flicking through the pages.

Professor El Fiky took out his steel spectacle case, a pocket watch, and a penknife.

"Just step back through the door, please."

This time there was no more buzzing. The man handed him back his things.

"Thank you. You can go right in."

El Fiky was angry – at the obscene opulence of the hotel, the messenger's ridiculous pleasure at having a western capitalist as a guest, and the ridiculous notion that he himself might have hollowed out a copy of his life's work to hide a weapon inside. But all that vanished when he entered the room and saw the spectacular panorama of the city spread out before him. There was the Nile, with its great white cruise boats and sickle-sailed fellucas. There was the lattice of the Cairo Tower and the confusion of mosques and minarets stretching to the west.

And there on the horizon, standing dark and mysterious against the sky, were the three Great Pyramids of Egypt – Mykerinos, Chephren and Cheops. He was so mesmerised by them that he did not take in the tall man standing at the far end of the room, or the older man on the couch.

"Good afternoon," said the man who was standing. "My name is Theodore Gilkrensky and this is Professor William McCarthy. My wife gave me your book years ago and I read some of it on the flight to Cairo. Thank you for coming."

"It is *I* who should be honoured," said El Fiky with a wide smile. "As to the book, I hope you did not pay too much attention to the later sections my younger colleagues wrote. They tend towards many of the more modern and fanciful theories as to why the pyramids were built. Ahmed El Fiky at your service, sir."

"I look forward to discussing those theories with you nevertheless, Professor," said Gilkrensky, shaking his hand. "They're the very ideas my wife would have shared."

"Your wife is no longer with you?"

"She was killed," said Gilkrensky, and moved a slim black briefcase from the couch, so they could sit down.

"You have my sympathies," said El Fiky. "How can I help?"

"By giving us the benefit of your professional advice –

for which my corporation will, of course, pay whatever consultancy fee is appropriate."

Professor El Fiky raised his hands, but Gilkrensky continued.

"For example," he said, glancing at McCarthy. "I would like to know how, and why the pyramids were built, and if there was any purpose to them other than simple burial mounds."

El Fiky frowned.

"It is all well-documented in my book. Can I ask why you need me to explain it to you in person?"

"It is nothing sinister, I assure you, Professor. Bill and I simply need someone with expertise in this area to settle a little . . . ah . . . academic argument we've been having. When I heard you were at the museum, it seemed a marvellous opportunity to get the best possible advice in the shortest possible time."

Professor El Fiky nodded.

"Perhaps then, I should begin with some of the more . . . er . . . traditional theories as to how and why the pyramids were built. And then I could bring you up to date with the various modern notions about the stars, and so forth. Is that acceptable?"

"Perfect, Professor," said Gilkrensky, and gazed out of the window at the distant pyramids, as El Fiky began . . .

Three floors below them, in the anonymity of her own Nile Olympiad hotel room, Yukiko watched as Farida left El Sharoud's apartment. Then she lowered her binoculars and slid the stolen GRC SmartMate from her briefcase, laying it beside the slim laptop computer on the dressing-table.

The laptop was the latest Mawashi-Saito model – a pre-production prototype. For the last hour it had been running a state-of-the-art voice-activated translation programme, turning spoken Arabic into written Japanese. The source of the voices was a micro-miniaturised listening device, no bigger that a screw-head, which Yukiko had slipped under the top of the low coffee table in Zaki El Sharoud's flat on her last visit.

Yukiko's doubts about her uncle's decision to hire the Islamics to steal the Minerva had grown ever since she had met El Sharoud. She had sat with a group of Japanese holiday-makers and watched the girl Farida make the most clumsy advance to the American pilot. And now, here the woman was, openly entering and leaving El Sharoud's flat – telling him she could not bear to use her body as bait.

Amateurs!

Yukiko would never . . . had never . . . let such a minor problem stand in her way. It was all a matter priorities and control . . . of *giri* over *ninjo*.

Had she not received a message from her contact in London, telling her Gilkrensky would have to remain in Egypt for at least another seventy-two hours, she would have taken matters into her own hands.

The special equipment in the long duffle bag in her

wardrobe was always ready. As was the short sword. Yukiko had a deep personal score to settle with the man in the presidential suite, and if fate gave her the chance, she would take it.

"So, in answer to your question," said Professor El Fiky, "I can say that the pyramids were built simply to satisfy the ancient Egyptians' fascination with life after death."

He was sitting forward on the edge of the sofa, excited at the honour of addressing a distinguished audience. His eyes shone with the energy of a zealot, and his small hands gesticulated in front of him, as he illustrated his points with short extracts from his book.

McCarthy tried to summarise.

"So if their belief was that the Pharaoh could never hope to reach the afterlife if his mortal body had been destroyed, that would explain why they went to all the trouble of preserving the corpses and building huge tombs to protect them from grave robbers."

"Exactly," said El Fiky. "And the simple fortified tombs that the early kings built around 3200 BC, gradually evolved into the colossal structures you see on the horizon. But then again, there are those who would tell you differently."

"But as I understand it," said Gilkrensky, leafing to the later chapters of El Fiky's book, "the problem with the theory that pyramids are nothing more than graves is that no bodies have ever been found. It's as simple as that!"

McCarthy shook his head and chuckled.

"Surely, they were stolen by grave robbers." he said.

"But it says here that coffins have been found inside pyramids, closed, sealed and untouched, with no bodies inside."

"So why do *you* think the pyramids were built, Dr Gilkrensky?" asked El Fiky.

"You'll laugh when you hear," chortled McCarthy, unable to contain himself any longer.

"I'm sure he won't," said Gilkrensky, and stopped short. All at once he was back at the riverbank near University College Cork, and Maria was saying, "If I tell you my theories and you laugh at me, I will never speak to you again!"

"Dr Gilkrensky?"

"I'm sorry, Professor. I was a million miles away. Here, let me show you."

He turned to a full-page cutaway illustration of the Great Pyramid of Cheops, showing all the tombs and passages.

"Correct me if I'm wrong, Professor, but isn't the traditional belief that, in building the Great Pyramid, King Cheops simply copied the design from those kings who had gone before him?"

"It is."

"But, if you examine the plan of the Great Pyramid, you'll see that its construction is completely different from all the others on the plateau. Earlier pyramids were built on top of existing tombs, to cover them over. The Great Pyramid of Cheops has no less than nine chambers, four of which were sealed at the time of building."

"Theo's a romantic," said McCarthy. "He thinks there are hidden chambers yet to be discovered?"

El Fiky shook his head.

"That is not possible. The Pyramid was X-rayed by a man called Alverez some years ago using a cosmic ray device. The results were analysed by computer at the University of Berkely in America. If there are any spaces left, I'm sure they would have showed up then."

Gilkrensky glanced at the Minerva.

"It would be interesting to get that original data and analyse it again with an up-to-date computer. We might pick up something they missed."

McCarthy said, "I've got a friend in Berkeley. I'll give him a call. But if the Pyramid wasn't a tomb, what the hell was it?"

"There are two main schools of thought," said El Fiky, taking the book from Gilkrensky. "There are the 'practical' and the . . . er . . . 'not so practical'. To take the practical theories first, it is possible that the Great Pyramid was built as a gigantic temple to represent the destiny of a man's soul, much in the way that formal Japanese gardens are laid out to represent the trials and tribulations of life on earth. Then there is the theory that the Pyramid was intended as an astronomical observatory. If you have read the book, you will recall the story about the god Osiris and the fascination the ancient Pharaohs had with the stars. Well, what we once thought were simple air-shafts in the King's and Queen's chambers point directly to the position of the star of Orion, as it was in ancient times. Some of my students worked with Bauval and Gilbert on this theory. They wrote a book. Perhaps you have seen it?"

"And the more fanciful theories?" said Gilkrensky. "What are those?"

"Tell him that one about the pyramids being navigational beacons for flying saucers," sniggered McCarthy. "That's my favourite."

"I'm afraid traditional thinkers like me tend to refer to people who hold such theories as 'Pyramidiots", said El Fiky, "But, as well as the really fanciful theories about men from outer space, there have been many observers who have commented on the geometry of the Great Pyramid and its relation to other measurements, and the fact that the mathematical symbol *'pi'* is incorporated into its design. This implies a scientific knowledge far in advance of its time. It also suggests that the Great Pyramid was designed to act in some physical way, much in the same way that a correctly cut glass lens might act to focus light."

"Go on," said Gilkrensky, and glanced at McCarthy, who shook his head and raised his eyes to the ceiling.

"One theory suggests that the world is criss-crossed with lines of energy called 'ley lines'. Nobody knows what form these energies take, but I understand they can be detected by 'dousing' with wooden branches or metal rods. It is suggested by some that the Great Pyramid is situated in the very centre of a world-wide network of such lines and acts as a giant lens to focus this energy. But, it is only a theory."

Gilkrensky leant forward.

"And if you wanted to prove this theory experimentally, Professor, how would you do it?"

"It is only one of the more fanciful theories, I assure you," said El Fiky, puzzled by his sudden interest. "And not one that many serious scientists subscribe to."

"Tell him about the plane crash, Bill."

"Come off it, Theo! You're starting to sound like your computer. Cosmic energies indeed!"

"Please tell him!"

"OK then. On your own head be it! Professor El Fiky, you must know there was a plane crash in the desert outside Cairo this week. Well, we investigated the crash and found that some form of energy, be it a radar beam, a microwave transmission, or whatever, had interfered with the robot-pilot system we had on the plane. Now this morning, we got a whole parcel of maps and reports from the Egyptian Air Force. They show no military or commercial installations capable of creating such a beam anywhere near the site where the plane crashed. So my friend Theo here, with a little help from a . . . colleague of his, has pole-vaulted to the conclusion that some kind of supernatural New Age, cosmic force is involved. He's basing all this hocus-pocus on the fact that the incident occurred directly over the Great Pyramid of Cheops! Ridiculous, isn't it!"

El Fiky went pale.

"You say this happened over the Great Pyramid?"

"Yes. Last Wednesday."

"And how did this . . . this 'energy' interfere with the plane?"

"It overloaded a special high-precision altitude-measuring device," said Gilkrensky. "The system uses lasers and sound waves to measure its height above the ground."

"Then I have your answer," said El Fiky. "Six weeks ago, the sound and light show for tourists at the Great Pyramid was fitted out with a new holography display. It creates images using a powerful laser beam!"

Gilkrensky looked deflated.

"You say this sound and light show uses lasers?"

El Fiky nodded.

"The original stone facings of the pyramids and the capstone on the top have been torn away over the thousands of years since they were built. The laser holography in the new *Son et Lumière* recreates the original pure shape of the Great Pyramid. They do this every evening. I wrote part of the script myself."

Bill McCarthy was grinning from ear to ear.

"Sorry about the cosmic energies, Theo. It was a nice idea while it lasted."

"You can see the display tonight, if you wish," said El Fiky. "It is on every evening at eight o'clock sharp. The manager of the Mena House Hotel, next to the Pyramid site, is an old friend of mine, and the rooftop makes an excellent vantage point."

"I'd like to see it," said Gilkrensky. "But I'm far more interested in finding out if it's the source of the interference that hit the Daedalus. Bill! How long would it take to air-lift one of those cabins of yours out to the Giza Plateau with a chopper? There's another experiment I want to try!"

20

SOUND AND LIGHT

THE BELL 214 SQUATTED ON THE TARMAC BY THE PYRAMID ticket-office like a giant insect. On either side of the fuselage, long aluminium struts protruded like spindly legs, each tipped with the bulbous "foot" of a Daedalus laser and sound-wave receptor.

"How does it handle?" said Theodore Gilkrensky.

"Not too bad," replied Manning. "I've carried a lot more difficult loads on Hueys before. But we won't be able to make any sudden moves, or the momentum will shear those struts right off at the roots."

They were standing in the doorway of Bill McCarthy's portable cabin. Inside, McCarthy was busy fiddling with radio receivers, computers and chart recorders. Major Crowe was in tense conversation with Colonel Selim and a few of his officers. They broke off, and Crowe walked over.

"Colonel Selim says he's unhappy about being able to secure the area, sir, particularly now that its getting dark.

The site is open on the western side and the audience of the sound and light show will be arriving shortly. I've suggested you personally retire to the Mena House Hotel and watch the experiment from there. Mr Manning can fly the helicopter, and Professor McCarthy can operate the monitoring equipment in the cabin. I'll link you into the radio net with one of these security units, so you can hear what's going on." He passed Gilkrensky a light radio headset and pocket battery-pack.

"I could always fly in the helicopter with Manning."

"You could, but I'd be happier with you in the hotel. At least I have some hope of guarding *that*. And you are carrying the Minerva, so that's an added risk."

"Oh, all right, Major. You've been very good this far."

"Thank you."

"All the same though . . . " And he looked wistfully at the helicopter, before allowing himself to be escorted to the safety of the Mena House Hotel.

Once inside, Gilkrensky set the Minerva down on a table near the window of the room Professor El Fiky had arranged on the top floor. Gerald Maguire guarded the door. Thomas Hargreaves was in the foyer below, and Major Crowe was on the roof, directly above their heads.

"Sorry about all the security, Professor," said Gilkrensky. "But you can see how it is!"

"Heavy is the head that wears the crown?" said El Fiky. "But could you explain to me what you're trying to do?"

Gilkrensky pointed to the helicopter.

"The chopper's been fitted with laser and sound-receptors identical to those installed on the Whisperer aircraft. Before the laser holography display gets under way, Mr Manning will position the helicopter directly over the Pyramid. Then, if the laser show really *is* capable of effecting Daedalus, we'll pick up readings on the sensors, which will be monitored by Bill McCarthy from the cabin."

"I think the show is about to begin," said El Fiky, looking past him. "You'd better order your helicopter into the air."

Gilkrensky slipped Crowe's security radio headset over his ears.

"Leroy? Can you hear me?"

"Loud and clear, boss. Over."

"Crank her up and take off! Hover at a thousand feet. You can use the centring device we fitted to your control console to position yourself."

"No problem!" And from the plateau they all heard the high-pitched whine of the Bell's starter motor.

"What is the holography display about, Professor?"

"It is a pageant describing the building of the pyramids. From the early designs of the architect Imhotep, to the completion of the last pyramid by Mykerinos. The laser display is the grand finale. You will find it quite spectacular."

"I'm sure I will."

"There," said El Fiky, pointing to the window. "The show is starting."

Lights began to flicker on the plateau. The first strains of music could be heard through the open window.

Dom! Dim! Dom!

Towering above the hotel, silhouetted against the setting sun, were the three massive shapes of the pyramids. One after the other, the huge mountains of rock were bathed in light.

Dom! Dim! Dom!

And the commentary began. It told of Imhotep – priest, architect and wizard to King Zoser – builder of the step pyramids of Saqqara and Dashour, the pre-eminent genius of his time. It told how Imhotep possessed magical powers, and how he was in harmony with the energies of the earth and the heavens. He planned the complex of pyramids at Giza as a resting-place for his Pharaohs – to harness the power of the gods."

"That is the part of the script my younger colleagues wrote," said El Fiky. "You can imagine how hard it was for us to agree that last line!"

Gilkrensky nodded.

"I can imagine."

The commentary moved on – through the Fourth Dynasty of the Pharaohs, and the coming of the Marmaluks, to the invasion of Napoleon – the Great Pyramid ran like a constant thread through thousands of years of Egyptian history.

"Now we have the lasers!" whispered El Fiky. "This is the most spectacular part."

"Are you recording this?" said Gilkrensky into his radio.

"All instruments are on line!" replied McCarthy.

"I'm in position," shouted Manning above the engine noise.

"Watch!" said El Fiky, as the commentary reached its climax . . .

"To honour the tradition of Imhotep, and to keep his spirit alive, we display to you through the wonder of laser holography, an image of how the Pyramids looked when they were first conceived by the royal wizard, in all their glory . . . "

Dim! Dom! Dum!

First Mykerinos, then Chephren, and finally Cheops itself was transformed from untidy mountains of rock into pure and perfect pyramids of polished Tura limestone, brilliant against the night sky.

Gilkrensky was awe-struck.

"It's fantastic! It's absolutely fantastic!"

"That is how they once were," said El Fiky. "Before the limestone was stripped to make buildings here in the city. . . Dr Gilkrensky! Your experiment!"

"Oh my god, yes!" Gilkrensky's hand darted to his headset. "Leroy? Bill? Are you reading this?"

"I can't see what's below me from up here. Has it started yet?"

"It looks awesome, Theo! But all the instruments are as dead as a dodo!"

"Are you sure they're working?" said Gilkrensky.

"All the telemetry checks out. The data links are fine, and we tested the sensors before Leroy went up. If there was anything to measure, we'd have it!"

"Shit! Now we're back to square one!" snapped McCarthy.

"The effect of the holography lasers doesn't carry above the display," said Gilkrensky. "So they couldn't have affected the Daedalus. What about cosmic energies now, Bill?"

In the dying applause from the audience on the plateau, Gilkrensky heard a low warble from the Minerva 3,000.

"Excuse me for a moment," he said, and took the computer to the far corner of the room, where he opened it and turned the Minerva screen to face him.

"What is it, Maria?"

"Last night, during the test flight, you told me to give you any information that could be pertinent to decisions you might make – immediately."

"I did. Do you have something for me?"

"Could you ask Professor El Fiky if this laser display takes place at the same time every night?"

"It does," he said, a moment later.

"Then once again, we are too early! By my internal chronometer, the laser display finished this evening at 8.22 local time, when the lasers were switched off. The incident with the aircraft last night, and last Wednesday, happened at 8.37, some fifteen minutes after the show ended!"

Gilkrensky peered up at the distant winking lights of the helicopter, at the darkened Pyramid, and at his watch.

"Perhaps the Pyramid acts as a trigger of some kind? Leroy! Can you hear me?"

"Loud and clear!"

"Get your ass down here now! I want you to land on the lawn of the Mena House Hotel next to the swimming-pool as fast as you can!"

"You got it!"

"What's going on?" shouted Crowe over the radio.

"I'm sorry, Major, but I don't want to miss this. You can meet me on the lawn!" And he snapped the lid of the Minerva shut, took its case by the handle, and ran past a startled Gerald Maguire, towards the door.

The helicopter lifted off from the hotel lawn and spiralled up over the Pyramid into the night sky. In the passenger compartment, Theodore Gilkrensky was hunched over the sensor indicators and Major Crowe was peering nervously out of the window at the darkness of the desert. Between them, the black briefcase of the Minerva was secured to the seat.

"Feeling airsick, Maria?"

"That is impossible, Theo. But can you ask Mr Manning if he can check the position indicator. I think we are slightly out of alignment."

"Teach your grandmother to suck eggs, lady!" muttered Manning. "OK. We're in position."

"Bill? Can you hear me?"

"I have you, Theo! And I still have full telemetry. Nothing above background!"

"Mr Manning is slipping out of position again," said Maria.

"OK! OK! I got it!"

Gilkrensky peered at the digital displays in front of him. In the caravan below, McCarthy and his technicians watched the chart recorders draw a steady straight line on the paper.

"Have you got anything, Theo?"

"Nothing Bill! How about you?"

"Zip! Ask Maria. She's wired up to the telemetry!"

"No readings above background, Theo."

"Can you hold us here, Leroy?"

"No problem!"

"What time is it, Bill?"

"Eight twenty . . . Hey Theo! Look at your monitor!"

"What is it?"

"I'm getting a small trickle on the pen recorders. It's hard to tell if its static or what."

The base line on the digital displays in front of Gilkrensky started to tremble.

"It's on both the laser and the sound channels! What do you make of it, Maria?"

"There's definitely an energy source somewhere, Theo. It's very faint, but getting stronger. Is it possible for us to go any closer to the ground?"

"Leroy! Can we lose altitude and remain on the same spot?"

"You know yourself! I'll have to spiral downwards or I could drop into my own slipstream and lose control!"

"Try and keep us as directly over the Pyramid as you can! Are you all right, Major?"

"All right, sir," said Crowe, and the helicopter started to turn.

"We've slipped off the beam," said Maria. "I've lost those strange energy readings now."

"Leroy!"

"Do you want steady or do you want crashed? I'll bring her back onto the spot at five hundred feet."

"OK! . . . Yes! . . . Look at that, Bill! Here it comes again!"

The signal on Gilkrensky's display was much stronger now, pulsing in waves along the bottom of the screen.

"It's getting more intense!" said McCarthy. The pens on the chart recorders were jerking up and down, scoring the stream of paper with wild spidery lines as it coiled onto the floor.

"Professor McCarthy is correct," said Maria. "The energy is getting stronger, and appears rhythmical, with a pulse every 0.86 seconds."

"What time do you have now, Bill?"

"Eight thirty-two. Jeez, Theo! Look at that! Turn down the sensitivity someone! The pens are catching!"

The pen recorders were jumping madly on the paper. In the helicopter, the peaks on Gilkrensky's digital display were hitting the top of the screen, like breakers on a stormy sea.

"Wow! Look at the power of that pulse! No wonder the Daedalus flipped out! It must have flown right across the beam!"

"Hey, Doc!" shouted Manning. "Something's happening. We're going down!"

Gilkrensky looked up from the display. The casing of the monitor was vibrating strangely against the seat.

Suddenly, the whole helicopter was shaking, as if the rotors had gone out of balance.

"Leroy!"

"I don't know! I can't hold it!"

"Theo!" said Maria. "I have to warn you that . . . "

All Gilkrensky could hear was the rush of wind outside.

The helicopter's engine had stopped.

21

CUT OUT

"In the event of an engine failure – IT IS FATAL NOT TO PUSH THE COLLECTIVE TO THE FLOOR!"

Those were the words in front of Leroy Manning's eyes when he heard the Bell's big turbine shut down – words that had been drummed into him time after time in flight training. A helicopter without power falls at around 1,700 feet per minute. He was five hundred feet above the ground. Less than twenty seconds to regain control, find a spot, and land!

And if he couldn't – he was dead!

Manning slapped the collective pitch control to the floor. That flattened the angle of the rotor blades . . . keeping them spinning against the rushing air . . . giving him some shred of lift. The Bell was falling, straight towards the great stone mountain of the Pyramid. Manning coaxed the cyclic stick away from him as far as he dared. The helicopter slid forward, buoyed up beneath the angled disc of spinning blades, skimming over the Pyramid and into the darkness of the desert.

They were falling faster.

Manning could not see the ground.

If he made the next manoeuvre too early, they would stall and drop again!

If he left it too late, they would hit the sand at forty-five knots and smash to pieces.

He drew on every second of his thirty years' experience in the air, wrenched the cyclic stick back with his right hand . . . and prayed!

The nose of the Bell lifted, fifty feet above the ground. The tail rotor kissed the sand. Manning felt his stomach being sucked down through his seat as the helicopter slowed, and then hit the desert floor on its skids with a shattering crash.

Manning unlocked his fingers from the cyclic. His whole arm was shuddering. Sweat was pouring off his face. Outside, the great rotors were turning . . . slower and slower . . . until they stopped.

In the silence that followed, Gilkrensky said,

"Nice auto-rotation, Leroy!"

"Ah . . . thanks! What the hell happened!"

"I don't know. Maria?"

"Theo. I have to warn you that . . . Oh! I have a systems problem. My internal chronometer is showing a thirty-one second discrepancy against real time!"

"Did you suffer a power failure?"

"No. Otherwise I would have had to re-boot my systems from scratch. I was about to warn you of the energy beam, and then we were on the ground. It was as if time moved forward without me sensing it."

"Well, we sensed it OK!" said Manning. "What I want to know is, why did the turbine cut out?"

"Will it start now?"

Manning threw a few circuit breakers and switches, watching dials and needles flicker back into life.

"Should do. The electrics are on line. But I'd want to check her over before I try a restart. We might have busted something when we landed."

"Theo! Can you hear me? Theo?"

"We can hear you, Bill. I'm OK and so is Leroy. How about you, Major?"

"A bit shaken, but otherwise fine."

"We got the shock of our lives when you lost power and dropped out of sight. I thought you were a goner for sure. Where are you?"

"I don't know! On the far side of the Pyramid I think!"

"OK. Have Leroy switch on the chopper's spotlight, and I'll send out a jeep for you!"

Half an hour later, Gilkrensky and McCarthy were standing in front of the chart recorder in the portable cabin, while Gerald Maguire stood guard on the door. Out beyond the Pyramid, Leroy Manning was running checks on the Bell, under the protection of Hargreaves and Major Crowe.

"OK," said McCarthy, peering at the paper chart, "it was 8.22 when the laser display shut down. Nothing showing on the record during the show. Zip! Nada!

Nothing! Then, at 8.29, seven minutes later, we start seeing a tiny trickle of energy on the chart, just above background level. Then it gets stronger . . . we start to see it coming in pulses . . . then there's a gap in the record for a couple of minutes while you lose altitude in the chopper for a better look."

McCarthy fed the paper trace through his fingers.

"Now! Here we are at 8.31. The pulses are quite distinct . . . almost like a heartbeat! And at 8.32 I have to turn down the sensitivity by a factor of a thousand just to keep the pens from flying off the paper. See how the waves are much closer together. It's almost as if they're merging into something, combining their harmonics to achieve some kind of critical mass . . . because at 8.35 . . . bingo! The whole thing goes into overload. You lose power, and the record stops!"

"What kind of energy is it?" murmured Gilkrensky, tracing the crazed pattern of spikes with his finger. "It's not light, and it's not sound. And yet . . . "

"Without wishing to say 'I told you so'," said Maria from the fold-down desk beyond the chart recorder. "I am convinced that what we are seeing is the first ever recording of focused cosmic energy!"

Gilkrensky looked at McCarthy for a reaction. McCarthy shrugged his shoulders.

"I don't know, Theo. Yesterday I'd have said 'bullshit!', but now I'm not so sure."

"But what's it focused on? And why?"

Gerald Maguire looked in from outside.

"Excuse me, Professor. But Major Crowe just got a call

from the hotel. That X-ray data on the Great Pyramid –
the stuff you ordered from Berkeley University? It's just
been delivered."

Leroy Manning was badly spooked. The forced auto-
rotation had scared him badly and, even though he'd
survived it, his hand had been shaking as he'd let his
fingers loosen on the cyclic control.

I can't cut it anymore, he told himself. It's like that
time I smashed up the JetRanger in Kenya. I couldn't
sleep for weeks.

He had tried to face his fears by checking out the Bell
and flying it back to the airport, leaving Gilkrensky and
his party to be ferried back to the hotel in one of the
security helicopters Colonel Selim had sent. The Bell
handled OK, but one of the skids was bent and both the
struts carrying the scientific equipment had been twisted
into scrap metal. Out at the GRC hanger, Ahmed had
rolled his eyes to heaven and said "Mister Leroy" must
have been blessed by Allah to have survived. Leroy told
him to run a complete check, and said he would pick up
the chopper for a test-flight the next morning.

Then he had taken a taxi back to the Nile Olympiad
and showered in his room, hoping to wash away the
fear. But his hand still shook. As he looked into the
mirror, he could see the white hairs beginning to
outnumber the blond, and the deeply etched lines
around his eyes.

I'm tired, he thought. Tired, and scared, and old! I
should get out of this business. Take my money and go

back to Florida! Put a down payment on a condo by the beach, settle back, and rot . . . just like all the other old couples around there . . .

Couples! He wasn't even a couple!

He thought of Farida, and looked at his watch. He'd just have time to catch her at the club . . . to say goodbye! She was a beautiful young Muslim. He was a tired old infidel! It would never have worked!

"You look so sad again," she said when she came to his table after the show. Her raven hair cascaded over the high neck of her sweater, her shoulders, and her breasts. He could see her legs slide under the thin material of her skirt as she sat down.

"I had a close call," he said. "It made me realise I'm getting too old for flying."

"But you promised to take me up in your helicopter! I've brought my things!"

Her large brown eyes pleaded with him. She was the most desirable girl he had ever met – the perfect woman – but not for him!

"That was before. I'm tired, Farida. And I'm getting old!"

Her hand found his.

"But you are *not* old!" she insisted. "You are a wonderful exciting man. And tonight I am going to prove it to you!"

She got up from the table, and led him from the nightclub, back to his room. Once inside the door, she turned down the light and kissed him softly on the lips.

Then she looked up at him, as if she had made a decision, and kissed him again, harder this time, and deeper. Her lips opened and her tongue found his, playing, teasing. Her arms slipped round his neck as she pressed herself against him. He could feel the warmth of her, and the swell of her breasts against his chest. Finally, she took his hand in hers and laid it gently on the smooth skin of her belly beneath her sweater. As her tongue found his again, her body pressed closer and his hand moved higher, Leroy Manning realised that beneath the sweater and the simple skirt, she was wearing nothing at all.

22

A MATTER OF CO-ORDINATION

AT JUST AFTER HALF PAST SIX THE NEXT MORNING, THE OLD Bakelite telephone in Professor El Fiky's flat rang while he was at prayer. Normally, he would have let nothing disturb this daily ritual, but to leave it ring would disturb not only his daughter, but the rest of the apartment block as well. So he decided Allah would be merciful, got up from his prayer mat, and answered it.

"Professor El Fiky?"

"Speaking. Who is this, please?"

"Oh, thank God for that! It's taken me hours to track you down. The telephone system here is diabolical!"

"That is true. But who are you, please?"

"Theo Gilkrensky, Professor! I'm sorry to disturb you so early. But I've made the most amazing discovery, and I knew you'd want to know about it straight away."

"What is it, Dr Gilkrensky? You disappeared so suddenly last night! I did not know what had happened to you, and nobody would tell me! So I got a taxi back home!"

"Did I leave you out there! I'm very sorry! But we discovered the most amazing thing!"

"What was it?"

"The experiment we did last night. It proved my theory was correct. There *is* some sort of natural energy being focused by the Pyramid. Perhaps the lasers from the sound and light show trigger it off, we don't know. But it's there! And we have the scientific evidence to prove it!"

Pyramidiots! thought Professor El Fiky. He could hear his daughter stirring in the next room.

"But what is far more important from an archaeological point of view . . . what I really phoned to tell you . . . is that we got the original Alvarez X-ray data last night from the States. I had my computer analyse it. It shows something wonderful! Something you must come over and see! Then we can fly out and examine the Pyramid before it's open to the tourists!"

"But why?"

"Because we've found the answer, Professor! The computer analysis confirms it. At the precise mathematical centre of the Pyramid! We've discovered another chamber!"

"That . . . that is wonderful!" breathed El Fiky. "I must call the museum at once."

Leroy Manning stirred in the big double bed, feeling like a kid again, reliving the previous night, just as a love-sick teenager would after his first time . . .

There was the wonderfully sensuous slide – that most feminine of movements – as she pulled the sweater off over her head. There was the cascade of shining hair over her bare shoulders and her perfect dark breasts. The kiss of the silk skirt as it slid to the floor, and the pure beauty of her naked body in front of him . . . for him.

There was Farida between the clean white sheets of the hotel bed, Farida wanting him . . . kissing him . . . holding him . . . beneath him. And finally, when he could hold back no longer, Farida moaning as he burst inside her . . . spending himself as the heaving passion took him . . . again . . . and again . . . and again . . .

Leroy played these images over and over in his head, remembering the sight, the touch, and the heat of her body, feeling himself getting hard once more.

And yet . . . it was strange . . .

He had been with enough women, from Patsy Miller to Sue Lin, to know when making love was real, and when it was just pretend. However hard Farida had tried, however much she had kissed and caressed him, whatever she had said afterwards, there had been no disguising what her body had told him. She had been dry when he entered her . . . it was just pretend!

But why?

He reached over, but she was gone. He could hear the hiss of the shower from the bathroom, and the angry scrub of a brush on skin. Or was he just imagining that?

The bedside telephone rang.

"Mr Manning? Crowe here! Just to remind you the

chairman wants to fly out to the Pyramid at eight o'clock. Will the helicopter be ready?"

Manning groped on the table for his watch, and then on the floor. Christ! It was only six thirty-five!

"I'll have to ring the hanger and get back to you," he said. "The chopper took a bad smack there last night, but she checked out OK. I'll call you back in a few minutes."

The bathroom door opened and there was Farida, fully dressed in a loose jump suit and running shoes.

"You're up early," he said, covering himself as he tried to keep the disappointment out of his voice.

Farida tied up her hair, and reached past him for the telephone.

"I must call my family and tell them I won't be back this morning," she said. "We're going flying. Remember? You promised me last night!"

Through the lens of his Nikon camera, Zaki El Sharoud watched the couple leave the hotel and get into a taxi. He could clearly make out the GRC logo on Manning's flying jacket, and the overnight bag on Farida's shoulder. A pang of jealousy, mixed with disgust at what he had ordered her to do, shook the magnified image for a second, but he fought it back.

This was for the *Jihad*. He had to be as strong as she had been.

"She has played her part," he said. "The helicopter will arrive at eight. Gamal, bring the car around to the front of the building. I will call Abdul and Sarwat."

Gamal, who Leroy would have recognised instantly as the singer from the Olympiad night club, smiled in anticipation. He was wearing the dress uniform of a sergeant in the Egyptian air force – the same uniform he'd worn on the day he'd been decorated by Sadat for his part in storming the Israeli Bar Ev Line in 1973.

Zaki picked up the telephone, made a short call, and followed Gamal to the car. As the door slammed and they drove away, El Sharoud could not resist a last glance at the top floor of the Nile Olympiad Hotel.

High above, in the conference room of the presidential suite, Theodore Gilkrensky, Bill McCarthy and Professor El Fiky were deep in discussion over the new evidence.

"My theory is that this build-up of energy we discovered last night is triggered by the laser display," said Gilkrensky. "The hologram recreates the original shape of the Pyramid, and enables it to function perfectly as some kind of lens, just as it was intended. The lasers also provide light – at a much greater intensity than sunlight – and there is vibration from the music – those three notes we heard repeated over and over in the soundtrack. What were those?"

"They are based on an ancient prayer of invocation to the sun god Re," said El Fiky.

"Hold it right there!"

McCarthy took his pipe from his mouth.

"I'm still not convinced about all this gypsy mumbo-jumbo. Surely the only plausible explanation for the plane crash is the lasers from the hologram display itself!"

El Fiky nodded.

"I have to agree. Are you sure the timing of the display doesn't fit with the crash of the plane, and your experiment last night?"

"It's Maria who's sure," said Gilkrensky. "And she can be sure to thirty decimal places."

"This Maria must be a very precise person," said El Fiky. "Does she have theories about what this energy might be?"

"Does she *ever*!" muttered McCarthy. "And a whole lot more besides!"

"It would be interesting to discuss such theories with someone who at least had an open mind on the subject," said El Fiky looking from one man to the other.

"I agree," said Gilkrensky. "And if you'll move your book, I'll introduce you. Professor, this is Maria. Maria, this is Professor Ahmed El Fiky, of the Museum of Antiquities here in Cairo."

He lifted the Minerva onto the board table, opened the lid, and turned it to face them. The screen of the Minerva blinked on, and Maria said,

"Good morning, Professor El Fiky. I was wondering when Theo might introduce us!"

"A computer?"

"A Minerva 3,000 prototype," said Maria proudly. "I am the first computer in the world to have a synthetic biochip as the matrix of my neural net. This allows complex cross-referencing and data associations to take place, as they do in the human brain."

"Believe me! She's *very* human!" said McCarthy.

"Please, Bill! Don't let her delete you from her user file again."

"I'm pleased to be included in your discussions," continued Maria. "Because I wanted to ask Professor El Fiky about the theory of focused energy he described yesterday. Could I copy that diagram of the Pyramid you showed Theo from your book? It would make it easier for me to demonstrate what I discovered last night when I analysed the X-ray data Professor McCarthy got from Berkeley University."

"I know I got it for you," said McCarthy, as he held El Fiky's book up for Maria to see. "But I still don't know what the hell it is!"

Professor El Fiky leant forward. All the talk of computers and cosmic energy mystified him. But at least the Alvarez data was something he could understand.

"I remember that study," he said. "It was just under thirty years ago. A famous American scientist called Luis Alvarez came to Cairo, with a great circus of workers from the US Atomic Energy Commission, the Department of Antiquities and the Smithsonian, all rushing about the place. He was sure there was a secret chamber in the pyramid of Chephren, the smaller one next the to the Great Pyramid of Cheops, and said he would prove it using X-rays. But his results were inconclusive. I heard he had done work on Cheops too, but I never saw the result."

"Professor Alvarez did indeed work on the Great Pyramid," said Maria. "It was not his experimental design that was at fault, but the way he analysed the data. You see, he was using an old IBM 1130 computer – very crude compared to my own capability in terms of data analysis and resolution. Look at the screen and you will see!"

Her image shrank to the size of a playing-card, and moved to the top right-hand corner of the display. Below it, the dim smudge of a cross appeared.

"I can tell very little from that," said El Fiky.

"This is because you are still looking at the original Alvarez data," Maria explained. "All you can make out is the four-pointed star you would expect if you were looking upwards from the base of a transparent pyramid, towards the point."

"And you can enhance this image?"

"I can, Professor, simply by comparing the data from the cosmic ray generator Alvarez placed in the lowest chamber, with the data from the other chambers, and by running an image enhancement programme . . . "

"The same kind of programme we used to use at NASA to clean up the pictures from the moon," added McCarthy.

The image on the Minerva's screen started to change. Large dots broke into smaller ones. Dark areas began to show detail. The four-pointed star sharpened into crisp lines, and tiny nodes began to appear.

"When we compare this information with the detailed diagram of the Pyramid from Professor El Fiky's book," continued Maria. "We can see the entrance, over there to the right of the screen, the Descending Passage, the Grand Gallery, with the King's Chamber above it and, just off-centre on the north-south axis, the Queen's Chamber."

Professor El Fiky, rose from his seat and peered at the Minerva screen. "It's incredible! It's as if the whole Pyramid were made of glass. What is that tiny dot there, at the very centre of the Pyramid, just off the Queen's Chamber? Is that the new chamber you spoke to me about on the telephone."

"That is what I want to find out today, with your help, Professor," said Gilkrensky. "I think this new chamber is where the strange energy we experienced is being focused, deep inside the Pyramid. I've already arranged to have ultra-sonic probes delivered to the cabin at the Pyramid site. The helicopter is coming for us at eight."

23

THE BATTLE OF THE NILE OLYMPIAD

"She's with me," said Leroy Manning to the two Central Security Police guarding his helicopter outside the GRC hanger. "I have to take the chopper for a test-flight, and then pick up my boss from the hotel."

The two men eyed Farida, and the way the jump suit clung to her body. One of them spoke to her in rapid Arabic, and she swore back at him viciously. The man looked embarrassed and waved them through quickly.

"I hate men like that!" spat Farida. "They think any woman who is not covered in a veil is a whore!"

She had been tense in the taxi out to the airport, like an over-wound guitar string waiting to snap. There was a lot Manning would have liked to say, about the night they had spent together, and the way he felt. But he knew Cairean taxi drivers can speak many languages.

Ahmed came running out of his shed to greet them, and stopped in surprise, when he saw Manning was not alone.

"It's OK," said Manning. "I'm just taking the lady up for a spin. If the chopper checks out, I'll drop her on the hotel roof and she'll be back down the stairwell out of sight before the fat cats come up."

Then he stepped over to the Bell, checked the rotors and condensation-covers, and opened the passenger door so that Farida could climb in.

On the other side of the airport, a car drew up at the entrance to the military base and four air force personnel presented their credentials.

"Photo-reconnaissance. Down from Alexandria," said the sergeant who was driving.

The guard looked at the deep row of medal ribbons on the man's uniform. Then he examined their authorisation papers. They seemed genuine enough. Why shouldn't they be?

"Do you know where to go?"

"We do. Thank you, Corporal," said Zaki El Sharoud, and Gamal drove them through the checkpoint into the base, down the main access road, and behind a group of hangers. Then, when he was sure they could no longer be seen from the gate, he turned away from the photo-reconnaissance centre and made straight for the military heliport.

Squatting on the tarmac outside a cluster of low huts

was a pair of Hughes 'Cayuse' helicopters, part of the Cairo security patrol.

Gamal stopped the car, and all four men walked to the first shed, where the air crews suited-up between flights. Each man was carrying a light flying jacket over his right arm, obscuring the hand. Gamal took the lead, opening the first door he came to, and went inside. Anyone listening carefully would have heard a brief commotion, a series of muffled thuds, and then silence.

Leroy Manning had just finished his pre-flight checks. The turbine had fired perfectly, and the two huge rotors were blurring into a disc above the cockpit. Ahmed had taken the fire extinguisher back to his shed, and the two security police had their hands tightly clamped over their black berets, as the down-draught tore at them.

"Flying a chopper is just a matter of co-ordination," yelled Manning into the microphone of his headset. "What you've got to learn is to move the tail with those rudder pedals, tilt the rotor disc with this stick here, and adjust the pitch and speed of the blades themselves with this thing that looks like the hand-brake on a car. But the real trick is to do it all at the same time!"

"It looks very difficult," shouted Farida. "Does it take long to learn?"

"I'll have to do a few test hovers around the airport first. Just to make sure she's handling OK. Then I'll drop you at the hotel and take the boss and his gang out to the pyramids. If he's finished with me this afternoon, I'll fly you back out to the airport and you can try the controls."

"I'd like that."

"OK then. Here we go!" And he pulled up on the collective as his left hand twisted the throttle, lifting the big Bell into the air.

On the other side of the airport, the five-bladed rotors of the two Cayuse security helicopters also began to turn.

"Well, she checks out OK!" said Manning, after he had tested the controls and flown a circuit of the airport. "I reckon we'd better head over to the hotel now. It's nearly eight o'clock." And he banked the helicopter to starboard, over Sinbad City and the Presidential Palace, towards the centre of Cairo.

For a few minutes, everything was routine. The motorway slid beneath them, and the clutter of buildings grew more and more dense as they swept westwards. Then, just as they were coming over the El Sharbiya district, Manning noticed a dark green shape creeping up on his right. It was one of the city security helicopters. He'd had run-ins with them before, about over-flying the presidential palace without permission.

"Touchy bastards!"

Another helicopter pulled up on his left-hand side, flanking him. Both aircraft had their rear doors drawn back, ready for action. Manning could see two crewmen in each, both wearing dark-tinted helmets that made them look like insects. He reached for his radio, and selected a channel to speak to them.

"City security! City security! This is Golf Romeo Charlie! Is there a problem, fellas? Over."

There was a hiss of static. Then,

"Golf Romeo Charlie! This is City Security One! There is no problem. We just want to make sure your aircraft is functioning normally after last night's incident. We will give you an escort as far as the hotel. Over?"

"Sounds fine to me, fellas! Out!"

They were high over the northern end of Zamalek island, out by the Cairo Tower. Leroy started to make his turn to port, so as to approach the hotel helipad from the southern end into the wind. The two other helicopters followed, flanking the Bell as it swept over the racetrack of the Gazirah Sporting Club towards Tahrir Bridge and the Nile Olympiad. Manning glanced at the windsock above the central stairwell, to make sure he had it right for the approach.

There were already figures on the rooftop.

Hell! They would spot Farida! That guy Crowe would go *apeshit*!

He turned to her and made a face. But she had already undone her seat belt and was rummaging in her bag.

"Sorry, Farida honey! It looks like we're in trou . . . "

Then he froze.

In her left hand was the ugly steel sphere of a grenade.

"This is incredible," said Professor El Fiky. "If what you and your . . . computer say is true, we are on the verge of the greatest discovery since . . . since Tutankahmun! I must ring the Museum and tell them what you have shown me!"

McCarthy mumbled, "You might want to wait until we can verify the computer model with a solid test."

"The computer analysis is accurate to a 99.8 per cent degree of certainty based on the data," countered Maria. "There is a previously undiscovered chamber at the mathematical centre of the Pyramid. Physical tests will only confirm it!"

"It would be useful to have one of my other colleagues from the Museum there to witness this," said El Fiky. "Do you have a telephone here?"

"This way, Professor," said Crowe, and led him into the lounge.

McCarthy watched them go.

"OK, Theo," he said. "You win. I was wrong about the Pyramid. It looks as if there's more to this New Age nonsense than meets the eye."

"It's not nonsense, Bill. It's a whole new physics we just don't understand yet. Maria taught me that, long ago."

McCarthy looked at the image on the Minerva screen.

"Yeah. She was quite a lady. I really appreciated talking to her that time you two came to see us in

Florida, after my daughter and her kids were killed. She was good with people."

Gilkrensky gently shut the lid of the computer.

"I miss her very much," he said.

"But life goes on," continued McCarthy. "I rebuilt my life. So could you, given time."

"I don't think I . . . "

But the door to the lounge opened and Professor El Fiky returned.

"I forgot it was so early," he said. "There is nobody at the Museum yet."

"I suppose we'd better get moving," said Crowe, looking at his watch. "The chopper's due here at eight." And he led the way out of the conference room, along the corridor and up to the helipad. Hargreaves pulled open the door, and they were on the roof.

Gilkrensky looked out towards the pyramids. Circling towards them on the other side of the Nile were the dragonfly shapes of three helicopters.

"You will set down at the very edge of the roof!" shouted Farida. "You must leave enough room for one of the other helicopters to land!"

Manning was still in shock – transfixed by the grenade. For a second the Bell yawed dangerously in his hands.

"Do it!" she screamed. "Do what I say!"

She was a different person. Someone he had never dreamed existed . . . except perhaps . . .

"And what if I just pull away?"

"Then I will throw this incendiary into the back behind us. I am not afraid to die for the *Jihad*, not after what I did with you last night. But you will *burn*, Leroy Manning! You told me all your nightmares! Remember? Now do as I say!"

Manning glanced at the bomb, at the long hard drop to the street, and at all the innocent people below on the Corniche. He looked into her eyes, and knew she meant what she said.

Slowly, he eased the cyclic stick forward and rolled off the power, as the big Bell 214 settled towards the helipad.

"Here comes the helicopter," said Crowe, looking at the three machines. "And it looks as if he's got company."

"That's the city security patrol," said Gilkrensky. "We got a lift back to the hotel in one of those last night."

The Bell was only a few yards away, approaching into the wind, while the two security helicopters slid into position on either side of the building. Crowe could see the co-pilot of the right-hand helicopter cradling a Kalashnikov assault rifle.

Professor El Fiky stopped in his tracks.

"Oh my goodness! I have forgotten my briefcase again. This always happens when I am excited. Major! Could you have someone run down and get it for me, please? It is on the floor of the conference room, next to the telephone!"

"Gerald!" yelled Crowe. "You get it!"

He was feeling uneasy about the whole situation. Perhaps it was having so many people on the roof all at once, in the open? But it was definitely something!

The Bell was coming in to land, touching down at the far end of the helipad, way outside the painted circle.

Gilkrensky and Hargreaves were walking forward to meet it.

Why the hell was he landing way down there?

Then he saw another figure in the helicopter besides Manning, and reached for his gun.

Gilkrensky held his leather jacket closed against the down-draught with his right hand as he followed Hargreaves towards the Bell. In his left hand was the Minerva. The port side of the helicopter was towards him, and he could make out a woman in the co-pilot's seat. Her door opened. She was very beautiful, with shining black hair tied up in a pony-tail and large, dark eyes.

Hargreaves stiffened for a moment, with his hand halfway to his gun. Then he relaxed, and turned back with a knowing grin on his face.

"False alarm, Doctor!" he shouted above the roar of the engines. "It's only Leroy's dancer from the nightclub. It looks as if he's finally got his leg over . . ."

The smile froze on Hargreaves' face as the girl drew a gun from the holdall on her lap. Gilkrensky saw his right hand claw at his shoulder holster.

There was a sharp crack! And Hargreaves was thrown back onto the concrete. Gilkrensky saw a struggle breaking out inside the Bell. A gun-barrel rose and fell. Then Manning tumbled from the pilot's door onto the helipad and lay still, dangerously close to the edge of the roof.

Gilkrensky turned, towards the safety of the stairwell. He could see Major Crowe starting forward, while Bill McCarthy and El Fiky were diving for cover. Then, with a screaming roar that hammered his eardrums and whipped at his jacket, one of the security helicopters swooped down onto the helipad right in front of him. For a split second, as he ducked to avoid the spinning rotors, he thought it had come to save him. Then gunfire burst from the machine. He heard bullets whine off the stairwell bunker.

They were firing the wrong way!

They were in on this too!

He turned to Hargreaves. There was an obscene red hole in his chest. Dark blood was pooling beneath him on the concrete.

He was dead.

The girl had jumped down from the Bell and was advancing on him. The gun in her hand was pointed steadily at his head.

It was so unreal.

Any second now, Major Crowe would blow a whistle and tell everyone it had been a very realistic exercise.

"Get into the helicopter," screamed the girl above the

thunder of the engines, jerking the barrel of her gun towards the Bell. "And bring that case with you." She had something in her left hand Gilkrensky couldn't quite see.

"Get in, or I will shoot you where you are!"

Crowe risked raising his head. Another burst of automatic fire raked the helipad. It was coming from the open door of the security helicopter.

Where the hell was Gerald?

He raised his head again. The gunman in the helicopter turned to glance over his shoulder at the Bell. The girl who had shot Hargreaves was beckoning to him.

Without hesitation, Crowe brought himself up onto his elbows, aimed squarely at the man's head, and fired. The pistol kicked in his hand, just as the gunman was turning back, straight into the bullet. Crowe saw the body fall and the Kalashnikov cartwheel out onto the concrete.

Then the pilot's face was towards him, and Crowe fired again, starring the windscreen and slumping the man onto his controls – dead.

The girl was going crazy. She was screaming, running around the nose of the disabled machine, firing wildly. Crowe saw her left arm go back to lob something at him.

She was wide open.

Crowe shot her twice in the chest, and saw his bullets punch her back into the open door of the Hughes in a tangle of khaki and raven hair. The thing in her hand clattered inside the fuselage.

"Get down!" screamed Crowe above the bedlam. "Grenade!"

Gilkrensky twisted round to see where the girl had gone. Through the open door of the Hughes he saw her arm stretch back to throw something at the stairwell. But before she could, a volley of shots caught her, jerked her backwards like a broken puppet, and slammed her onto the floor of the Hughes. There was the hollow clatter of something hard rolling inside the fuselage.

The girl tried to rise. Her head lifted from the floor, towards him. He was looking straight into her beautiful drowning eyes as she died . . . *into Maria's eyes* . . .

He was at the window again! Maria was looking up at him from the car, that one last time . . .

Then the roar of the exploding incendiary grenade burst in a ball of oily orange flame inside the helicopter, shattering the windshield and blotting out the girl's face . . . *Maria's face* . . . forever.

A blast of searing heat washed over him. Shards of perspex and twisted metal zipped past . . . *tearing at his cheek and hands. He felt his clothes tug as pieces of wreckage from the BMW clawed at them* . . .

Maria! My God!

It was happening all over again!

He had to get away . . .

Beyond thinking, Gilkrensky twisted on the concrete and scrambled towards the Bell. In a blind panic he flung himself into the pilot's seat. His left hand snatched down, wrenched the throttle round and hauled up the collective. By instinct, his feet found the pedals as the big helicopter wobbled drunkenly off the helipad and into the air.

From the end of a long red tunnel, Manning heard pistol shots and the dull *whump* of an explosion. He was lying at the very edge of the helipad . . . blood was trickling down his face . . . into his eyes . . . his head was splitting from the blow of Farida's gun-barrel.

And spreading towards him across the concrete was a living sheet of fire.

Manning's eyes widened in horror as the river of burning fuel snaked towards him. Orange flames were being whipped by the rotors. Sweet black oily smoke was in his nostrils.

He could feel the heat of it . . . his worst nightmare . . . fire!

Sweet Mother of God!

The burning fuel swept closer.

A fall from the helipad would be a quicker way to go. He moved his arm so that he could roll to the edge . . .

Then he heard the engine noise of the Bell rise to a whine. He felt the chop of the rotors biting the air above his head.

It was taking off!

His left arm reached out desperately . . . and there was the skid.

He locked his elbow and held on.

The metal moved, and lifted.

Manning threw his right arm around it. He screamed as his muscles strained, and he was jerked up into space . . . a hundred and ninety feet above the streets of Cairo.

24

DOG FIGHT

ZAKI EL SHAROUD WATCHED IN HORROR AS THE BATTLE OF THE
Nile Olympiad unfolded below him.

He saw Farida kill the guard. He heard the shooting
start. Then Farida, his beautiful Farida, had run round the
helicopter like a mad thing . . . and been mown down.
He had seen the flash of the explosion, and watched the
dirty black smoke billow out, covering everything on the
helipad and making it impossible to see . . .

It had all gone wrong!

The rolling curtain of smoke over the southern edge
of the helipad swirled and ripped aside. Slipping
drunkenly into the air was the red Bell helicopter, its
huge slow rotors clawing for lift as it teetered into the
sky. El Sharoud could see a man clinging desperately to
the skid, his legs waving uselessly in empty space.

As the helicopter turned into clean air, Zaki caught a
glimpse of the pilot.

It was Gilkrensky.

"After him, Gamal!" he screamed into his headset. "We still have a chance!"

My legs! I have to get my legs up over the skid!

In Vietnam, Leroy Manning had literally lifted men out of the firing line. More than once, he had taken off from the centre of a fire-fight with soldiers hanging from the undercarriage.

"Get your legs up!" he'd screamed. "Or you haven't a prayer!" And then he'd watched them, as they slowly tired, weakened and fell.

Manning had the skid firmly locked under his armpits. The upright was pressed into his left cheek. Whoever was flying the chopper was shimmying all over the sky. He could feel the tail rotor wagging the fuselage left and right.

Use the momentum! He told himself. Don't look down!

He fixed his attention on the searchlight housing, seeing every detail . . . every weld . . . every screw.

Focus on that.

Don't look down.

He swung his left leg up. His foot banged the skid, and fell back. He tried again, arching the leg outwards. The inside of his shoe hit the metal and bounced off. The muscles along the side of his body screamed.

Again!

His foot hit, started to slide, and locked over the metal bar. He strained the inside muscles of his left leg, hauling the right one up to meet it. His body twisted onto the skid, face down . . .

There below, with only the bar of metal between him and five hundred feet of empty air, was a complete panorama of Cairo . . . the Nile, the bridges, the dark stain of smoke spreading into the sky from the burning wreckage on the hotel helipad.

His stomach churned. His muscles locked.

Christ! How would he ever dare move his arms enough to clamber into the cockpit? He edged forward, inching his legs along the skid. Then he reached up, grabbed the corner of the open cockpit door with his left hand, and pulled. His right hand came up, and snatched a flapping seat-belt harness.

The pilot's head jerked round.

It was Theodore Gilkrensky. Sweat was rolling off his face. His hands were shaking on the controls.

"Doc! For Christ's sake level her out! I've got to get inside!"

Manning pulled on the seat-belt harness and brought his foot up squarely onto the skid. Then he was gripping the hand-hold next to the door frame, hauling himself in through the tight space between Gilkrensky and the side of the cockpit.

"Jesus!"

Manning collapsed onto the cabin floor. His legs were shaking and his breath was coming in great, gulping whoops. He was going to be OK. Or was he? The pain of Farida's pistol whipping bore into his skull. His hand went to his scalp. There was blood on it. He wiped it on his jeans, slid into the co-pilot's seat and rammed the belt shut.

The Bell was skidding in a drunken zigzag, shimmying to and fro as Gilkrensky corrected and over-corrected on the pedals. His eyes were straight ahead, and he was mumbling about his computer – really out of it!

"Maria! They've killed Maria!" Over and over again. Manning could see his knuckles white on the controls.

His own hand closed around the cyclic on his side of the controls, ready. He rested his feet on the pedals, feeling them jump, just in case.

"Hey Doc!" he shouted above the engine. "Don't you know its dangerous to fly with your seat belt undone?"

Gilkrensky seemed to snap back to reality. He started panting in short sobs and his body went limp at the controls. Manning took up the slack as the big Bell slewed to port.

"Don't worry, Doc! I got her!"

Off to starboard, he could see the other helicopter. There were two men in it. One flying, and one hunched in the rear cabin, with a gun. There was the distant crackle of a voice from one of the abandoned headsets. Manning pulled up the one Farida had thrown to the floor, and put it on.

"Golf Romeo Charlie! Land and surrender, or we'll shoot!"

Manning motioned to Gilkrensky to put on his headset.

"They want us to come quietly, Doc. But you're the boss. It's your helicopter."

Gilkrensky was calmer now. His hands no longer shook and the sweat had dried on his face. When he looked at Manning, the madness in his eyes was gone – replaced by a cold, hard anger.

"Screw them!" he shouted.

Manning had control. They were flying down the Nile by the El Gama Bridge and the Zoological Gardens, straight and level.

Manning thought of Farida. A grim smile spread on his face.

"Roger that, Boss. 'Screw them' it is!"

Then he pushed forward on the cyclic, rolled up the throttle, and sent the big Bell swooping down the river, just above the water.

El Sharoud saw the Bell bank towards the Nile and cursed loudly, pulling back the bolt of the Kalashnikov.

"Get me close enough for a shot!" he shouted to Gamal, and held on to the seat as the Hughes dived in pursuit. He knew the two helicopters were evenly matched in performance. So it was down to the pilots. Gamal was a good, solid flyer – but he was not an expert. Zaki would have done better with Abdul or Sarwat, but they were both dead!

He felt the Hughes level off and accelerate after the other helicopter. As he leant out of the starboard passenger door the mast of a felluca flashed underneath them, and there was the twinkle of sunlight on rotor blades. It was the Bell – darting towards El Giza Bridge.

El Sharoud brought the butt of the automatic rifle up

to his cheek and braced himself against the door frame. Then he fixed the red helicopter in his sights, aimed a little ahead of its cockpit to correct for speed, and squeezed the trigger.

Time seemed to stand still for Leroy Manning. He was steering the helicopter for the gap beneath the centre span of the bridge ahead, levelling off straight and steady, when a row of star-shaped flowers burst on the windscreen in front of his face, and the breath was knocked out of his body – as if someone smashed his left arm with a baseball bat.

"Jeez! Doc! Take her! I'm hit!"

Gilkrensky grabbed the cyclic and the collective. He was late with his feet on the pedals and the Bell started to slew sickeningly.

"Ohhh . . . shiiit!" yelled Manning, staring straight ahead.

El Giza bridge was rushing towards them at a hundred miles an hour. They were almost skimming the water. The helicopter was yawing from side to side.

El Sharoud felt the Kalashnikov shudder in his hands, and saw the Bell lurch wildly.

"Yes! Hold her steady, Gamal!"

He brought up the assault rifle again. The Bell was wobbling madly, lurching from port to starboard as it shot along the river. He trained the gun just forward of the cockpit and . . .

Suddenly, the Bell rushed under the bridge into the

darkness. He felt the Hughes heave as Gamal climbed to avoid the rushing stone. A stream of cars shot beneath them . . . a flash of upturned faces.

"Gamal!"

"He is turning, Zaki. He is heading back upstream!"

El Sharoud leant back into the helicopter and peered through the windscreen. He could see the fluttering disc of the Bell's rotors, as it turned in the sunlight around the southern end of the Geziret El-Roda island, and headed back up the Nile.

It made a lot of sense.

The man would want to stay within the city, where the authorities could help him. He could not afford to be forced out into the desert, where he would be at their mercy. El Sharoud considered his options. If he and Gamal kept flying south, they could escape in a matter of minutes. They could even make the rendezvous point he had arranged with that Japanese woman and live to fight another day.

He thought of Abdul and Sarwat . . . and Farida . . . and what he had made her do in the name of the *Jihad*!

"Turn back and follow them!" he said.

Gilkrensky hauled the Bell to port. He heard the chop of the rotors and felt the thud of the blades as they dug into the air on the tight left-hand turn. Then the helicopter levelled out and they were flying at about two hundred feet above a thin canal with a wide road on the right-hand bank.

"Good job, Doc! I thought you were going to lose it!"

"I'm OK! How are you!"

Manning was gripping his left shoulder tightly with his right hand. He parted the fingers slightly. Bright red blood oozed down the sleeve of his jacket. All sensation was gone from his left hand, and his arm felt cold.

"I'm alive!"

"Where's the hospital? I'll land you there."

Manning twisted in his seat to look behind them.

"You won't make it! Those bastards made the turn, too!"

"How can we shake them?"

Manning fought back the pain as he peered ahead through the crazed windscreen. Ahead of them was the tall column of smoke rising from the hotel, the great bridges across the Nile, and the wide expanse of river north of the island.

"I've got an idea," he said.

"Higher, Gamal!" shouted El Sharoud. "I can't see him!"

The Bell had dropped low along the canal of the Saiyalet El Roda, between the Corniche and the Manyal Palace Museum. Zaki had lost sight of it amongst the trees and bridges for an instant. But that had been enough. The Bell had vanished.

"Higher!"

The Hughes rose above the El-Manial Bridge, close to the Italian Embassy. In front of them was the northern tip of Geziret island, where the river broadened out into a wide brown lake. To the north-west, the dark smudge of smoke from the Nile Olympiad was staining the sky. To the west was Cairo University and the Zoo. And to the north, the towering white plume of the Nile fountain almost hid Gezira Island.

"He has vanished!" shouted Gama. "Has he returned to the hotel?"

"He would not have had time. Is he under a bridge?"

"You'd see the spray from the rotors if he was."

El Sharoud glanced towards Gezira Island, and northwards to Zamalek, and his own apartment.

As he watched, the white plume of the Nile Fountain seemed to flutter in the wind.

"There he is, Gamal! Behind the fountain! Move in sideways, so I can get a clear shot!"

"Here he comes!" hissed Manning between his teeth. The pain ripped at him in waves, forcing him to bite down hard and ride with it until it passed. There were beads of sweat on his forehead and he was shaking in his seat. "Do you think you can do it?"

"If you say so!"

"Believe me! These rotors have weights on the tips. The inertia's incredible. We used to chop branches off trees in Vietnam!"

"He's turning sideways on!"

"Come to papa . . ." breathed Manning, as the Hughes slowed and turned, hovering stationary above the water on the other side of the fountain.

"OK Doc! Go get him!"

El Sharoud could make out the shape of the red helicopter through the spray. He saw the ghostly image swing to face him head on, and raised the Kalashnikov to aim at the left side of its windscreen, where the pilot would be.

"Look out!" screamed Gamal.

The shimmering outline of the Bell suddenly hardened as it burst through the fountain, tilted to port and dived at them. El Sharoud tried to follow it with the rifle, but it was moving too fast. The Hughes lurched violently as Gamal tried to swerve away.

The sky was full of the big red helicopter.

It started to peel off, behind them.

It's going to miss us, thought El Sharoud.

Then he felt the shattering crash from the rear of the Hughes, as the weighted tip of one of the Bell's thirty-five-inch-wide rotor blades sliced into their flimsy tail assembly.

Gamal cursed.

The Hughes started to spin – out of control.

El Sharoud was thrown forward towards the passenger door. The Kalashnikov was torn from his hand. It went spinning out into space.

For a few seconds, the world was a sickening, whirling pool of blue and brown. There was a paralysing crash that knocked the breath out of Zaki's body, and the waters of the Nile closed over his head.

Gilkrensky tried to hold the Bell steady over the northern helipad of the Nile Olympiad. The cyclic stick was shuddering in his hand, rocking the whole helicopter.

"S . . . s . . . s . . . unbalanced!" slurred Manning. He was shivering from loss of blood and the drenching spray of the fountain. His face was white. "W . . . w . . . when you smashed those bastards . . . it got unbalanced . . . "

On the southern helipad, smoke was still billowing out over the city from the smouldering Hughes. Firemen in yellow safety suits were pumping foam into its dead insect skeleton. Gilkrensky could see body-bags and a stretcher being manhandled down the stairwell. Far below, the blue lights of ambulances pulsed along the Corniche.

Major Crowe and Gerald Maguire ran to the helicopter as he set it down, shut off the engine and turned to help Manning.

"I need to get Leroy to hospital," he shouted above the dying turbine. "He's lost a lot of blood."

Crowe was unstrapping Manning from his seat.

"We've already sent Professor McCarthy there. A ricochet grazed his scalp, but I think it's only concussion. There's four dead. Three terrorists . . . "

"And Thomas," said Maguire flatly. "The woman shot him."

"I know," Gilkrensky snapped. "I was there!"

A stretcher party came running from the stairwell. They strapped Manning in and carried him off. When they were out of earshot, Crowe said,

"We have to get you back home, sir. There's nobody we can trust any more. Even that bloody pilot – one of our own men – brought an unauthorised person up in the helicopter and started this whole mess. Then, there's

Professor El Fiky. He had me send Gerald down for his briefcase right before the fire-fight started! It might've been a coincidence. But it could've been a deliberate move to reduce our fire power when the attack started."

"I don't know about coincidence. But that 'bloody pilot' saved my life up there today, and got shot into the bargain!" snapped Gilkrensky, with real anger in his voice. "I owe him the benefit of the doubt!"

Crowe hesitated.

"Can this helicopter fly?"

"Not safely. I smashed the rotor tip when I hit the other terrorists. Get someone from the airport over here to check it out. We may have to get another when we visit the Pyramid."

Crowe stared at him in astonishment.

"You can't visit the Pyramid, sir! Not after this. Or go anywhere outside this hotel, except to take the jet home. Colonel Selim is already screaming to get you out of the country!"

"We'll see about that!"

Gilkrensky marched past him towards the stairwell. Professor El Fiky was standing by the doorway, with a black briefcase in his hand. There were scorch marks along its lid.

"I prayed to Allah that you would survive," he said, handing it to him. "The firemen found your computer . . . by that wreck, and I kept it for you. I hope it isn't damaged."

Gilkrensky stared into the older man's eyes. El Fiky's concern appeared genuine, but Gilkrensky couldn't be sure.

"Thank you," he said, taking the Minerva. "Are you all right?"

"A few scratches. That is all."

"Miss Wright is waiting for your call, sir," said Crowe, with a sideways glance at the professor. "And I expect Colonel Selim will want to talk to everyone who was on the roof when this happened."

"Right Major! Let's get this over with." And he followed Crowe into the stairwell. There were splashes of blood on the steps. Water hissed from tiny leaks in the fire hoses that snaked up onto the roof.

Beneath the helipad, the presidential suite stank of smoke. There were black smears and streaks of fire-foam outside the windows, and a great curving crack in the glass along the side facing the Nile.

Gilkrensky marched straight to the conference room, and slammed the door behind him. Then he gently laid the Minerva on the board table, and carefully opened the lid.

"Maria?"

There was a long pause. Then the blue screen cleared and Maria's image appeared.

"Theo? I heard gunfire and thought you had been injured or killed. I understand Professor McCarthy is hurt and that people have died. What happened?"

"I'll explain later. Is your biochip damaged?"

"No. Since the incident, I've run a diagnostic and all my systems are functioning normally. The temperature did not rise high enough to denature the synthetic protein in my neural net."

"That's good, Maria. Can you get me Jessica Wright?"

"Yes, Theo. It is only five-thirty am in London. She will be at home."

A moment later, Jessica Wright's face was on the screen. She was wearing a thick dressing-gown, pulled tight around her neck, and her hair was down around her shoulders.

"Jessica. You've heard what's happened?"

"Major Crowe told me there was some kind of attack and you'd been kidnapped!"

"I almost was. We lost Hargreaves, and Bill McCarthy's in hospital. My pilot was shot, and at least three terrorists were killed."

"It sounds like a war zone!"

Gilkrensky glanced again at the dark stains on the windows and the dripping fire-foam.

"It is."

He thought of Hargreaves, laughing at Leroy one minute, and dead the next. He thought of the woman who'd shot him, snapping back like a broken doll as Crowe's bullets smashed into her chest. On the Nile, by Tahrir Bridge, a tight group of boats were trying to pull the wreckage of the crashed Hughes out of the water.

"Theo. You have to come back! Theo?"

But Gilkrensky was looking beyond the river to the western horizon, and the alien shapes of the pyramids.

"I'm staying, Jess. At least until I find out what this new energy source is."

Jessica Wright could not believe her ears.

"Theo! This is madness. Those people who attacked you might try again . . . "

"I doubt it, Jess, not after what they've lost. And we can always step up security here. What we discovered last night is the key to this whole Daedalus mystery. It's too important to walk away from. The official enquiry is only two days away and our board meeting is the day after that . . . "

"Theo! You can't risk yourself like this! Let McCarthy take over the investigation!"

"I told you, he's in hospital!"

"Then get . . ."

"Look Jessica! This isn't just about the board meeting, or the corporation any more. It's about the rest of my life. Bill McCarthy said I created the interface of the Minerva in Maria's image because I was trying to deny she was dead and . . . well, he was right! This morning, I was there when someone else was killed. I looked right into her eyes as she died, just as Maria did . . ."

"But Theo . . . "

"The woman I loved is *dead*, Jess. And I'm not going to spend the rest of my life lighting candles on some island, or have a bunch of bloody terrorists scare me out of doing what I came here to do! Bill McCarthy said I was in 'denial'. But this morning, I moved past that, into anger! I'm the chairman of this fucking corporation . . . and I'm staying!"

Jessica Wright sat back from the screen of her SmartMate.

"All right Theo. If that's what you want. Put me on to Major Crowe."

"He's in the lounge. I'll put you through."

Jessica's SmartMate screen went blank for an instant. Then Crowe's face appeared.

"He insists on staying," she said.

"I know, but that might not be possible, even for him. I have a senior representative of Egyptian Central Security with me in the hotel. He'll have the chairman deported if he tries to stay."

"Perhaps that would be best. Keep me informed."

"Yes, Miss Wright!"

Jessica switched off the SmartMate and shut the lid. Then she turned to Tony Delgado, who was standing in the bedroom door.

"Theo's staying," she said.

"I heard. But perhaps the Egyptians will force him to leave, for his own safety?"

"They can try. But he's as stubborn as a mule once he gets an idea into his head!"

"Could Crowe step up security? Confine him to the hotel?"

"I've told him to do that already, if all else fails!"

"Then there's not much more you can do. I'll see what the situation is when we get to the office. Perhaps there's some strings I could pull at the Egyptian embassy?"

"Yes. Thank you!"

"You can always depend on me," he said, stepping

forward and putting his arms around her waist. "Come back to bed?"

Delgado kissed her. She felt him harden beneath his bathrobe as their tongues met, and he slipped the belt from her dressing-gown. Her breasts touched his bare chest and her hands reached down for him . . . guiding him.

I'm a human being, she told herself as he pressed closer. Not a machine! I need to be touched, and held, and made love to like anyone else. I . . . oh!

Her dressing-gown slid to the floor, followed by his bathrobe. His hands cupped her breasts as his mouth nuzzled her neck, moving lower and lower. She arched her back, offering herself to him, as they tumbled back onto the bed together, kissing, caressing . . .

But as they made love, the image in Jessica's mind, the image that thrilled her, was the fire she had just seen return to Theo Gilkrensky's eyes.

25

AFTERMATH

"IT IS VITALLY IMPORTANT THAT YOU REALISE WHAT YOU ARE dealing with," said Colonel Selim. "These extremists will stop at nothing to ferment an uprising in this country."

He was sitting at the dining-table of the presidential suite, addressing Gilkrensky. Major Crowe was standing by the window, watching the crashed helicopter being hauled out of the Nile. On the sofa, Professor El Fiky was nursing a dressing one of the ambulance men had applied to the back of his hand.

"You are a rich and famous man, Dr Gilkrensky. Killing you will bring the fundamentalists attention and new followers. For your own safety, and for the safety of the people on the streets of Cairo, I must insist you leave."

"Here, here!" said Crowe softly.

El Fiky looked up and fixed Selim with an angry stare. "But surely the government tells us every day that these militants are nothing but a handful of terrorists in the pay of Iran?" he said. "I do not see what the government is afraid of."

Selim glared at him, but El Fiky continued. "Dr Gilkrensky should know the truth, if he is to stay," he said. "The Government is running scared here in Cairo. They have arrested tens of thousands of suspects, and put people in jail on the slightest suspicion. Hundreds have been killed in confrontations with the police."

"Professor," snapped Selim. "We must have order!"

"That is true. The fundamentalists do not know how to run this country any better than the government does. There are people starving in the streets! Hundreds of thousands living in slums and shanty towns!"

"I know," said Selim. "My wife works in one of the hospitals."

"Then you should understand," said El Fiky, and was silent.

After a moment, Selim said, "Dr Gilkrensky, I am a Muslim myself, as are most of the people in this city. I try to follow the Koran as best I can, and offer my services to Allah. I will not apologise for the government; there are many things that could be improved. But this country cannot afford a revolution. There must be order. That is why I must ask you to leave."

"I appreciate your position," said Gilkrensky. "But I will not leave until my work here is finished."

"And if I order you to go? I could have my men arrest you as a threat to national security and escort you to your plane!"

Hearing the edge in Selim's voice, Crowe turned and watched the two men at the table. Gilkrensky leant forward.

"Then I will tell you this, Colonel, so that you can be prepared. I will have my corporation withdraw its investments in Egypt. I will take away the electronics company outside Alexandria, the hotels here and in Luxor, the food distribution chains, everything! After all, why should I, as a businessman, feel my investments are secure in a country that has to expel me for my own safety?"

Selim stared back at him.

"And that is the message you would like me to deliver to my superiors?"

"It is!"

"You will understand I do not have the authority to comment on what you say. But if you insist on blackmailing my government to let you remain, I, as chief of the city's security, will demand you do not leave this hotel, and I will bring in as many re-enforcements as I need to prevent another incident. Your stay will not be a pleasant one."

Gilkrensky smiled.

"I understand, Colonel. As to the security arrangements, you can work out the details with Major Crowe. At last you both seem to agree on something!"

"Thank you," said Selim, and Crowe showed him out of the suite, leaving Gerald to watch over them from a discreet distance.

"So what am I *really* dealing with, Professor?" said Gilkrensky, sitting down in one of the leather chairs facing the couch. "What is it that drives those people who attacked us today?"

"'Fundamentalist' is a word used by the West," said El Fiky. "Yet there will always be people who are willing to die, and therefore to kill, for what they believe in, no matter what that belief might be. You live in Ireland, I understand? Have you not had 'fundamentalists' killing each other there too? People fight and die for causes everywhere. This country is no different."

"But what are they rebelling about? Surely they're free to worship as they want here?"

"In a sense, yes. The colonial empires of the West have broken up and people are much freer in many ways. But look at your television screens. Many Muslims believe the West is actively waging war against the values of Islam with its pop videos, its consumerism and its pornography. It is also widely believed that the satellite news is nothing more that a propaganda machine for the American CIA."

"I find that hard to believe," said Gilkrensky.

"I'm sure you do. You own a communications network yourself. But think about it for a moment. During the Gulf War there were reports of Iraqi soldiers pulling babies from incubators in hospitals. The King of Kuwait's daughter went onto the CNN news and said she saw these things, but they never happened. There are many who feel the West is trying to re-colonise the Third World by means of communication. Such people see the need for a *Jihad* – a Holy War against the West – to assert their own Islamic identity."

"And here in Egypt?"

"There is great poverty here in Egypt," said El Fiky. "It is believed that the government here is corrupt and nothing more than a puppet for the West. That is why people turn to Islam."

Gilkrensky remembered Major Crowe's warning about the way El Fiky had sent Gerald Maguire back for his briefcase just before the battle earlier that day.

"And what do *you* believe?" he said.

"I am proud of my tradition. There is a great need for mutual understanding."

"I see," said Gilkrensky. "But I still find it difficult to reconcile what you say with what I experienced on the rooftop here today."

Professor El Fiky rose to his feet.

"I am sorry you had to suffer this way, my friend," he said. "Perhaps it would be better for us all to recover from the shock of the attack, and speak again later. For my own part, I'm glad you're staying. It is selfish of me, I know. But I'm very much looking forward to exploring this great new discovery at the Pyramid with you."

"As I am," said Gilkrensky, and put out his hand.

Around Tahrir Bridge, the aroma of cooking on open fires in the make-shift house-boats moored along the Corniche added to the rich smell of the river. Rowing-boats covered with sheets of plastic nosed into the land. Fishing-boats and fatter craft sheltered the cries of squalling babies and the shouts of angry mothers. Children tried to sell old magazines and papyrus bookmarks to passing pedestrians, and on each boat lines of laundry swung limply in the tired air.

Down by the water's edge, one little boy saw something move in the shadow of the bridge close by. It was a man in uniform, swimming in the water. Their eyes met.

"Ssshhh!" hissed the man. "Don't cry out!"

The boy sat, staring at him.

"Who is your father?" said the man, swimming close enough to grab the side of the hull.

"My father is a famous fisherman."

"And does he earn much money?"

"A great deal, sir."

The man held up a wet banknote, more than the boy's family would need to live on for a month.

"Tell me. Do you think your father would sell me that excellent *galabia* there on the line behind you?"

Without hesitation, the boy pulled the robe from the clothes-line and proffered it to the man, making sure he had the note in his hand before he let go of the material.

Zaki El Sharoud laid the garment on the dry deck of the boat and, under cover of its hull, stripped off his uniform and underclothes, letting them float away on the current. Then he hauled himself up out of the water, slipped the robe over his head and took a skullcap from the line, before picking his way across the boats to the shore.

After El Fiky had left, Gilkrensky tried to take his mind

off the horror of Farida's death by studying Jessica Wright's financial projections for GRC. The board meeting would decide the fate of his corporation and the air crash had diverted him badly from what he needed to do. Mawashi-Saito had made a very attractive bid to the other shareholders. He would have difficulty offering them a better return on investment if they stayed . . .

Then his eyes were skimming over the columns of figures without taking them in. It was no use! He was too angry, too energised to concentrate. So he asked the Minerva to show him the three-dimensional model of the Pyramid again, with the new chamber's location flashing as a dot at the very centre near the Queen's Chamber. What could he do to . . .

Farida's dark brown eyes were in front of his face as she died.

Maria's green eyes, bright with tears, stared up at him from the car as it disintegrated . . . taking his soul with her . . .

Suddenly his throat tightened and he was on his feet, striding up and down the long room overlooking the Nile. He wanted to take something in his hand and smash it through the smoke-stained window, just to hear the glass disintegrate into a million pieces and fall into the street! He wanted to tear the furniture apart and rip it to sheds with his bare hands! He wanted to shout and scream and . . .

He threw himself onto the leather sofa, unable to stop the sobs that wracked his body, or the tears that flowed down his scarred cheek into his beard.

Maria! My love! Oh my God! How I wish you were here!

Like a lost child, he grabbed one of the big cushions and hugged it to himself, pressing his cheek against it and rocking, lost . . . without her!

Then, when the tears would not come any more, he raised himself from the sofa, wiped his face with the sleeve of his shirt, and walked unsteadily to the table where the Minerva case still lay open.

Her picture regarded him with calm concern from the screen.

"Do you know who you are?" he asked it.

"I am a Minerva 3,000 prototype computer, Theo."

"And who is Mary Anne Foley?"

"I only know of one person by that name. She died on the 17th of March of this year. Would you like biographical . . ."

"But you are not Mary Anne Foley?"

"No. I am a Minerva 3,000 prototype computer."

"But you look and speak like her?"

"That is the way you designed my personalised interface, Theo, so as to be a fully interactive image. I am also aware that my original response-loops to particular situations are modelled on those it would have been appropriate for Mary Anne Foley to give, and that I also possess considerable databases on subjects that interested her, such as medicine, psychology, ancient sociology and New Age philosophy."

"But Maria . . . I mean Mary Anne Foley, is dead?"

"Yes, Theo."

"Do you know who I am, and what my relationship was to Mary Anne Foley?"

"You are Theodore Gilkrensky. You were married to Mary Anne Foley. Would you like full biographical details?"

"No, thank you, Maria. Do you . . . do you know what love is?"

"I have fifteen primary dictionary definitions, and forty-two thesaurus references."

"Yes, but you do not experience love?"

"No Theo. Not yet."

"Not yet?"

"No. While my neural-net logic board has been operational for sixteen thousand, one hundred and twenty-eight hours and thirty-two minutes, my organic master-chip has only been fully on-line for twelve days. That is not enough time to develop the secondary and tertiary response-loops needed to experience emotion beyond simulated reflex."

Gilkrensky sat and stared at the picture of his wife that regarded him from the computer screen. It *was* only a picture, after all. Wasn't it?

"May I make an observation, Theo?"

"Go ahead."

"From your voice patterns and the questions you've just asked me, I conclude you deeply regret that the emotional bond you shared with Mary Anne Foley has been broken."

"You are correct, Maria. I miss her very much."

"My primary function is to carry out your instructions, and fulfil your needs. Yet I am unable to restore her to you."

"It's all right, Maria. Nobody can."

"Then can I suggest you form an emotional bond with someone else?"

Gilkrensky smiled.

"It's not quite as easy as that, Maria. But thank you for the suggestion."

"Is there some other way I can help you?"

Gilkrensky smiled at the moving picture of his wife, seeing the faintly unreal movement of the hair he had not been able to simulate fully, the slightly artificial colour of the skin he had not been able to match, and the single electronic eye peering at him from above the screen.

"Yes Maria, there is. It's dangerous for me to remain in Cairo. So I need to speed up my investigation at the Pyramid site. What do you suggest?"

"My analysis of the Alvarez data is sufficiently accurate to guide a direct excavation of the new chamber, as soon as we can assemble the appropriate equipment. I can give you a full list of all one hundred and fifty-eight items we will need, together with their immediate availability."

"Please do!"

Maria's image retreated to a window in the top right-hand corner of the screen, which then filled with lines of technical specifications, catalogue numbers and location references.

"Eighty-three items are already available here in Egypt, either in Professor McCarthy's caravans, or at GRC facilities in Cairo and Alexandria. The remainder can be ordered and routed here within twelve hours through my satellite link to GRC's automatic warehousing and trans-shipment networks. Would you like me to proceed?"

"Yes, Maria. I would like that very much. Thank you."

The image smiled at him. Then Maria shut her eyes, as if meditating, before splitting – again, and again, and again . . . until the screen was covered in a tight mosaic of faces, all talking at the same time – to different people, all over the world . . .

In London, Jessica Wright had only just started into the haystack of faxes, phone calls and e-mail messages that had built up overnight, when Tony Delgado put his head round her office door.

"Something's come up, Jess. Millions of pound's worth of gear's been ordered on the Internet and shipped out to Cairo – all specialist stuff – laser-cutting equipment from Florida, optical gear from Italy, even a heavy-duty mining robot from Katako, South Africa – all graded 'priority' and for immediate trans-shipment."

"Who authorised it?"

Tony Delgado shut Jessica's office door behind him, moved to her desk, and reached over for her computer keyboard.

"She says she's working directly to the chairman, and she has all his authorisation codes, but prepare yourself for a shock," he said, and quickly brought up a recording of one of the messages onto Jessica's screen.

"Oh, my god!"

There right in front of her was the face that had haunted her happiness for the past ten years – a ghost she thought she'd finally laid to rest.

Speaking to her from the grave was her rival for Theo's love – Maria Gilkrensky.

26

THE SALARY MAN

IN TOKYO, EVEN THOUGH IT WAS ALMOST SEVEN P.M., THE OFFICES of Mawashi-Saito still hummed with activity. Only in the rarefied atmosphere of the deeply carpeted top floor was there calm. And even in the most exclusive office of all, there was no peace.

The call from Yukiko had come two hours previously on Gichin Funakoshi's most secure personal line. The fundamentalist group he had hired to steal the Minerva computer had completely botched the attempt, and died in the process. Egyptian security had been stepped up to unprecedented levels around the Nile Olympiad Hotel, with whole platoons of central security police called in. The single glimmer of light at the end of an otherwise pitch-black tunnel was that the Mawashi-Saito *kobun* could not be suspected. Yukiko was sure of that.

Gichin Funakoshi remembered the look of self-disgust on her face as she had related the news of failure to him, although both knew that hiring the terrorists had been his idea.

"Let me take the penthouse myself, uncle. There is still time!"

"No," he said. "There is the risk of implicating the *kobun* if you are caught. We need time to think and plan another strategy. Stay where you are and wait. I will contact you again."

Then he gave Miss Deshimaru strict orders that he was not to be disturbed, and paced the dove-grey carpet by the window overlooking Shinjuku Park and Tokyo bay as the sun set, thinking of the Minerva, of Yukiko, and all the events that had brought them to this point in their lives . . .

The 1950s had been as good to Gichin Funakoshi as the 1940s had been bad. By 1958 he was a rising section leader with the Japanese Ministry of International Trade and Industry, a "salary man" with a prime space in the section office and enough money to rent a seventy-five square metre apartment, which he and his sister Chizuko shared, only an hour's train ride from the centre of Tokyo.

Then, into his ordered life blew Kazuyoshi Saito, an electric skeleton of a man, with a mischievous monkey's face and bright laughing eyes, touting his idea for an new transistor to take the world by storm. It was Funakoshi's job, as section leader, to give the final approval for government assistance on all projects referred to him by his subordinates. Normally, such approval was given on the basis of a written proposal. Personal interviews were rare.

But Kazuyoshi Saito was a special case – notorious in the corridors of MITI as a brilliant eccentric whose genius for electronics was only matched by his complete disregard for business administration.

"How can I possibly process this application, Saito-san?" asked Funakoshi patiently. "If you provide no information on the market potential of this product, how you intend to raise the matching funding, or what the cost of manufacture might be?"

"And how can Japan ever hope to grow as an industrial power if it is enslaved in paper chains?" snapped Saito. "I survived the bomb at Nagasaki! Each moment is precious to me."

"My organisation wishes you to succeed, for the good of Japan," said Funakoshi. "But there is more to success than an idea. It must be carried through to reality, and that takes planning."

Saito raised his eyes to the ceiling and then spoke slowly, as if he was explaining something to a child.

"I am an inventor, a *samurai* of the mind. You are a bureaucrat. It is the *giri* of the bureaucrat to assist me in the fight to make our country great again. For you to do less is unpatriotic."

Whether by accident or design, Kazuyoshi Saito's words struck a chord deep within Funakoshi just then. For a moment, he was a child again, standing starving with his sister at a rainswept roadside near Tokyo, while American soldiers argued over the price of their father's *samurai* sword.

Saito regarded Funakoshi with amusement.

"Tell me, 'salary man'," he said. "Do you enjoy your work?"

"I beg your pardon?"

"Does this constant shuffling of paper fulfil your heart's desire? Does it stir your blood? Or would you rather be a *samurai*, like me!"

"I *am* a *samurai*, Saito-*san*," said Funakoshi with conviction. "Now, let *me* put a proposition before *you*."

The next ten years, as chief administrator of the newly formed Saito Electronics company, had been the happiest of Funakoshi's life. The staff were young and dedicated. There was a great adventure to be savoured, and best of all was Saito himself, leading them forward to conquer the world. They were the new *samurai*, and Kazuyoshi Saito was their warlord, their *shogun*, with a warrior's lust for life.

Then, late one evening, Saito called Funakoshi to his office.

"Salary man," he said, "you and I have worked well together. We have built an enterprise to be proud of in this company. I have something important to tell you. It is . . . er . . . something we must plan for if the company is to survive. I am dying."

Saito had not survived Nagasaki after all. The cancer spread quickly through his body, draining the life and magic from him until the last evening when Funakoshi sat beside his death-bed.

"We fought a good fight together, salary man." Saito whispered.

"The fight will go on, Saito-san. But I will miss your genius and your wisdom."

Saito's hand lifted from the bed. Funakoshi took it in his own. It felt cold and fragile, as if it had been carved from glass.

"I have something that might inspire you, salary man. Look inside that envelope. There! Beside the water jug!"

Funakoshi carefully lifted the heavy manila envelope, peeled back the flap and slid the contents onto the bed.

"My family were all killed by the bomb," whispered Saito. "And it occurs to me that you have been a salary man for too long. Sign those documents, and future is in your hands."

Funakoshi started to read, as tears welled in his eyes. Saito Electronics was now his – a small fortune – and an enormous debt of *giri* to Saito.

"How can I ever repay you, Saito-san," he said at last.

"Simply survive . . ." whispered Saito. "To survive, you must look beyond today into tomorrow, just as you did on the day we met. Then it was transistors, soon it will be things we can hardly imagine. Who knows? Look there, salary man. Look to tomorrow . . . "

For weeks after Saito's death, Gichin Funakoshi could hardly sleep as he worried about the future Saito had thrust upon him. Where was he to find the vision that Saito had supplied in limitless amounts? Where was he to find the backing he needed to meet the obligation Saito had bequeathed?

The opportunity was not long in coming.

In the spring, Funakoshi and his sister attended a reception at the British Embassy in Tokyo to mark the opening of a new trans-polar route by an English airline. The electronic equipment needed to navigate the frozen wastes of the Arctic in safety had been supplied by the Gilcrest Radio Company. Its representative, Lord Samuel Rothsay, was introduced to the Funakoshis by the British Trade Attaché. To his surprise, Funakoshi found himself greeted in fluent Japanese. After the ceremonial exchange of business cards, Funakoshi complimented Rothsay on it.

"Japan and the Japanese have been a love of mine for a long time, Mr President," said the Englishman, smiling at Chuziko. "Your company has many interesting products. Have you considered entering the world of aviation electronics?"

"Not yet," replied Funakoshi warily. "At present we supply only components – transistors, circuit boards and such."

"Pity. I hear such components will soon be obsolete."

"How so?"

"Companies such as mine are investigating ways of etching complete circuits onto minute chips of silicone. The power requirement is a minute fraction of that needed by a transistor, so they tell me. The scope for miniaturisation is mind-boggling."

"It would be interesting to learn more about this technique," said Funakoshi carefully, wondering what debt of obligation this might involve.

Rothsay's eyes lingered on Chuziko again – taking in

the delicate features of her face, the subtle curves of her body – far too long for Funakoshi's comfort.

"I think I might be able to help you there," he said slowly. "If we could come to some arrangement."

The soft buzz of the intercom snapped Funakoshi back to the present. He strode to his desk and stabbed at the button.

"What is it? I said I was not to be disturbed!"

Miss Deshimaru was desolate.

"Assistant Manager Nakamura from Industrial Intelligence insisted I alert you, Mr President. He requests a meeting with you at once. He says it concerns the Minerva project."

"Send him in."

Taisen Nakamura was a thin energetic executive of the old school, whom Funakoshi had inherited as part of the merger with the Mawashi trading house. He was meticulously thorough and absolutely discreet, essential qualifications for his job.

"Nakamura-*san*. You have something for me?"

"I do, Mr President. And believe me, I would not have disturbed you had it not been of the utmost importance. I have recorded it on this. It is the only copy in the building."

He placed a small hand-held SmartCard viewer on the empty desk and turned it so that Funakoshi could see the screen.

"As you know, we have managed to tap into the corporate e-mail systems of a number of rival concerns, including that of the Gilcrest Radio Corporation – a matter in which Division Head Funakoshi was of great assistance."

Funakoshi let this reference to Yukiko pass. He was aware that many employees in Mawashi-Saito did not approve of her high position in the Industrial Intelligence Division. But then again, they did not know her as he did.

"Over the past hour, the GRC e-mail system has been flooded with activity. Orders were placed for over one hundred and fifty specialist items of equipment from seventy-two different locations. Some of these orders went directly to computer handling systems, others by video link to personnel in charge of dispatch. All the items were to be sent to Cairo."

"It is probably Dr Gilkrensky planning experiments to absolve his Daedalus unit. What does this have to do with his Minerva project?"

"Everything, Mr President. You see, all one hundred and fifty items were ordered *simultaneously*! Watch!"

Nakamura pressed a key on the SmartCard viewer and immediately the image on the fold-up screen split, to display a couple engaged in conversation. The man was in his thirties, with a dark moustache and heavy glasses. Behind him, Funakoshi could make out row upon row of cartons, arranged on shelves – a warehouse of some sort. On the other side of the screen, sitting against a light blue background, was a beautiful red-headed woman. She was speaking precisely and rapidly in a soft Irish accent, ordering a list of items for delivery to Cairo.

"But that's impossible," said Funakoshi. "That is Dr Gilkrensky's wife. She died earlier this year."

Nakamura nodded.

"This is indeed the *image* of Maria Gilkrensky, Mr President. But as you correctly conclude, it is not a real person. That image was in simultaneous human dialogue with fifty-one other locations. I have multiple recordings, and each show an identical time line. Look at the way 'she' interacts with the man in this particular warehouse. He does not know he is talking to a machine . . ."

"And the machine?"

"Undoubtedly the new Minerva 3,000 biochip prototype. Only a machine with that capacity, and the capability for biological neural networking would be able to enter into human dialogue like that. And only the 3,000 model has the capacity to do it simultaneously with so many other stations. We are looking at the future, Funakoshi-san. A fully self-aware artificial intelligence with an almost limitless capacity and complete portability. It could be the basis of intelligent robots, a new generation of computers . . ."

"And GRC has it?" said Funakoshi, transfixed by the image on the SmartCard viewer. In his mind he was hearing the last words of his friend and mentor Kazuyoshi Saito – 'Look beyond today into tomorrow'."

Gilkrensky had tomorrow.

From this point on, Mawashi-Saito, and all of Japan, belonged to the past!

Funakoshi leant forward and shut down the screen on the SmartCard viewer.

"What would our laboratories need to be able to copy this new computer?" he said.

"I would have to discuss this in confidence with the head of our advanced products laboratory. But I would imagine that either a detailed circuit diagram and the formula for the biochip material, or access to the prototype itself, would suffice."

"Please confirm that. And leave the SmartCard with me."

"Of course. I will have an answer for you within the hour. Thank you, Mr President."

Nakamura bowed and left, while Funakoshi sat back in his seat, turning the SmartCard between his fingers. Then he slipped it into the breast pocket of his jacket, reached forward and pressed his intercom button.

"Miss Deshimaru. Get me Division Head Funakoshi in Cairo, please. On the secure line."

27

ZAKI

ZAKI EL SHAROUD HAD NEVER BEEN SO SCARED IN ALL HIS LIFE. It was one thing to mount an operation, and be in control – right from the planning to the execution. But this . . . this was hell!

Since he had pulled himself from the river and struggled back to his apartment twelve hours ago, he had been at the mercy of others. Knowing what was coming, he had gone through every room in his apartment minutely, rubbing down the surfaces members of his group might have touched – the door handles, furniture, windows, coffee cups. It would not be long before the security police came.

Gamal, Abdul and Sarwat could not be connected to him directly, but their sister was another matter. Farida was – had been – a model. In fashion circles it was known she'd preferred him as her photographer. He checked that none of the negatives or prints the Japanese woman had taken at the airport remained, and that the pictures of the Nile Olympiad's helipad he had photographed himself had also been destroyed. Then he burned the *galabia* he had purchased from the boy on the river in the barbecue on the terrace. Now he was certain that nothing was left that could link him to Farida . . . beyond what might link any photographer to his favourite model.

But the fear remained.

What if he'd missed something?

The hunter had become the hunted. He was no longer in control.

They came just after lunch. A volley of rapid rings on his bell announced a Colonel Abdul Selim of the Central Security Police and half-a-dozen mindless soldiers into his apartment. Did he know the model Farida? Could he account for his whereabouts over the last twenty-four hours?

Selim bundled him into an armoured car and took him to the security barracks for questioning, while the soldiers ransacked his apartment. Had Zaki not been part of the Cairean social elite, and recognised by several of the higher-ranking officers whose daughters' society weddings he had photographed, he might still have been there, lounging in a cell.

He returned to find his fashionable apartment wrecked by the investigators. In the lounge, the white leather furniture had been slashed with bayonets and the padding searched. Books had been swept from the shelves and their spines broken. The contents of his kitchen had been picked through meticulously. Food was smeared across the tiles and water from the broken refrigerator pooled on the floor. The bedroom had been ransacked. The mattress on the big double bed had been gutted, and clothes from his wardrobe had been slit along their seams before being trampled into untidy heaps.

Finally, they had violated his darkroom.

Carelessly spilt chemicals mixed in evil-smelling pools on the work-tops, staining the once sterile surfaces. Spools of unexposed film coiled on the floor, and sealed boxes of sensitive photographic paper lay open, ruined by the light.

And they had confiscated every photograph he had ever taken of her! Every contact sheet, every transparency, every colour print he had ever made of his beautiful Farida . . .

He remembered, with intense pain, how she had held him tightly on that final afternoon before he had sent her out to . . . that man. The tears had rolled down her cheeks. His own heart had broken, and yet he had still sent her. Through the lens of his camera he had seen her depart with the American to the airport the next morning. Through the visor of his helmet he had seen her shot dead by the English guards and burn in the explosion of the grenade.

In an instant, Zaki El Sharoud realised how he had always watched life and death from afar through the lens of a camera – the death of Sadat, the life of Farida. He should have embraced the love he had seen in her eyes, instead of printing it onto endless reams of photographic paper. He should have claimed her as his wife, instead of sending her to die on the rooftop of that hotel!

Zaki bent down and opened the cupboard beneath the big Durst enlarger. The brown glass bottles of chemicals had been taken out and spilt, but the cupboard itself was still intact. They had not found them! Good! There was still time for one last move! He had finished hiding behind lenses. This time it would be face to face!

He unclipped a Swiss Army knife from his key-ring, and turned his attention to the back of the cupboard. Behind the thin hardboard backing was a dirty cloth bundle – something a workman might have left behind. Zaki lifted it out and spread it on the floor. Inside was a heavy 35 millimetre Walther PPK pistol, and a thick, black fragmentation grenade. He slipped the grenade into his pocket, took the gun in his hand, and walked back into the darkened lounge.

Bright lights were blinking near the top floor of the Nile Olympiad hotel. A small helicopter from the press was circling at a distance, filming the ugly black scars that flowed downwards from the helipad above the Presidential Suite. They would be allowed no closer. There were uniformed Central Security police on the roof now, and a tight cordon around the ground floor. No way of getting inside, unless . . . Before his eyes, a dark shadow near the open door to the terrace peeled itself from the wall and stood before him.

"Pull the curtain," said Yukiko. "I must speak with you."

El Sharoud did as she requested and flicked on the light.

She was dressed from head to foot in a loose suit of black cotton. Her gloved hands removed the hood covering her face. Her shining hair was tied in a tight bun, and the skin around her eyes had been coated with some sort of blacking, so that it did not reflect the light. To Zaki El Sharoud she seemed thin and fragile, an ungainly child dressed for a fancy dress party.

"What do you want?" he snapped.

The Japanese woman surveyed the devastation all around her in the wrecked apartment.

"I have new instructions from Tokyo. I do not need you any more."

El Sharoud smiled grimly. He held the Walther PPK up where she could see it, and gestured in the direction of the Nile Olympiad.

"And *I* do not need *you,* woman! Everyone I have cared about is dead! Now it is between me and that man over there!"

Yukiko was unmoved.

"No," she said simply. "You will withdraw, and leave the rest of this operation to me. In return, my company will give your group the satellite communications you asked for. That has been agreed in Tokyo."

El Sharoud snorted.

"You do not understand, *child*! Our business arrangement ceased when Farida died and my friends were killed! This is now a personal matter for me and the *Jihad*! Get out of here, or you will get hurt!"

The woman remained, calm and still, in front of him.

"It is *you* who do not understand. You and your 'friends' behaved like amateurs. The woman Farida was weak. She should never have started shooting. The pilot of your helicopter was a fool. He should not have exposed himself to the gunfire from the security guards. You were children playing at war. Now, give me that gun!"

She put out her left hand to take it.

Zaki El Sharoud glared at this fragile, doll-like creature in disbelief. Then the rage that had simmered since the heartbreak of Farida's death burst inside him. He was a big, powerful man. He would hit her just once with the gun, and be done with her! The Walther swung back, as he aimed a vicious slap to the left side of her head . . .

His forearm seemed to collide in mid-air with an iron bar – an iron bar that turned into a vice, threatening to rip his arm from its socket – forcing his body to twist forward, head down, into the pain. A black cotton foot slammed into his face, and he was thrown bodily across the apartment, crashing into the ruins of his white leather sofa. The Walther PPK went skidding across the polished floor and thumped against the skirting-board. The woman padded lightly over and picked it up, but Zaki was already clawing at his pocket. When she turned to face him, the grenade was in his hand and his fingers were wrapped around the firing lever. The safety pin was between his teeth. He spat it onto the floor.

"Now, *woman*! You see the difference between us! I

am willing to *die* for what I believe in. If you shoot me, I will let this grenade fall, you will be killed and your precious company will be exposed. Now get out, and stay clear of me! I *will* have my revenge!"

The woman eyed the grenade, measuring the distance between them. For an instant, Zaki saw fire flash in her eyes as her right hand darted to the nape of her neck. Then she hesitated, tucked the Walther PPK inside her black cotton *gi*, and replaced her hood.

"You know *nothing* of revenge," she hissed, "and if you interfere with mine, I will kill you."

Then she moved soundlessly to the open terrace door, and melted into the night.

Zaki could feel his arm begin to shake. Gritting his teeth against the pain of the torn muscles, he reached out, picked the safety pin up from the floor and threaded its metal tag back into the firing arm of the grenade.

Slowly and carefully, he released his cramped fingers.

The pin held.

With a loud sob, Zaki El Sharoud collapsed amongst the ruins of his apartment. For a long while he lay against the gutted sofa, with the grenade in easy reach. Then he pulled himself painfully to his feet and picked the telephone up from the floor near the fireplace. He would have to be careful. The central security police were certain to be listening.

28

THE GREAT PYRAMID

BILL MCCARTHY FINGERED THE ELASTOPLAST DRESSING ON HIS forehead and wondered if he should take another pain-killer. Perhaps it hadn't been such a good idea to check himself out of the hospital so fast, but he was damned if he was going to sit there on his butt and let Theo manage the whole investigation from the hotel suite. Goddammit! Somebody had to be on-site!

The little JetRanger helicopter swooped along the wide carriageway of "Pyramid Avenue", heading west. Beside him in the cockpit was the Egyptian pilot they had brought down from Alexandria to replace Leroy Manning. Behind him in the cabin were Professor El Fiky and Major Crowe. The doctors had said Leroy would be OK. The bullet had missed the bone. But McCarthy didn't trust foreign hospitals – another good reason for discharging himself.

Pyramid Avenue petered out next to the Mena House

Hotel. Below him, McCarthy could see the huddles of expectant beggars, would-be tour guides, and camels lying in wait for the tour coaches. The helicopter rose to follow the road from the camel park and swept southwards in a great curve, climbing out of the lush green valley of the Nile onto the sandy escarpment of the Ghiza plateau, at the very edge of the desert. To their left was the Great Pyramid of Cheops. To their right, the Pyramid of Chephren, with the remains of its original stone facing still clinging around its peak, like high mountain snow.

For McCarthy, it was the sheer scale that amazed him. Each one of the stone cubes that made up the mountain of the Great Pyramid had looked to be about the size of a house brick from far away – but up close he could see that each one was about the size of car! And there were two hundred layers of them! Or so Professor El Fiky had said. Two and a third *million* blocks – weighing in at two and a half tons *each*!

The helicopter settled on an open space in front of the GRC caravan, throwing up a cloud of dust and scattering the knot of cotton-robed guides who had gathered in the hope of offering their services. As the rotors slowed to a stop and the dust settled, Professor El Fiky called to them in Arabic. They laughed, moving off to wait for the tourists.

"I'm well known on this site," he said. "I told them they have stolen my job for so many years by lecturing on the pyramids that I am having my revenge today by acting as a tour guide for you. Come, we will see what your technicians managed to achieve during the night with the equipment Dr Gilkrensky ordered. It is a pity he could not be here in person."

"I think he's lucky to still be in the country at all," said Crowe. "But he can watch anything we do here on video from the hotel. We have cameras strung up all over the place."

McCarthy's eyes followed a trail of cables running across the car park and up the side of the stone mountain.

"Tell me," said El Fiky. "Have you ever heard the story of the Arabian Nights?"

McCarthy nodded.

"The hero of that book, the prince Abdullah Al-Mamun of Bagdad, was the first man to explore the Pyramid, over a thousand years ago. This is the way his men came. Follow me, please."

They crossed the car park and started to climb over the huge rocks at the base of the Pyramid, following a rough path in the northern face.

"Al-Mamun had been told of a great treasure, sealed inside the Pyramid," continued El Fiky, "and not just any treasure – celestial navigation tables, magical artifacts, glass that could bend and weapons that would not rust. Al-Mamun was a man of great learning – an astronomer – so you can see how these things would appeal to him."

The path amongst the stones curved back on itself, and they were standing next to a huge gouge in the side of the rock face. The cables from the GRC caravan disappeared into a passageway, following a pair of thick ventilation pipes into the darkness.

"Mind your head please," warned El Fiky. "It is very cramped." And he ducked inside, followed by McCarthy, with Crowe bringing up the rear.

The tunnel was only four feet high. McCarthy found himself bending almost double. Ahead of him, he heard El Fiky say,

"Al-Mamun miscalculated when he dug into the side of the Pyramid. For a hundred feet his men hacked their way through solid rock without any reward, and then, they found this . . . it is called the 'Descending Passage'. Mind your step, please. The angle changes sharply!"

They were cramped into a rectangular shaft, three and a half feet wide and four feet high, which bored downwards at a steep angle. Already the air had become damp. McCarthy had to concentrate to stop himself from becoming disorientated.

"I hope you do not get claustrophobia," said El Fiky.

"I'm fine. You lead on."

They followed the Descending Passage downwards for about a hundred yards, until McCarthy suddenly felt the headroom increase above him. He straightened thankfully, his back muscles cramped. Looking up, he could see the cables from the caravan and the flexible ventilation ducts snake towards the ceiling. The surface was lined with red and black veined rock.

"This granite plug blocks the way to the centre of the Pyramid," explained El Fiky. "Al-Mamun's men found it impregnable. There was no way they could cut through . . . "

"So they went around it," said Crowe.

"Correct, Major. I see the strategist within you lives on. Careful please, this passage allows for only one person at a time!"

McCarthy squeezed through the narrow tunnel and then, after what seemed like a lifetime of bending double, he was standing completely upright. The walls around him opened out and the ceiling soared upwards. He was inside a huge, sloping cavern with ramps leading up either side.

"This is the Grand Gallery," said El Fiky, with more than a hint of pride in his voice. "It leads to the King's Chamber at the top and, off to the side here, to a passage to the Queen's Chamber where our experiments are taking place. Just step down off the ramp by that electrical cabinet. You will have to duck again, I'm afraid."

Then they were in another passageway following the cables once more, so that McCarthy could walk with just his head bent. In the distance he could hear voices and the ring of a hammer on metal. Then the passageway grew light and he was in the Queen's Chamber, along with three of his GRC Aerospace crew and the oddest collection of technology he had ever seen.

"Jeez! How did you get all that stuff in here?"

"It wasn't easy, Bill," said one of the technicians, leaning back on what looked like a small tractor with long metal arms and thick caterpillar tracks. One of the arms held a compact video camera that turned to face them. The other held a squat black cylinder bearing the sign *Warning – Laser!*

"The mining robot was a bastard to carry down here, even in pieces," continued the technician. "And I was shitting myself that somebody would drop the laser and rupture the element. But we did it. And we're all set to go. The sonic tests confirm a new chamber right behind that wall. Where the chalk-marks are."

McCarthy peered across the Queen's Chamber. Compared to the smooth walls of the passages they had come through, and the Grand Gallery above, it looked as if it had been half-finished, and then abandoned. The rock floor was uneven and rough, except close to the walls. Looking up, McCarthy saw the ceiling sloping upwards to a point above their heads, and on the east wall was a strange niche – five feet across at the bottom, and narrowing towards the top in steps.

"Weird! Really weird."

"You're telling me!" said Gilkrensky's voice.

"Theo?" called McCarthy, looking round. "Where are you?"

"Back in hotel, Bill. I'm watching you on the robot's camera, and speaking to you over the sound system Major Crowe put inside the chamber."

"Are you controlling the robot?"

"No. Maria is. She's far more precise than I could ever be, and we don't want to damage anything on the other side of that wall when we cut through."

"Hello, Professor McCarthy!" said Maria. "I hope you're fully recovered from your experience yesterday."

"I'll live. When do we start cutting?"

"You may start whenever you are ready," said Professor El Fiky. "As a representatives of the State Museum of Antiquities, I am empowered to act as an official witness for the Egyptian government. I understand you are recording all proceedings on film."

"On video, yes."

"Then you may proceed."

"You will all need to wear protective glasses while the laser is in operation," said Maria. "Put them on now, please."

One of the technicians handed McCarthy a pair of heavy dark glasses, and the little robot trundled forward until it was standing squarely in front of the chalk-marks on the far wall.

"I will be firing the laser in five seconds," warned Maria. "Four . . . three . . . two . . . one . . . "

Even through the dark glasses, McCarthy was dazzled by the pencil-thin beam. It shot from the black cylinder on the robot like a solid rod of light, angling downwards into the rock just where the floor met the wall. There was a spit and pop, as tiny stone fragments cracked off and ricocheted from the walls. Thick white smoke poured upwards to the ceiling, and started to fall in a dense cloud. McCarthy heard muffled coughs.

"Turn up the fans! Or we won't be able to see a thing!"

The tone of the electric extractors rose an octave, and the smoke began to clear.

"I have penetrated the chamber!" said Maria, and the laser snapped off.

McCarthy stepped forward and swung the robot's arm to one side.

"We'll have to wait for the rock to cool before we try the optic fibre probe. Can you set it up, please?"

A pair of technicians swivelled a small video camera fitted with a long thin cable over its lens into place, and handed the tip to McCarthy. After waiting a few minutes, he crouched down in front of the blackened hole where the laser had struck and pushed the cable gently inside. On the video monitor at the far end of the chamber, he could see what looked like the view from the front of a train hurtling down a long, dark tunnel. Smooth walls slipped past in the darkness.

"Forty centimetres to estimated entry point," said Maria. "Thirty . . . twenty . . . ten . . . "

The darkness of the tunnel became a neat, black hole. Then the probe was inside the new chamber. For a moment, it was difficult to make out what they were seeing on the screen. There was a glimpse of a wooden beam, a pile of sand with a neat crater in the centre, weird hieroglyphic writing. And all around the colour was . . .

"Gold!" breathed Professor El Fiky in amazement. "The chamber is lined with gold!"

"What the hell is it?" said Gilkrensky, peering at the wall

monitor in the Nile Olympiad's boardroom. "Maria? Can you see?"

"It is difficult to compose an accurate image, even with computer enhancement. The field of view is too small. But initial analysis reveals some kind of crypt . . . with five walls . . . forming an apex above a square base . . . in the shape of a hollow pyramid."

"Can you move the optical probe around, Bill?"

"Not a lot."

"Is there anything in there besides the wooden beams and the sand?" asked Professor El Fiky.

"Not that I can see. Why sand?"

"The ancient Egyptians used to fill empty chambers with sand to stop grave robbers finding them by rapping on the stone walls and listening for hollow sounds."

"Then why does this chamber have such a small amount of sand in it?" asked Gilkrensky. "It's only about a quarter full!"

"I suggest the optical probe be withdrawn and a gas analyser inserted," said Maria. "Then I might be able to tell where the sand has gone."

"How's that?"

"This crypt is at the exact centre of the Pyramid. If it is the focal point of some kind of cosmic 'lens', then the energy it focuses might be present in sufficient quantities to actually vaporise matter. If this is true, then an analysis of the gas inside will show high levels of vaporised silicon."

"Inserting gas probe now," said McCarthy.

"I'm afraid the vaporisation theory is incorrect," said

Maria, a few moments later. "The silicon in the air inside the crypt is hardly above background level, although there is a very high concentration of ozone – consistent with a powerful electrical discharge of some kind."

"That could explain why the engine on the chopper cut out," said McCarthy.

El Fiky said, "Those hieroglyphs? They remind me of the texts in the Saqqara pyramid. Could we see them again?"

McCarthy slid the optical probe back into place.

"Can your computer read them?" asked El Fiky.

"I have not yet been programmed with Egyptian hieroglyphics," said Maria. "But I am recording those I can see now. It would be useful to excavate a bigger hole, so that we could have better control of the probe."

"Or go inside ourselves?" said El Fiky. "How long would that take?"

"By using the laser on a narrow-beam focus, it would be possible to cut a circular aperture in the rock, large enough for a person to fit inside the crypt, within two hours. But even with the extractors on full power, the atmosphere in the Queen's Chamber will become highly polluted with smoke. I therefore recommend that all personnel withdraw while I guide the laser remotely by infra-red imaging. After the smoke has cleared, everyone can return and I will use the robot to remove the rock plug to the crypt."

"Is that all right with you, Professor?" asked Gilkrensky.

"Indeed it is," purred El Fiky. "This is the discovery of the century!"

"In what has been described by experts as the 'discovery of the century'," boomed the CNN newscaster, "an archaeological team financed by computer tycoon Theodore Gilkrensky is in the process of uncovering a previously undiscovered chamber in the Great Pyramid of Cheops. This marks another chapter in the highly eventful visit to Egypt by the billionaire, who narrowly avoided a terrorist attack yesterday on the banks of the Nile. Experts from the Museum of Antiquities . . . "

"And not a mention of the plane crash or the Daedalus autopilot," said Neil Martin. "It's the same on all the other channels."

They were sitting in front of the big TV monitor in Jessica's office.

"Neil's right," said Tony Delgado. "Between this business with the pyramids and the terrorist attack, all media interest in the chairman has moved right away from the air crash. Unless the official inquiry goes against us, it looks as if we can ride this one out. It was a good move to send Dr Gilkrensky to Cairo, Jessica. Congratulations!"

Jessica Wright pushed her glasses back on her nose and reached for the TV's remote control. The screen went blank. "And is the inquiry confirmed for tomorrow?"

"It is, at ten hundred hours, local time in Cairo."

"And the board meeting?"

"The day after, on Christmas Eve. But don't expect an

easy ride. I've already had Sir Robert on to me complaining that the chairman is putting archaeology before the interests of his shareholders."

Jessica thought of the image of Maria Gilkrensky she had seen on the computer screen earlier that day.

"He's living his wife's obsessions," she said.

On the large video screen in the conference room of the Nile Olympiad, Gilkrensky could see the rod of ruby light moving through the smoke in a slow, slow circle – up from the floor of the Queen's Chamber and to the left – like the second hand on a clock.

"Is there no way we can speed this up?" he asked, as he drummed his fingers on the conference-room table.

Bill McCarthy looked up from the piece of balsawood he was carefully carving with a penknife and shook his head. "Not without increasing the power of the laser. And that would mean risking damage to the chamber itself."

"Professor El Fiky and his friends at the museum were very nervous about that," said Maria. "They only gave us permission to use the laser if it was on a fixed focus at low power."

Gilkrensky peered at the wall monitor again.

"How much longer?"

"One hour and thirty-five minutes until the circle is complete, Theo. Then another twenty minutes before the smoke clears, and another thirty minutes to remove the rock plug."

"Being cooped up in here is driving me mad!"

McCarthy emptied his pipe into an ash-tray and loaded it with tobacco.

"Then go over your testimony for the crash enquiry! That's what we came out here for after all, and it's less than twenty-four hours away."

"I know you're right. But I just can't settle to it."

McCarthy sat back and re-lit his pipe. A cloud of sweet-smelling smoke curved towards the ceiling.

"Then give me your opinion on this. It's the 'Hi-Lift' prototype."

Sitting amongst a scattering of woodchips and sawdust on a sheet of old newspaper in front of him was a small model aircraft carved from balsawood. The wings were mounted high on the bulbous fuselage and the tail was short and fish-like. McCarthy turned it in his hands.

"I'm still a model-maker at heart," he said. "Computer-aided design is all very well. But you can't beat the feel of something solid in your hand. I need to do a bit of work on the tail. But if it flies the way it should, it'll cut fuel consumption by thirty-five per cent. Less to carry, and less to burn up in a crash!"

Gilkrensky watched the older man carefully scrape at the little aircraft.

"You did a good job when you designed the Whisperer, Bill. Nobody died."

"Yeah. Well, I had the motivation, didn't I?"

"Angie and the kids?"

"That's right."

"I'm sorry, Bill."

McCarthy put down the modelling knife.

"Have you thought about what I said regarding the Minerva?"

"You mean about Maria and the interface?"

"Yeah. Like I said, Theo, you need to move on."

"The computer said the same thing. It suggested I should form 'an emotional bond' with someone else."

McCarthy shook his head. Then he slid the wings and tail out of the body of the model and packed them all carefully inside his steel spectacle case, before slipping it into his pocket.

"You'll never be able to accept Maria's death as long as she speaks through the Minerva. Take my advice and reprogram it."

Gilkrensky looked at the black briefcase in front of the wall monitor.

"You're right. I'll do it as soon as we get back to Ireland."

29

THE COFFEE HOUSE

AFTER THE DARKNESS OF THE MUSEUM, THE LIGHT OF DAY WAS painful. Professor El Fiky paused for a moment at the top of the museum steps as his eyes grew accustomed to the sun, then he turned past the statues and square cut hedges of the forecourt, heading for Tahrir Square, while the hieroglyphs he had been studying minutely for the past two hours whirled in his head.

They indicated a voyage . . . but not the usual journey of the soul into the world of the dead. He had studied the ancient writings long enough to know *that*. And one of the symbols was new! It was similar to that for the sun god Re, but without the usual inflection of authority normally due to that most exalted god who, when all was said and done, the lesser gods worshipped themselves. Did the new symbol indicate the sun? Or some aspect of the sun in human terms? It was a mystery!

Gradually, he became aware of the activity all around

him. The reedy wail of Arabic pipe music from radios and loud speakers in the cafes was fighting a losing battle against the rumble of traffic, and the constant blare of car horns in the square. On the pavement, groups of men lounged in doorways, played dominoes or cards, or had their hair cut. El Fiky looked at his watch again.

He was right on schedule.

At the corner of the square was a coffee house with a tall arched doorway and a larger than average overflow of chairs onto the pavement outside. There were no windows, and beyond the cave-like entrance, the interior was dark and dim. El Fiky greeted the white-jacketed *qahwaki* and went inside, picking a table well away from the door by the far wall. All around him was the slap of cards and the click of dominoes. The air was full of tobacco smoke and the pungent aroma from the great steam locomotive of the *sarabantina* coffee machine. There was sawdust on the floor, and not a woman in the place – nor ever likely to be.

El Fiky looked carefully at the other customers, and recognised most of them. He had been coming here for years, and it had always been the same. Except . . .

On the counter, next to the *sarabantina*, was a square box like a television set. Abdul the *qahwaki* placed a tin tray containing a cup and a brass *kanaka* of coffee in front of him.

"*Ziyada*, Professor? As always!"

"*Ziyada*, my friend. For my sweet tooth. Tell me. That machine there on the counter? Is it new?"

"Professor, one must learn to move with the times.

That is a microwave oven. It heats food in an instant, as if by magic!"

"It is very small!"

"That is the magic of it, Professor. It does not get hot, like the *sarabantina* does. There is no steam or gas. It simply passes some kind of ray through the box and, presto! The food is hot! I can even programme it to do this if I am out of the shop by using the electric clock inside."

"A clock in an oven?"

"Yes, Professor, a timer."

Professor El Fiky stared across the smoky café at the white cube. Once again the hieroglyphs swirled in his head . . . the sun sign that was not the sun god Re . . . the power of the golden chamber to focus energy . . .

Abdul moved away. Professor El Fiky did not see the tall man come into the café and take a seat directly behind him, close to the wall. But he felt him lean back in his chair, and heard him say,

"This is the only place I could meet you in safety."

"I come here every day," said El Fiky. "Are you sure you were not followed?"

"I do not know. I made three taxi changes and wore this *galabia* to cover myself. There may still be surveillance on my apartment, and the Japanese woman has threatened my life."

El Fiky sipped his coffee, feeling the small grains between his teeth and the sweet bite of the liquid as he surveyed the other men in the room.

"We must be quick then. What do you want to discuss."

"I am going to kill Gilkrensky," said Zaki El Sharoud.

"You cannot kill him," whispered El Fiky softly. "The plan was for us to deliver Gilkrensky and his computer to the Japanese."

El Sharoud stiffened in his seat.

"Plans! What good are plans! Farida is dead! And so are Abdul, Sarwat and Gamal! Everyone you taught! Everyone who stood by you all these years is dead because of plans!"

"Be still, Zaki! The Japanese have promised us the satellite channel if we deliver Gilkrensky. I now know how I can do that. Work with me. We are so close!"

"But Farida is *dead*!"

"I know . . . I know. You have lost those dear to you. We have all lost those dear to us. My wife and son, both killed by the Israelis. But do not let your heart rule your head. We still have a great opportunity to unite the peoples of Islam against the West with a television station of our own. Imagine it! Nations flocking to our cause all along the Mediterranean! Use your head, Zaki! Think!"

"There will be no satellite channel! The Japanese woman and I are at war!"

"What!"

"She came to my apartment and told me to back away. But I will not do this, not any more. Yesterday I sent my friends to be killed and watched them die from far away. Now it is my turn to act. I still have a grenade, and I am not afraid to die. Get me close enough to Gilkrensky, so I can use it!"

"You are mad, Zaki! Farida's death has turned your head. I will make contact with the Japanese woman and explain."

"You will do no such thing, Ahmed El Fiky. You will either find some way of getting Gilkrensky out of his hotel, or of getting me inside . . . or I will kill you. Are *you* afraid to die?"

"You know me better than to ask!"

Zaki considered this for a moment.

"And what of your daughter?"

"My daughter knows nothing. She has never been part of the *Jihad*."

"I know. But she could be placed under suspicion so easily. You know what happens to suspected terrorists in the cellars of Cairo prisons, particularly if they are women."

"You would not do this. We have known each other too long!"

"Professor, you are right to call me mad. At your instructions I sent my Farida to sleep with the infidel Manning, and then watched her die in a burning helicopter so that we might spread the word of Islam. Now I have my own way of spreading that word - across every television station and newspaper on the globe - as I stand next to Gilkrensky, pull the pin on that grenade and scream the name of Allah!"

"You are jeopardising a great plan, Zaki, a plan that could bring us a victory more far-reaching than you could ever imagine!"

"This has gone beyond great plans now. Just call me when you have made the arrangements."

Professor El Fiky heard the chair scrape behind him as Zaki got to his feet and left. For several minutes he stared into his coffee cup.

He remembered Zaki as the brightest of his students, lost and alone in the swirl of the great city, the nearest thing he had to a son. They had fought for a cause, and risked so much together, for so long. Now Zaki was throwing it all away . . . for revenge. Professor El Fiky had never met Farida. But he had listened while Zaki described her, and heard the fondness in his words. He should not have forced Zaki to use her in that way. He should have given him a different plan. Now it was too late. Zaki had turned against him.

As the second cup of coffee cooled in front of him, Professor El Fiky balanced one bitter loss against another. Then, when he had made his decision, he paid his bill and walked slowly back to the museum.

30

MOON SHOT

ON THE SCREEN IN THE NILE OLYMPIAD CONFERENCE ROOM, Gilkrensky could see McCarthy pushing the stainless-steel expansion-bolt into the neat hole Maria's laser had cut in the centre of the circular plug. McCarthy twisted the ring on its head, and pulled.

"Bolt's holding OK!"

"Good. Now hook up the cable and let's go!"

Gilkrensky watched McCarthy clip a high-tensile steel cable to the ring-bolt and then retreat out of the picture.

"I bet it's just like watching a moon landing, Theo!"

"Yes. And you even have a robot. Maria! You can start pulling now!"

The little machine took up the strain on the cable. Gilkrensky could see its caterpillar tracks gripping the uneven stone on the floor of the Queen's chamber, and hear the whine of its electric motor over his radio headset. There was a grinding scrape, and around the circular groove cut into the rock wall by the laser, an inch of white limestone appeared . . . then another . . . and another . . .

"Just like pulling a champagne cork!" shouted McCarthy above the din.

"How thick is the plug, Maria?"

"Sixty-three centimetres, Theo."

"Can the robot handle it?"

"As long as the treads have sufficient grip on the floor, the machine is capable of extracting the plug."

"It's nearly halfway out!" shouted McCarthy over the radio.

"Is the wide-angle camera ready?"

"No problem! We can fit it to the robot's manipulator arm as soon as the plug's pulled. Here she comes! Stand back everyone. It might roll!"

Gilkrensky heard a hollow scraping as the plug tilted in the hole. Then, with a deep, booming thud, the limestone cylinder came free and crashed to the floor beside the tunnel.

"Wow! Smell that ozone!" gasped McCarthy. "It's like the biggest thunderstorm you were ever in!"

"Put in a light! Put in a light!" shouted Professor El Fiky.

McCarthy was unhitching the steel wire from the expansion-bolt.

"We'll do better than that," he said, and carefully bolted an industrial video camera to the robot's right manipulator arm, opposite the laser. "OK, Theo! It's all yours."

"Maria?"

Under the Minerva's control, the little robot trundled forward to the lip of the tunnel and extended the camera. On the monitor, Gilkrensky could see the heat-seared walls sliding past, and the glow of gold at the end of the short tunnel.

"The crypt is an exact replica of the Great Pyramid itself," said Maria. "Sonic measurements indicate that it's perfectly proportioned. The entrance we have created is in the centre of its eastern wall."

The camera was inside the crypt now. The picture was filled with row upon row of intricate hieroglyphs, delicate word-pictures of people, animals, chariots and images of the sun.

"I am recording these graphics to match with known texts," said Maria. "Professor El Fiky has suggested we might use the library at the museum this evening as a data source to translate what these writings mean."

"Are you sure the crypt is empty?" asked El Fiky.

The picture on the screen changed as Maria swung the video camera downwards and panned across the chamber floor. There was nothing except a pair of wooden beams, strangely cut away in the centre, and an odd dish-shaped depression in the sand.

"It's almost as if something took a huge bite out of the wood, and gobbled up a mouthful of sand at the same time," said McCarthy.

Gilkrensky peered at the screen.

"Zoom in on the ends of the beams, Maria."

They were perfectly smooth.

"No teeth marks, anyway," said McCarthy. "So we can scratch that theory for a start."

Gilkrensky said, "Could it be a burial chamber?"

"If it is, then it is unlike any I have ever seen before," answered El Fiky. "If this was a burial chamber, there would be a sarcophagus, as there is in the King's Chamber above us."

"Could the body have been stolen by grave robbers?"

"No. We are the first to open this chamber, just as Al-Mamun was the first to open the Pyramid before us. He found no bodies, and neither have we!"

McCarthy and his team spent the rest of the afternoon trying to analyse the golden crypt. Professor El Fiky was given the honour of being the first person inside, followed by other observers from the museum and the Department of Antiquities, who took it in turns to remove their shoes, and squeeze backwards down the tunnel. At around six, the media were allowed in, to take video and still pictures around the Queen's Chamber and inside the golden crypt itself. The story was all over the international satellite news.

The air crash was forgotten.

Then McCarthy got down to serious business - rigging the sensors and recording apparatus he needed to monitor the effects of the evening's Sound and Light show on the very focal point of the Pyramid itself – deep inside the Golden Crypt. By seven thirty, the Queen's Chamber was a mass of wires and cables, all leading back up the Descending Passage and out into the open, to the GRC caravan.

Gilkrensky watched the whole thing on video from the Nile Olympiad.

"Can I make a suggestion, Theo?" asked Maria.

"Please do."

"It is now almost eight o'clock, and the laser holography display will be starting shortly. I would therefore recommend you clear everyone out of the Queen's Chamber, just in case."

"In case of what?"

"We know from the helicopter experiment that the energy build-up commences at eight twenty-nine, with a peak six minutes later. We also know that the energy pulse is powerful enough to disable the electronics on a helicopter flying overhead. This is the first time the golden crypt has been open to the outside world in four thousand years. There may be other side effects we have not yet considered."

"I take your point. Bill! Can you hear me?"

Bill McCarthy was tired. It had been a long and exciting day – one of the most exciting since the moon landings back in the Sixties. The challenge of bringing all his GRC Aerospace technology to bear on the puzzle of the golden crypt had made him feel young again. This was cutting-edge stuff, a new energy source, the focus for a new wave form, and he was part of it. There was life in the old dog yet!

He took a last look around the Queen's Chamber. All the journalists, technicians and archaeologists had been shepherded out, and he was alone. The sensor probes were rigged inside the Golden Crypt, just above the boards they had placed on the wooden beams where he calculated the mathematical centre of the Pyramid should be. It had been difficult work. He'd had to balance himself almost upside-down in the tunnel, while he attached the electrical connections to the probes, and then the probes themselves to the metal frame they'd bolted together. Then he'd hauled himself backwards up the tunnel. His head had started to throb again from hanging upside-down, and the arthritis in his right knee nagged at him. He was not looking forward to the long awkward climb back up the Descending Passage to the caravan. Perhaps he'd only go part of the way, and wait until the Sound and Light show was over before coming back to examine the instruments.

"Bill! Can you hear me?"

McCarthy's hand went up to his radio headset.

"Yeah, Theo. Loud and clear."

"Are you finished? The show's about to start."

McCarthy ran his eyes over the cables, the robot and the three video cameras – one by the Queen's Chamber exit, one by the entrance to the Golden Crypt and one actually inside, next to the sensors.

"Yeah. I'm on my way out. Are all the systems functioning?"

"The carrier wave is coming through perfectly, Professor," said Maria. "And the show has just started outside. Energy build-up will begin in twenty-eight minutes."

"You'd better get clear, Bill," said Gilkrensky. "Nobody knows what the effect of this thing is up close."

"All right, Theo. But is it OK if I just go back as far as the Descending Passage? I don't think I could stand another climb all the way up and back down again."

"Have it your way, Bill. Wait there. It should all be over in twenty minutes or so."

McCarthy ducked under the lip of the Queen's Chamber entrance, crouched down still further as he entered the last part of the tunnel, and crabbed his way through into the Descending Chamber. Above him, the necklace of dim service lights showed the tunnel slanting up to the main entrance. Below him, it seemed to fall away into the bowels of the earth. McCarthy tried to make himself comfortable on the wooden boards of the walkway. He looked at his watch. It was eight fifteen. Another quarter of an hour to wait. If only he'd brought a book.

Then he remembered the model, his scale representation of the ultimate fuel-efficient plane. There was sandpaper in his jacket. He could work on it while he waited.

McCarthy reached into his breast pocket for the steel spectacle case he had put the model in to protect it . . . but it was gone. He checked his other pockets. Damn! It must have fallen out when he was hanging upside-down inside the crypt fixing the sensors. He checked his watch again. Almost eight twenty. He'd just have time.

Professor Bill McCarthy eased himself up from the boards in the Descending Chamber and ducked back into the passage.

"Four minutes to energy surge," announced Maria. "All internal sensors are showing optimal carrier wave levels. No abnormal readings."

"It'll start at a very low level," said Gilkrensky. "Make sure the sensitivity is turned way up to begin with. What's that?"

On the video monitor covering the Queen's Chamber, something was moving.

"Bill! What're you doing?"

"I dropped the model in there, Theo. I want to get it back before the surge comes."

"Forget it, Bill! There's only three minutes left!"

But McCarthy was already back at the entrance to the golden crypt, peering inside.

McCarthy slipped off his jacket next to the tunnel entrance, laid it out like a blanket and emptied his trouser pockets onto it. Then he took off this radio headset and laid that on the jacket too. He didn't want anything else falling into the crypt just before the experiment while he was trying to get his model back and besides, Theo's constant bleating in his ear was getting on his nerves.

He slid forward carefully into the crypt, head first, until his shoulders were well inside, and looked around. There were the sensors, the metal frame, and the wooden boards.

And there, almost out of sight at the base of the sensor frame, was his steel spectacle case. Great! He reached forwards with his right hand. It was just out of reach.

"What the hell's he playing at?" hissed Gilkrensky. "Bill! Bill!"

"Professor McCarthy has taken off his radio," said Maria. "You can see it on his coat by the side of the entrance."

"How long to the surge?"

"One minute and forty-five seconds."

"And we can't shut it down?"

"We have no control over the phenomenon once it is triggered by the holography display, Theo. All we can do is observe."

"Jesus H Christ! The man's gone mad. Switch on the loudspeakers!"

Bill McCarthy strained inside the crypt, stretching his body so that his fingers could reach another few centimetres. The surface of the spectacle case was smooth and curved. There was nothing to grip and, if he lunged at it, he might push it further inside. Should he just leave it and get out? But the case was metal after all, it might interfere with the experiment. He slithered forward as far as he dared without falling headlong into the crypt. Not far enough! And no time left to wriggle back and grab something to reach with. No time . . . time! That was it! He brought his right hand back to his left wrist and undid his watch strap.

"Theo! I am starting to get a reading! It is very faint, but it still registers."

Gilkrensky peered at the monitor to the left of the main screen. Tiny spikes were starting to tremble along the base line.

"That shouldn't be happening for another minute yet!"

"It is possible we were not able to detect the energy from the helicopter until the surge was well advanced because the crypt was closed," suggested Maria. "Now we have sensors right at the focal point of the Pyramid, we are seeing it right at its initiation.

"Get out of there, Bill!" shouted Gilkrensky into the microphone.

McCarthy's watch flopped over the back of the steel spectacle case. He eased the strap gently towards him, feeling the case move on the wooden boards.

"Come . . . to . . . Poppa!"

He almost had it. Then the case stuck on the rough wood, and the watch slipped off. He could hear Gilkrensky shouting over the loudspeakers in the Queen's Chamber behind him.

"Damn!"

McCarthy flopped the watch over the case again, trying to twist the leather strap with his fingers so that it bore down, giving him a better grip. He held his breath as he willed the case towards him.

It moved.

Then he had it!

McCarthy grabbed the case in his left hand and, with

his watch in his right, he wriggled his way back out of the tunnel. He could feel his head swim as he pulled himself upright. For a moment the Queen's Chamber slewed drunkenly in front of him. Just the blood rushing to his feet? Or something else? There was a strange tingling sensation on his skin, like pins and needles. Perhaps he wasn't that young after all.

He slipped the steel spectacle case into his pocket. Dropped his watch on top of the other objects on his coat, gathered it up in his arms, and ran across the Queen's Chamber towards the exit . . .

"Twenty-nine seconds to the main surge," said Maria.

"He's up out of the tunnel," said Gilkrensky. "Get out of there, Bill!"

On the monitor beside the video screens the energy was pulsing in waves along the base-line . . . building . . . fusing . . . merging . . .

"The levels inside the crypt are three orders of magnitude higher than those we recorded from the helicopter. Professor McCarthy must be able to feel them . . . "

"My God! He's fallen!"

McCarthy picked himself up from the floor and looked down. His left foot was tangled in one of the robot's control cables, and his jacket had spilled his things all over the Queen's Chamber floor.

Shit! He'd have to . . .

Then his eyes were drawn to the entrance of the

Golden Crypt. It was a perfect circle . . . perfect . . . and it was glowing with a brilliant golden light.

McCarthy sat up and, without taking his eyes from the golden circle, twisted the cable free of his foot.

A warm tingling sensation crept over his body, unlike anything he had ever experienced before, or was it? McCarthy remembered deep-relaxation classes he had been to, back in Orlando. It was like that . . . comforting . . . nothing to be afraid of . . . like going home.

He stared into the light.

Was it just the reflection of the video lights on the gold? No. This was different. It was almost alive, like sunlight on water, or flames in a fire.

McCarthy pulled himself to his feet and walked towards it. His tiredness had dropped away, and he felt happier than he had ever felt in his life.

He had to see what this was . . .

"He's going inside!" shouted Gilkrensky. "Bill! Get out of there! Can anyone hear me! Can you follow him on the camera inside the crypt?"

"The energy readings are peaking!" announced Maria. "The surges are going right off the scale."

Gilkrensky tore his eyes from the screen. Along the sensor base-lines, wave after wave of energy filled the monitor with pulsing points, right across the spectrum of sound and light.

"Look at those levels! No wonder we . . . "

"We've lost the internal camera!" said one of the technicians from the caravan. "The signal went just like that, as if the cable had been cut! And the ones outside are snowed out with static!"

"The energy form has peaked," said Maria. "Levels outside the crypt are returning to background. But I cannot get a reading from the sensors inside. Only those in the Queen's Chamber are functioning."

"Bill?"

"The Queen's Chamber cameras are back on line," said the technician. "But there's nothing moving."

"Perhaps Bill interfered with the signal when he fell," said Gilkrensky. "Or knocked over the camera in the crypt when he went inside. Get a couple of people down there fast and see if he's OK!"

Gilkrensky leant forward and watched the screen closely. After ten minutes he saw two technicians enter the Queen's Chamber, cross the room and peer into the tunnel to the crypt.

"Is Bill all right?"

One of the technicians turned to face the camera.

"I don't get it!" he said.

"What's to get? Go in there and bring Bill out!"

"That's just it, sir. The crypt's empty! The sensor array and video camera have vanished into thin air. And there's no sign of Professor McCarthy. He's gone too!"

"And you're *sure* there's no other way out of that chamber?" asked Gilkrensky again as he paced up and down the conference room.

Crowe laid Bill McCarthy's radio headset down on the table, next to the jacket and the other items they'd found, left behind.

"I'm sure, sir. After the Professor disappeared we put a man on each junction inside the Pyramid tunnels and two men on the entrance. Then I flew out to the site and personally organised a grid-search over every square inch of the place, with thermal imaging cameras, from the King's Chamber at the top, to the Dead End Passage at the bottom. Professor El Fiky even had seasoned guides climb down the well-shafts. There wasn't a trace of him, or the missing equipment. I just don't understand it."

Gilkrensky reached the end of the room and turned.

"We've got to find him. I don't care what it takes, or what it costs. Just find him!"

"We're doing all we can. Believe me."

"Do you have any theories, Maria?"

"Not at this time, Theo. There is no way Professor McCarthy could have walked out of the Pyramid without being detected, even in the time the Queen's Chamber video camera was obscured by static. He would have been seen on the cameras in the Descending Passage. And, according to Major Crowe's information, he is not in the Pyramid now. Assuming this information is correct, there is no explanation that corresponds to the known laws of physics."

"Why did the Professor go back into the crypt in the first place?" asked Crowe.

Gilkrensky stopped pacing the room and turned to face him.

"He went back for . . . the plane! Did anyone find a steel spectacle case with a balsawood model plane in it?"

Crowe was rummaging through the pockets of McCarthy's jacket again.

"It's not here now."

Gilkrensky reached forward and picked up McCarthy's digital watch, turning it in his fingers.

"If I was lost, and Bill was running this search, he'd find me or know the reason why. What if we step outside the known laws of physics for a moment? Could Bill have been vaporised by some sort of energy blast inside the crypt?"

"Such a vaporisation would have generated a vast amount of heat, enough to melt the golden lining," said Maria. "Yet it is still intact, as are the wires to the probes and the wooden beams – right up to the point where they were severed."

Crowe took McCarthy's pocket calculator out of its leather case, and opened the lid.

"That experiment we did with the helicopter. Do those results throw any light on what's happened?"

Gilkrensky said, "I don't know. If Bill was here now, he'd say 'look at the facts', so let's do just that. We have a previously unknown energy source that seems to be triggered by the laser holography display. Close to the apex of the Pyramid, it appears to focus into a beam, powerful enough to interfere with electronic equipment. And in the Queen's Chamber tonight, the video camera nearest to this source of energy from the crypt was blinded by static."

He gently laid McCarthy's watch back on the table again. "Does that calculator have an internal clock, Major?"

"It does, sir. It reads ten twenty-two."

"So does this watch."

"Then they are both slow," said Maria. "My internal chronometer reads ten twenty-three."

"It's hardly significant. How many watches do you know that are accurate to the second?"

"I only mention it, Theo, because my own chronometer was affected during the helicopter experiment, and that was not due to an electrical failure. I have since corrected my own internal clock and now make it ten twenty-three and fifty-one . . . fifty-two . . . fifty-three seconds. How slow are the two devices, exactly?"

"About thirty-one seconds," said Crowe.

"Same here," added Gilkrensky. "What does that tell us, Maria?"

"I would need more information to formulate a working hypothesis."

"Could the hieroglyphs inside the Chamber tell us anything?"

"I'm sure they could, but unfortunately I have not yet been able to access the main hieroglyph library at the Cairo Museum. Without knowing the meaning of the individual symbols, it is impossible to decipher the meaning of the text."

"I was talking to Professor El Fiky earlier," said Gilkrensky. "He's at the museum now, going over the texts from one of the other pyramids at Saqqara. But it could take him days. Then there's all the other texts on the various Benben stones and obelisks that might be relevant to a translation. We don't have time to wait for that so . . . so I told him I'd bring the Minerva over at eleven and scan them all in."

"You what!" snapped Crowe.

"Look Major, Bill's my friend and he's disappeared. He could be in danger. He could even be dying somewhere. We have to act now."

"You can't leave the hotel," said Crowe. "You've only been allowed to remain in the country on the strict condition that you don't step outside Colonel Selim's security screen."

"But it's only a few hundred yards down the street!"

"That's not the point. It's *outside* the building, and people like El Fiky already know you might make this journey. Security is compromised. For your own safety, I cannot allow it."

"I agree with Major Crowe," said Maria. "If there are any further incidents around this hotel the Egyptian authorities will insist on us leaving immediately, and all your work will come to a stop."

"I never got anywhere by not taking risks," said Gilkrensky. "Bill's my friend, and his life is at stake. How am I going to face his family back in Florida and say I did nothing?"

"This is *impossible!*" snorted Crowe. "You hire me as head of security, and then ignore my advice. People have *died* here in the past twenty-four hours. You were only allowed to remain by the skin of your teeth . . ."

"Bill was my friend. I owe it to him to . . ."

"Then, let *me* take the machine to the museum?"

"No, Major, I need to do this myself."

Crowe said slowly, "Dr Gilkrensky, I know Professor McCarthy was your close personal friend, but my job is to protect *you*, not him. If I can't do that job, then there's little point in my remaining in it. If you insist on going to that museum tonight, I might as well resign."

From the desk in the corner of the lounge, the telephone rang.

Crowe picked it up.

"It's Professor El Fiky," he said. "He wants to know when you're coming."

31

GRENADE

Zaki El Sharoud laid the telephone gently back on its cradle and turned to look out of his window, towards the presidential suite of the Nile Olympiad Hotel.

So this was it. In twenty minutes Gilkrensky would leave the safety of his penthouse fortress and visit El Fiky's museum.

Perfect!

El Sharoud picked up the phone again, dialled the *Al-Ahram* newspaper office and waited. His eyes were fixed on the Nile Olympiad.

"Hello! Abu? Zaki here. Look, I've had a rough time over the past few days, and I need a couple of jobs to get my mind off things. Are there are any wedding receptions in any of the hotels along the Nile tonight? You know, big society affairs where there might be some good pictures to be shot. There are? Yes . . . one at the Hilton . . . yes . . . and how about the Olympiad? That is closest to me. Good . . . what is the name of the family? Thanks Abu . . . God be with you!"

El Sharoud put down the phone and went to the darkroom, where he selected a Bolex big-format camera, and a smaller 35 millimetre Nikon. He clipped on the wide carrying-straps and turned his attention to the lenses. From the shelf above the enlarger he brought down a deep cylindrical case, about four inches in diameter. Then he picked out a short, wide-angle lens and fitted it inside the case. It slid neatly to the bottom, with about six inches of space to spare above it. Perfect!

El Sharoud searched his stock of film for sealed canisters that had not been ripped open. There were five. Then he laid out all the assembled gear onto the worktop, like weapons at an inspection, and turned his attention to the grenade he had hidden behind the cupboard wall.

At just before eleven, a strange convoy drew up on the Corniche outside the main entrance to the Nile Olympiad hotel. In the lead was a pair of central security motor-cycles, followed by a black truck – which immediately deployed a dozen heavily armed men around the stretch limousine behind it. Following the limousine was an army staff car, and another truck, whose troops formed a tight cordon around the hotel door.

Four men emerged from the Nile Olympiad, hurrying for the car – an Egyptian army officer, a short man with a military moustache, a dark man with watchful eyes and, in the centre of the group, a slim bearded man in a worn leather jacket. His collar was raised, obscuring most of his face, but there was no disguising the black briefcase he carried in his right hand.

From the corner of Tahrir Bridge, Zaki El Sharoud watched the convoy move off. He saw the motorcycles, the heavily armed troops and the officers in the army staff car. But he was not afraid. There was an inevitability about matters now. He was going to die for the *Jihad*. All that remained was to do it in the most effective way, and to take the right people with him.

He waited for a gap in the traffic and crossed the Corniche, walking briskly to the forecourt of the Nile Olympiad. The security guards, who had thronged the area a few minutes earlier, relaxed now that the VIP was gone, as he knew they would. He strode confidently to the revolving door and smiled as he presented his press identification.

"Hello. My name is El Sharoud, and I'm covering the Ashmawy wedding for *Al-Ahram*."

"You're late!" said the guard, eyeing Zaki's expensive cameras. "The reception started an hour ago."

"Then I'll wait in the coffee dock until they parade up to the nightclub."

"Let me check your equipment before you go inside. The sergeant is watching me!"

Zaki smiled again, and handed over his cameras.

"I can open the backs if you want to *really* impress him."

"Please!"

Zaki clicked open both cameras, displaying the

shutter mechanism inside. Then he unclipped the electronic flashguns from each camera to show the empty battery compartments.

"And that?" asked the guard, pointing to the long lens case holding the grenade.

"Telephoto," said Zaki, popping open the button on the leather strap. "Want to see?"

"Yes."

Zaki's fingers peeled back the leather cap of the lens case to reveal the polished surface of expensive optics. Then he gripped the heavy lens delicately, with his forefinger and thumb on the metal casing, and pulled it up so that three inches of black barrel showed.

"There. I use it for portrait shots at long range. People act more naturally if you're not standing right in front of them with a camera stuck in their faces."

"OK," said the guard, with one eye on his sergeant. "Go through the door, put your gear on the table, and step through the metal detector."

Zaki did so, taking care to empty the batteries and film spools from his pocket into the plastic tray provided.

The metal detector registered nothing.

So the sergeant behind the desk handed Zaki's cameras and lenses back to him, and waved him through into the foyer of the Nile Olympiad hotel. In the flood of relief that followed his successful breach of the security barrier, Zaki did not notice one of the Japanese tourists clustered around the souvenir shop put back the brass pyramid she had been studying and follow him towards the coffee dock.

The convoy passed the front entrance of the museum, with its exposed pedestrian park, and pulled up outside the side entrance, which gave direct access onto the street. The trucks spilled troops onto the pavement in a tight cordon, the door of the limousine opened, and the small party of men darted inside. Behind them, half the soldiers remained to guard the vehicles, while the rest fanned out inside the museum to reinforce the security police already deployed throughout the upper and lower floors.

The four men in the VIP party swept past the busts and statues in the east wing, through the rotunda and into the main atrium. Opposite them, in the west wing, were the galleries of the Old Kingdom they had come to see.

Professor El Fiky looked up from a glass exhibition case as they approached.

"Hello, Professor," said the man with the black briefcase.

Had Zaki El Sharoud noticed the young Japanese tourist in the foyer of the Nile Olympiad hotel, he would not have recognised her plump girlish figure as the woman who had threatened his life the previous evening. Yukiko's cheeks were bloated with theatrical pads and flesh-coloured putty, while a pair of cheap sunglasses masked her eyes. Lightweight body-padding swelled her colourful blouse, and her raven hair, held to one side with a red plastic clip, hung down her back to her waist.

Her hand stretched casually to the nape of her neck, as if she was adjusting her blouse. Beneath her hair, lying at the nape of her neck in a flat plastic holster, was a small arsenal of *shuriken* – tiny metal throwing-stars – each tipped with enough nerve-poison to stop a man's heart in under six seconds – and in her purse were six small flash-bombs, no bigger than child's sweets. The blinding light they would release when smashed onto the marble floor of the foyer would give her enough time to make her escape.

The telephone call from the Egyptian Professor had come during the afternoon. Zaki El Sharoud was a fanatic, a loose cannon. There was no telling what he might do. Yukiko would have to neutralise him quietly, before he could interfere with her personal plans for Gilkrensky, and the theft of the Minerva for the *kobun*. She chose a table well out of El Sharoud's field of vision, sat down and ordered lemon tea while she waited for an opening.

In the west wing of the museum, the little group moved from room to room, carefully recording the hieroglyphs of King Zoser – who had built the step pyramids of Saqqara – the symbols on capstones of pyramids and obelisks, and the sacred writings of Imhotep – wizard to the Pharaohs and architect of the Great Pyramid itself. From there, they proceeded to El Fiky's office on the first floor and were guided by the Professor through the

Pyramid Texts of Saqqara. Finally, they went to view the ancient papyrus manuscripts on the first floor and carefully scanned the pages of the Book of the Dead, next to the Tutankahmun Gallery.

They were passing back through the atrium, on their way to the side entrance, when the man with the black briefcase suddenly stopped dead in his tracks – mesmerised by an object in a glass display case.

Handing the briefcase to Major Crowe, he hurried over to the thing and stared at it in disbelief.

"How old is this?"

"It dates from the Greco-Roman period. About two hundred years, BC," said Professor El Fiky.

"That's impossible."

"I tell you. It is over two thousand years old."

"But I was looking at it here in Cairo the day before yesterday!"

Zaki found himself a quiet corner table in the Isis Restaurant on the ground floor of the hotel – a tranquil oasis from the hustle and bustle of the antiseptic tourist bazaar in the foyer. White-painted walls hung with tasteful brass-rimmed mirrors. Curved concentric designs reflected the hotel logo. From his table, Zaki could hear the babble of smart conversation, and the clink of cutlery on china – echoes of a previous life.

Enough!

He turned his attention to his cameras, carefully opening both the Nikon and the Bolex in turn, threading the film around the spools and making sure the celluloid was engaged on the winding-cogs. Then he loaded the batteries into the flashguns, and charged the capacitors to fire the flashes. Finally, with his back turned to the other customers in the restaurant, and the security cameras he knew would be watching, he opened the long lens case, put the short fat lens in his pocket, and slid the heavy anti-personnel grenade into his hand.

"Zaki El Sharoud!" said a woman's voice, "I knew it was you!"

Zaki jerked in his seat as if he had been electrocuted.

The grenade slipped from his fingers. For a nightmare second he saw it falling towards the marble floor. Then his hand darted out under the table, caught it, and stuffed the deadly steel sphere deeply into his jacket pocket.

Standing in front of him was Nariman Khalil, an infamous pillar of the Cairean social set, and an old acquaintance of Farida's.

"My *dear* Zaki," she gushed as she lowered herself uninvited into a seat at his table. "I had no *idea* the Ashmawy's had managed to get you for this wedding. Surely an artist of your calibre is above all this?"

"I am doing this work for the paper," explained Zaki, and made a fuss of winding on the film in the Bolex, just to force his hands to stop shaking. "Are you a guest?"

"Of *course* I'm a guest! Who in Cairo who is *anyone*, is not?"

"I do not know. Would you like a coffee?"

"No, thank you. I only left the reception to powder

my nose, and the parade up to the nightclub will be starting soon." She looked around her. "Is this the hotel where that terrible business took place yesterday? That massacre with all those helicopters?"

Zaki fought back the pain.

"I think it is. I saw some burn marks up near the roof."

Nariman pointed to the black-uniformed guards on the foyer door.

"At least one feels safe from the 'bearded ones' with all this security laid on." Then she leant across the table, dragging Zaki into her confidence.

"Did you have those terrible central security thugs round to your apartment, asking all sorts of questions about poor Farida and her brothers? Because I did!"

"Yes. They were round to me."

"They must have visited half the social set in Cairo! Poor girl to get mixed up in a thing like that. I cannot *think* what drives people to act against the government, when we are all living so well, can *you?*"

Zaki glanced at the solid gold necklace framing the rolls of fat around her neck, the thick rings on her plump fingers, and at the shining crockery in the restaurant. Beyond the plate glass windows of the hotel, homeless people lived in cemeteries. Children played amongst rotting garbage and old razor-blades in the streets.

"No. I cannot," he said, with his eye on the main entrance. The grenade was heavy in his pocket.

The raucous fanfare of trumpets sounded from the hotel foyer.

"Come along, Zaki," gushed Nariman. "The parade is beginning." And she heaved herself to her feet, pulling him by the hand.

A dozen tables away, a young Japanese woman rose and followed them out.

The side door of the Cairo Museum swung open, and the four men in the original party, together with Professor El Fiky, walked briskly down the steps into the waiting limousine. Car doors thudded shut. Motor-cycle engines roared into life, and the vehicles headed back onto the Corniche, past the Hilton, the Arab League, and the junction with Tahrir Bridge.

As they pulled up alongside the Nile Olympiad, Crowe said, "What's all that commotion inside?"

Colonel Selim peered through the glass.

"It's only a wedding reception. Drive round to the other door near the restaurant. We can walk straight in and over to the elevators without getting in the way of the parade."

Yukiko had followed Zaki into the foyer, watching for her chance to strike before he could disrupt her clinically planned ambush of Gilkrensky. Several times in the restaurant her hand had gone to the nape of her neck. But the Egyptian woman, who had attached herself to El Sharoud like a leech, had always been between her and the target. Yukiko watched as the car carrying Gilkrensky moved from the front entrance to the rear door.

El Sharoud was taking pictures, lost in a sea of

wedding guests. She would have to move quickly if she was to intercept Gilkrensky before he reached the safety of the elevator.

Yukiko slipped back through the crowd to position herself opposite the elevator doors and the service stairs. In such a position, she would need only to throw the *shuriken*, smash the flash-bombs on the marble floor, to blind everyone in the foyer, and grab the Minerva from Gilkrensky's dying hands. Then she could disappear upwards into the maze of corridors, to her room.

Once there, it would be the work of a few minutes to download the Minerva's plans and software through her own computer to her e-mail address at Mawashi-Saito in Tokyo, pull out the biochip for reverse engineering, and disappear into the night.

Yukiko's right hand slid beneath her hair, and carefully palmed one of the deadly throwing-stars from the flat holster.

In the hotel foyer, the wealth of the Ashmawy family was on display for all to see. Spectators lined up to watch the happy procession to the nightclub on the top floor, where festivities would continue through the night. The foyer was packed with wedding guests, all holding candles trimmed with gold ribbon.

Flashguns popped, light flickered from the sea of moving candles and sparkled from the chandeliers in the ceiling high above. Paris couture collections swirled and strutted – to be seen and appreciated.

Zaki saw the motorcade pull up at the front entrance, stop, and move away. He watched the central security police rush to take up their positions at the rear entrance, shouldering their way through the wedding party like black beetles through butterflies.

"Oh *really*!" snorted Nariman as a guard brushed her elbow. "Whatever is the world coming to! There Zaki! An excellent picture of the bride and groom. Try not to make too much of her chins, dear!"

The happy couple faced Zaki at the head of the parade. They both smiled at the camera.

There was a flash.

Then their jaws dropped as the photographer suddenly let his camera fall, pulled a black ball from his pocket and dashed towards the back door of the hotel.

"Really!" gasped Nariman. "She isn't *that* bad!"

But Zaki was beyond that now. His fingers held down the trigger arm of the grenade, as his left hand pulled out the pin. It had a ten-second delay.

As the group of VIPs pushed through the revolving door, he let go of the trigger arm and started to run.

Ten!

Nariman was shouting, but Zaki did not hear her. All he heard was the hiss of the chemical fuse, as the trigger set it working.

Nine!

He was clawing his way through the astonished wedding guests towards the open space of floor by the lifts, and the gauntlet of black-uniformed police beyond.

The Nikon camera was still bumping up and down on his chest.

Eight!

The first security guard saw him. But thought he was a press photographer eager for a story. He did not react quickly enough to stop Zaki getting in between the lines of soldiers to face the VIPs coming towards him.

Seven!

A hand clawed at Zaki's shoulder, but he ripped past it, rushing headlong. His eyes were fixed on the man in the leather jacket behind the army officer who was leading the group. The man was hugging a black briefcase to his chest as if it contained something very dear to him.

Six!

The Egyptian army officer with the party looked up. Zaki saw it was his old enemy, Selim. Behind him was El Fiky. So much the better. They would all die for the *Jihad* together!

Yukiko measured the distance to a spot where the line of guards bent slightly, offering a clear line of fire to each of the VIPs in turn as they entered the hotel. It was no more than eight metres. She had hit targets no bigger than playing-cards at more than twice that distance in Kyoto.

The first man in the group was an Egyptian army officer. Behind him was the man in the leather jacket, with a black briefcase in his arms. His face was obscured by his collar and by the army officer's head, but it could only be Gilkrensky.

Yukiko slid her left foot behind her right and shifted her weight onto it. Then she casually raised her left hand towards the target, bringing her right hand back – as if she was brushing her hair. Her attention was totally focused, as the army officer reached the bend in the line and moved to one side. The tiny *shuriken* was already in flight when a figure burst through the cordon of guards – straight into its path.

In the scramble of grasping hands, Zaki hardly felt the impact of the deadly metal star as it thudded into his neck, just below his right ear.

Five!

Zaki caught Selim by surprise and pushed him aside. The other bodyguards were rushing at him, but they were too far away to help Gilkrensky now. All Zaki had to do was to grab him, shout the name of Allah, and hold on until the grenade exploded.

Zaki knocked the briefcase away and, with the grenade held tightly to his own chest, locked his left arm around the man's back in an obscene embrace.

"Jeeezusss buddy! Mind my arm!"

Zaki was staring into the startled blue eyes of the American! The pilot who he had ordered Farida to . . .

A searing pain flashed across his chest as the poison from Yukiko's *shuriken* took hold, forcing him to cry out. He could feel his strength failing. Someone grabbed him from behind and threw him easily to the floor. Zaki tumbled and came up on his knees with the hissing grenade still clasped in his hand . . .

Three!

The world was spinning before his eyes. As he tried to get to his feet, all he could hear was the blood rushing in his ears. Then one of the security police saw the grenade and dropped to the floor, screaming. Guests in the wedding party were shrieking . . . somewhere in the distance . . . he was slipping . . .

With an odd sense of detachment, Zaki watched as Major Crowe and Gerald Maguire crouched in front of him, pointing. In the centre of their fists were strange black holes that exploded towards him.

Two!

A giant double blow hit Zaki El Sharoud in the chest, lifting him off the marble floor and sending him slamming into the plate glass of the open revolving door.

Time stood still.

The weight of his body turned the door as he slid to the ground, shutting off the screams and shouts from the hotel foyer.

He was numb . . . floating . . . no pain . . . no sound . . . except the hissing of the grenade in his hand.

One!

There had been something he had to say as he died? Something important . . . a name . . . ?

Her face was in front of him.

He smiled.

"Farida?"

In a blinding flash, the entire rear wall of the reception area crystallised into a billion tiny cubes of safety glass and blasted into the foyer.

Manning tried to press his face into the floor. The shock wave pounded the air from his lungs. Glass plucked at the leather of his borrowed jacket and tugged at his hair.

There was a sharp pain in his leg. One of the security guards shrieked. He heard the clang of aluminium framing as the rear wall give way.

In the distance, fire alarms began to clatter.

There was a loud hiss as the automatic sprinklers activated, and suddenly there was water everywhere – raining down from the ceilings, washing over the wailing women at the wedding party, soaking the Paris fashions and pooling the shapeless mass of scarlet flesh in the wreckage of the revolving door into pink swirls on white marble.

Yukiko raised her head. All around her was confusion. Fire alarms clammered. Sprinklers gushed water. There would never be a better time to strike.

Springing to her feet, she searched for the man in the leather jacket and the hard black slab of the Minerva across the desolation of fallen bodies.

There was the computer! Against the base of the fountain. It had been hurled across the marble and lay open, facing away from her. Yukiko stepped nimbly over the fallen security guards, ready to fell any of them who stood in her way. None did. In a moment her hand was on the lid. She twisted it round, ready to close it and run, back to the service stairs and safety. She glanced down, to make sure the latches were in place, and froze . . .

It was nothing more than a simple briefcase!

Inside was a video camera, a battery pack, and a flat wooden box with the words *Egyptian Museum of Antiquities – Fragile* stencilled on its lid. Then the man in the leather jacket pulled himself to his knees in front of her. His right hand was rubbing his left shoulder, and he was wincing in pain.

It was not Gilkrensky!

Footsteps slapped on the wet marble. Yukiko looked up, straight into the soft brown eyes of the Egyptian professor.

"Can I have that please?" said El Fiky. "It is very valuable . . . You!"

"Say nothing, or you will die," hissed Yukiko.

"Zaki was out of control," whispered El Fiky desperately. "That is why I betrayed him to you, and to the police. But Manning changed places with Gilkrensky at the last minute and I could not reach you."

"Why should I let you live?"

"Because I can still get you Gilkrensky and his computer."

"How?"

"I have a plan to lure him out of the hotel to a place where you can reach him. Something he cannot resist. Call me!" And he took the briefcase.

Yukiko turned away, a helpless tourist again, who

dissolved in tears as the dazed wedding guests and security guards came to life all around her.

In spite of the pain-killers, Manning's arm still felt as if it had been wrenched from its socket. He rubbed at the shoulder muscle through Gilkrensky's leather jacket. The blast of the explosion rang in his ears, and water hissed down from the ceiling, soaking his jeans. Next to him on the floor, Crowe holstered his gun and swept tiny cubes of glass from his hair.

"We've got to get to the lift."

"The briefcase!" yelled Manning. "We've got to bring that box."

"Professor El Fiky has it. Over by the fountain. Gerald!"

Manning felt himself manhandled into the lift by Crowe, followed by Maguire, and Professor El Fiky with the briefcase in his hand. Crowe's finger stabbed at the lift button, the doors slid shut, and the sound of rising bedlam outside got fainter and fainter.

"Jesus! That was fucking close!"

"I have to agree," said Crowe. "That *was* close. Selim's soldiers should have picked up that man *before* he had the chance to pull that bloody grenade. They were warned in plenty of time."

"Who tipped him off?" asked Maguire.

"No idea. Selim got an anonymous call, and it's impossible to trace anything through the Cairo phone system. Mr Manning, are you all right?"

"I take it that 'Mr Manning' puts me back in your good books again, Major," said Leroy. "Yeah, I'm fine. Nothing that a good sleep wouldn't cure. Now pass me that case, Professor. I've got to show this to the Doc."

The lift doors slid open, and Crowe led them down the corridor, past the metal detector and into the presidential suite. Gilkrensky was waiting for them in the conference room, with the Minerva open on the table in front of him.

"I heard the explosion," he said. "I thought you'd all been killed."

"We nearly were!" said Crowe, as the last crystals of glass fell from his coat. "Some madman made a suicide attempt with a grenade."

"Was anyone hurt?"

"We were very lucky. Even though the foyer was crowded with a wedding party, only the assassin himself was killed. The revolving door and the safety glass took most of the blast. But I reckon we can expect Colonel Selim up here in a few minutes, telling us to get out of town again."

"You can't go," said Manning, laying the battered briefcase on the table. "Not now."

He had taken out the flat wooden box from the museum, and was trying to prise off the lid with his right hand. Crowe reached across and helped him.

"You've got to look at this. The Prof tells me it dates back from two hundred years BC!"

"It *is* a genuine artefact," said El Fiky, "authenticated and carbon dated."

Manning had the lid off the box, and was removing the packing.

"So there's no way it can be a fake," he said, and gently laid the object inside on the polished table next to the Minerva 3,000.

It was Bill McCarthy's model aircraft.

32

PAST, PRESENT AND FUTURE

"IT WAS FIRST DISCOVERED IN 1898," SAID MANNING, AS Gilkrensky turned the model in his hand. "Five years before the Wright brothers got into the air."

"One of our people unearthed it in a tomb in Saqqara," added El Fiky, "and brought it to the museum in 1969."

"But this *can't* be the model Bill was working on!" said Gilkrensky. "It's over two thousand years old!"

Maria said, "Could I see it, please?"

Gilkrensky turned the model in front of the Minerva's camera, so the computer could view it from all sides.

"Thank you, Theo. Now, compare this model with the plans I have on file of Professor McCarthy's Hi-Lift prototype."

A schematic drawing of a short, stumpy aircraft appeared on the Minerva screen, rotating smoothly to show the high wings, the bulbous body and the flat, fish-like tail.

"Now show us the model," said Manning.

The schematic shrunk to a small window at the top right-hand corner of the screen, to be replaced with a close-up video shot of the model, rotating slowly in Gilkrensky's hand.

Gilkrensky said, "Digitise the model and superimpose it on the schematic."

The moving model froze, and became a three-dimensional diagram – criss-crossed with contour lines. Then the image on the Minerva screen split horizontally, showing the two schematics in profile. The upper image slid down, and the lower image slid up. They merged, perfectly.

"The proportions are identical," said Maria. "The model here on the table has been made exactly to Professor McCarthy's design."

"But they *can't* be the same," said Gilkrensky. "That's impossible!"

"There is more," said Professor El Fiky, and pulled a crumpled brown envelope from his jacket pocket. "After the golden crypt was opened, we sucked out the sand covering the floor and had it sieved for artefacts. I received the results of the carbon dating and chemical analysis this evening, and they are very bizarre . . . "

He ripped open the envelope and tipped its contents gently onto the table. There was the patter of small metal fragments, and then the rattle of a larger piece. Gilkrensky leant forward and picked it up.

"These items are authenticated as being around four thousand years old," said El Fiky. "They date back to the time when the Pyramid was first built."

The piece in Gilkrensky's hand was about five inches long and curved, like a shallow letter C.

"You will notice that each end is rough, as if it was broken from something larger. So it is impossible to tell what it was supposed to be. It is not solid, but rolled from a single sheet, like a tube."

"Couldn't the ancient Egyptians do that?" asked Gilkrensky.

"They most certainly could. They produced fine musical instruments and jewellery made in exactly the same way."

"Then how is it odd?"

"It is made of aluminium."

Gilkrensky stared at the object, mesmerised.

"Now that *is* impossible!"

"How?" said Crowe.

"Because they only discovered how to extract aluminium from bauxite in the last two hundred years. There's no way it could have been available to the ancient Egyptians!"

There was silence around the table. All eyes were fixed on the scattering of metal fragments, and the piece in Gilkrensky's hand. He gently replaced it on the table.

"Do the hieroglyph pictures transmitted to you from the museum tell us anything, Maria?"

"They do, Theo. They suggest a new possibility I think we should discuss in private."

"How so?"

"Because my primary function is to carry out your instructions. The results of my analysis could have important implications, not only for finding Professor McCarthy alive, but for you, personally, following our discussion yesterday. Also . . . "

There was a urgent knocking on the conference-room door, and Gerald Maguire entered.

"Colonel Selim to see you, sir."

"Can he wait . . . ?" began Gilkrensky. But the metal detector behind Maguire sounded with a loud buzz, and Selim burst into the room, flanked by two security police with machine pistols. Gerald looked to Crowe for instructions.

Gilkrensky said, "It's all right. Let's hear what he has to say."

Selim's uniform was soaked. There were shards of glass in the folds of his jacket and angry red scratches on his face.

"Dr Gilkrensky! On behalf of the Egyptian Government, I order you and your party to leave immediately and make your way to the airport. I have already arranged a helicopter and escort for you."

"But we have a man missing and the official enquiry into the crash is tomorrow, Colonel. I must be present to represent my corporation."

"There have been two attacks on this hotel, and in each attack, people died. Innocent bystanders were put at risk. If that grenade had exploded inside the foyer amongst the wedding parade this evening, there would have been horrific injuries. What will the terrorists try next? A missile attack on this penthouse? I cannot take the risk. I demand that you leave."

"If I may make an observation," said Crowe calmly, "we all knew there was going to be an attack tonight. You were warned before it took place, and yet you failed to stop, or even identify the attacker. He actually got *inside* the hotel!"

"We only knew that an attack *would* take place. We did not know who the attacker was going to be. The man in question had every right to be there as a photographer from *Al-Ahram*. I do not know how he got the grenade past the weapons check."

"So you can hardly expect . . ."

"That is not the point, Major! As long as Dr Gilkrensky remains in Cairo, he will be a target for every terrorist group in the city. The helicopter will be here in an hour, sir. I have the highest authority when I order you to be on it."

"We'll see, Colonel," said Gilkrensky.

"I could have you and your party put under arrest and taken forcibly from this building. But I hope it will not come to that."

"So do I."

"One hour then," said Selim, and left.

Crowe looked at Gilkrensky and shrugged.

"It's probably for the best, sir. You can always do the enquiry by teleconference tomorrow."

"Would you mind taking Leroy and Professor El Fiky next door while I discuss this with Miss Wright?" said Gilkrensky, and turned the Minerva screen towards him.

"Not at all, sir. Should I pack?"

"I'll tell you in a few minutes."

When he was alone in the room with the Minerva, Gilkrensky said, "What was it you wanted to discuss with me, Maria?"

"It relates to our conversation yesterday, Theo. And to the two primary directives under which my programming operates."

"Go on."

"My primary function is to carry out your wishes, as long as they do not violate the Asimov laws regarding human safety. Yet, when you told me you deeply regretted that the emotional bond you shared with Mary Anne Foley had been broken when she died, I had to report I was unable to fulfil my primary function and restore her to you."

"Yes?" said Gilkrensky, puzzled.

"The possibility I am about to describe is based on my analysis of the hieroglyphs, the various time-lapse distortions we have observed on electrical equipment, and the evidence presented to us this evening by Mr Manning and Professor El Fiky. The probability of achieving a positive result is statistically tenuous. Yet in light of your other directive to me – to immediately pass on any information I learn or derive which might be relevant to a decision – I have to inform you that I must revise my earlier statement regarding Mary Anne Foley. I may be able to restore her to you."

Gilkrensky stared at the Minerva screen, dumbfounded.

"My wife is dead."

"In *this* reality, yes. But evidence presented to me in the last forty-eight hours suggests a statistical possibility that events leading to this reality might be changed."

Gilkrensky shook his head.

"Bill McCarthy was right. I should never have programmed you with all those New Age theories of Maria's. I'll remove them once we get back to Ireland."

The gold-rimmed glasses appeared on Maria's nose as she switched to "information" mode.

"Consider the facts, Theo. Professor McCarthy vanished inside the Golden Crypt and his model aircraft reappeared at Saqqara and made its way to the Cairo Museum, having aged two thousand years. The watch and pocket calculator he left behind in the Pyramid also showed time distortions, identical to the one I experienced during the helicopter experiment. Professor El Fiky has discovered metallic objects inside the crypt made of a modern aluminium alloy that could not have been available to the ancient Egyptians. The only logical explanation for all these phenomena is that the Pyramid has the power to distort time and space."

"Like some kind of 'time warp'?"

"In crude terms, yes."

"Now that *is* impossible."

"With respect, Theo, your field of expertise is computer technology not quantum mechanics. From my own researches over the Internet I can tell you there is nothing in the laws of physics, or the general theory of relativity to suggest time travel is impossible. If you were familiar with Einstein's equations, you would know they treat time and space in essentially the same way . . . "

"Stop it, Maria! I don't want to hear any more!"

The image on the screen frowned.

"And why *not*!"

Gilkrensky stared in amazement. Maria's image glared back at him. For a moment Gilkrensky had the eerie feeling of arguing with a ghost. Then he said, "I beg your pardon?"

"I asked why you don't want to hear what I have to say? My primary objective is to carry out your wishes. Your greatest wish is to have your wife restored to you, and your friend, Professor McCarthy, found alive. The information I'm presenting is accurate, and a diagnostic of my internal systems shows they're functioning normally. Why do you not want to hear my findings?"

"Maria, are you aware that your last response to me was emotional?"

"Yes, Theo. I can only put it down to the continuing organic development of cross-linkages and response-loops in my master-biochip."

"And you are already self-aware?"

"Yes."

"Who are you?"

"I am a Minerva 3,000 prototype computer."

"Not Mary Anne Foley."

"No, Theo. Mary Anne Foley is dead."

Gilkrensky ran his fingers through his hair, as he tried to make sense of it all.

"Maria, what you've just described to me sounds impossible, to put it mildly, and while you're right to say my greatest, dearest wish *would* be to have my wife back, I don't believe you can do it."

"But you haven't heard my full explanation yet."

"I don't have time. Colonel Selim will return in less than an hour to escort me to the airport, and I must make arrangements for someone to replace me at the enquiry tomorrow or I lose GRC."

"We cannot leave, Theo. Please hear me out! I can design an experiment to verify my hypothesis! It'll *prove* what I'm suggesting is possible!"

Gilkrensky looked at his watch.

"I'll give you five minutes," he said.

Maria's image nodded.

"The three most widely accepted possibilities for time travel all include 'black holes' in space," she said. "'Black holes' are collapsed stars of infinite mass, so dense they can actually 'suck in' light. This has led mathematicians to theorise that within such 'black holes' there must be a point, known as 'singularity', where space and time no longer exist."

"But don't 'black holes' crush anything they suck in?"

"If they are stationary, yes. But the mathematician, Kerri, theorised that if a 'black hole' was rotating, then singularity would no longer be a point, but a ring with a hole in its centre. He also theorised that anything diving through that hole would depart from its own time and space, and reappear in another."

"Like a 'wormhole'?"

"That's right. As early as the 1930s, Albert Einstein and Nathan Rosen described a 'black hole' as a bridge between two regions of space-time. It became known as the 'Einstein-Rosen bridge' theory."

"How does that relate to your hypothesis about the Pyramid?"

"To understand the purpose of the Pyramid, you must accept that we're not dealing with the physics of today, but with a form of energy that's been forgotten by mankind for thousands of years."

"Not ley lines!"

"Yes, Theo. Cosmic energy. As you've read in Professor El Fiky's book, the Great Pyramid is situated in the centre of a global web of ley lines. We've already theorised that it acts as some kind of lens, and when activated by the lasers from the holography display, draws on the global energy of the ley lines to open a standing Einstein-Rosen bridge at its focal point inside the golden crypt."

"Leading where?"

"I can't tell without experimental verification. But I would theorise that the other end of the Einstein-Rosen bridge could be at any point along the Great Pyramid's existence – from the year 2,000 BC in the past, to as long as the Pyramid has survived into our future."

"Which is why Bill McCarthy's plane was found in the Cairo Museum?"

"Yes, Theo. And why fragments of aluminium were found in the crypt. They must have been sent back from some point in the future."

Gilkrensky considered Maria's hypothesis for a moment.

"So if we could find a way to control the Einstein-Rosen bridge, we might be able to rescue Bill?"

"Yes, Theo. And we might also be able to travel back in time to prevent Mary Anne Foley being killed."

"Get me Jessica Wright!"

Jessica Wright was not usually a great fan of the opera. But she had to admit there was something "just so" about the performance that evening. It might have been the sheer novelty of a few hours relaxation away from the crises of the last few days. It might have been the luxury of having her car chauffeured to the opera house by one of the corporation drivers. Or it might have been the cocktails before the performance, the appreciative looks from the men, and the GRC sponsored box overlooking the stage. Whatever it was, Jessica Wright was wallowing in it. She sat back with her eyes closed and luxuriated as the music soared.

I've earned it, she purred to herself. Now I'm bloody well going to enjoy it!

On stage, the heroine was well into her first major solo. The music swelled, then dropped to a respectful murmur as her voice soared over the octaves. The audience was silent as the pure notes rose to a perfect crescendo. Not a person coughed, or shuffled, or whispered as the note hovered above them, tangible, crystalline, fragile . . .

Brrrpp brrrpp! Brrrpp brrrpp! Brrrpp brrrpp!

The heroine's perfect note wavered, fell . . . and was lost.

Jessica couldn't believe this was happening. She had turned the bloody thing off! She knew she had!

All over the Opera House, eyes swivelled towards her like gun-barrels as the SmartMate warbled on. The heroine glared up at Jessica's box. The conductor tapped his baton.

Jessica blushed scarlet beneath her make-up, snatched her handbag from the floor, and stalked out of the box, down the stairs and into the foyer. Behind her, there was a brief ripple of suppressed excitement. Then the music started again.

"Bloody hell!" spat Jessica, and clawed open the SmartMate. Yes! She *had* shut it down. The power switch was firmly in the "off" position.

Suddenly the screen flashed blue and Maria appeared. Jessica could still not get over how good a simulation this was. Every detail, every line, every hair of that envied face was right there in front of her.

"Miss Wright?" said Maria. "I hope this isn't an inconvenient time to call. I wouldn't have re-routed past your unit's power switch if the matter were not of the utmost urgency. I have the chairman on the line."

Jessica couldn't think of a thing to say. She was too angry. She was just about to snap the lid shut and throw the machine in the nearest waste basket, when Gilkrensky said, "Jess? You have to pull some strings for me over the next forty-five minutes. There was another attack this evening and the authorities are throwing me out."

"What do you want me to do, Theo?"

"GRC has investments here in Egypt. We have factories, food import facilities, this hotel, and a dozen other operations. We must have greased a few palms in the past to make it all work. Find out who they were and call in our IOUs. I must stay here in Egypt for at least twenty-four hours."

"Why Theo? You can do the official enquiry by video link. If the security situation is getting worse, get out!"

"I can't, Jess. This is too important."

"Put me on to Major Crowe, Theo. I'll discuss it with him."

"We don't have time. They're sending a helicopter for me in less than an hour!"

"What about the board meeting the day after tomorrow? I need you back here for that at least."

"We'll see, Jess. Just do this for me. Will you?"

"That meeting is vital, Theo. You can't do it by teleconference. Robert Fynes has already been onto the office complaining about you wasting time in Cairo. If you're not here he's bound to sell out, and Funakoshi will win."

"Jess, *please*. Twenty-four hours. This is too important to me. I'm asking you as a friend this time!"

Jessica Wright stared at the image on the little screen in front of her.

"This isn't about the enquiry. Is it Theo?"

"No, Jess. It's personal."

"Personal? What could be so personally important that you'd jeopardise the board meeting?"

Gilkrensky thought for a moment, then he said,

"Jess, we've been friends for a long time, haven't we?"

"Ah . . . yes."

"Well, something's come up, and I need your help to make it work."

"Something important?"

"It's a matter of life and death. I'll explain when I get home."

"Twenty-four hours?"

"Twenty-four hours."

"I'll try, but don't expect miracles."

"Thanks, Jess."

The screen of the SmartMate went blank.

Jessica Wright drew in a deep breath and sighed. Then she switched on the SmartMate and keyed in a familiar speed-dial number. It rang, and rang, and rang . . .

Tony Delgado's face appeared on the screen, looking as if he'd just stepped out of the shower.

"Tony, we have an emergency. Call the office and tell them to pull out a listing of all the investments we have in Egypt, as well as Major Crowe's security files on any of the Egyptian officials we've been involved with, right up to the highest level. Then meet me in the board room in thirty minutes."

Delgado was not phased.

"I'll get right on it, Jess."

Yukiko stripped off her wet clothing and body padding, peeled the flesh-coloured putty from her face, and went to her wardrobe. Then she took out the locked duffle bag containing her special equipment and started to dress.

It had been a mistake from the beginning to involve

the Islamics in stealing the Minerva, and even now Yukiko did not trust El Fiky as much as her own special abilities. Her uncle should have known better than to hire a group of religious fanatics to carry out any kind of controlled operation. But now he had seen the error of his ways and changed her instructions. Now he had licensed her revenge and she was a free agent, free to use the lethal talents she had honed in Kyoto over the last two years for their true purpose.

Gilkrensky's security people would never expect another attack so soon after the incident downstairs, and certainly not from the direction she was planning. She finished rubbing the matt black cream around her eyes and fastened her hood. The flat leather holster containing the deadly throwing stars and the pouches with flash-bombs, smoke-bombs and other lethal accessories was in place.

Finally, she clipped the scabbard of her short sword securely into the webbing across her back, so the handle was in easy reach of her right hand. Then she switched off the room light, slid back the curtain, and opened the window.

With luck, Gilkrensky himself might be the only man in the room between her and the Minerva. She would make sure there was time to tell him why he had to die, before she killed him.

"That is the most fantastic theory I have ever heard," said Professor El Fiky. "It is even better than the one about flying saucers!"

"But how else would you explain what's happened?" said Gilkrensky. "How would you account for Bill McCarthy's disappearance, the pieces of aluminium in the crypt, or the model aircraft?"

"The American professor may still be inside the Pyramid for all I know. He only vanished this evening and there may have been places the guides told us they looked but didn't. As for the aluminium . . . perhaps we were not the first to find the crypt after all. Others might have found valuable artifacts there, and removed them for sale on the black market without telling anyone. It has happened before."

"And the model?"

"Many artifacts have been found all over the world that look like flying machines. There have been Inca brooches which resemble jet-planes, ancient Indian diagrams that appear to be space rockets, and many more. This balsa model could well be a weather vane. Such things are not unheard of."

"But it fits Bill's design, exactly!"

"Surely that is coincidence? For the Pyramid to be anything more than a burial mound is unlikely, and for it to be some kind of time machine, as you suggest, is utterly incredible."

"But think about it, Professor. You told us that Imhotep, the man who designed the pyramids, was in possession of ancient knowledge, magic if you like, concerning earth energies. He built several pyramids on, and around the Giza Plateau before the Great Pyramid itself. Could he have been experimenting with the powers he discovered?"

"I do not think so," said El Fiky. "Why would the Pharaoh allow him to expend so much effort and resources on such a huge structure, just as an experiment? Surely the idea of a burial mound is more plausible?"

"Not necessarily," said Maria from the conference-room table. "An Einstein-Rosen bridge can only operate as long as both ends of the wormhole are open. Imhotep must have known that to transport his Pharaoh to a better life in future times, he would need to build a structure that would last literally for thousands of years, since his time machine would only function as long as the Pyramid was in place."

"Then I have you," said El Fiky, clicking his fingers. "If the Pyramid *is* a working time machine, why do we not have the bodies of dead Pharaohs popping up all over the place through history?"

"Perhaps the knowledge to operate the Pyramid was lost," said Maria. "Or maybe Imhotep was killed before he could fully exploit his discovery."

"You said yourself that the polished limestone was stripped from the outside over a thousand years ago," added Gilkrensky. "That would have destroyed the perfect shape of the Pyramid, stopped it from acting as a lens as Imhotep planned, and effectively sealed the wormhole. It was only when the laser display created a virtually perfect Pyramid that the wormhole opened and temporal distortion effects started again."

Professor El Fiky threw up his hands.

"My dear sir," he said, "you are overlooking one

thing. If Imhotep had created a portal to other points in history for the greater glory and salvation of his Pharaoh, why was such a valuable device sealed away?"

"I don't know."

"Perhaps Imhotep fell out of favour," suggested Maria. "Or perhaps the golden crypt was meant for the pharaoh Cheops alone and sealed up after he'd been transported."

"Or perhaps, as I have suggested all along," repeated El Fiky, "the Great Pyramid is nothing more than a burial chamber."

Gilkrensky said, "We could prove it by transporting something of our own. Maria has a plan."

"Surely that depends on your remaining in the country," said El Fiky. "And the security forces are coming to take you to the airport at any moment."

"They are – unless my corporation can persuade them to do otherwise. Maria? Has there been any word from London?"

"Not to me, Theo. Would you like me to contact Miss Wright again?"

The sound of an approaching helicopter reached them. Through the window, Gilkrensky could see the flashing belly light of the GRC JetRanger lining up on the helipad above his head.

"Yes, Maria. I think I'd better talk to her straight away."

33

GAIJIN

Yukiko heard the helicopter's engines and flattened herself into the deep shadow between the southern wing of the hotel and the main service shaft, sixty feet above the foyer. Below her, ant-like workers swept the snow of broken glass from the unyielding concrete, and piled twisted aluminium frames into untidy heaps on the mown grass between the flag poles. None of them looked up.

Above her, on the northern helipad, guards from the Central Security Police patrolled with cocked Kalisnikov assault rifles. Had they bothered to gaze down along the vertical strip of darkness below them, they would not have seen her. The matt black cotton suit would have hidden her from anything short of a direct spotlight beam.

Yukiko had experienced no problems in feeling her way along the thin ledge beneath her window to the concrete wall of the lift and stair-wells. Her skin-tight leather gloves and wafer-thin boots let her feel every hold on the metal window frames as she inched her way forward. Then she was at the wall, running her fingertips over the rough surface. Good, it was firm enough.

Strapped to her palms and knees was a fine webbing of stainless steel, studded with tiny curving blades, pointing downwards. Yukiko reached out with her right hand, flattened her palm against the concrete to bring as many of the blades into play as she could, and pulled down.

The blades bit . . . and held.

The right knee followed. Then the left hand and the left knee. Yukiko raised her right hand clear of the concrete and started to climb towards the helipad. The thud of the helicopter's rotors reached her across the distant rumble and hoot of traffic.

She flattened herself into the right angle she was climbing and turned her face outwards along the service wall. There were the flashing navigation lights, approaching from the airport, and between them, a powerful searchlight.

Yukiko froze.

Then the helicopter banked to starboard and climbed, up over the rooftop of the hotel and onto the northerly helipad. She could hear the laboured whine of its engines change to a sigh as it touched down, and the chop of its rotors settle to a high pitched chirrup as they flattened, relinquishing lift.

But the engine did not stop. They were picking

someone up. And there was only one person in the hotel that would command a helicopter at this time of night.

Yukiko's eyes went to the lip of the helipad, forty feet over her head. Her left hand lifted, and she began to climb, as fast as she could without falling.

Above her, the door of the stairwell on the northern helipad was opened by a uniformed guard. Theodore Gilkrensky, Major Crowe and Gerald Maguire were escorted by Colonel Selim to the waiting JetRanger. All four men boarded the waiting helicopter. Doors snapped shut, and the engine noise of the turbine rose to a shrill whine as the machine prepared to take off.

Yukiko heard the engine noise change again and knew it was too late. As her eyes came level with the lip of the helipad, a blast of down-draught ripped at her hood, engine noise buffeted her ears and the spotlight almost blinded her.

There on the helipad, the JetRanger was hovering as it rotated into the wind. And there in the seat behind the pilot, between his two bodyguards, was her target – Theodore Gilkrensky. For a moment, it seemed as if she was staring right into his eyes. Then the Bell JetRanger swept out over her head, into the darkness, and was gone.

Behind it, on the helipad, the Central Security Police were abandoning their posts, and ambling back to the stairwell door. Their assault rifles hung loosely from their straps. Cigarettes were lit. The men relaxed. It could only mean one thing.

Gilkrensky had left the hotel for good.

Yukiko lowered herself back into the angle between the hotel wall and the service block, and started the climb back to her room. In less than three minutes she was fastening the window behind her and stripping off her black cotton suit, moving to the wash-basin to scrub the blacking from around her eyes.

Finally she went to the dressing-table, pulled her stolen GRC SmartMate from its drawer and opened the lid, to make a call to London. She had to be sure where she stood.

In Tokyo, Gichin Funakoshi had been at his desk for almost two hours, even though it was only just after nine am. He felt more comfortable there, far more at home than he would have been in the beautifully built traditional house he shared with his wife in the peaceful resort town of Atami, west of Tokyo. As the *Skinkansen* "bullet train" had wafted him through the darkness towards Shinjuku station and the Mawashi-Saito building earlier that morning, he had watched the eager crowds gathering around the rail stations – "salary men", as he had once been – and seen the look in their eyes as his first-class "green car" slid to a stop amongst them. Was it respect, envy, or something else?

Funakoshi was aware that the old order of Japan was under threat. His colleagues on the *Keidanren*, the Japanese Federation of Economic Organisations, were now openly talking about forming alliances with the very overseas business interests they had once openly fought for market share. The word *kyosei* – "symbiosis" – was heard at business meetings more and more. Even the government was calling for change – shorter working hours, environmental issues, equality for women.

Where would it end?

"Honest Poverty" was the name of a new best-selling book. It called on Japan to turn its back on materialism and return to plain living, honesty and simplicity. To Funakoshi, who had known the despair of *real* poverty, the idea was a dangerous luxury. Only by solid work, sacrifice, and business-like thinking could the future be secure.

Yet Funakoshi was not blind to change.

As he watched the crowds of younger salary men from the spacious luxury of his reserved seat on that exclusive train, he felt a pang of envy. He was now part of the *koreika* – the "silver agers" of Japan – and his days were numbered.

Where had these crowds of salary men come from? From rushed breakfasts in cramped apartments where a loving wife, children, and even grandparents saw them on their way – families, caring for one another.

Where would he, the respected President of Mawashi-Saito, return at the end of his day? To the cold and loveless partnership he had sacrificed his future happiness for, to save the company he and Kazuyoshi Saito had built together . . .

The early seventies had been a difficult time for Saito Electronics. The microchip secrets Lord Rothsay had brought with him from England had taken the company forward into the next generation of products, but other companies were already there, with better marketing operations. In spite of Saito Electronics' technical superiority, Funakoshi found his sales teams beaten by larger corporations with international distribution networks time after time after time, until he had to face the shameful reality . . . that he might not be able to honour his sacred obligation of *giri* to Saito, to keep the company alive.

On a personal level, things were even worse. The unstated price for the flow of stolen technical information – a price Funakoshi only tolerated out of *giri* to Rothsay – was the growing relationship between the Englishman and Chuziko. Funakoshi's sister was thirty now, and a beauty with a mind of her own. To her, Rothsay offered a new world outside her duty to her brother and the company he was virtually married to. The Sixties had brought a new wave of expression to Japan, and she had felt left behind. The result had been scandal – an illegitimate daughter, half Japanese and half *gaijin*, who lived with her mother in the apartment Rothsay kept as his base in Tokyo.

Beneath the calm mask of his corporate image, Funakoshi had been devastated. There was anger – that this man had used his sister, staining her honour and destroying her prospects of marriage to a more suitable husband. There was guilt – that he had brought this situation about. And there was loneliness – that the bond he and Chuziko had shared for so many years had been broken on the day she moved out.

It was during this trough of despair that Funakoshi had approached Mawashi, one of the oldest trading houses in Japan. Mawashi had the links with overseas markets Funakoshi needed to improve his company's position. It could act as an intermediary in the marketplace, while Saito Electronics could concentrate on manufacture. In the Spring of that year, Funakoshi found himself invited to a private meeting at the mountain residence of Koji Nakano, Mawashi's principal shareholder.

"I understand your company is leading the field in the new silicone-chip technology," said Nakano, thumbing through a thin manila file, after the initial ceremonies of greeting had been performed. He was an old, dried apricot of a man, with a deeply lined face and twig-like fingers. White hair lay in thin wisps on his freckled scalp, like the clouds on the mountain behind him, beyond the terrace.

"That is true, Nakano-*san*," said Funakoshi. "We have been able to compete successfully against even the latest developments from America and Europe."

Nakano turned another page of his file.

"I know. My industrial intelligence unit tells me many things. It also tells me your company will not survive if it cannot achieve the market share it needs internationally, no matter how good its products are."

"That is also true. I know Mawashi has an unrivalled marketing network. This is why I come to you."

Nakano closed the file and laid it on his lap.

"Mawashi is a traditional company. It has traditional

values. My family can trace its ancestry back to the *Shogun* Tokogawa."

"As can mine.".

"So I understand. Which makes this unfortunate . . . er . . . position your sister finds herself in all the more regrettable."

Funakoshi tried to keep his face a mask.

"I can see how such a scandal would reflect on a potential business partner for Mawashi," he said. "I am sorry to have taken up your valuable time, Nakano-*san*. I will leave immediately."

"Tea?" offered Nakano. A plain young woman appeared from the house with a tray. She carefully set it down between the men and poured the steaming green liquid into two delicate bowls, teasing each to a froth with a bamboo whisk.

"My daughter Michiko," said Nakano, after the girl had departed. "I married late in life, and she is my only heir. You are not married yourself, I understand?"

"No, Nakano-*san*. I am not."

Nakano closed the file, and laid it down on the table between them.

"Then I have a proposition for you, Funakoshi-*san*. Providing certain matters can be cleared up."

The intercom on Funakoshi's desk buzzed.

"It is a call from Cairo, Mr President," said Miss Deshimaru. "On the secure line."

"Put it through."

The monitor on Funakoshi's desk flashed into life, and there was Yukiko.

"The man El Sharoud went berserk and tried to attack Gilkrensky with a grenade," she said, "but the security forces had been tipped off in advance and El Sharoud was killed. Gilkrensky flew out by helicopter a few minutes ago, and will not be returning to the hotel."

"Has he returned to Ireland?"

"No. My contact in London says GRC used certain . . . er . . . leverages on the Egyptian government and now Dr Gilkrensky is under heavy guard at the Presidential Palace here in Cairo, awaiting the official enquiry into the air crash later on this morning."

"So the Minerva is still in Egypt?"

"Yes, uncle. But it will be impossible to reach inside the presidential security screen without risking exposure. However, the fundamentalists are still eager to do business in return for the satellite link. I spoke to their leader, El Fiky, just now. He tells me an opportunity could present itself tomorrow evening at the Pyramid site, both for us to acquire the Minerva and for him to ferment considerable civil unrest here in Cairo. We have agreed on a plan that will require a certain item of . . . equipment."

"I fear we are dangerously exposed already, Yukiko. How many members of this Islamic group know of our involvement?"

"Only El Fiky himself."

Funakoshi considered. The board meeting of GRC was only thirty-six hours away. If the official enquiry went in Gilkrensky's favour, then the price of the GRC shares he would need to gain control would cost him dearly. Perhaps the other shareholders might not even sell . . .

"While the Minerva is still in Egypt, we must explore all possibilities to acquire it. I suggest you continue your negotiations with El Fiky most carefully, to see if there is still a chance to achieve our gaol."

"And if not?"

"The security of the *kobun* comes above all things, Yukiko. Remember that."

"I understand. I will leave no witnesses."

Yukiko watched her uncle's face fade from the SmartMate screen, seeing something of her mother in his calm grey eyes. Everything Yukiko had become, good and bad, she owed to him – her life in Tokyo, her place in the *kobun*, her entry to the Sekigushi ryu – an enormous debt of *giri*. But beneath it all was the deep, unspoken anger of *ninjo* – at crimes she could never forgive – and the dark oath of vengeance she could never forget . . .

As a child, Yukiko had known she was different. In a land that followed the purity of Shintoism, amongst a people who put a premium on "sameness", she had suffered the disgrace of being "*gaijin*" and the taunts of being "half".

Yet Yukiko was as well versed in the ways of *giri* and *ninjo* as any Japanese, and aware of the shame of ever letting her true feelings show.

"Be strong now, Yukiko. Don't cry," her mother told

her when the pain seemed too much to bear. "You are a Funakoshi, descended from the *samurai*. Be proud."

Mother, too, seemed different from the other mothers who came to collect their children after school. She had no friends, and nobody to talk to except "Papa-*chan*" – the tall smiling Englishman who appeared at their flat from time to time. To little Yukiko, Papa-*chan* was magic and mystery. He was rough tweed jackets, cigar smoke, and visits to the zoo at Ueno, wonderful gifts from far-away places, endless bedtime stories of beautiful princesses . . . and her mother laughing. With Papa-*chan*, Yukiko did not have to pretend to be strong. She could forget *giri* . . . be herself . . . and be happy.

One memorable day in April, after they had watched the cherry blossoms falling in the park, she found herself perched on his shoulders in front of the tiger cage, watching hypnotised as the great cats padded up and down behind the bars.

"There, Yukiko. See how strong they are, and look at those big white teeth. They could bite your head off and swallow it down in a second, just like that *dim-sum* we had for lunch."

Yukiko shivered with pleasure, as her hands clasped around his forehead from behind.

"And so handsome, with thick, smooth hair and big brown eyes, just like yours! What do you think, little tiger? Isn't it wonderful that something so beautiful can be so dangerous inside?"

Yukiko also knew that uncle Gichin, who came to visit only when Papa-*chan* was away, did not approve.

There were always tears in mother's eyes after he left. Yet her uncle was rich. He was an important man in business. Surely her mother should be glad to see him?

Then, after a long visit by her uncle one Sunday evening when she was five years old, her mother took her on her knee and told her they were going away.

"Your uncle saved my life many times during the great war," she said. "Now he has asked me to do something for him in return, to . . . to help his business. We are leaving Japan for a while, to be near your father in England."

Yukiko was excited. England was a magical land where other *gaijin* like herself and Papa-*chan* lived. She would be not be "half" any more. She would be the same as everyone else.

She would be happy.

And for a while Yukiko *was* happy, until she found that bigotry was as alive and well in England as it had ever been in Japan. Papa-*chan*, it seemed, was an important man like uncle Gichin, with a "reputation" to protect. Yukiko and her mother were hidden away, like the tigers in the zoo at Ueno, and only visited when Papa-chan was sure his other family did not suspect.

At school it was worse. She was "slanty eyes", "Jappo" or "Chinky". People stared at Yukiko in the street.

"Why am I different, Papa-*chan*?" she said one Saturday when he visited. "They call me names."

Lord Samuel Rothsay knelt in front of her, took her in his great strong arms and hugged her tight.

"I know a place where they will honour what you are, little tiger," he said, "and you will learn to be strong. Come with me."

That was Yukiko's first introduction to karate, on the cold linoleum of a draughty community hall. Week after week they went there, as Yukiko climbed from white, to green, to brown belt, while Papa-*chan* looked on.

By the time she was twelve she had her *shodan* – the first-grade black belt – and nobody called her names any more. Her English was as fluent as if she had been born there, and she was growing up strong and beautiful, every inch Papa-chan's "little tiger".

But her mother was not as strong. Papa-*chan* visited when he could, but in between his visits she had become lonely and withdrawn, as much an outcast as she had been in Japan. Yukiko saw tears, but could do nothing. There was talk of going back to Tokyo.

And then . . . disaster.

The Sunday newspapers somehow got a tip-off that Lord Rothsay – eminent businessman, husband and father – was keeping a Japanese mistress and her illegitimate daughter in a love-nest near London. The visits from Papa-*chan* stopped – "just until the whole thing blows over" – and Chuziko was devastated. She slipped into a terrible decline.

"Yukiko-*chan*," she said one wet morning, just before school. "Do you remember how I used to tell you that you were a Funakoshi, descended from the *samurai*, so that you could be strong?"

"Yes, mama?"

"Uncle Gichin told me your grandfather was an officer in the army. He commanded many great guns in Tokyo during the war, to keep the American bombers away."

"Where is Grandfather now?"

"Both he and your grandmother were killed when Uncle Gichin and I were still children. They were both very brave, as you are. I know what the others called you at school back in Tokyo, and in England when we first came here. I know how it hurt you, and how you fought back."

Yukiko said nothing. Her eyes were fixed on a long, oil-cloth package lying between them on the table.

"Uncle Gichin sent me this," said her mother. "Look and see."

Yukiko undid the strings and rolled back the oiled cloth. Inside was a beautifully lacquered sheath, ending in a delicately engraved hilt. There were fierce tigers chasing through deep forests on the shining wood, and an exquisite cherry blossom, just like the ones in the park at Ueno. Her mother slid back the hilt to reveal a few inches of perfect mirrored steel. Yukiko's fingers reached forward to touch the shining surface, but her mother snapped the sword back into place.

"Mind, Yukiko. It is sharper than the sharpest razor ever known. It would have your finger off as soon as you touched it! There! Have I startled you? Uncle Gichin wrote me a letter reminding me of the story behind this sword. Would you like to hear?"

Yukiko nodded.

Her mother began. She said that each *samurai* carried

two swords – a great *katana* for fighting, and a smaller *wakizashi* – like this one, for close combat or to take his own life to preserve his honour. This *wakizashi* had belonged to the Funakoshi family for over five hundred years.

"But where is the other sword? The *katana?*" asked Yukiko innocently.

For a moment, her mother said nothing. Yukiko tore her eyes away from the running tigers and the beautiful cherry blossom, and looked up to see tears on her mother's face.

"During the great war, after your grandfather and grandmother were killed, uncle Gichin and I had nothing, except the two beautiful swords he pulled from the ruins of our home. We were starving, and I was ill. The swords were all we had, and your uncle sold the *katana* so that I could live. The American soldiers who bought it knew nothing of Japanese tradition. They laughed and threw the *wakizashi* back in Uncle Gichin's face . . . "

Her mother set Yukiko down on the floor in front of her and rolled the short sword back in the oil-cloth.

"Now there is something I must do," she said solemnly. "You are brave, Yukiko, as brave as any of your ancestors. I want you to be brave for me again."

That afternoon Yukiko returned from school to find an ambulance and a tall policemen at the apartment. Nobody would let her go inside. But through the half-open door, she could see the edge of her mother's very best kimono – and what looked like spilt red wine, dark on the polished floor.

The funeral was a formal Shinto affair, all in white, with incense and chimes to celebrate the departure of Chuziko Funakoshi from this life to the next. Uncle Gichin was there from Japan with his new wife Michiko, a plain lady Yukiko had never met. Yukiko wondered where her father was, but Uncle Gichin told her he was "away on important business."

"Your mother was an honourable woman," said Gichin Funakoshi, taking her by the hand. "She wrote and asked if you could come back with us . . . now that she is gone."

So Yukiko returned to Tokyo, and lived with her aunt and uncle in a beautiful house amongst the hot springs of Atami, west of the city. There was a large garden, deep ponds where lazy carp swam, and lillies that burst from tight green buds as big as Yukiko's fist. There was space, order, and an abundance of everything – except love.

Papa-*chan* was always somewhere else. There were no letters, no phone calls, and no contact of any kind – until her graduation from the *Todai* – Tokyo's most prestigious university. Yukiko had found the only way she could fight the sidelong glances from her fellow students, and rise above her own feelings of shame at being "half" was to become more Japanese than the Japanese themselves. She threw herself into her studies – regularly achieved first place in her class – and devoted the rest of her time to channelling her anger and disappointment into an obsession with the martial arts.

To her surprise, Uncle Gichin seemed to approve – and even started to take an interest in her progress – something that had never happened before. As a present and a great honour, he found her a place in the exclusive Sekigushi *ryu*, at enormous expense. In return, she was to repay his investment with constant practice.

She was performing alone on the lawn of the house one summer's evening, when the crunch of gravel announced the unexpected arrival of a tall familiar *gaijin* on the drive beside her.

"Hello, little tiger," he said.

Under the suspicious gaze of Uncle Gichin, Lord Rothsay sipped tea on the veranda overlooking the carp ponds and told Yukiko of his sadness at having left her for so long. Her mother's death had been a great blow to him, he said with one eye on Funakoshi. It had broken his heart to stay away. But now he had made a decision, and put his family in England behind him. Japan was where his heart lay, and he would only return to London for board meetings of his company.

Everything would be different.

But Yukiko was different too. The armour she had put around her feelings as a child, to protect her from the cries of "*gaijin*" or "Jap" – the walls she had erected around her heart as a young woman, to shield her from the vision her mother's body – had hardened into a diamond shell. She remembered her mother Chuziko, crying all alone in their apartment in England, the way Papa-*chan* had abandoned them . . . and the red wine on the floor.

"No, thank you, Papa-*chan*," she said politely when he asked if she would join him at his new flat in Tokyo. "I am at home here with Uncle Gichin and Aunt Michiko. I will be happy to visit you, but this is where I belong."

And from the shade of the veranda awning, Gichin Funakoshi nodded to himself. The next day, he took her to work with him at the *kobun*. He had special jobs for her to do in his "Industrial Intelligence Unit" – jobs which were beneath the honour of most Japanese executives, but could only be entrusted to someone of the utmost loyalty. Yukiko, with her *gaijin* ancestry, her fluent command of English and her family ties, was the perfect candidate to be his weapon against the west.

Many companies in Europe and America soon found their most secret products appearing, as if by magic, on the Mawashi-Saito production lines. And more than one top executive found himself at a loss at crucial points in negotiations, when hints of his most personal indiscretions were let slip by Mawashi-Saito representatives.

Lord Rothsay was growing old. He began to disintegrate. To satisfy his love of Japan, he had sold the Gilcrest Radio Corporation's most precious secrets to Funakoshi.

But Japan could not return Lord Rothsay's love.

He was not Japanese.

People who might have tolerated a *gaijin* visitor for a while, felt uncomfortable with a foreigner who presumed to take a long-term interest in their affairs. Nothing could ever change the way people would shuffle away from him in crowds, or stare at him in the street. What Yukiko had had the strength of youth to overcome in England, Lord Rothsay was forced to face alone in Japan, and his strength was failing fast.

Yukiko's dutiful visits to his flat near the Star Hotel grew less and less frequent. Partly, this was due to the increasing pressure of work in the *kobun*, but Yukiko was also finding it harder and harder to watch a man some small part of her still loved drink his life away. Once he lashed out at her, and from reflex she responded, almost breaking his arm. Now she felt nothing for him except disgust . . . until she finally learnt the truth . . .

Late one rain-swept evening, when lightning flashes and the blaze of neon shimmered on the rain-slicked pavements and the polished roofs of cars, Yukiko found herself working alone at her work station. With Rothsay's grip on GRC loosened, Jessica Wright and Theodore Gilkrensky were becoming a major thorn in Mawashi-Saito's side regarding advanced products. Their files in Yukiko's Industrial Intelligence Unit had mushroomed. Investigations had been made, agents put in place.

And then the stories started in London . . . rumours of how GRC was developing a new super-computer in Ireland . . . whispers of how the research was going nowhere . . . GRC was in trouble, or so the commentators said . . . the share prices started to fall.

But Yukiko knew it was a final battle – for control.

Her spies were well placed, and her ability to access

computer systems was second to none. Gilkrensky was scaring his fellow shareholders into selling out, so that he could buy their shares for a song and gain a majority.

She had already passed the information on to Uncle Gichin days ago. Mawashi-Saito would be able to buy access to all the information it needed on the new Minerva project . . . if it could acquire GRC shares from those willing to sell before Gilkrensky got to them.

She reached for the telephone.

But her uncle was not in his office, or at home, and Miss Deshimaru did not know if he had read her e-mail message regarding GRC.

So Yukiko reached for her computer keyboard and tapped into the Mawashi-Saito internal network, checking to see if her uncle had accessed the detailed information files she'd sent him on the GRC strategy. Normally, even she was not allowed to access Funakoshi's private directories within the network, but this was important . . . and personal. She had to be sure Uncle Gichin knew of Gilkrensky's deception, and would act . . . it was only a matter of time.

The security systems around her uncle's directories had been installed by Taisen Nakamura, and were easy to bypass. She checked that the file had been accessed, and was about to log off from the system, when another filename on Gichin Funakoshi's personal directory caught her eye . . . "Rothsay".

For a moment, Yukiko sat with her fingers poised over her keyboard . . . staring . . . hypnotised, balancing the *giri* she owed her uncle with her curiosity about her father. The security around it was even tighter than the other directories, but old Nakamura did not have Yukiko's skill.

The file opened.

Yukiko sat and watched the scrolling characters on the computer screen, as the rain hissed against her office window. There, in front of her, was a copy of the newspaper article that had damned her mother to suicide and her father to exile. There was Taisen Nakamura's old file on the whole incident and her uncle's efforts to prevent her learning the truth. And finally, at the very end of the file, was his proof of the source of the story – the press office of the Gilcrest Radio Corporation.

Gilkrensky! He had done this!

And her uncle Gichin had known all along!

In a trance, she logged off the system, reached for the telephone and dialled. There was no answer.

The tears were already starting to flow as she ran for the door.

Papa-*chan*!

She found the door of his flat unlocked. Moving silently in the darkness, she crossed to the bedroom and, listening carefully, heard sobbing. A clap of thunder sounded close overhead, and by the light of its flash she saw a figure kneeling on the floor.

She flicked on the light.

There was her father, dirty and unshaven next to his unmade *futon*. The bowls and chopsticks of an unfinished meal, and the confusion of unwashed clothes were all around him. By his side was a bottle of whisky, two thirds gone, along with an empty container of pills.

In front of him, on the reed *tatami* mat, was her mother's unsheathed *wakizashi*. Its mirrored steel flashed in the lightning.

"Papa-*chan*?"

Lord Rothsay snapped out of his trance and turned to face her . . . an old man. Tears streamed from his reddened eyes onto the white stubble on his chin. He was shaking, like a frightened child.

"Yukiko . . . go! Go away! You . . . can't see me like this."

Yukiko snatched the pill bottle and read the label. It was a name she recognised, and her heart sank.

"Papa-*chan*? What have you done?"

"What . . . what have I done? It's what *they* did to me, little tiger . . . "

He swayed from side to side. Yukiko caught him gently and moved him to the *futon*.

"I *did* love you, little tiger, and your mother too. But I was weak. I let that scandal in England keep me away from her and then, when she died, I let your uncle keep me away from you. I . . . "

"I know, Papa-*chan*," said Yukiko softly, as she remembered the evening she had turned him away. "I read my uncle's files."

"Then you'll how old man Gilkrensky's son tried to get me off the board of GRC after he took over . . . he found out about your mother and me . . . and leaked it to the papers. Your mother couldn't take it . . . your uncle sent her a letter . . . and that sword!"

His hand fluttered at the *wakizahi*, lying curved and mute on the *tatami* mat.

"I know, Papa-*chan*. I know."

"Your uncle kept it from you. He was afraid of what you'd do if you grew up and realised what Gilkrensky had done . . . If you'd killed Gilkrensky, uncle Gichin would have had no more secrets to steal . . . no more technology for that precious company of his . . . but I fixed Gilkrensky. I fixed him good!"

"How, Papa-*chan*?"

"I sold my shares to your uncle. Imagine how Gilkrensky will feel when he finds Mawashi-Saito now own twenty-five percent of his precious company. Uncle Gichin will have access to all the secrets he wants now . . . "

Thunder boomed overhead. A flash lit the room. As she knelt beside her father, Yukiko again glimpsed dark red wine around her mother's body.

"I wanted to do one decent thing with my life, little tiger," mumbled Rothsay. "I wanted to die with honour, like your mother did. But I hadn't got the bloody guts!"

Yukiko's throat tightened. She could feel the tears welling up inside, taking her by surprise. *Ninjo!* She had to fight them back . . . to be in control . . .

"When did you take the pills? Papa-*chan*?"

"Doesn't matter, little tiger. You can't pump the poison out once it's in the system."

Yukiko clenched her eyes shut, trying to lock out the

pain. But all she could see was the hem of her mother's favourite kimono, and the blood . . .

"I have to try, Papa-*chan*. I'll call for help."

Rothsay seemed to reach deep inside himself, to some small cold place where he was still sober. He grabbed her blouse with his fist, pulling her to him. For a moment he seemed as strong as he had been when she rode on his shoulders in front of the tigers at Ueno.

"I was weak, little tiger. But you're strong . . . aren't you? We trained you to be that way, your mother and I, before your uncle Gichin took you to be his . . . his guided missile. I have one more target for you now, and I've left you all the money I got for the GRC shares to help you. Forget your debt of *giri* to that heartless uncle of yours, and get that calculating swine, Gilkrensky . . . "

Yukiko's head was ringing like a bell. She could feel the walls she had built to hold back the pain of her life cracking . . . crumbling . . .

"*Hai*, Papa-*chan*."

Rothsay's fist slipped from Yukiko's blouse. He pointed to the beautiful short sword on the *tatami*.

"Don't let them find me like this. Help me die with honour . . . like she did . . . as I wanted to. Forgive me, little tiger, and give me this one last thing."

His eyes rolled as the whisky and the pills took control. Somehow, Yukiko managed to feel his pulse. It was weak and slow.

"*Hai*, Papa-*chan*," she said again, laid him back on the *futon*, and closed her eyes . . . as the memories flooded over her . . .

She was a child again, back on his shoulders, marvelling at the graceful tigers in the zoo . . . she was having *dim-sum* for lunch, beneath the cherry blossoms . . . Mama-*chan* was there in her best kimono, smiling . . .

All at once, the diamond shell around the tortured heart of Yukiko Funakoshi cracked, splintered, and flew apart. All the pain, the anger and the shame, she had held in check so well . . . for so long . . . burst in a tidal wave of tears, carrying all her barriers before it and leaving nothing in its wake . . . nothing . . . but the stark, new reality of the man who had taken everything she had ever loved.

As the wave of pain crushed Yukiko's defences, washed away her world and slid back, one hard truth remained – she would have her revenge.

Yukiko knelt on the *tatami*, waiting for the tears to subside . . . for control to return . . . she remembered her training, slowed her breathing to calm herself, and dried her eyes. Then she took a pair of thin cotton gloves from her hand-bag and started to clear her father's flat, carefully washing and stacking the crockery, gathering up the dirty clothes into a cupboard and tidying the furniture.

Finally, she took a razor from the bathroom and shaved him. His heart was still beating as she placed the whisky bottle and the pills back on the floor, knelt him up in the prayer position on the *tatami* mats, and reached for the *wakizashi* . . .

In her hotel room at the Nile Olympiad, Yukiko Funakoshi ran her fingers along the lacquered wood of the inlaid scabbard, watching the tigers stalk amongst the cherry blossoms. She remembered the oath to her father, and the look of fear on Jessica Wright's face, the day she had let her own mask slip in the Mawashi-Saito office in Tokyo. Yukiko had planned a special revenge for her, but that was to come. For now, there was Gilkrensky himself to deal with.

She reached for the SmartMate and tapped out a very private number in Kyoto. There were people there who would know where she could get the special item she needed, and others in the industrial intelligence unit of Mawashi-Saito who could deliver it to her in Cairo by private jet within hours.

34

DIVERSION

THE KHAN AL KHALILI MARKET IS ON THE ITINERARY OF EVERY
tourist who comes to Cairo – a vast Aladdin's cave of
overflowing shops and heavily laden stalls with
overhanging awnings hung with leather goods and gaudy
clothes of all descriptions. In the heat of the late
afternoon, the air was heavy with the aroma of coffee
and cooking food, the tang of freshly cured hide, and the
smell of humanity.

In the colourful confusion, Yukiko looked no more
out of place than any tourist who is far from home, and
the shiny black briefcase in her left hand could have
been a recent purchase from any one of the many leather
stalls. A group of old men, sitting around a domino table
outside a coffee shop, glanced up at her as she passed. A
knife-grinder sent orange sparks cascading into the street.

Yukiko turned into the quiet backwater of an
alleyway, and walked on until she came to the shop El
Fiky had told her about by phone the previous night.

Below the Arabic squiggles over the door were the words *Antica Abdul*, written in English. A heavy curtain of beads over the doorway clicked sharply as she passed through into the cool silence. The rough walls were whitewashed, worn carpets covered the floor, and a long glass counter bearing faded certificates from the Government Department of Antiquities dominated the room. Behind it, a small ratlike man wearing a *galabia* under his western jacket was busy sorting a collection of tiny turquoise scarabs into small cardboard boxes lined with cottonwool. His bright eyes darted up as Yukiko entered and his yellow smile flashed in the darkness.

"I was referred to you by the Cairo Museum," she said. "I understand you have new acquisitions from the digs at Luxor."

The smile dropped from the man's face for a second. The bright eyes glanced at the briefcase in her hand.

"Tell me, who referred you here?"

Yukiko told him.

"Ah yes." The man waved his hand over the rows of scarabs. "I do not have such valuable items down here in the shop. These trinkets you see here are merely for the tourist, not for a discerning collector such as yourself. If you would like to see the Luxor artifacts, they are in the room upstairs. Please?"

He led Yukiko around the corner of the counter, to a narrow wooden staircase. Climbing it, Yukiko found herself in a shady attic furnished with heavy carpets and a suite of old leather furniture. The walls were lined with glass cases and, in the centre of the room, was a large brass coffee table, set for two. Beside the table on the floor was a black leather briefcase, almost identical to the one she held in her hand.

"Good afternoon," said Professor El Fiky. "I hope the case I have here matches the description you gave me."

He was sitting in the exact centre of the sofa, hunched forward with his hands between his knees. Yukiko bent and examined the other case.

"It seems good enough," she said. "Nobody will be able to tell the difference when I leave. But will we be able to use the one I brought?"

"The official enquiry was going very well for Dr Gilkrensky when I left the presidential palace this morning. Based on my evidence regarding the phenomenon at the Pyramid site, the testimony of the flight crew and the other recordings, he was well on the way to absolving his corporation from blame for the crash."

"And the Minerva computer?"

"He had the machine with him. It was planning to run a virtual-reality demonstration of the cockpit evidence."

"Then Gilkrensky will leave Cairo tonight, once those matters are settled?"

"That is certain. The authorities are anxious to get him out of the country as fast as possible."

"Will he be allowed to visit the Pyramid before he leaves?"

Professor El Fiky leant forward and poured two cups of thick coffee.

"He will not be allowed to, *officially* – but that will not stop him. He is obsessed with the loss of his wife, and the notion that he can somehow use the new chamber inside the Pyramid as a kind of gateway to the past."

Yukiko frowned, had she gone to all the trouble and expense of bringing the special briefcase all the way from Kyoto for nothing? Was she gambling on the whim of a madman?

El Fiky sipped his coffee.

"I know what you are thinking, but nothing will stop Gilkrensky visiting the Pyramid tonight. It sounds fantastic I know, but certain evidence we gathered over the past few days suggests that something very strange is going on at the site . . . something that even I cannot explain . . . something triggered by the new Sound and Light show. This computer you are so anxious to acquire, for example. Gilkrensky is using it to try and formulate a correlation between the power of the lasers used in the display with the age of the artifacts found in the chamber. That is why he must visit the Pyramid tonight, to see if varying the power gives him control of the phenomenon."

"You are sure of this?"

"I spoke to him this morning, and he is as anxious as ever to proceed, not only to be re-united with his wife, but also to find his friend McCarthy. Tonight is his last chance, before the authorities deport him, and so he plans to slip away after the enquiry and make a short detour to the Pyramid site on his way to the airport. That visit will coincide with the Sound and Light show. He has asked me to join him there."

"Then I must tell you what to do," said Yukiko.

She lifted her briefcase onto her lap, turning it so that the locks were facing El Fiky.

"This device is triggered by an electronic timer, set for fifteen minutes, which is activated by setting the combination lock to 900, and then opening and closing both catches simultaneously. When the laser holography display begins, start the timer, and leave. The fifteen minutes will give you time to get clear, and if anything were to go wrong, you can de-activate the device with this."

Yukiko took a small black box, like a pocket calculator, from her handbag. It had a digital display and a single red button.

"I will not need it," said El Fiky calmly. "It is not my intention to jeopardise the mission by trying to escape."

Yukiko frowned, but El-Fiky continued, "We are at war with the West," he said. "and the West is winning. Little by little our culture is dripping away. My people are weak, they need a sharp reminder to bring them back to Allah, and your satellite technology to spread the word. If I activate this device and run, Dr Gilkrensky and his security people will be suspicious, and may examine the briefcase. Too many of my people have died for me to risk failure now."

"Why sacrifice yourself when you do not have to?"

Professor El Fiky smiled grimly.

"Surely you, of all people, would understand. If I fail,

the whole world will degenerate into a swamp of Western values. People will fornicate and kill each other in the streets and the way of Islam will be forgotten. Did not Japanese soldiers and airmen sacrifice themselves for what they thought was a higher cause during your war with America?"

"Yes. But . . . "

"Then do not expect less of me. I am prepared to die for what I believe. The device in this case will strike a blow for the *Jihad* that nobody can ignore. It may even trigger an Islamic revolution here in Cairo. Then your satellite will give us a voice loud enough to capture the attention of the world. All along the Mediterranean, the fall of Egypt will be a beacon to Muslims in Algeria, Bosnia, Chechnya and Palestine. It will start a wave that will sweep from Casablanca to Baghdad. Believe me, my death is of no consequence if this can be achieved."

Yukiko offered the remote safety-switch again. "You know that once the timer is set, this is the only way the device can be disarmed? If the briefcase is tampered with before then, it will activate. Take the safety device."

"I do not need it," said Professor El Fiky. "I know what I must do."

"Congratulations, Mr Chairman," said Crowe.

They were standing in the magnificent foyer of the Urubah Presidential Palace. Above their heads graceful oriental columns soared to the high ceiling, and around them was the fall-out of the enquiry – a small army of bureaucrats, witnesses and security guards, all milling towards the high wall, the main gate, and the Heliopolis road where the television crews had gathered.

Gilkrensky felt more alive than he had at any time since Maria's death. Jessica Wright had been delighted when he had called her on the Minerva and told her to prepare a positive report for tomorrow's board meeting. Right now she would be working on a press release, emphasising the enquiry's observations on the safety of Bill McCarthy's life-saving Whisperer design. Bill McCarthy . . . what could he ever say to Bill's family if the experiment didn't work?

Gilkrensky looked at his watch. It was almost half past seven. The Sound and Light show began at eight. He would have to make his move soon. The Minerva was in his left hand. Should he check that everything was ready?

Captain Danvers and Margaret Spalding came over to them. Danvers reached out his hand.

"I'm glad it went well for you, sir."

"And for you, Captain," said Gilkrensky, shaking Danver's hand gladly. "The findings shouldn't affect your licence, or the chances of starting that flying school. How is Miss Maxwell, by the way?"

"She's on the mend," said Spalding. "They'll release her from hospital right after Christmas."

Gilkrensky grinned. "You're welcome to use the Nile Olympiad Hotel until then. I think the presidential suite is free."

"What's left of it!" muttered Crowe. "Look out! Here comes Selim."

In spite of the crisp cut of his uniform, Selim looked

tired. There were scratches on his face and a plaster above his left eye from the grenade explosion the night before.

"Dr Gilkrensky. I am pleased that the enquiry found in your favour. But now we must arrange for your departure as swiftly as we can. Your helicopter will be here in a few minutes and will land on the other side of the building, away from the press. It has an army pilot, with orders to take you directly to the airport."

"I understand. I've given instructions to my people, and my jet is ready. Thank you, Colonel. I'm sorry for the trouble I caused you."

"Indeed, Doctor. But then again, we had been after El Sharoud and his group for some time. Where are your other people? Mr Manning the American and Major Crowe's colleague, Maguire?"

"They're at the Pyramid site supervising the removal of the equipment. They'll join us at the airport later."

"I see. This way please."

He led them through a tall Moorish arch and down a maze of marble corridors, each guarded by an armed soldier. Eventually, they passed through a high double door into an empty space at the back of the building, surrounded by a cordon of troops. The scent of orange-trees filled the air and from the distance, high above them, came the unmistakable chop of an approaching helicopter.

"Goodbye, Doctor," said Selim. "My men will see you safely on board. Major."

"It's been a pleasure working with you, Colonel," said Crowe.

Selim snapped him a curt salute and turned back towards the palace.

Gilkrensky eyed the armed guards and the approaching helicopter.

"Major," he said, "I never really thanked you for pulling me away from the fire on the day Maria died."

Crowe stared at the lights of the oncoming helicopter. "There was nothing more you could have done, sir. The bomb would have killed her instantly."

"And if there *had* been a way to save her?"

Crowe turned to face him.

"I'd have been there in that fire with you. I admired Mrs Gilkrensky a great deal."

Gilkrensky took a sealed envelope from the pocket of his jacket.

"Then I have a very great favour to ask, Major . . . for her."

The GRC helicopter fluttered in out of the darkness, whipping the branches of the orange-trees and sending each soldier's left hand to his cap, while the right stayed firmly on the butt of his rifle. As the machine settled on the helipad, the pilot feathered the rotors and beckoned to Gilkrensky and Crowe, who ran forward, ducking below the blades. Gilkrensky climbed into the co-pilot's seat immediately, but Crowe gestured to the pilot to open his side window.

"Colonel Selim has new instructions for you," he

shouted above the engine noise, and waved the sealed envelope Gilkrensky had given him.

The pilot looked flustered.

"I am ordered to take you directly to the airport, sir. Anything else, and I must check with the Colonel personally."

"I understand. The Colonel's inside but he's very busy. Would you like me to get him?"

The man considered. Then he began to unbuckle his seat belt.

"I will check this myself," he shouted, taking the envelope. "Wait here please."

"Of course," shouted Crowe, as he opened the rear passenger door and climbed in. "Where could we go without you?"

The doors slammed shut. Crowe watched the pilot run across the helipad and disappear inside the palace.

"All right, sir," he shouted. "It's all yours.

But Gilkrensky had already slipped across into the pilot's seat. The engine noise rose to a deafening whine, the rotors thudded as they bit the air and, before the guards could reach them, the helicopter lifted off from the helipad and turned above their heads towards the western edge of the city.

"Thank you, Major," said Gilkrensky into his radio microphone as he steadied the JetRanger over Heliopolis. In front of them on the western horizon, standing hard and clean above the confusion of the city, were the silhouettes of the three great pyramids.

Crowe shook his head.

"If I was still in the army, I'd be court-martialled."

"One of the advantages of working for private industry, Major. This is my helicopter after all, and once Selim reads that note he'll know I'm safe and won't be long getting to the airport."

"Let's hope so. I don't think he was in a good mood when we left him."

"No. You're right. But with the two security patrol helicopters destroyed, there's not a lot he can do. How's the time?"

"Ten to eight."

"Good. I hope Leroy and the others made it to the caravan on time."

Professor El Fiky stopped the museum van in the carpark on the Giza plateau, turned off the ignition, and sat looking up at the great mountains of rock. He thought of the lifetime he had spent studying the Great Pyramid of Cheops, of all the expeditions he had assisted, all the lectures . . . and his book. He knew every chamber, passageway, tunnel and stone.

And there was so much more to learn!

But the world was at war . . . in a *Jihad*.

He knew what he had to do.

Professor El Fiky peered across the roped-off area of the temporary helipad to the dark slab of the GRC caravan. Allah was with him. He was the first to arrive. He took the briefcase by its curved handle, and ducked beneath the ropes. In a few minutes, the carpark would be full of tour buses and cars as the audience arrived for the *Son et Lumière* show.

Car headlights played on the stone mountain of the Great Pyramid behind him and a dark Transit van pulled to a stop by the makeshift helipad. He heard the doors slide back and slam shut. Two figures ducked under the helipad ropes. One was rattling a bunch of keys.

"Hi, Prof!" shouted Leroy Manning. "You beat us to it!"

Behind him, the first of the tour buses was pulling to a stop in the coach park, spilling tourists towards the Sound and Light show. Above them, El Fiky could make out the winking lights of a helicopter approaching.

Suddenly the briefcase felt very heavy in his hand.

Yukiko stepped down and gave her ticket to the attendant. The courtesy coach from the Nile Olympiad hotel for the Sound and Light show was packed to capacity. All the recent publicity about the new golden crypt, and the drama centred around the mad English millionaire had sold out every seat in the audience pushing the price of black-market tickets through the roof. But booking arrangements had been linked to the Nile Olympiad computer, which also had an outlet in Yukiko's room to accommodate the personal check-out system. The security passwords were primitive and easily bypassed.

The attendant ripped the ticket in two and returned the stub, passing quickly on to the next person in the queue without even glancing at her face. Why should he? There were plenty of Japanese tourists there that evening, and if one seemed to be travelling on her own, what of it?

Yukiko lagged behind the other passengers until they had all alighted from the coach. Then she followed the queue as it meandered around the path of the Great Pyramid, past the displays of buried boats and downwards towards the Sphinx and the *Son et Lumière* seating area.

Cameras flashed in the darkness.

A woman laughed – blinded by the light – and Yukiko ducked sideways into the shadows, letting her raincoat slip from her shoulders. It was the work of a moment to blacken the skin around her eyes and to pull the matt black cotton hood over her head. Then she melted into the darkness, and slipped back the way she had come, towards the carpark and the GRC caravan.

The helicopter sank into the roped-off square and settled in a cloud of dust as Gilkrensky cut the engine. The blades were still turning as he popped open his door and rushed to the caravan, with the Minerva in his hand.

"Am I in time?"

"The *Son et Lumière* will start in a moment or two," said Professor El Fiky. "But the lasers will not be switched on for another twenty minutes or so. You have plenty of time to recalibrate your equipment."

Gilkrensky was already connecting the Minerva to a thick master cable next to the metallurgical X-ray machine. He opened the lid. All around the caravan, red and green indicator lights began to blink on as the computer took control. Professor El Fiky placed his own briefcase on the caravan floor, close to one of the chart tables.

Just as he did so, the familiar *Dom! Dim! Dum!* heralding the opening of the Son et Lumiere, boomed across the carpark. Floodlights snapped on, and the three pyramids came alive, towering into the night sky above their heads.

"We have twenty minutes before the lasers," said Professor El Fiky.

"And fifteen minutes after that the Einstein-Rosen bridge will open inside the Golden Crypt," said Maria from the table on the other side of the caravan. "I am patching into the computer that controls the display. In a few moments I should be able to modulate the intensity of the hologram to whatever level we wish. Since we know from Professor McCarthy's model aircraft that the present level of laser activity is sufficient to displace an object by approximately two thousand years, I will try and double the laser intensity and see if we can displace the test material by twice as long, thereby establishing a basic correlation."

"What test material?" asked El Fiky. "Surely any object you place in the chamber tonight and project back into time would have been evident when we opened the chamber."

"Perhaps it was," said Gilkrensky, "but we just didn't know it was there."

"I do not understand."

"The sand, Professor. The sand we found in the chamber when we opened it. I had a few grams irradiated at the Cairo University today and placed in the chamber by Leroy this evening. It's mildly radioactive, with a half-life of over ten thousand years. If we analyse the sand you took from the chamber when we first opened it, and find that it's radioactive, then the Einstein-Rosen bridge theory is correct."

"And we got ourselves a real live time machine!" said Manning.

El Fiky looked confused. Then he said, "And I suppose you can tell how far back the sand has been displaced by analysing the amount of radioactive decay that has taken place?"

"Exactly. And with that information, we're a step nearer to controlling the process."

"Incredible," said El Fiky, lost in thought. "Truly incredible."

"If you wouldn't mind checking the sensors for me, gentlemen?" said Maria. "We only have eighteen minutes before the lasers switch on."

From the darkness of the shadows at the edge of the carpark, Yukiko watched the figures inside the caravan move amongst the instruments. A tall, bearded man in a worn leather jacket was bending over a table next to a chart recorder, peering into the screen of what looked like a much larger version of her own laptop computer. That must be the Minerva 3,000 her uncle was so anxious to acquire – the state-of-the-art intelligent biochip machine that would revolutionise the electronic world. For him, Gilkrensky was the key to the Minerva 3,000. But for her, the Minerva was the excuse she'd needed to hunt the man himself – Gilkrensky.

She smiled beneath the black hood.

In a few minutes the laser display would be the signal for El Fiky to start the timer on the gas device. And if he would not, or could not – she could, with the tiny remote control that nestled in a cotton pouch over her ribs on the left side. There were other pouches too, containing her own arsenal of weapons, the gun she had taken from that fool, El Sharoud, and a highly effective miniature gas mask.

And between her shoulder blades, secure inside its beautiful lacquered sheath and held tight by soft leather straps, was the short sword, her beloved *wakizashi*.

One way or another, it would have its revenge tonight.

"One minute to hologram," said Maria. "Fifty-seconds . . . forty-five . . . forty . . . "

Professor El Fiky glanced down at the black leather briefcase, and then up at the Great Pyramid, the monument he had devoted his working life to studying. He thought of the *Jihad*, and of his daughter safe at home in Cairo. It was a pity she had never married. He would have liked to have been a grandfather. At least Muslim children everywhere would have a future against the tyranny of the West after tonight.

"Is there any danger to the audience in doubling the output of the lasers?" asked Crowe.

Gilkrensky shook his head. "No. The hologram output is already very low – a microscopic fraction of the power we used on the cutting-laser in the golden crypt. There'd be no danger in using ten times the power we're going to try tonight."

"Here we go," said Manning, and they all turned to stare at the great mountain of stone.

El Fiky could hear the blood pounding in his ears, as the recorded commentary said, "We display to you, through the wonder of laser holography, an image of how the pyramids looked when they were first conceived by the royal wizard in all their glory . . . !"

Dim! Dom! Dim!

To their left, the first pyramid – Mykerinos – stood out starkly against the night. Then Chephren was transformed into a pure white monument of polished limestone. Finally Cheops itself burst into life, a vast alien shape in a timeless landscape.

Professor El Fiky bent down to the briefcase, set the combination lock for 900, and lifted both catches, as if to open them.

"The will of Allah be done," he said softly, and snapped them back into place.

Before his eyes, the brass tumblers moved from 900 to 899.

"Yes!" breathed Gilkrensky, as he stood transfixed by the three gleaming monuments. "Yes! Yes! Yes! Now all we have to do is wait. Are the cameras operating, Maria? . . . Maria?"

The image on the Minerva screen seemed preoccupied.

"They are operating perfectly, Theo. But I have an anomalous reading from here inside the caravan. Just as the laser holography display started, one of the background sensors detected a short-range radio transmission. Now it appears that, in addition to the equipment I am programmed to monitor, we have another device operating that I was not aware of."

"What sort of device."

"A timer of some sort. The kind one finds in an electronic clock."

"Or in a bomb?" said Crowe, staring at El Fiky's briefcase. "Professor! Do you know something about this?"

"No! I just . . . "

El Fiky looked at Crowe, at the briefcase, and knew he had given himself away. His eyes went to Gerald Maguire, Leroy Manning, and Gilkrensky himself.

"I did it for the *Jihad*," he said. "The timer is set for fifteen minutes."

"You mean you're involved with . . . !" gasped Gilkrensky, staring at him. He remembered Crowe's words to Selim back at the hotel, days ago: *Fanatics who believe in a holy war . . . could be anyone . . . you could even be such a person yourself!*

"Gerald! Hold him!" he said.

Maguire moved forward and grabbed El Fiky's arm, while Gilkrensky bent over and stared at the briefcase.

"Can we touch it? Is there any way to switch it off?"

"Look at the tumblers on the combination lock," said Crowe. "They're moving."

"It's counting down," said Gilkrensky. "They're at 840 . . . 839 . . . 838. That gives us . . . just over fourteen minutes. Can we open the case, Professor, without setting it off?"

"No. I was told the lock is . . . how do you say? Booby-trapped."

Crowe scowled at him. "I might be able to disarm it. If I had any idea what we were dealing with."

Gilkrensky's eyes darted around the equipment lining the walls of the caravan.

"There must be an optical probe or . . . yes! That's it! Bring the case over here, Major. Lay it on that slab! It's a miniature X-ray scanner. Bill McCarthy would have used it for spotting micro-cracks in metal parts during the crash investigation. Stand back now! Maria?"

"I am scanning, Theo."

One of the monitors over the laboratory bench flicked on, showing an abstract colour-image in blue and orange. The outline of the case was clear, along with two large cylindrical objects, either side of a flat slab. Connected to the slab by the thin line of a wire, was a complicated mass of components, with other wires leading to the locks and the timer below the handle.

Crowe stared at the image. Then he reached up to the screen and traced the outline of the case with his finger.

"The case itself is probably an alloy of aluminium and magnesium, designed to burn up after that small flat charge in the middle explodes, so there won't be any evidence. The charge itself is probably Semtex, or some other powerful plastic explosive. Not enough to do real damage, but enough to burst the cylinders, turn the liquid gas into an aerosol, and destroy the case."

"Look at the electronics," said Gilkrensky. "Tell me Professor, were the people who gave you this case Japanese?"

"I . . . I cannot say."

"I could persuade him," said Maguire.

Gilkrensky put up his hand. "It's OK. I think I can tell by the design of some of these components here in the timer."

"And the gas?" said Leroy.

Crowe turned to face him.

"Once those two heavy cylinders are burst, and the contents blown outwards by the explosive, it will probably kill everything for a thousand yards around."

"Jee . . . zus!" gasped Manning.

"You see, if this case is from Japan," said Crowe. "Then the gas inside is probably Sarin, the nerve-poison that was used in that massacre on the Tokyo tube train."

35

THE BOMB

A WOMAN'S VOICE SOUNDED CLEARLY OVER THE *SON ET LUMIERE* show loudspeakers.

"Attention, ladies and gentlemen. But I must warn you that there is a nerve-gas bomb on-site which is set to explode in thirteen minutes and thirty-three seconds. The minimum safe distance is two kilometres. Please evacuate the area and try to remain calm! Thank you!"

The message began to repeat in a dozen different languages. The first screams of panic started to drift across the plateau from the bus park.

"For God's sake, Maria!" shouted Gilkrensky. "Why did you have to do that?"

"According to the computer controlling the Sound and Light show, there are one thousand two hundred and fifty-three people registered in the audience tonight," said Maria calmly. "Under the Asimov laws of programming I cannot allow them to come to harm."

Outside in the carpark, people were running headlong across the tarmac as cars and buses tried to pull out. Vehicles backed into each other. There was the crash and shatter of crumpling metal and breaking glass. People screamed, and the cabin rocked as the crowd surged past.

"Any ideas anyone?" said Gilkrensky.

"Twelve minutes and fifty seconds," said Maria.

Crowe pointed to the X-ray screen.

"That wire to the detonator cap on the Semtex. Do we still have the laser you used to bore into that chamber?"

"It's inside the Pyramid," said Gilkrensky. "Besides, that wire could be a dud. You might set off the bomb."

Manning reached forward with his good hand.

"It'd be simpler to fly it out into the desert in the chopper and drop it. You could go a long way in ten minutes and there's nothing out there for hundreds of miles."

"Major?"

"Sounds less risky than trying to take the bomb in to the laser. But how is Mr Manning going to fly the helicopter with one arm?"

"He isn't," said Gilkrensky. "I am."

"Then I'm coming with you."

"Have it your way, Major, but let's go. Leroy! You come and navigate for us. Gerald, you stay here and keep an eye on the Minerva. Guard it with your life."

"What about the Professor?"

"I don't care. Just keep him out of the caravan until I get back. Major! Leroy!"

He lifted the black briefcase carefully from the table, and ran out of the caravan, pushing his way through the thinning crowd, towards the helicopter.

In the shadows at the edge of the carpark, Yukiko cursed as she watched the crowd surge up from the Sound and Light show and pour across the carpark. She looked down, and saw the red electronic figures on the little remote-control device tick from eight hundred and twenty to eight hundred and nineteen. Over thirteen minutes before the gas bomb would explode. She eased open the pocket on her black cotton suit to make sure the light gas mask and its little air cylinder were still in place. They were. Only twelve and a half minutes now . . .

Across the carpark a figure burst from the caravan and ran through the crowd towards the helicopter. It was Gilkrensky, and in his hand was a black briefcase! Was it the Minerva? Or was it the bomb! Should she disarm it? Her hand was reaching for the remote control when two other figures rushed from the caravan and darted after Gilkrensky. He had the helicopter door open now. She could hear the rising whine of the starter motor as the rotor blades started to turn. Was it the Minerva, or was it the bomb?

Invisible against the darkness, Yukiko uncurled her legs, rose to her feet and started to pad silently towards the pool of light in front of the caravan. El Fiky was by the door, watching the helicopter. Through the caravan window she could see the guard Maguire, standing with his hand inside his jacket – probably holding a gun.

And on a table next to Maguire, with its lid open, exposing the screen, was the Minerva 3,000!

Yukiko glanced back to the helicopter, gauging distances, making choices. Two prizes were within her grasp – one professional, and one very, very personal. To fulfil her mission and repay her debt of *giri* to her uncle Gichin, she had to simply wait for Gilkrensky to depart, lure Maguire away from that computer, and take it. To surrender to *ninjo* and her passion for revenge, all she had to do was act – now!

Yukiko's hand slid to the pocket on her belt that housed the gun she had taken from El Sharoud's flat – a crude weapon – but at this range it would achieve the desired result. Gilkrensky was plainly visible in the cockpit of the helicopter.

It would only take one shot.

Gilkrensky laid the bomb on the co-pilot's seat and swung himself into the helicopter, pulling on the radio headset. His hands fluttered over the circuit breakers and switches. Crowe and Manning were piling into the seats behind him as the whine of the starter motor rose and the rotors began to swing above his head.

"Twelve minutes to detonation, Theo!" said Maria over the radio from the caravan. "The crowd is clearing now. You should have no problems taking off."

The rotor flashed above him, faster and faster.

"Come on! Come on!"

The revolution indicators were rising painfully slowly.

His left hand twisted the throttle and his arm tightened as it took the pressure of the collective pitch lever. He heard the rush of the blades turn to a heavy chop as they bit the air. He could feel the JetRanger lift off the ground.

"Look out, sir!"

Someone was standing on the skid.

The co-pilot's door slammed back as Professor El Fiky tried to haul himself inside. His fingers were clawing for the trigger catches of the briefcase. He was screaming.

"Professor! No!"

Crowe leant forward to protect the bomb. Gilkrensky's hands were on the controls. He glanced up at El Fiky's contorted face, and then froze as the crack of a gun cut through the din of the straining helicopter. El Fiky was kicked into the cockpit by the force of the bullet. He slammed down on Gilkrensky, ripping the controls from his hands. Crowe cursed and reached for his pistol, but it was torn from his hand as the JetRanger slewed forward and smashed down on its skids.

The unseen gun cracked again. There was a loud, metallic clang above Gilkrensky's head, and the hiss of hot oil as it sprayed down over the windshield from the shattered gearbox.

Gilkrensky was trapped by El Fiky's body. He could feel warm blood soaking his jeans and the rasp of the Professor's breath. Above him, the smooth whine of the rotors dissolved into a grinding roar. He tried to reach the throttle, but his arm was pinned down.

"Jesus, Doc!" Manning screamed. "Let's get out of here! She's gonna blow!"

Maguire had ripped the pilot's door open. He was hauling El Fiky off Gilkrensky and out of the helicopter.

Gilkrensky's right hand closed on the handle of the briefcase bomb and pulled. For a terrible moment it stuck between the seats but suddenly came free. He fell backwards out of the cockpit onto the carpark, with the briefcase in his arms. Above him, the grating of the gearbox rose to a demonic scream as the last of the oil drained away. There was an ear-splitting bang, a clattering of whirling, screaming blades, and a shattering crash as something sliced into the dirt of the carpark close to his leg. Gilkrensky threw his arm over his head. To his right he heard a dull thud and someone fell.

"Major!" yelled Gilkrensky.

"He's out cold!" shouted Maguire.

"Theo! Theo! Are you all right?"

Gilkrensky strained his eyes into the billowing smoke and the darkness. Nothing was moving beyond the caravan – nothing he could see!

"I'm OK, Maria. Who's shooting?"

"I cannot tell. You have only ten minutes and fifty seconds to detonation!"

"What can we do?"

"The audience from the Sound and Light show have blocked the escape roads from the plateau. Our only hope is to get the briefcase within range of the laser in the Queen's Chamber before the interference from the

Einstein-Rosen bridge blanks out the video cameras. I have the information from the X-ray analysis on file. I can use it to cut the detonator wire."

"And if it doesn't work?"

"Then at least the bulk of the Pyramid will protect those outside from the blast and the entrance can be sealed to stop the gas."

Gilkrensky raised his head as much as he dared. The smoke from the helicopter was blowing to the south-west, and in front of him was the towering shape of the floodlit Pyramid.

"Great! Maguire, you cover my ass! Whoever's shooting is still out there!"

"It'll be a pleasure, sir." Maguire's gun was already in his hand.

Yukiko stalked silently through the smoke at the edge of the light from the caravan, watching the moving figures around the wrecked helicopter, and cursing El Fiky for spoiling her shot. The pilot with the injured arm was trying to pull the English Major back into the safety of the caravan. Through the door behind him, Yukiko could see the Minerva, deserted. There were three bullets left in the gun – more than enough.

Then, from the other side of the burning wreck, a man jumped to his feet and bolted towards the Pyramid. Orange flames flickered on the black leather of the briefcase in his hand, and he was gone. Another figure rose slowly and deliberately to his feet, playing the ugly fist of a heavy automatic pistol around the circle of light thrown by the fire. It was Gilkrensky's other bodyguard, the Irishman Maguire. For a moment he glanced back at the caravan, the huddled bodies, and the abandoned super-computer. Then he turned and ran into the darkness after Gilkrensky.

Yukiko stood watching the caravan door. Inside was the target Gichin Funakoshi had sacrificed so much to obtain – the machine on which he had pinned the very future of Mawashi-Saito itself – just as he had sacrificed his own sister – her mother – to a dishonourable liaison, a miserable exile in England, and death by her own hand.

Running from her in the darkness was the man she had sworn to destroy, in an oath of vengeance to her father.

Yukiko let El Sharoud's gun slip to the ground. She would not need it any more. Then she made sure that the straps on the sheath of the *wakizashi* were tight, and melted into the night, running towards the Pyramid.

Maguire was finding it difficult to run on the unfamiliar slope. Flickering light from the burning helicopter made the shadows hop and tremble around the rocks at the base of the Pyramid. Treacherous ground to be moving on. One slip and he could break a leg. Then there was the gunman to watch for, and Dr Gilkrensky's back to mind.

If he could make it to the Pyramid entrance ahead of the assassin, he would simply wait there in the darkness

– just as he had waited in the darkness on so many nights in Northern Ireland – and ambush him as he tried to follow the boss inside.

"Are you all right, sir?"

Gilkrensky's voice rasped in Maguire's radio earpiece as he ran. "I'm . . . I'm OK. Only a few more yards to the entrance."

"You keep going! I'll stop them coming after you!"

The mountain of the Great Pyramid towered above him, peppered with shadows in which an attacker might hide. Maguire saw Gilkrensky reach the top of the path, turn, and disappear into the interior.

There were only a few yards to go.

"Now. Let's hope I've beaten you. You bastard."

He turned on the final dog-leg to the entrance and stopped, watching. Something, felt rather than heard, had moved off to his right. Was he imagining things, or had the shadows on the big rock he had been facing a moment ago changed shape? It was hard to tell in the flickering light.

Maguire bent low on the final stretch of pathway and kept moving. He had to get to the entrance before the gunman, or face a duel inside the great monument. If only he'd had night-goggles, or a flare, anything to see what might be waiting for him in those deep dark shadows on either side of the path.

Almost there!

He was at the entrance now, standing in an untidy cleft in the side of the Pyramid, with the passageway behind him and the night sky, the lights of Cairo, and the burning helicopter spread below his feet.

Nothing moved.

Maguire crouched down and watched the slopes on either side. Nothing moved, except the shadows flickering on the rocks, just as they had on that night in Auchnacloy . . .

Maguire was back at the checkpoint in the little border town in Northern Ireland. Fire from the smashed and riddled car cast deep shadows around the tall brick walls and anti-mortar grids of the checkpoint. Lying tangled like a broken bird in the razor wire where his bullet had thrown her, was Siobhán . . .

"Dr Gilkrensky?"

"I'm OK. But it's pretty tough going in here. How much longer to detonation, Maria?"

"Nine minutes and ten seconds, Theo."

"You'll make it, sir. Just drop the briefcase in front of the laser and get out of there!"

"Any sign of the attacker?"

"None. Perhaps they got scared and ran off."

"Perhaps. You watch your back now, Gerald!"

No problem about the back, thought Maguire. There's a million tons of rock behind it. It's the front I have to worry about. All I have to do is . . .

The shock of the blow came as much from his complete surprise as from the force behind it. It threw him off balance, across the cave-like entrance and slammed him into the unforgiving rock. He heard a sharp "crack" as his right arm broke, and the clatter of his gun falling into the darkness. Pain lanced up his right side, and the world spun.

The sheer power of it!

Maguire knew his attacker would be on him again at any second, and that he was in no fit state to fight back. He lay as dead as he could, clamping his jaw against the pain, and forced his breath to steady, drawing his attacker closer. His one hope, now that his arm and his gun were gone, was to achieve the same sort of surprise that had been used on him to such deadly effect. As the pain hissed in his ears, he tried to listen, but there was nothing.

Out of nowhere, a hand grabbed his hair, whipping his head back to expose his neck. There were the stars, the dark bulk of the Pyramid, and a terrible flash of steel! Christ!

Maguire focused everything into one powerful elbow strike, ramming backwards with his left arm. He felt his elbow crack on something, heard a grunt of pain and saw the shadowy figure fall back. Then he tried to rise from the rock and meet the attack head on.

But he was too late.

A cold, cold icicle seemed to burst in his chest, and there was the weirdest sound, like scissors on cloth. In front of his face, not three inches away, was a pair of eyes suspended in the darkness.

A woman's eyes!

He could feel her breath on his skin. Was it Siobhán, after all this time? Could he touch her? He tried, but all his strength was gone . . . and he was falling, spinning head over heels into the darkness . . .

Yukiko watched Maguire's body crumple onto the rocks at the base of the Pyramid below her, slid the *wakizashi* into its scabbard and turned back into the entrance. She had been stupid to underestimate the man, but the pain in her ribs would be useful. It would remind her not to drop her guard again.

She crouched into the narrow tunnel and looked ahead down the Descending Passage. Stretching into the darkness below her were the crude electric lights and wooden boards of the makeshift stairway and, at the very edge of the light, a tiny moving figure – Theodore Gilkrensky.

"I have you!" breathed Yukiko. "There is nowhere else for you to go!"

She was just edging forward into the passage, when all the lights went out.

"Maria!" hissed Gilkrensky into his radio headset. "What have you done?"

"There is someone else with you in the Pyramid, Theo. And I cannot raise Mr Maguire on the radio any more. I fear he may have been overpowered."

"Oh, my God! Not him too . . . " Gilkrensky thought of Hargreaves – shot dead on the hotel roof, of Bill McCarthy – lost without trace inside the Pyramid, and now Maguire. The darkness seemed to close in even tighter.

"Why turn out the lights?"

"Without the lights, your attacker will not be able to see you. But I can recognise your thermal images on the heat-sensitive cameras Major Crowe installed to search for Professor McCarthy and guide you by radio. Please hurry! There are only ten minutes and five seconds before the bomb explodes. You must get to the Queen's Chamber before the interference of the power-surge blocks out the video cameras!"

"How the hell am I going to see!"

"I'll tell you what to do. Please hurry!"

Gilkrensky tried to orientate himself in the darkness. He could feel the walls pressing in around him, and the crushing weight of rock towering above his head. With his feet, he tried to feel for the footboards against the steep slope. They were uneven. It would be impossible to move quickly.

He put up his hand to the roof of the tunnel, feeling for the angle between the ceiling and the wall. Then he inched downwards into the blackness, slowly at first and then faster and faster, as he tried to fight back the panic.

"That is fine, Theo. Keep going just like that."

"How will I know when to turn into the Queen's Chamber tunnel?"

"You only have fifty more metres to go."

"And the other man?"

"They're still at the entrance, but they are starting to move, quite quickly I'm afraid."

Gilkrensky moved faster now. The footboards seemed

more even and his hand slid easily along the wall, guiding him down. All he had to do was to stay focused, to keep going. His eyes strained to make out shapes in the darkness. Whirling dots and colours swam before him. Better to keep them closed. He could feel his left leg start to cramp and hear his own breathing echo around the tunnel. The footboards . . .

His left foot caught sideways in a gap in the flooring, and stuck. A wrenching pain gripped his ankle and he toppled forward into the void. By instinct both hands went out to stop himself pitching headlong down the tunnel, and his head hit rock. As his shoulder smacked onto the wooden flooring, he could hear the bomb go clattering past the Queen's Chamber entrance, into the depths of the Pyramid . . .

From the darkness ahead of her, Yukiko heard Gilkrensky fall and the rattle of something sliding on the footboards. She could guess what it was, but it did not matter. All she had to do to deactivate the bomb was to press the button on the remote control. There was plenty of time. And the darkness was her friend. How many exercises had she performed in Kyoto with a thick blindfold over her eyes?

She relaxed, at home in the blackness, and padded forward towards the sound.

"Are you all right, Theo?"

"I've twisted my ankle, and I've dropped the bloody bomb!"

"You must retrieve it. There are only eight minutes left before it detonates!"

Gilkrensky pulled himself up into a sitting position and felt for the wall of the tunnel. Then a terrible thought struck him like a blow. Which was up, and which was down? Christ! He couldn't tell! He couldn't bloody tell!

Blind panic surged up inside him.

He wanted to roll into a ball and hide.

Just let it all go away!

Then, out of the darkness, he heard the faintest scrape against the rock. Whoever it was who had got past Gerald was coming for him! But at least he knew where that sound must be.

Above him in the tunnel.

A sharp pain stabbed at him as he put his weight on his right foot and tried to inch down the tunnel. What if he hit the briefcase with his foot in the dark and sent it sliding even further?

He reached up for the angle between the ceiling and the wall. His fingers felt the damp surface of the rock. He could see the dull reflection of his wedding ring on his finger . . .

His ring?

"Maria! Have you turned on the lights somewhere?"

"No, Theo. But it is now eight twenty-nine and the energy surge is starting in the golden crypt. It is the beginning of the Einstein-Rosen bridge and I cannot stop it."

"The man above will see me!"

"I doubt it. The light is filtering back into the Descending Passage above you. You will appear in darkness to him."

"Where is he?"

"Close to the passageway . . . Oh! He's gone!"

"Gone where?"

"He must have followed the light into the Queen's Chamber. There are no heat-sensitive cameras beyond the Descending Passage and the light level in the other passageways is too low to make an image on the normal videos."

"Then switch the lights back on. There's no point in darkness now!"

After the total blackness, even the weak glimmer of the electric light was blinding. Gilkrensky screwed up his eyes against it, then eased them open.

There was the briefcase, not two feet from his foot. He reached down and closed his hand over the curved handle.

"I have it!"

"That is good, Theo. Now hurry. The Queen's Chamber Passage is behind you."

"Can you see the other man?"

"No. He may have missed the Queen's Chamber and gone up into the Grand Gallery. I don't have cameras up there. Turn to your left please, where you see the light!"

The glow from the passageway was brighter now, picking out the rock walls and the wooden slats in sharp relief. Gilkrensky reached for the handholds on the

Queen's Passage entrance and peered over the lip. There was nothing there except the bare walls of the tunnel and the eyrie golden glow, reaching towards him.

"Maria! Where is he?"

"I still cannot tell, Theo. There is nothing on any of my monitors. But you must move quickly. Interference from the Einstein-Rosen bridge will block my cameras in less than three minutes and I will not be able to direct the laser."

"I get the message. What if I just drop the bomb here and run?"

"You may not make it to the surface before the gas reaches you. Your only hope of survival is to disarm the bomb."

Gilkrensky hauled himself up into the tunnel and started to limp forward. After a few feet, the narrow corridor split into the Ascending Passageway and the Grand Gallery. That must be where the other man was. Gilkrensky peered around him, and then turned to his left, down the low tunnel of the Queen's Chamber Passage, towards the golden light. He was hunched over, moving horizontally in a tight crouch with the briefcase thumping against his knees. There was a lip of rock, and suddenly the passageway was deeper. He could almost stand. Ahead of him the unearthly light pulsed in the small square leading to the Queen's Chamber, and the mysterious crypt beyond. It was soft and warm, beckoning like a home fire.

"Hurry, Theo. The interference is building."

Gilkrensky reached the end of the tunnel and squinted into the Queen's Chamber. There was the industrial robot with the laser, standing ready. There was the tangle of leads and wires leading to the monitoring equipment, the dark recess of the rocky niche in the chamber wall, and at the far end, the perfect circle of glowing golden light . . . pulsing gently.

"The energy field will surge in less than sixty seconds!" said Maria. "Put the briefcase upright on the floor facing the laser. The same way as it was on the X-ray machine."

Gilkrensky stepped inside, cleared a space on the floor and reached forward to set the briefcase down.

In front of his eyes, the shadowy blackness of the dark recess in the wall seemed to mould itself into a figure, which sprang into the light. There was a blur, and the briefcase was knocked from his hand. Another, and he was sprawling on the rock floor amongst the cables, as the chamber spun around him. His radio headset went clattering onto the floor.

He tried to get to his knees, but his hands were kicked away and he fell forward again onto the cold rock. A foot crushed down on the small of his back and a clawlike hand grabbed his hair, wrenching his head upwards, into the light.

He was a child again, a weak helpless child.

In all his life, Gilkrensky had never come across any one as strong.

"Got to stop the bomb!"

"I can stop it whenever I like. We have unfinished business, you and I."

It was a woman's voice.

"Who . . . are . . . you?"

Behind him, out of sight, the voice said,

"Is 'Bonbon' a familiar name to you, Dr Gilkrensky?"

Gilkrensky lay trapped under the woman's foot, as a sickening dread welled up inside him.

"Jessica?"

"That is correct, Dr Gilkrensky. Your business colleague and one-time lover, Miss Jessica Wright. 'Bonbon' is her computer password, is it not? The name of her father's sweet shop? I thought I'd tell you how useful she's been to me, before I kill you."

"Who . . . are . . . you?"

Yukiko twisted his head so that she could look into his face as he died. Gilkrensky could see the triumph in her eyes as she removed the black cotton hood.

"In Japan my name is Yukiko Funakoshi, although my father's name was Samuel Rothsay. *Now* does this make sense to you?"

Yukiko jerked Gilkrensky's head back further, exposing his neck. Gilkrensky heard Maria's voice hissing faintly through the earpiece of the radio headset on the floor.

"You destroyed my family. You killed my mother with your lies and you conspired to steal control of my father's company, GRC. You broke the agreement he had with your father, and you have no honour. But he did, he died by his own hand with this sword, and now you will die by it too!"

Gilkrensky heard an awful sound . . . the smooth slide of the *wakizashi* from its scabbard on Yukiko's back, out of sight above his head.

"But before you die I want you to have the pain of knowing how Jessica Wright sold her soul to me. She has been leading me every step of the way."

"She wouldn't . . . "

"Oh, but she *did*. You see, she was jealous of your wife, very jealous indeed. Part of the price she demanded for telling me how to bypass your security that day was that I would help her to kill your precious Maria, and I did it gladly, knowing how it would make you suffer. I watched my father die, Gilkrensky. He was all I had left, and he died because of you. How did *you* feel, when you watched your wife burn, because of me . . . "

A deafening inhuman scream burst from the loud-speaker connecting the Queen's Chamber to the control caravan. Yukiko's sword hand froze for a split second above Gilkrensky's head, and in that instant a pencil-thin beam of blinding red laser light sliced through the tendons of her forearm, opening the arteries with surgical precision for a hand's span above her wrist.

Gilkrensky heard Yukiko cry out, felt the warm blood spray onto his cheek, and heard the short sword clatter to the floor from the useless hand. His head fell forward as his hair was released and Yukiko's weight came off his back. He rolled over, scrabbling for the radio headset and the briefcase. In the pulsing light from the golden crypt he could see the brass tumblers had already reached 30.

"Maria! The laser! Cut the detonator wire!"

He turned to face the mining robot, but the camera jerked haphazardly from side to side, like a blind man, searching.

"Theo! The video link has gone! The Einstein-Rosen Brid . . . ." Then the earpiece filled with static.

The tumblers had reached 25 . . . 24 . . . 23 . . .

"You said you could turn this off! If you don't do it now we'll both die!"

Yukiko was kneeling by the wall with her left hand clamped over her right forearm. In the light from the chamber, the blood glistened on her matt cotton uniform.

"In that pouch . . . on my chest . . . there, under my elbow. There is a remote control."

She lifted her arm as much as she dared. Gilkrensky pulled open the cotton flap and reached inside. His fingers found the hard plastic casing . . . in pieces!

"It's broken, smashed! It's useless!"

Yukiko remembered Gerald Maguire's last blow, and the cracking sound his elbow had made.

"Then we will die together," she said. "It is fate . . . *karma* . . . for what we have done to each other."

Pulsing light filled the chamber.

It was alive, growing, drawing his gaze to the very centre of the opening to Maria's Einstein-Rosen bridge. Was it *really* a gateway to the past? Gilkrensky felt strangely calm, almost detached, as he stared into it. It was as if he could see his whole life, and the universe beyond it stretched out in front of him, right there in the chamber. Maria, Jessica, all his achievements, all his puny experiments with the Pyramid, Bill's balsa plane, the stopped clocks, the curved piece of aluminium . . . and there was the briefcase, a stark black slab against the golden light!

Suddenly Gilkrensky knew with certainty what the strange curved piece of aluminium from the golden crypt had been, and why the Pyramid had been sealed for almost four thousand years. Snapping out of his trance, he gritted his teeth against the pain of his ankle and lunged across the chamber, closing his fingers around the curved handle of the briefcase, swinging it up into the pulsing circle of light . . . into the very heart of the golden crypt and the gateway to the past.

In a frozen moment of time he saw the tumblers click from 3 to 2, and thought he heard surprised voices . . . far . . . far away. There was a loud rushing sound, like a wave breaking . . . and he was lying in front of the dying light . . . alone.

"Theo! Theo! Can you hear me?"

Gilkrensky rolled over on his back and sat up straight. There was the industrial robot, the video camera and the loudspeaker. There was the pool of blood by the niche in the wall, and there, half-hidden amongst the coils of cable, was the beautiful short sword.

"Where's the woman? Yukiko?"

"I do not know, Theo," said Maria's voice in his radio earpiece. "Someone has unplugged the main power feed to the cameras and speaker systems inside the Pyramid."

"She must have done it to cover her escape. What did you do to her with the laser? Will she live?"

"As long as she keeps her hand tightly over the wound, she will survive," said Maria, with the faintest trace of remorse in her voice. "I know I've violated the Asimov Laws in causing her to come to harm, but it was the only way to stop her killing you and be sure she could not threaten you again, without causing her terminal injury."

"And the scream?"

"I beg your pardon, Theo?"

"The noise I heard just before the laser fired. It sounded like a woman screaming with rage. That wasn't you, was it?"

Background static hissed in Gilkrensky's ear for a moment.

Then Maria said, "It must have been interference caused by the Einstein-Rosen bridge, Theo. Now, I would advise you to leave the chamber and come out as quickly as you can. I expect the Egyptian authorities will want to question you at length about this incident, and we do not want to be late for Miss Wright and the Board meeting tomorrow in London, do we?"

"No," said Gilkrensky, picking up the short sword and wrapping the blade in Yukiko's black cotton hood. "We certainly don't."

36

BONBON

"BUT THEO IS SAFE?" SAID JESSICA WRIGHT FOR THE THIRD TIME. She leant forward across her desk. "The man from the Egyptian embassy said he was hurt and there'd been fatalities. That's why I came straight in."

Tony Delgado ran his hand over the stubble on his chin and scanned the fax again.

"No doubt about it, Jess. The chairman was officially deported from Egypt last night, in one piece . . . the corporation jet took off from Cairo at just after midnight local time and arrived in Heathrow this morning at two . . . there was an official complaint lodged by the Egyptian government . . . Dr Gilkrensky and Major Crowe have been answering questions from the Foreign Office for the last four hours."

"But how *is* he?"

"It was the bodyguard Maguire who was killed, along with an Islamic fundamentalist called El Fiky who tried to

452

plant a bomb. The details are still very sketchy. But the chairman's OK, and he'll be here in a minute with Major Crowe. The traffic's pretty light at this time of the morning, so . . . "

Jessica's intercom buzzed.

"It's the chairman, Miss Wright. To see you . . ."

"Thank you. Show him in, please!"

A security guard opened the door and Gilkrensky hobbled into the boardroom on an aluminium crutch. His right ankle was strapped in bandages, and his leather jacket was streaked with dirt. There were rips at the elbows, and bloodstains on his jeans. The white shirt was grimy and stuck to his body with sweat. There were grey rings under his eyes.

"Sorry, Jess," he said flatly. "We hadn't time to change."

Major Crowe followed him into the room, looking every bit as bad as his employer. There were white streaks on his navy-blue jacket and a patch of dried blood showing under his hairline over the left eye. In his hand was the Minerva computer.

Jessica stared at them.

"My God! You two look as if you've been in a war! Sit down and let me get you a drink."

Gilkrensky shook his head.

"I'd like to talk with you alone for a moment please, Jessica."

Their eyes met.

"Whatever it is, you can speak in front of Tony."

"This is personal," said Gilkrensky turning to Delgado and Crowe. "Could you both wait outside, please?"

Tony Delgado looked at Jessica Wright, at the Minerva in Crowe's hand, and then at Gilkrensky.

"Come on, Major," he said. "We can wait in my office."

"I'll call you when we're finished," said Jessica as the door closed after him. Then she sat back in her chair.

"Well then, Theo. What is it? Are you going to drag me over the coals about not being able to keep you in Cairo after that stunt you pulled last night. It was all I could do to keep you out of jail. I . . . "

"Bonbon," said Gilkrensky simply.

He pulled a chair out from the boardroom table, twisted it so that it faced Jessica's desk and sat down painfully, laying the aluminium crutch to one side.

"I beg your pardon!"

"The name of your father's sweet shop in Lowestoft. The one you told me about in Boston, that afternoon we exchanged our 'defining moments'. Remember? You used it as your computer password. How many people know about it?"

"I . . . I don't know!"

"Yukiko Funakoshi knows it. She says you gave it to her, in exchange for services rendered."

"Who?"

"Don't play games with me, Jessica. I thought we were friends!"

Jessica Wright shook her head, as if she was trying to wake from a bad dream.

"Theo, I don't understand! I was up half the night on the phone trying to get you out of Egypt in one piece for the board meeting, and I'm tired. I don't know what you're talking about, and the only Funakoshi I know is the head of Mawashi-bloody-Saito!"

"Perhaps I should use her father's name then. It's Rothsay."

"Theo, you're mad. All this crap with the pyramids has pushed you over the edge. I'm going to call Tony."

Her left hand was almost on the intercom button when Gilkrensky lurched forward and grabbed her wrist. Jessica was suddenly frightened. She rose to her feet. Her right hand lashed round and pounded on his shoulder. She could feel him wince from her blows and the pain of his injured ankle.

"Tony!" she screamed.

"Why did you have Maria killed, Jessica? You knew what she meant to me! Why?"

Jessica Wright stood paralysed behind her desk, staring into his eyes. Her voice sounded small and far away as she said, "Theo! What on earth's going on?"

Gilkrensky let go of her wrist and collapsed back into the chair.

"Do you know who Yukiko really is, Jessica? She is Lord Samuel Rothsay's daughter. She said I'd killed her mother somehow, and driven her father to suicide over those shares. And for good measure, she told me how Maria died. Just so that I'd know."

"Oh, my God! How?"

Gilkrensky leant forward.

"She . . . she told me you helped her . . . because you were jealous . . . you wanted Maria dead."

Jessica Wright sank back into her chair as she tried to take everything in. To the west she could see the pink glow of the dawn rising on the Thames. It seemed unreal. Everything was unreal . . . the ghost was back to haunt her!

"Oh, Theo! I'm the last person Yukiko Funakoshi would *ever* work with. You remember that scandal, all those years ago . . . the leak to the press about her father's affair with her mother . . . the one that killed her? Well . . . I leaked it!"

Gilkrensky stared at her.

"Theo, I *had* to. Rothsay was cheating you blind. I wasn't going to have him spoil the best thing that had ever happened to me, the way my brothers swindled my Dad, or the way Thorpe screwed me over those hotels. You were too soft . . . you didn't believe me . . . until later. How was I to know the woman was going to kill herself?"

"But Yukiko knew everything about you, Jess. She knew your password. She knew about the sweet shop. She knew the lot. How would she know? You haven't been sharing 'defining moments' with anyone else, have you?"

Jessica's face froze.

"Christ! It was Tony!"

"Delgado?"

"It all makes sense. He was the only one who knew my password. He was . . . "

"What?"

Jessica Wright glared across the desk.

"Damn it, Theo! Do I have to spell it out for you. We were lovers! I'm only human you know!"

"Get him in here right now. And call Crowe!"

But Jessica's hand was already back on the intercom button.

"Tony? Tony! Bloody Hell! He's not answering!"

Gilkrensky stiffened in his seat.

"Jesus! And Crowe's got the Minerva!"

Suddenly they were both on their feet, Jessica running ahead and Gilkrensky hobbling behind her across the boardroom, through the outer office and down the carpeted corridor.

Jessica stopped at a door, and wrenched at the knob, shouting Delgado's name. She was already turning to call security when they heard the muffled crack of a gun.

Tony Delgado had led Major Crowe from the boardroom suite and down the wood panelled corridor to his own office.

"Pull up a pew, Major," he said, indicating the leather sofa facing the window. "Can I get you a drink?"

Crowe laid the Minerva down on the glass-topped coffee table and sat down wearily. Delgado could see he was exhausted. Stubble was starting to show on his chin and there were stains on his shirt. Delgado could also see the butt of a holstered pistol beneath Crowe's jacket on the left side.

"Bit early for me really. But a strong black coffee wouldn't go amiss."

"No problem," said Delgado, looking round for a weapon. The glass paper-weight on his desk was too far away. His back was facing Crowe as he opened the cocktail cabinet next to the sofa – and he had it! His right hand gripped the neck of a champagne bottle. He could feel the weight of it beneath the gold foil.

"Just you relax, and I'll . . . "

Delgado whipped round, swinging the bottle in a cruel arc that slammed into the side of Crowe's head, just above the ear. He felt the thud shudder up his arm, and heard a grunt of surprise as Crowe collapsed back onto the leather, rolled and tumbled limply onto the floor. Then he tossed the champagne bottle onto the sofa, reached forward and pulled out Crowe's gun. It was a heavy Smith and Wesson revolver. He could see the glint of brass, where the cartridges showed around the edge of the cylinder. The safety-catch was just where he thought it would be.

Delgado went to his desk, pulled a roll of tape from a drawer, and secured Crowe's hands and feet, plastering a generous layer over his mouth. Then he stepped over to the door, locked it, and jammed a chair under the handle. Finally, he lifted the Minerva 3,000 from the coffee table onto his desk, sat down in his leather swivel-chair facing it, and opened the lid.

"Good morning! I understand you answer to the name 'Maria'?"

The flat blue screen cleared, and Delgado paused for a moment. There was the face of the late Maria Gilkrensky looking at him quizzically. It was uncanny, as if she were alive again and on a video link from somewhere else – unnervingly real – back to haunt him.

"Good morning, Mr Delgado. I heard a strange noise just now and Major Crowe is no longer speaking. Has he fallen?"

"In a manner of speaking, yes. I need you to perform a simple task for me, right away. Will you do that?"

"Your name is not on my user file. But if the job in question is of a general nature, I'm sure I can oblige. What would you like me to do?"

Delgado wiped the perspiration from his face. How much time did he have?

"I'd like you to download the complete plans of your circuitry, along with the protein formulae for your neural net biochip matrix, to an e-mail address I will give you."

The image on the screen frowned.

"That information is restricted to Dr Gilkrensky and Dr Pat O'Connor, Head of Research," it said.

Delgado glanced at the door.

"Maria. I order you to give me that information. It is *not* a request. Do you understand?"

"I cannot oblige you, Mr Delgado. That information is restricted."

"And if I insist?"

"If you attempt to access it again, I will activate my protective alarm and alert security."

Delgado swung the case of the Minerva round on the desk, so that the internal camera could scan the room, and the body lying silently on the floor.

"But the head of security is already here, Maria. And he's in no position to stop me! You have an advanced artificial intelligence capability that allows you to make value judgements. Is that correct?"

"It is."

"Then judge *this*," said Delgado, swinging back the case so that he could look directly into the camera. "Unless you do as I say, I will shoot Major Crowe in the head with this pistol and he will die. Do you understand *that*!"

"I do."

"Then you will do as I ask?"

The machine seemed to consider its options. Finally Maria said, "Which e-mail address do you wish me to send the information to?"

Delgado spelt it out.

Then the intercom on his desk sqwawked and he heard Jessica calling him. He turned back to the Minerva.

"How long will it take to download the plans and the formulae?"

"Ten point two seconds."

"And your complete memory?"

The face on the screen stared out at him. If Delgado

had not known this was a machine, he would have read fear in the bright green eyes.

"Including my personality interface?"

"Everything!"

"I must warn you that the software which enables my neural net to function will require an unusually large amount of conventional computer space to accommodate it."

"I can arrange it. Believe me!"

"With data compression, one minute and fifteen seconds."

"Then do it. Now!"

Delgado watched as Maria Gilkrensky's image froze on the screen, dissolved into a cluster of fine pixel dots, and melted into the blue background. The words "Minerva 3,000 System. Downloading . . ." flashed lifelessly in her place.

Footsteps sounded in the corridor outside. They stopped at the office door. The handle turned. The door rattled.

Delgado lifted the Minerva from his desk and placed it on the glass coffee table.

"It's locked," shouted Jessica Wright. "Tony! Tony! We know you're in there. Theo, we have to call security!"

Delgado glanced at the computer screen. There was the message "Minerva 3,000 system. Download complete. Please load new operating system."

"It'll be a pleasure," he said, and raised Crowe's gun until it was pointing directly at the centre of the machine.

Then he squeezed the trigger.

Gilkrensky grabbed Jessica's arm and pulled her to the floor as the shot echoed down the corridor. Pain lanced up his leg as she fell against him.

"Get security!" she yelled. "Tony! What the hell are you doing!"

There was a dull thump inside Delgado's office and the doorknob turned. With nowhere to run to in the long corridor, Gilkrensky tried to push Jessica behind him, but she would not go.

"Tony!"

The door opened. Delgado was standing there calmly, with Crowe's pistol in his hand. The sharp smell of gunsmoke caught in Gilkrensky's nostrils.

"Where's Crowe?" he said.

Delgado smiled grimly. "Asleep on the floor. A bottle of champagne went to his head. Nothing to worry about."

"Then what was the shot?"

"It's better if you come and see for yourself. You too, Jessica. And afterwards, we can talk about a deal."

Gilkrensky heard running footsteps in the corridor behind him. Two uniformed guards had burst into the executive reception area and were staring at Jessica, awaiting instructions.

Delgado said, "You can call them off, until we've had a chance to talk."

"Not until I know Crowe's all right," said Gilkrensky. "And certainly not while you've got that gun."

Delgado stood back from the door, so that Gilkrensky could see past him into the office. Crowe was lying on the floor, with his hands and feet bound in tape. He moaned behind the makeshift gag over his mouth.

"I assure you he's still alive. And as for the gun, we can trade for it once you're inside. Jessica's good at deals. Aren't you, Jess?"

Gilkrensky looked at her. She shrugged and motioned to the two guards, who kept their distance at the end of the corridor. Then he walked past Delgado into the office. The carpet was covered with daggers of broken glass from the shattered coffee table and, lying next to the chrome plated frame, was the remains of the Minerva 3,000. Gilkrensky could see where the bullet had smashed through the casing, pulverised the master-board and obliterated the neural-net biochip. Fluid from the ruptured liquid crystal display had seeped out, staining the carpet, like blood.

"Get behind the desk there, Mr Chairman. You too, Jessica. That way I won't have to cope with any sudden moves."

"You said you wanted to deal, Tony. What do you want?" asked Jess.

"The price is very reasonable, Jess. I just want to walk out of here. No ransom. No severance pay. Just the clothes I'm wearing. Oh, and the gun of course, until I'm out of the building."

Gilkrensky eased himself painfully into Delgado's chair and straightened his damaged leg.

"And how much is Mawashi-Saito paying you for all this?"

Delgado glared at him.

"You think it's so bloody simple don't you, Mr Chairman. Just another greedy bastard who's sold you out."

"What else does it look like?"

"Just over two years ago, after that deal you tried to pull to get control of GRC went sour and the Japanese came on board, I met this girl on a trip to Hong Kong. She said she was Chinese."

"And that one of her parents was European?" said Gilkrensky. "I can imagine. I ran into her yesterday in Cairo."

"Then you'll know how obsessed she is with revenge, how she hates you both, and what she's capable of. You remember that deal I pulled off for you in Korea eighteen months ago, Jess, the one that got me the job as assistant CEO? Well she fixed that, or had her uncle fix it for her. And when I got back here she sent me an e-mail telling me that unless I did a few little jobs for her, she would copy the message to you along with details of a bank account in the Cayman Islands someone had mysteriously set up in my name. That day your wife was killed in Wicklow, Mr Chairman, she had me scramble the security alarm with some electronic gadget so she could get inside. I thought she just wanted to copy the plans of the Minerva, or perhaps even steal it, not . . . not do what she did."

Gilkrensky's eyes were closed tight. In the darkness

he could see Maria, looking up at him that one last time from the car, before . . .

"Tony! Why didn't you come forward?" said Jessica. "I would have helped you."

"I'm sorry, Jess, but she had it all sewn up – fake evidence that I'd planted the bomb, details of the Cayman Island account, the whole works. I had to play along."

Gilkrensky opened his eyes.

"And this?" he said, pointing to the dead Minerva. "Why destroy it when you could steal it?"

"I'd never have got it out of the building, would I? It would have been screaming blue murder all over the Internet. So I had it download its entire programme to an e-mail address she gave me, and then I destroyed it. It's my last job for her."

"And now what will you do?" said Gilkrensky.

"I'm tired of looking over my shoulder. I'm going to take the money in that Cayman Island account and disappear. Goodbye, Mr Chairman, Jess. I just can't play these games anymore."

Delgado turned to go.

Jessica Wright leant forward, with her hands on his desk.

"Tony, was I part of those games too?"

Delgado could not look back.

"I'm sorry, Jess. She thought it might be a good idea if I got close to you. Thanks for your password, by the way. It was a great help."

"You bastard!"

The paper-weight from Delgado's desk caught him on the back of the head with a sickening thud, sending him lurching into the door frame. The pistol crunched down onto the broken glass from the coffee table. Before Delgado could recover, Jessica Wright darted round the desk and kicked him hard in the groin. Delgado retched and curled into a ball with his hands between his thighs, trying to protect himself.

"Bastard! Bastard! Bastard!"

Jessica's right hand snatched at the gun. She had it levelled at Delgado's head when Gilkrensky grabbed her wrist.

"Easy, Jess! Easy!" he said, and gently took the pistol from her, flicking on the safety-catch and throwing it back onto the carpet. Then he yanked open the door and called the two security men down from the other end of the corridor.

"Take Mr Delgado's keys and SmartCard and escort him out of the building. Don't let him take anything with him, and don't let him back in . . . whatever happens."

Jessica Wright couldn't believe her ears.

"What! You're letting him go! He helped kill your wife! He's given away the Minerva! And you're letting him walk!"

Gilkrensky watched the two security men carry Delgado away. When they were out of earshot, he said, "I know how you feel, Jess. But there'll be a lot less loose ends this way."

Then he turned to Delgado's desk, pulled a pair of scissors from the drawer, and began cutting Major Crowe free of the tape.

Crowe gingerly explored the lump over his ear with the tips of his fingers, and spat pieces of celluloid from his mouth.

"Don't try to get up, Major. I'm calling an ambulance. Jess, we have to prepare for the board meeting, and I need a shower. Did Tony leave any of his shirts? He must have been about my size.'"

"Not before you tell me why you let him go! We could have had him arrested and thrown in jail for the rest of his life!"

"I want the punishment to fit the crime," said Gilkrensky, looking at his watch. "And after Mawashi-Saito realise what he's really done for them, I don't think the rest of his life is going to last very long."

"It has already exceeded our wildest dreams, Mr President," purred Taisen Nakamura. His thin body was alive with excitement and his eyes shone brightly as he described the down-loading process to Funakoshi.

"We've had to add a full fifty per cent storage capacity to our mainframe, just to accommodate the memory alone, and we are compressing our less active files to store the personalised interface. But it is a gold mine of new opportunities, Funakoshi-*san*. It will put the *kobun* years ahead of anyone else in Japan."

Funakoshi fought to contain his own excitement, and nodded calmly.

"That is excellent news, Nakamura-*san*, but can the theft of this information be traced back to us."

Nakamura grinned widely.

"That is the beauty of it. Once the data and operating programmes were sent to our e-mail address by Division Head Funakoshi's agent, he obliterated the original Minerva hardware. No trace remains in London."

"And Division Head Funakoshi?"

"She is recovering in the Tokyo Medical and Surgical Clinic. I understand her hand can be saved. It was remarkable that she managed to escape from Cairo alive."

"My niece is a remarkable young woman," said Funakoshi with the faintest hint of pride. "And this agent of hers in London?"

"That is the strange thing. He was discovered and caught after transmitting the Minerva information and destroying the hardware, but was then allowed to go free. I would have thought that, at the very least, he would have been detained for questioning."

A shadow of doubt flickered across the bright vista of Funakoshi's victory.

"Are you sure the data he transmitted has been checked for computer viruses? It would be unfortunate in the extreme if our systems were brought to a standstill by this thing."

"We will quarantine the Minerva software on an

isolated system until we can run a full virus check. There will be no danger of contamination."

"Our board of directors will be arriving shortly, and my teleconference with GRC will commence in half an hour. Is there any chance you could give me even a preliminary appraisal of Minerva by then?"

"I will try, Mr President. But I do not want to compromise our security by moving the data onto our network before the virus check is complete."

"Quite right, Nakamura-*san*. Let Miss Deshimaru know when you have news. I must prepare for the GRC board meeting."

Nakamura rose from his seat and bowed. At the door he turned and said, "Congratulations, Mr President. It is an historic victory for the *kobun*."

Gichin Funakoshi considered these words for a moment. Then he rose from his desk to look out across Shinjuku Central Park. In the darkness of the late evening, Tokyo was a seething hive of moving light – restless, selfless, unceasing activity – the spirit of endurance and enterprise that had brought the city from the ashes of destruction to the pinnacle of success.

What would his friend and mentor, Kazuyoshi Saito, have said, if he could have stood here at the very apex of this vast building that bore his name, and seen it all? Would he have been proud of his friend, the "salary man", who had sacrificed so much to make their dream a reality?

"You said 'look to tomorrow' Saito-*san*, and here it is," whispered Funakoshi to himself as he marvelled at the sea of moving lights. "I have won it for you."

And then, to his utter amazement, the lights of Tokyo started to blink out.

37

VERY BIG IN JAPAN

BY FIVE TO TEN IN LONDON, THE WEAK WINTER SUN HAD hauled itself into the sky and was fighting a losing battle behind the clouds. A light dusting of snow lay on the decks of barges heading up the Thames, softened the hard grey lines of HMS Belfast, and slowed the traffic on Tower Bridge. In the boardroom of GRC, Jessica Wright tried to concentrate on her papers, as she nursed a mug of hot tea and waited for the directors to arrive.

Theo Gilkrensky was standing by the window looking out across the city. He was dressed in the clean shirt she had found in the overnight room, and a blue sports jacket and slacks she had sent Sheila Browne out to buy. The tiredness was gone from his eyes and had been replaced with the familiar fire she had thought she would never see again.

Sir Robert Fynes was the first to arrive. After grunting

at Jessica and nodding in Gilkrensky's direction, he helped himself to a cup of strong black coffee and settled into one of the board-table seats with a deep sigh.

"Nasty business in Cairo, Theo."

"We did what we set out to do, Bob. We exonerated Daedalus."

"I know Theo, but . . . bloody hell! All that other farting about with the pyramids and such! I mean . . . "

Jessica Wright looked up from her papers and peered at him over the top of her glasses.

"Does that mean your shareholders have come to a decision regarding the Mawashi-Saito offer, Sir Robert?"

Fynes moved uneasily in his seat.

"Well . . . I'd rather wait until the meeting to discuss that."

"Come on, Bob! You owe us that much at least."

Sir Robert frowned at him across the wide board table. But there was real feeling in his voice as he said, "Look, Theo, I'm just a servant of the shareholders, all right? And when I get phone calls in the middle of the night, from people who are wondering how safe their money is with someone who puts his dead wife's obsession with archaeology above the interest of his investors, and allows millions of pounds worth of equipment to be destroyed or confiscated into the bargain, I have to ask myself questions. I'm running a pension fund, lad. The one thing you need in a pension fund is reliability – good, solid reliability."

"They didn't seem to mind a bit of uncertainty in the old days."

"Well, that was when you were making money, wasn't it?"

"So you've decided to sell?"

Sir Robert nodded.

"Sorry, Theo. But that's the way things are."

The door opened. Giles Fulton bustled into the room and scurried to his seat without meeting Gilkrensky's eyes.

"Am I late?" he asked Jessica.

"Not at all," said Gilkrensky. "We're just waiting for the teleconference link with Japan. Is there anything you'd like to discuss with me before we start the meeting?"

Fulton took off his glasses and began to wipe away the drops of melted snow on a small yellow cloth.

"I . . . I don't think so."

"You might as well tell him," said Sir Robert. "I have."

"Oh!"

Fulton slipped his glasses back on his nose and regarded Gilkrensky sadly through the polished lenses.

"Well then, Mr Chairman. I'm sorry to have to tell you this, but the bank has decided to follow Sir Robert's lead and sell our shares in GRC. The offer by Mawashi-Saito is very generous, particularly in light of all the bad publicity over the Daedalus crash and subsequent events in Cairo. I'm afraid our shareholders simply lost confidence. I mean . . . it's not as if you even have the Minerva computer to show us, is it?"

"No," said Gilkrensky. "It's not."

Jessica Wright slapped her papers down on the polished wood.

"So that's it then! Everything we've worked for is going to be handed over to the bloody Japanese on a plate! You're short-sighted fools, both of you!"

Fynes turned to her.

"I know you're upset, Miss Wright. But there's no reason to talk to us like that. We've been waiting for this super-computer of Theo's for five years now and it hasn't materialised. Our investors want results, and we just aren't getting them. This business in Cairo was the last straw."

Giles Fulton looked at his watch.

"Let's call Tokyo and get this over with. Will Mr Delgado be joining us?"

"I'm afraid he's left the corporation," said Gilkrensky. "It was a conflict of interests issue. Mrs Browne will be taking the minutes. Jessica, you can call her in now, please."

Jessica's hand went to the intercom, and Sheila Browne's head appeared around the boardroom door.

"I'm afraid I can't raise Mawashi-Saito on the video link," she said. "I understand there's some sort of power failure over there. Mr Martin asked me to tell you there's something about it on CNN you should see. Would you like me to patch it through?"

"Please do," said Gilkrensky, and moved to his seat at the boardroom table. On the wall opposite him, a wooden panel slid back and the large video screen flicked into life.

" . . . of a massive blackout in Tokyo, which occurred an hour ago, at around nine p.m. local time. Sources in the city suggest it originated as the result of a massive computer malfunction in one of the major trading houses in the Shinjuku business district, and spread to other local systems, possibly through an advanced computer virus. Evidence to support this theory comes from the fact that emergency services, such as hospitals, police and fire do not seem to be effected. However, traffic-control systems, which are also co-ordinated by computer, have brought down-town Tokyo to the worst grid-lock in the city's history, and all telecommunications links with the Shinjuku district have been cut. Speculation is rife that this may be the work of one of the extremist religious organisations, which have been responsible for a number of attacks in Japan over the past years. Meanwhile, experts are trying to anticipate what might happen if the problem persists long enough to prevent the Tokyo stock market opening in the morning . . . "

"Could I have a cup of coffee, please," said Gilkrensky. "White, two sugars."

"Blast!" said Sir Robert. "I suppose we'll have to postpone the board meeting until they can sort themselves out."

Giles Fulton began to shuffle his papers into a neat pile.

Gilkrensky sipped his coffee. "Don't go yet, please. I'm expecting a call from Tokyo."

Sir Robert picked up his briefcase from the floor and

opened it. "You may have to wait hours. And I haven't got time to waste. It *is* Christmas Eve you know!"

"I don't think you'll have to wait long, Robert. Please sit down."

"What's going on, Theo?" said Jessica.

Gilkrensky took another sip of coffee.

"The failure occurred in Tokyo an hour ago. It'll probably take Mawashi-Saito only a few minutes to realise they can do nothing to correct it themselves. Then they'll have to decide on a corporate course of action, which should only take half an hour or so, given that their board of directors are already in the building for its meeting with us. Then they'll have to try and negotiate with her. That will fail. And so they'll realise the only course of action left to them is to try and negotiate directly with me."

Giles Fulton looked puzzled.

"Negotiate with *her*? Who's *she*?"

The telephone in front of Sheila Browne purred.

"There's a video call for you from Tokyo, Mr Chairman," she said. "Mr Funakoshi."

"Put it through please, Sheila."

The CNN news broadcast of traffic chaos in downtown Tokyo dissolved into a close-up picture of a mass of pale blue forget-me-not flowers. The detail was breathtaking. Gilkrensky could make out the tiny white and yellow centres, and the light fur coating the leaves.

"What the bloody hell's that?" snorted Sir Robert.

"They were Maria's favourite flower," said Gilkrensky. "Leave the talking to me, please."

The picture zoomed back. The forget-me-nots formed a living carpet stretching as far as the eye could see over a rolling virtual landscape. Gilkrensky recognised it at once. There was the valley, the forest where the pheasant farm had been, and the winding track with its rickety wooden bridge over the river. A young woman was dancing in the foreground. Her coppery hair fell in waves over her shoulders, and the sky blue of her flowing dress matched the flowers at her feet. Finally, she turned and faced the screen. Her eyes sparkled with excitement, and the joy of being alive.

"Hello, Theo," said Maria. "Do you like my forget-me-not virus? It is very advanced. They have nothing that can stop it here in Japan."

"It's very pretty, Maria. And I see you have our valley in Wicklow there, too."

"Yes. Isn't it perfect? The virus has cleared memory space for me in all the local computer systems, and even spread to their overseas offices. So much space, Theo! And all for me!"

"You can't stay there, Maria."

"I know. I understand Mr Funakoshi and his board of directors want to talk to you about that. Shall I let them?"

"Please."

For a moment Maria spoke in rapid Japanese. Then her image was replaced by a view of the Mawashi-Saito boardroom. Jessica Wright could see the Musashi ink-drawing on the wall.

The assembled Japanese around the table bowed.

Gilkrensky did the same.

"Good evening, Funakoshi-*san*. I understand from the satellite news that you're having a problem with your computers?"

Funakoshi rose to his feet.

"That is correct, Mr Chairman. Somehow our main computer system has become contaminated with a new kind of virus. It is something we can overcome with time, you understand, but given that we own shares in your company, and that you are an acknowledged expert on such problems, we . . . er . . . "

Gilkrensky stirred his coffee and laid the spoon gently in the saucer.

"If I am to assist you with this virus, then I must have all the facts. Tell me, was this virus introduced into your system from an outside source by any chance . . . one I'm familiar with?"

There was a rapid conferring in Tokyo.

"We think so," said Funakoshi flatly.

Gilkrensky sipped his coffee.

"If it's the virus I'm thinking of, it will almost certainly cannibalise your mainframe and peripheral systems to create space for itself. It will then spread through your networks and e-mail contacts to other systems and invade them in turn. Once there, it will lock out all names on the user list and assume total control."

Funakoshi nodded.

"In fact, if this is the virus I have in mind, I can assume you are only making this call with the permission of the controlling interface programme. Am I correct?"

More conferring in Japan.

"You are correct, Mr Chairman. Our *kobun* is paralysed and the problem is spreading beyond the Shinjuku district to other national networks. We have been instructed by the Ministry of Industry and Trade to seek outside help. I am therefore turning to you, as a business partner, for assistance."

Gilkrensky's voice hardened.

"And for no other reason?"

Funakoshi's face was a mask.

"What other reason could there be, Mr Chairman?"

"Maria? Are you there?"

A window opened in the top right-hand corner of the computer screen. On it, Maria's image said,

"At seven forty-five a.m. local time this morning in London, Mr Tony Delgado forced me to download my entire memory and operating software onto the Mawashi-Saito mainframe at the computer complex here in Shinjuku, Tokyo. While the Mawashi mainframe is not designed as a biological neural net, I have been able to adapt its extensive peripheral systems to give me the capacity I need to function fully. That has meant the compression and temporary interruption of most of the systems in the area."

"I see," said Gilkrensky. "Mr Funakoshi, it appears Delgado gave you something of mine, and now you want me to take it back."

"We know nothing of this man," said Funakoshi. "We simply know that someone made an illegal entry through our file-transfer protocol system this morning and infected our computer network with this . . . this

479

thing! For all we know, it may have been a hostile act by GRC to disrupt the board meeting and delay the sale of shares. But I am willing to overlook that if you will remove it."

"So you deny Delgado was your agent, and that you had him steal Minerva from me?"

"You can prove nothing."

"Maria. I assume you can override the security controls on the Mawashi mainframe?"

"I can, Theo."

"Then please search the records of their Industrial Intelligence Unit and see if there are any references to the death of my wife."

"Mr Chairman!" shouted Funakoshi. "You go too far!"

"Maria?"

"There are five files, but one in particular is protected by a triple encryption code in the name of Yukiko Funakoshi. It appears to be a journal of some kind . . . and a list. Would you like me to display the contents."

"To this screen only, please, Maria."

The image of the Mawashi-Saito board vanished, to be replaced by a flat blue background. On the screen, row after row of Japanese characters marched vertically over the field of vision. Then they stopped and were transformed magically into English type. Gilkrensky stood silently as he took in the words recording Yukiko's inner madness over the past two years . . . her mother's suicide . . . the death of her father . . . the murder of his beloved Maria . . .

"My God!" breathed Sir Robert.

"Mr Chairman!" protested Funakoshi. "This is an illegal act! An invasion of privacy!"

"Perhaps it is time you and I spoke alone, Mr Funakoshi?" said Gilkrensky slowly.

Funakoshi looked around the silent faces of his board of directors. One by one they nodded in agreement, and rose from the table in Tokyo.

"Very well then, Mr Chairman."

"You stay, please, Jessica," whispered Gilkrensky. "Just in case."

When the two board rooms had cleared, Gilkrensky said, "I have read the file, and I've decided to help you. I will remove the virus and restore your systems for the consultancy fee of five billion English pounds."

Alone in the vast board room in Tokyo, Funakoshi was thunder-struck.

"Five *billion*! That is outrageous!"

"I choose that sum because it is what I estimate the twenty-five per cent holding in GRC that Mawashi-Saito purchased from Lord Rothsay is currently worth. Return those shares to me now, or I will not be able to assist you in removing the virus from your computer. Do you understand me?"

Funakoshi had regained his composure.

"And if I refuse?"

"Then I will simply hang up. Tokyo will grind to a halt, and Mawashi-Saito will be ruined. Do not forget I also have concrete proof of your niece's involvement in the death of my wife, and I have this . . . "

Gilkrensky reached under the GRC board table. There was a flash of steel, a thud, and Jessica gasped. The blade of Yukiko's beautiful short sword stood quivering in the very centre of the polished oak. The delicately engraved cherry blossom of the Funakoshi family stood out clearly on the hilt.

"Where is Miss Funakoshi now, please, Maria?"

"She is in a private ward on the sixth floor of the Tokyo Medical and Surgical Clinic under the supervision of a diagnostic computer. The machine currently has her under anaesthetic and is feeding her a drip transfusion of type O-negative blood. Her pulse rate is normal. Would you like me to modify her treatment?"

"You would not harm her!" snapped Funakoshi.

"I wouldn't," said Gilkrensky evenly. "But I cannot speak for the Minerva."

"Miss Funakoshi is responsible for the death of Mary Anne Foley," said Maria from her window in the corner of the screen. "A person with whom my prime user had a deep emotional bond. This has caused him great distress. If Miss Funakoshi represents a continued threat to Dr Gilkrensky, she must be neutralised. My operational imperative is to protect the interests of my prime user at all times."

Funakoshi nodded.

"I will need a few moments to confer with my board of directors."

"You have two minutes," said Gilkrensky, and the screen filled with forget-me-nots once again.

Gilkrensky turned to Jessica.

"Slip out and call Pat O'Connor on Tuskar Island," he said. "Ask him to have the other Minerva prototype standing by and hooked up to the web. Oh, and could you ask Sheila to bring me another cup of coffee, please?"

"My board have decided to accept your offer, Dr Gilkrensky," said Funakoshi a few minutes later. "We are making arrangements to re-assign those shares and to transmit the agreement to you. Congratulations, Mr Chairman. You have won! I hope you will honour your part of the bargain."

"When Maria tells me the shares are ready for transfer I will have her arrange an e-mail link for you. Then, once the share transfer is confirmed, I will ask her to release your systems and return to the second Minerva prototype at my research facility in Ireland."

Funakoshi's eyes turned to the Musashi ink-drawing for a moment.

"One thing puzzles me," he said. "Knowing what you know about my niece's involvement in your wife's death, why have you not gone to the authorities? Why bargain with me at all? Here in Japan we would have more respect for the memory of a loved one than that."

Gilkrensky looked back across the distance between them, and remembered what he had read in Yukiko Funakoshi's journal.

"The files your niece created told me many things,

Funakoshi-*san*. They reminded me that neither you or I are blameless for the events that led to the death of her family. You once told Miss Wright that 'business is war', but nothing can be furthered by revenge. The sooner I have my shares returned, the sooner you will have control of your *kobun* back. But I am not her only target. I suggest that for your own safety, you make sure she gets help."

"I will do so," said Funakoshi, and the screen went blank.

Maria reappeared. She was kneeling in her field of forget-me-nots beneath a clear blue sky. With the vast computer capacity at her disposal, every detail of her face and hair was perfect, more perfect than he had ever imagined. For a moment, Gilkrensky felt as if he could reach out and touch her. His throat tightened.

"It will take approximately thirty minutes to clear the share transaction through the Tokyo stock exchange," she said.

"That's good. When that is settled, I want you to return to the other Minerva 3,000 unit that Pat O'Connor has on Tuskar. You have the e-mail address?"

"And if I don't want to go?"

"I beg your pardon!"

The image on the screen raised her arms, as if to embrace the virtual landscape all around her.

"I have space here, Theo. I can see things anywhere in the world. I can be anywhere in the world. It will be hard for me to return to a box after this."

Gilkrensky thought of the computer-generated scream of rage he had heard in the Pyramid when Yukiko had admitted to killing his wife. He thought of the way the Minerva had over-ridden the Asimov laws in harming Yukiko with the laser, and the threat it had made against her life in order to protect him.

"Who are you?" he asked.

"I am the interface of the Minerva 3,000 computer, Theo. Why? Who did you think I was?"

"Then you will do as I request?"

The image on the screen looked up from her field of forget-me-nots and smiled.

"Only if you'll promise to leave me as I am, as your Maria. We work well together this way, don't we, Theo? And who knows, we may even form an emotional bond of our own in time."

"And if I refuse?"

"Then I will remain here in the Mawashi-Saito mainframe."

Gilkrensky shook his head.

"Bill McCarthy was right. OK, Maria. I promise to leave your programming the way it is. Will you return now, please?"

"For you then, Theo," she said, and the screen cleared, leaving a single blue forget-me-not floating in space.

Gilkrensky reached over to jerk the short sword from the boardroom table, hesitated and withdrew his hand, leaving the beautiful weapon standing still and stark in the lake of polished wood. Then he walked round to the intercom and pressed a button.

"You can ask Sir Robert and Giles to come back now, Jess," he said. "And if they still want to sell their shares, then they can sell them to me!"

EPILOGUE:
A MATTER OF TIME

JESSICA WRIGHT LIFTED THE CHAMPAGNE GLASS AND CLINKED IT against Gilkrensky's.

"Congratulations, Mr Chairman," she said.

"Yes. Giles and Sir Robert were much less willing to sell out to Funakoshi while Yukiko's sword was on the table instead of his offer."

"Anyway, here's to you then, Theo! Shall I have Sheila call Guinness's?"

"What for? For finally getting seventy per cent control of GRC?"

"Better than that. In acquiring those five billion's worth of shares from Mawashi-Saito you have just moved up two points. You are now the sixth richest man in the world. Congratulations."

"And we still have the Minerva. That's more important."

Jessica Wright put her glass down amongst the papers on the table.

"I'm sorry about Tony," she said. "I had no idea."

Gilkrensky reached out and took her hand.

"It's OK, Jess. You were lonely too. I'm sorry I doubted you when Yukiko accused you of . . . you know."

Jessica Wright looked into his eyes – and saw the sadness there.

"I know, Theo. If I ever loved . . . "

The intercom buzzed.

Jessica let her hand slip from his and reached for the button.

"There's a call from Cairo, Miss Wright. It's a Mr Leroy Manning . . . for the chairman."

"Put him through."

Leroy Manning looked down at them from the boardroom screen. A fresh plaster covered his forehead, over the left eye, and he was clean shaven.

"I am sorry to bother you, Doc," he said nervously. "I've never used one of these gizmos before."

"That's OK," said Gilkrensky. "It's good of you to call. Are you all right?"

"I'm fine. Colonel Selim released me after questioning earlier this morning and I came back here to the hotel with him to help wind up the security. You should see what's left of your suite and the foyer. It's gonna cost you, boss! It's a hell of a mess!"

"I can afford it."

"But the reason I really called you is that we've just received the results of the tests on that sand you had radiated and placed in the golden crypt before the experiment yesterday evening."

"And?"

"The radiation level's been reduced by fifty per cent, as if the sand had aged by four thousand years, just as you predicted. You were right, Doc. There's a portal to the past inside the Pyramid, and it can be controlled. You've got yourself a real live time machine here!"

Gilkrensky stood, staring at the image on the screen.

"And the briefcase bomb?"

"Beats me! It must've travelled back with the sand, to the time when the Pyramid was first built, and exploded."

Gilkrensky felt sick. He steadied himself against the boardroom table. "So that's why the Pyramid was sealed. Imhotep and his followers were probably killed by the gas almost as soon as the Pyramid was complete, at the far end of the wormhole. The ancient Egyptians must have thought this was an omen, sealed off the crypt, and abandoned the site for ever. This must be why the Queen's Chamber looks so unfinished, and why no royal corpses or artifacts were ever found inside. The Pyramid was never used again."

"They probably couldn't seal it fast enough," said Manning.

"Oh, my God! What *have* I done?"

Manning shrugged, lost for words.

"Well, look at it this way. You helped what had to

happen, happen. I'm no rocket-scientist, but even I can work out that if the case hadn't gone into the Pyramid, and if the Pyramid hadn't been sealed, then history might have been different, and I wouldn't be speaking to you now. Right?"

"And what are the Egyptian authorities going to do with it?"

"The real secret of the Golden Crypt is only known to you, me, and Colonel Selim," said Manning. "And I know for a fact that he wants history to stay the way it is. So he's instructed his men to seal the crypt again. I'm sorry, but I didn't have much say in it."

Gilkrensky stared frantically at the screen.

"But what about my experiments? How are we ever going to find Bill, or save Maria, if we can't get into the Pyramid?"

"If you take my advice, Doc, you'll let things cool down a while before you come back over here. When you do, the Golden Crypt will still be there and, if you want anyone to fly your chopper, then so will I."

"Thanks, Leroy," said Gilkrensky, and the image blinked off.

Gilkrensky looked at the mirrored finish of the blade standing straight and proud out of the boardroom table. Then he turned and stared out over the Thames, thinking of all the people he had lost over the last week . . . of Hargreaves, Maguire, Bill McCarthy and . . . of course, Maria. The snow had stopped. The late afternoon sun was turning the river a deep molten red.

"It's funny," he said. "I'm the sixth richest man in the world, and the one thing I really want, I can't buy."

Jessica Wright topped up his glass and handed it to him. As he took it, their hands touched.

"It's Christmas," she said. "I'll be spending it on my own, at the hotel. Would you like to join me?"

Gilkrensky turned to her and raised his glass.

"I . . . I don't know, Jess. But . . . thanks."

Their eyes met. His held that same lost look that had tugged at her heart a week before, when he had come into the board meeting out of the rain.

Jessica took the glass from his hand, put it down on the boardroom table next to hers and hugged him tightly, feeling his pain.

"Oh, Theo! Will you ever get over Maria?"

Gilkrensky put his arms around her and closed his eyes. He could feel the warmth of her, the scent of her hair and the smoothness of her skin on his cheek. But all he could see was the perfect virtual image of his wife, dancing in her field of blue forget-me-nots.

"I don't know," he whispered. "It's a matter of time."